Bait and Switch

A Jessica Minton Mystery

Sharon Healy-Yang

To Alan,
A fellow laborer in the education vineyard and fellow writer. Enjoy!
Sharon Yang

TouchPoint
Press

BAIT AND SWITCH by Sharon Healy-Yang
Published by TouchPoint Press
4737 Wildwood Lane
Jonesboro, AR 72401
www.touchpointpress.com

ISBN-10: 0692597948
ISBN-13: 978-0-69259-794-1

Editor: Tamara Trudeau
Cover Design: Sharon Yang (concept); De-Ping Yang (compilation)

Visit the author's website at sharonhealyyang.com

First Edition

Printed in the United States of America.

The people who've helped me get this horse to the post have been innumerable; however, I'll try to number as many as I can. Over the years, I've had the encouragement, critiques, and advice of many friends and colleagues: Lisa McCarthy, Charmaine Kinton, Nancy Ferrell, Sonia Cintron-Marrero, Kathy Heal(e)y, Janice Trekker, Feenie Zeiner, Gina Barreca, Colleen Gresh, Carey Smitherman, Charlotte Gordon, Judy Jeon-Chapman, and Matt Ortoleva. If I've left anyone out, I'm sorry. Know that your input has been valuable to me. One person I need to cite for service above and beyond the call of duty is my buddy and colleague, Ruth Haber. Ruth's not just a great editor but she's a primo mystery buff who has a fine eye for what works. Her advice and suggestions have kept me on track all along, and her faith in me has been a mainstay. I'm lucky to be able to call her my friend. My parents, Grace and Leo Healy, were always there to encourage me in all my dreams, as well as to teach me to work my tail feathers off and never give up. My brother Leo, though a real wise guy, still had faith in my writing, listening to my ideas and respecting my abilities, even if he did it sarcastically. Yes, his practical jokes were the inspiration for Peter Hennessey. And Dusty was also a real life character. I hope that I captured all her "cattitude"! I'd also like to thank Sheri Williams for believing in me and accepting my work at Touchpoint, as well as Tamara Trudeau for her insightful, patient, and tactful editing. Finally, I want to thank my best friend in the world, De-Ping Yang, who has always supported and encouraged me, who always believes in me, and is also one hell of a ballroom dancer!

CHAPTER ONE

Damp, cold, dark. Jessica Minton wished she could feel that good about the play she was rehearsing. Cars splashed past. As if anyone in this city would ever slow down, even in this lousy weather. No lights illuminated the theater marquee behind her, and even the Desiree Café down the street had replaced its neon sign. It was late summer 1943, and most of New York's lively city lights had been darkened because of Nazi U-boats patrolling the coast and sinking ships — a thought that made Jess shiver even more than this chill storm.

Across the street beckoned the warmth and life visible through the plate-glass window of Shaftner's Drugstore. There hadn't been any warmth in the theater tonight, only a ragged rehearsal and a volatile director firing an even more temperamental young actor. Well, dwelling on how she'd been sucked into that emotional maelstrom wasn't doing her any good. Better to get across the street and restore herself with some of Harry Shaftner's good java and whatever pastry he could drum up at this hour.

Getting across the street didn't do anything to improve Jessica's mood, for her adept leap onto the opposite curb carried her over the gutter — into a puddle. Shaking a soggy black-sandaled foot, Jessica could almost admit that her beau Larry might be on to something when he pressed her to marry him and leave acting. After six years in the theater, she might be eating regularly; but she still wasn't exactly burning up the Great White Way. Life must, indeed, be going downhill if the only haven in sight was a stool at Shaftner's lunch counter.

Jess stepped into the drugstore. Shoot, no Harry. Worse, her companions were few and not exactly the comforting sorts she'd hoped for. At the four-seat counter to her left, a man was hiding from his blue plate special behind a newspaper. The view to her right wasn't any more appealing: three teenage girls crowded in front of the magazine racks. Bad rehearsals, a squishy shoe, no friendly face to welcome her. All she needed was to get hit by a random bolt of lightning and she would have officially hit bottom.

Okay, Jess inwardly ordered herself, *enough with the pity party, madam.* She pulled off her rain coat and folded it hastily over the empty stool next to Mr. Blue Plate Special. Harry must be in the back room behind the counter; soon enough, he'd be out to kid away her blues. He had a sixth sense about when a customer came in. Tonight it was just a little delayed. *So, go grab yourself a New Yorker,* she ordered herself. *If an article doesn't enlighten you, maybe the cartoons will wipe away your sour puss.*

Crossing to the magazines, Jess undid the scarf covering her head and shook out a mass of curly, shoulder-length dark hair. Those teenagers sure were intent on using the screen rags to buttress their arguments over the manly merits of Tyrone Power versus those of Victor Mature. Jess had to admit she was more in the Power camp. After all, how could a girl go for a guy who could fill out a top better than *she* could?

From behind her, a voice heavily flavored with Brooklyn cut through Jessica's cogitations, "Hey, Katherine Cornell, found out even genius has to eat?"

Jessica turned and smiled wryly, "Don't say 'Katherine Cornell' tonight, Harry. The way this play is going, that comparison is downright libelous to La Cornell."

Having heard it all before, Harry Shaftner only offered, "That bad?"

Somehow, the past several hours seemed less fraught in Harry's down-to-earth company. Jessica sauntered back to the counter and sat down, joking with her pal, "I'll say it was bad, Harry. Harold Vane voluntarily gave us a supper break."

"A couple more hours and you could take a breakfast break."

Jess smiled, "I guess he couldn't stand the sight of us anymore. I was beginning to sympathize with him. Anyway, I'll just have a coffee and a Danish. Cheese this time."

"There's a feast and a half."

"I can't eat much this early in rehearsals," Jess reminded him.

Harry shook his head, then raised a finger as he suddenly remembered, "Say, I got something to buck you up. Right in tonight's paper. I folded it up and put it under the counter, to save it for you. Did you see it?"

As Harry ducked down for his paper, Jessica, her interest piqued, leaned forward and queried, "See what, Oh Mysterious-Drug-Store Owner?"

"Take a gander at this, Miss Jessica Minton, Star of Page and Stage! Section C, page 23."

Harry plunked a newspaper down in front of Jessica, folded vertically to showcase a picture of her at the Stage Door Canteen, carrying a sandwich-laden platter as wide as her smile. But instead of cheering her up, the picture only reminded Jess how feeble her contributions to winning the war felt.

Harry went on, "Look at that. The caption even mentions your name and the play. Maybe I should cut it out, frame it, start a wall of stars who eat here, like in Schraff's — my own wall of fame."

"It might be more like a wall of shame," Jessica corrected, still feeling the blues.

"Knock that off right now, kiddo. Especially when you're doing something that's helpin' the guys who gotta win this war for us."

"Me?" Jessica was genuinely surprised. "Let's face it, Harry, when it comes to the war effort, I'm a pretty sorry customer. I wish I had the ability to do something worthwhile. All I'm good for is to serve some sandwiches, dance a few dances, try to make a few guys forget — but that doesn't change anything, does it?"

"Maybe making someone happy for a little while, giving a guy a good memory to carry overseas, that counts more than you know. Anyway, what about the U.S.O. shows you've done?"

"That's not enough, not really. I always feel... I should be doing more, don't you think?"

"Now stop stewing over not working in a munitions factory. You'll give yourself frown lines. You hostesses are supposed to make the boys want to come back, not scare them off," Harry teased her.

Jess smiled at him. He might be a bluff guy, but he always said the right thing.

"Harry, you're right. Each to her own talents! I'll save the heavy drama for my job across the street. Hey, at least if the play does come together, I'll be in my glory. I have the kind of role I love, a *femme fatale*. As much as I love to do comedy, I also like my art a little on the dark side, whether I'm reading it, watching it, or playing it!"

"Now about that cheese Danish..." Harry began, but before he could argue the virtues of nutrition with Jess an excessively loud chorus of giggles riveted his attention on the girls drooling over Tyrone and Victor.

"They been here an hour going through them rags," Harry scowled to Jessica.

Jess glanced briefly at the three girls, then queried, "Haven't they bought anything?"

"Why should they buy?" Harry returned with a shrug. "They read everything already." He poured a cup of coffee and slid it to Jessica. She crooked a smile that said, "Thanks."

Harry shook his balding head, "I better send the Andrews Sisters there out on tour. I think one magazine still has a page without their finger prints."

"I guess they'd better not take up a life of crime."

"Either that or they start wearing gloves the next time they hit my newsstand," replied Harry dismally as he took off his apron and tossed it under the counter.

Jess started to smile in response, but Harry had a parting shot for her. "It's lousy out there. When I come back you're gonna have something more than coffee and Danish to stand by you."

Jess knew better than to argue with Harry, at least just now. So, back to that coffee! Ugh! No sugar! Swell, the sugar canister next to her was empty. Even if there was a war on, did she have to be shortchanged on sugar tonight? Maybe the guy two seats down would pass her his sugar canister before her craving for sweet sent her off to mug a G. I. for his Hershey bar.

Jess turned, started to speak, but hesitated. When she'd come in, she'd barely noticed the man behind his newspaper. However, her curiosity was now definitely piqued by his tense behavior: intermittently smoking, staring past her out the window, tensely glancing down one of the aisles off to his right, then stubbing out a cigarette and lighting another.

Finally realizing he was being observed, he stared her down and demanded in a British-accented voice, "Haven't you ever seen anyone smoke before?"

"I've seen people smoke," Jess replied, settling her elbow comfortably on the counter.

He interrupted his nervous vigil to snuff out yet another cigarette and inquire sarcastically, "I imagine you've seen people extinguish cigarettes also?"

"Well, yes, but never in their food."

He blinked then stared into his plate, only now realizing that his mashed potatoes were gouged with cigarette butts.

"That's your third," Jessica pointed out. She couldn't help noticing that the lean-faced gentleman was easy on the eyes, in a Bohemian kind of way: tousled, longish dark hair and a mustache more full than Ronald-Colman-razored. Not that she was in the market, with an equally dark and handsome Larry Sanders in the picture.

Her companion opened his mouth for a retort, but froze. As he caught sight of something outside, his expression erased Jessica's impishness. She straightened, then instinctively followed his gaze out the window.

A car splashed by. Rain blurred the street lamp's illumination beyond the window. Jessica was slightly surprised to find herself relieved at *not* discovering anything fishy out there. But that relief evaporated as she sensed her companion was doing something to her coat on the chair between them.

Turning back sharply, indignantly, Jess started, "Say, just what...?"

Her companion cut her off by leaning forward and tensely, quietly instructing, "There's no time for questions. Just do as I say. I've hidden a brown-paper-wrapped package under your coat. After I'm gone, take it home with you. Try not to let anyone see you have it when you leave. If anyone does, convince him you came in with it. You're a clever girl. You can come up with a cover story."

Jessica snapped, "How did you know I was clever? Anyway, I most certainly will do no such thing..."

"Are you so truly concerned about not doing enough for your country, or were those just empty words I heard coming from you a few moments ago, Miss Minton?" the man demanded.

"Of course, I... How do you know my name?"

"Right here in front of me, I have the same section of the paper that you and your friend, the proprietor, were just talking about. And I'm not unfamiliar with your career. Now stop wasting time with questions and follow my instructions. Then you'll be doing the equivalent of thwarting a Panzer division."

He was on his feet, taking a cautious step past her, scouting through the window, trying not to be visible to anyone outside. And he seemed especially careful not to draw Harry's notice, who was completely wrapped up in giving what-for to the gaggle of delinquent bobby soxers.

"I don't understand," Jess protested softly. Crazy as it all seemed, for this moment she was drawn into the stranger's determination to remain undetected — but by whom?

Facing Jess again, he silenced her with his answer. "You don't have to understand. God forgive me for dragging you into this... but here we are. Just take the package and sit tight until it's safe for me to retrieve it. I'll keep an eye on you; low profile, of course. But for your sake, my sake, our countries' sakes, don't let anyone know what's passed between us. It's in your hands until it's safe for me to get it out of town."

"'It'? What 'it'?"

"Just keep a low profile."

Far from convinced, Jessica challenged the unnerving stranger, "Do you really expect me to buy this bill of goods? No soap, mister. If this were the real McCoy, why wouldn't you go for the police or the F.B.I.?"

"Haven't you heard of fivers, fifth columnists, traitors infiltrating the authorities? I'm on the run now because a German mole in this town liquidated my contact. I can't trust any of the regular authorities here. I need to leave this package with someone whom no one will suspect, but is easy for me to track down, until I can find a way to get safely out of the city."

"So, if this city is so chock full of Nazis, what makes you think I'm such a good bet? Why trust *me*?"

His features tensed with frustration. Fear, even? The man's quick glance out the window, followed by his sharp reply, suggested that only his desperation to convince Jessica kept him talking rather than beating feet, "Because my back's to the wall right now; and, long shot that you are, you appear to be the only chance I have. I got a pretty good idea of your patriotism from your conversation with the proprietor, so I'm placing all my bets on you're being right enough to help me. Don't let me down."

"But..."

"Someone *is* coming, and he doesn't look like my contact. Don't forget everything I told you. I'll be in touch."

"Wait! Where are you going?" she hissed after him. But his tall, wiry figure had moved rapidly into the maze of aisles leading to the rear of the store. Of course, out the back way — wasn't that always the exit strategy for a mysterious man followed by Nazi agents?

Jess was on her feet. What the devil should she do now? Of course, call the cops or the F.B.I. — who would probably say she was nuts. Or would they? Hadn't there been several high profile roundups of German infiltrators over the past two years, even right here in the city? If she believed that fellow enough to call in the authorities, she'd also have to take his word that they couldn't be trusted. Unless this was all some kind of practical joke in horribly bad taste.

That thought snapped Jessica Minton back to reality. Yes, the past ten minutes struck her as something scripted for a bad spy melodrama, and she'd almost been suckered right into it. Someone had gone to great lengths to play her for a sap, even tapping into her predilection for drama on the dark side. Someone who had to know her well: the roles she played, the books she read, the movies she watched. Someone who also understood exactly how much she worried about not doing enough for the war effort; someone like her brother-in-law, Peter Hennessey, a fellow all too well known as the king of grandiose practical jokes.

The beauty of his talent was that even if you expected some kind of gag from him, he knew your soft spot and set the stage so convincingly that you always fell for it. Peter was exactly the kind of smart aleck who would see the city's jitters over the recent arrests of German fifth columnists as the perfect basis for an elaborate gag. And manipulating her honor and sense of responsibility to trump her rationality would be exactly the kind of clever ploy he'd use to convincingly buffalo Jessica. That realization made her sore, good and sore. How dare Peter!

But Peter usually had a motive. You'd done something to annoy him, set him off. As far as Jess could figure, her brother-in-law had no beef with her. Or was he nursing a grudge over her sticking up for her sister during some of the couple's numerous marital quarrels? Jess slowly sat down on her stool, speculatively eyeing her raincoat. Had her mystery man left a package lurking beneath it?

Should she take a peek? Jess made a quick survey of the store. Nope, no Peter Hennessey, or anyone else, lurking in one of the aisles or behind a display to see if she'd taken the bait. She moved ever so slightly to check under her coat, and that's when the door slammed.

There he stood, with all the elegant lines of a fire plug, in an old trench coat, his hat stained with rain, his face with a scowl, a cigar clamped tight in a hard mouth — a new actor in this Looney Tunes farce. The black eyes, guarded by folds of flesh, scanned the room with cruel precision, and Jessica was glad she'd had a chance to get a grip on herself before they fastened on her. His gaze detoured to the cigarette-marred mashed potatoes, then back to her. Teeth grinding down on his cigar, he seemed to be running through the evidence with an expression too harsh for a player in a practical joke.

Jessica did some split-second calculations. If she looked away too fast, she might seem to have something to hide. But if she faced the guy, she could draw his attention — maybe not if she gave him the kind of once-over you'd give anyone who walked in, then just played it cool.

Removing the cigar in token deference, he opened with, "Hey, sister, maybe you can help me."

"You looking for something, Mac?"

Bobby soxers vanquished and magazines secured, Harry charged in for the rescue — drawn onto the scene by his sixth sense about trouble? Was that a tip off that his intercession *now* meant that the first stranger was on the level and this new arrival was not on the side of the angels?

"Yeah. Looks like you run this joint. Am I right, Pops?"

"This is my place all right. Been my place for twenty-odd years."

Jessica had the bizarre recollection of a Doberman and a pit bull in Central Park sizing each other up. She nipped her lip to keep from laughing — from nerves or humor, she couldn't say. The pit bull gave her a funny look, but at the moment his real interest was Harry.

"Yeah, well, great. I'm looking for a friend of mine. He was supposed to meet me here, but I don't see him. He was supposed to give me a package. It's important."

"This ain't the post office, Mac," Harry dismissed him, coming back to his side of the counter.

"I bet you must've seen him, lady."

"Me?" Jess came close to squeaking, ready to kick herself for that automatic reaction. Peter would have chortled if he were behind all this. She swiftly recovered herself for a casual, "I wasn't really paying attention."

"Not paying attention, huh? Well, you been sitting here awhile, right? There's a plate next to you, right? Who was eating there?"

"Oh, well, now that I think of it, I kind of remember some guy sitting at the counter," Jessica shrugged. "He didn't say anything about meeting anyone to me."

"Oh, he talked to you?"

Damn! Jessica cursed to herself. Maybe it was late, maybe she was hungrier than she'd thought, maybe she'd been through way too much melodrama on and off the stage back at the theater. Whatever the case, this guy who could give Edward G. Robinson the creeps seemed less and less like part of any gag. But she was not about to be rattled and nonchalantly answered, "Oh, no big deal. I guess I did ask him for the sugar, and he said, 'Here.' Not much of a conversationalist."

"Mmm." The fire-plug considered, looking at the floor by the seat next to Jess. "You notice what he looked like?"

"You here to buy something or play Edward R. Murrow?" Harry

interjected. "This here's a drug store. You buy things. You don't play twenty-question interviews."

Jessica didn't like the look the mug gave Harry, but Harry wasn't backing down. The tension felt too real even for Peter's deft stage management. Whatever this mug's motives, instinct told her to interject and act as if there was no big deal.

"He was just a guy. And I was hungry."

"You see if he was carrying anything when he left? Which way he went out?"

All Jess could think of was what might be hidden under her raincoat. Always the trouper, though, she kept her face a blank when she shook her head.

Harry cut in, "The guy paid his bill; he coulda been carrying a B-29 up the chimney for all I care. Now, maybe you ought to go out an' look for him yourself."

The visitor looked hard at Harry and moved as if to flick some cigar ashes on the floor. Harry's glare made him think better of it. Instead, he smiled — Jess thought his facial muscles had real trouble pulling it off — and said, "Sure, sure thing, friend. I'll do just that. I can always wait around outside and see what turns up."

"There's laws against loitering, Mac. My friends the beat cops like to keep the neighborhood peaceful and uncluttered, if you know what I mean."

The fire plug looked them both over, stared at the aisles of drug-store merchandise, then grunted as if coming to some conclusion and left.

Jessica couldn't stop a long sigh from escaping when the door closed on the fire plug.

Harry tried to ease the tension with, "Don't worry. I ain't about to let no small-time hoods turn my place into a drop-off joint. I got me a nice piece of pipe under the counter if he or his pal is dopey enough to come back between Sullivan's and Fiorello's rounds."

"He's a crook?" Jessica queried.

She was a little embarrassed that she'd only just remembered that a guy didn't have to be a Nazi spy to be a criminal.

"Sure. What did he look like, a G-Man? That's what the bit with the package was. They're dropping off bets or payoffs, but they ain't doing it here. So wipe them wrinkles off your lovely face, girlie. He won't be back. Now, have another cup of coffee. Oops, looks like you need more sugar in the canister, here. I gotta go in the back room to fill it up. Be right back. And don't you be nervous. Any trouble, not that I'm expecting any, and I'll be out here in a jiffy. Okay?"

"Thanks, Harry," Jessica smiled.

As soon as Harry disappeared into the backroom, Jessica's features tightened. Everything had happened so fast, but she realized that Harry's theory about everyday crooks did not jibe with what the mustached man had told her. His palaver about serving her country and then his dashing off, the second guy, practically on his heels, quizzing them about the package, all hitting her after twelve hours of brutal rehearsals and a confrontation with that fired actor — it was like being catapulted off the end of a roller-skating whip crack! Whatever the truth was, this last visitor had been no common criminal. He was either a "minion" of her nefarious brother-in-law or a Nazi fiver. Common sense insisted that the nefarious brother-in-law option was the most likely. She just wished that the fire plug hadn't been such an awfully disturbing player.

Jessica took a deep breath, then pulled her rain coat back. There it was, a medium sized, brown-paper-wrapped package, just as the mustached man had said. Well, that still didn't make the guy's claims legit. The package could be a fake, a prop.

Jessica was not about to waste time stewing over what a rotten trick Peter was pulling on her, playing on her guilt. No, better to come up with a scenario of her own to fix Peter's little red wagon, to turn the trick around on him. Someone had to bring home to him that you could go too far; a gag based on real dangers was no laughing matter.

So, let's see. No one else was still in the store this late. No one would see if she did grab the package. Even better, Harry had been in the back when she'd come in, so he wouldn't know whether or not she'd had the package then, if he did spot it. So, if she took the bundle away without Peter knowing and never breathed a word to him about the evening's events, wouldn't he go crazy wondering what *had* happened to the package? Getting away with playing a player was always sweet. It was about time someone taught her brother-in-law a lesson.

Still, affronted as she was with Peter's irresponsible choice for a rib, Jess had to commend him for his "actors." The mug had been a little too much central casting from Warner Brothers, but he'd still scared her — and buffaloed Harry, to boot! The first one, though, he'd played it right on the money. Jess was surprised she didn't know a local actor who could carry off the part that naturally — and he was easy on the eyes, too.

Pleased with the prospect of putting Peter Hennessey in his place, Jess found herself able to kid with Harry when he returned with her food, packed and ready to go. He'd seemed a little concerned that she had no more specific arrangement in mind for getting home than hailing a cab. Good old Harry, always a mother hen under the gruffness. To Jess's satisfaction, clearing skies gave her an excuse to drape her coat over her arm to try and conceal the package. Now, let someone outside Shaftner's try to report to Peter that she'd carried it off! That's all she was worried about, really. That man loitering further down the street only had the general build of the fire plug, right? She would not dignify Peter's attempt to scare her by letting this guy see she was checking him out. Jessica Minton was nobody's patsy. But she did wish she could figure out what had set her brother-in-law off.

* * * * * *

The Cherry Street Theater wasn't like any of the converted buildings or renovated old theaters Jess had played when she was working the subway circuit back in '38 and '39; this dressing-room wasn't damp enough to sprout mushrooms. The old building might not have had the best of heating, but a nice sweater or light coat could easily solve that problem in the occasional cool of late summer. All in all, except when the electricity occasionally cut out, it wasn't a bad place in which to work. And that problem would definitely be fixed before the play opened.

The last performer here, Jess sat in front of the mirror in her dressing room, wearing the requisite light coat, a cup of tea gone cold before her. Only the faint radio broadcast of the Andrews Sisters' harmonies told her that Gramps, the janitor, was somewhere off in the building. She ought to fix her make-up, brush her hair, pack up her things, and go back out into the night to hail a cab. Instead, Jess's eyes moved from her wan, tired face in the mirror to a shopping bag a few inches away on the dressing table, a shopping bag into which she had placed her "mystery" package. So why was she putting off stepping outside alone? Maybe because, as much as she hated to admit it, Peter's second player had gotten under her skin? Logic told Jessica that she had nothing to be nervous about, but at this time of night her exhaustion and imagination, attenuated by rehearsing her character's murder for several hours, undermined reason.

Restlessly, Jess got up and crossed the room to grab a slip hanging over the top of her changing screen. The lights and radio cut out together. She froze. Footsteps, audible in the sudden silence, were carefully, maybe even surreptitiously, moving down the corridor toward her door. They were *not* the weary shuffle of Gramps. Was Mr. Fire Plug back? Even if he was only part of Peter's practical joke, he still gave Jessica the willies, in spades.

The door slowly creaked open. Jessica tensed. Her hands twisted the slip into a cord of sorts, the lingerie her only protection. Could she strangle him? With a slip? This was exactly the kind of foolishness to which Peter was aiming to reduce her. Jess lowered her "weapon," embarrassed if not exactly reassured.

A lighter flickered on, and a male voice with a touch of an English accent called, "Jessica? Are you here?"

"Larry!"

Jessica would have been annoyed with herself for the relief in her voice if she hadn't been so determined to give the source of that relief a big hug.

Larry Sanders grinned as Jess's arms tightened around him, "This is a pleasant surprise. We haven't had this kind of a hello in quite some time."

With the room no longer dark and ever-dependable Larry here, Jessica stepped away, shaking her head, laughing at herself slightly.

"You wouldn't want to let me in on this joke, would you?" Larry inquired, his tone light.

Jess smiled as she sat down at the dressing table again. "I guess you really will have reason to think I'm crazy now."

"Jess, any time I get a greeting like that I'd prefer to know why, so I can inspire a similar response any time I choose."

That mischievously patrician face with those deep brown eyes warmed her. Should she let Larry in on Peter's prank and her intention of turning the tables? Still, he and her brother-in-law worked together and were close friends. Would Larry say something to Peter that might thwart her plans to undermine Peter's practical joke? Then again, maybe Larry could prove an adept ally for her.

"Well, if you have to know everything, I've had quite an entertaining evening."

Larry folded his arms and kidded, "I hope that isn't a jibe at a man who is nothing but a dull civil servant. I know I'm not part of the glittering theater world."

"Believe me, Larry, the least exciting thing that happened to me this evening was connected with the play. You see, I was eating in Shaftner's when I noticed that the man next to me was acting a little strangely."

"Strangely?"

"Would you call using his mashed potatoes for an ash tray strange?"

"I suppose it is. I was just thinking of how you tend to embellish facts."

She'd be gracious and let that remark pass, this time.

"Anyway, Larry, we had a little conversation, then he suddenly looked out the window.   I guess he panicked... and gave me the most incredible line of malarkey before beating it. It was bizarre, to say the least."

"You weren't discussing politics again, Jess? You've driven quite a few off that way, but they were mostly our friends. I'd hate to think you're starting on strangers now."

That was *not* the response she was looking for from Larry. Here she was trying to make him an ally, and he was getting cute at her expense. But that attitude *might* make sense if he were in on Peter's joke. Her brother-in-law was, indeed, silver-tongued, not to mention good buddies with Larry. Peter *might* be able to persuade even a stalwart fellow like Larry to help him rib her. A little probing was in order.

"Larry, I wasn't expecting you this evening. What made you decide to drop by?"

"Can't a chap drop by to see his best girl, see if she needs a lift home? I thought late at night, on an evening like this, all alone, you might be feeling a touch nerved up."

"Not that I mean to look a gift Galahad in the mouth, but how did you know I'd be here this late? Did someone tell you I'd be here waiting, alone, nervous?"

He hesitated. Bingo.

"Someone did tell you."

"Well, yes."

"And that someone would be...?" Jessica couldn't help feeling a little smug. She hadn't expected Larry to cave quite so quickly, but his loyalty *ought* to be stronger to her than to Peter.

"I promised not to tell."

"All right, Larry. I swear I won't tell that you clued me in."

"Right then. Harry. Harry Schaftner."

Jessica frowned. Definitely not the answer she'd expected.

Larry continued, "He called me. Let me know some rough sort had been in the drug store looking to make trouble. Harry thought you'd seemed unnerved and might be afraid of running into the fellow after you got out tonight. So he rang me up and dropped one of his not-so-subtle hints that I ought to play the knight for my fair lady. You won't tell him I spilled the beans? I must say that I'm glad that you left my number with him before, in case of an emergency, even if this little run in of yours only qualifies as an imaginary emergency."

Jess wasn't sure what to make of Larry's explanation. All she knew was that she'd better play it cool. If Larry were on the level, she didn't want to look as if she'd gotten rattled without good reason; if he were in cahoots with Peter, she certainly didn't want to give him the chance to report: mission accomplished.

"Larry, of course, I wouldn't get mad at Harry. He meant well, but I'd hardly say I was shattered. You can see I'm perfectly fine."

"A little jumpy."

"I'm fine, Larry."

"Certainly, if you insist, Jessica. So, what did the chap say to upset... to make Harry think you were upset? Nothing to make it seem as if he were going to follow you, right?"

Jessica folded her arms and considered Larry's words. He sounded as if he intended to lead her away from a worry she didn't want to admit she felt. That was a sign of concern, right? So, why didn't she feel calmed and comforted? Maybe because, whether Larry was part of her brother-in-law's plot or just trying to make up her mind for her once again, she still felt manipulated. Her best bet seemed to be leaving Larry out of any plan to outmaneuver Peter.

"Nothing important, Larry. Harry's a swell guy, but he's overprotective. He always thinks he knows people's business better than they do. What say we head out?"

"My carriage awaits, mademoiselle. May I carry anything for you?"

Jessica shook her head, sweetly smiling as she gathered up her things but thinking, *Like a brown-paper package? Ha! It's in my shopping bag! Just in case you* are *in league with my dastardly brother-in-law, you won't be able to report to him that I took his bait. So there!*

As Jess picked up the shopping bag, Larry thought a moment before querying, "Oh, shopping? Woman's sport. 'Bag' anything worthwhile?"

"Nothing you'd be interested in, my friend. Just girl stuff."

Her boyfriend only smiled in response.

Larry flipped off the lights and graciously closed the door behind Jessica after she'd passed him to exit the room. She was far too tired to make conversation as they headed for his car, parked in front of the theater. As they emerged through the main entrance, Larry reminded her, "Remember, tomorrow night is dinner and dancing with Elizabeth and Peter."

"Oh no, tomorrow I work at the Stage Door Canteen. It's the next night we make like Fred and Ginger... Oh, Mr. Bromfield!"

Jessica had caught sight of a heavy-set figure of medium height standing at the edge of the curb, his back to her and Larry. Hearing his name, the man turned. His slightly pudgy face was lined from over fifty years of living. The face would have been hard, even tough, if his smile at seeing Jessica had not transformed his features.

"So now you're finally going home," he lightly chided, coming forward. His voice was gravelly, but amicable, with an almost imperceptible middle-European tinge.

"Home at last," Jessica tiredly agreed.

"Hello, Mr. Bromfield," Larry greeted the older man. Frederick Bromfield was Jessica's co-star. Though certainly not a big name, he had a distinguished reputation that drew the more discriminating theatergoers. His accent was the only hint he allowed of the past he had escaped when the Nazis came to power. Despite a long line of theatrical credits from both sides of the Atlantic, his prestige had diminished in recent years. Friendly enough and certainly professional, Bromfield rarely joined in the camaraderie of his fellow players. Jess suspected the vague sadness she sensed in him stemmed more from the loss of his homeland than of past theatrical glory. Lately, though, he'd seemed more jittery than when she'd worked with him before. Bad news about the homeland, wherever that might be?

Frederick Bromfield shook Larry's hand and commented, "I'm glad you take care of this young lady. Every young woman needs a gentleman to take care of her."

"That's what I've been telling her," Larry agreed pleasantly.

Jess tilted her chin up in mock defiance to tease, "Mr. Bromfield, you seem to be here rather late yourself. Someone should be looking after you."

Strangely enough, Frederick Bromfield hesitated before saying, "I was waiting for someone."

"Oh?" Jessica responded, surprised. Glancing up and down the street and seeing no one, she offered, "If you've missed him, Larry and I will be glad to take you home. You don't mind, Larry?"

Frederick Bromfield shook his head. "No, no. That would take you out of your way. That's all right; you go ahead. I have to wait anyway."

"We don't mind," Jessica insisted, ignoring the slight glint of disagreement in Larry's eyes. Luckily for Larry, Frederick Bromfield was more insistent than Jessica. Having wished the older man a good evening, Jess walked off alongside Larry, too exhausted to wonder for whom Bromfield was waiting. She hadn't noticed Frederick Bromfield thoughtfully appraise her once she had turned away. All Jessica knew was that she wanted to go to bed, to sleep. After all, she'd already figured out that she had nothing more to fear than her brother-in-law's warped sense of humor.

Only much later in the game did Jess come to realize that she would not have been so confident, had she been able to see the tall, dark-haired, mustached man watching her tensely, hidden in the shadows of a nearby alley.

CHAPTER TWO

Jess was uneasy. She had just entered Shaftner's, the package in her hands. The drugstore was dimly lit, as if the lights could not draw enough power. Maybe the wiring was off?

Her eyes zeroed in on the lunch counter. Harry was not there. Jessica started to wonder where he had gone, but a trench-coated figure at the counter with his back to her nabbed her attention. Even before he turned to face her, she recognized him. Jess instinctively gripped the package as the cool dark eyes fastened on her. Looking for an escape route, she glanced through the window. A squat figure hulked outside, his face obscured by a turned up collar, a pulled down hat, and a peculiar arrangement of shadows. Jessica stiffened and turned back to the man at the counter, her lips parting but no words escaping. What was going on? What she should do? But there was no reassurance in this man's sharp features. Instead, an ironic smile slightly bared his sharp white teeth — and he meowed!

Jessica sat up with a start, eyes wide, her bed sheets twisted and bunched torturously. Looking down she was greeted by another meow, this time clearly from the gray tiger-cat on the bed gazing up at her.

Stroking the feline's comfortingly soft fur, Jess commented, "I suppose I should thank you for rescuing me from that nightmare, Dusty. Too bad my mind had to cook up such a creepy scenario."

Jessica shook her head to clear away the image of last night's mystery man "meowing." Untroubled by crazy nightmares, Dusty purred with lazy ecstasy while her neck was rubbed. If Jess hadn't known better, she'd have sworn the dream was her unconscious signaling her to take the previous evening's encounters seriously. But she did know better, and she wasn't about to let Peter take her for a buggy ride, even in her sleep. Smiling down at her gray cat, Jess started to say something more, when a new disturbing thought insinuated itself.

Her eyes whipping to the little clock on her bedside table, Jessica blurted, "Just great! Eleven o'clock and Elizabeth will be here at half past." Turning back to Dusty, she added, "Thank heavens the most dependable thing about my sister is that she's always late."

Dusty meowed with a trace of impatience, leaped to the floor, and exited for the kitchen at a trot. It was well past the feline breakfast hour.

Slipping into her robe and mules, Jessica indulged herself with a survey of her room. Definitely not the setting for nightmares: Wedgwood-blue wallpaper sprinkled with graceful white flowers, enhanced by the sunlight streaming through the room's two windows and the filmy white curtains. You didn't need to lower your blackout shades once your lights were out for the night.

Tying the belt of her robe, Jess looked out one of the windows into the New York street fronting her building. Damascus Place. One of those cobblestone cul-de-sacs lined with old, elegant buildings. Shady, with brownstones looming across a narrow way, Damascus Place was a refuge from city traffic, with only the occasional zipping surge of shifted gears drifting into the apartment. Jess threw open the window, and a warm breeze angled in from the street through the screen to send the curtains dancing about her. In the light of this delicious morning, while the late summer breeze brushed her face gently, the previous night's events seemed as silly as the conclusion of her dream. An amazingly drawn out cry from Dusty insinuated itself into Jessica's thoughts.

"Dusty, if you keep that up, I may rent you out to an air raid warden. You'd make a wonderful siren."

Dusty, who had returned to the bedroom, blinked coolly, as if to reply, "Foolish human, there are more important concerns at hand," then turned, marched to the doorway, and flicked her tail commandingly.

"You can wait, Dusty. I have to get ready for Elizabeth." Jess paused and muttered, "I'm conversing with a cat — no wonder I have strange dreams. I'm not in such great shape when it comes to reality."

* * * * * *

Dressed in a cream, button-down blouse with flowing sleeves and a belted, dark brown skirt, Jessica carried her breakfast tray out of the kitchen, past the bedroom and the cellar door, then down the short hallway leading into the dining area. The apartment was spacious by Manhattan standards, certainly beating the heck out of that flat on the East Side where she'd lived during her early years in the city. Jess almost felt guilty at times, being so happy and secure here when there was so much strife in the world. But paying, as her sister put it, "a pretty arm and a penny" in rent took a little edge off that guilt.

Jess set her tray down on the dining-room table, close to a window affording a pleasant view of the street. A glance at her watch told her it was nearly twenty past eleven. Almost time for Elizabeth. It would be just her luck if Liz suddenly developed punctuality; she wanted to have a chance to finish her tea.

Jessica removed the porcelain Blue Willow tea pot, her cup and saucer, and the plate holding her toast from the tray. All things considered, though, she was pretty darned lucky to have Elizabeth for a sister. Liz had pulled her through a broken heart or two that Jessica would rather not remember. Then, that year after the summer theater in the Adirondacks had folded, and she'd barely been able to make ends meet from her job in a department store, Elizabeth had been there to help, morally and financially. After Harold Vane had snapped Jess up from the subway circuit and two shows had put her in stable financial condition, her brother-in-law had advised her on a few investments to establish her security. So, she had to admit that Peter wasn't completely a bad egg, in spite of his practical jokes. Jess did her best to return the favor of Liz and Peter's past support, letting her sister stay at the apartment when things got too stormy in the marriage. That way, the couple had a little breathing space when they needed it.

About ten years ago, Elizabeth had met Peter Hennessey, a well-placed civil servant, and married him eight months later. Liz had been quite frank about her inability to resist a pink-skinned, sandy-haired mischievous Irishman. Born in the Big Apple, but raised in one of the southern counties of Ireland, Peter more than fit the bill. Her brother-in-law generally referred to their courtship as a case of his chasing Elizabeth until she caught him. Jessica really did like Peter's sense of humor, especially when they teased each other back and forth. It was just that his practical jokes, this gambit in particular, could go too far.

Looking up from her toast, Jess scanned the comfortable living room beyond the dining area. Down three steps from where she breakfasted, a comfy Queen Anne couch, upholstered with peach and apple-green sprigs, faced the bay window. On the couch sat her shopping bag holding the infamous brown package. How on earth could she have been silly enough to let something as pedestrian looking as that package drive her to a nightmare? For heaven's sake, how could anything brown be mysterious? Peter must have been daffy to think he'd really get her going for long. No one played on her emotions and got away with it, not even in fun — especially not in fun. Yes, it was definitely time someone gave Peter a good, strong dose of his own medicine, and she was just the clever girl to do it. That might save them all a great deal of future grief.

For a moment, Jessica considered opening the package, just to see how far her brother-in-law had gone to make his tale convincing. No, that wouldn't work. She could never redo it perfectly, and she would not give him the pleasure of thinking he'd aroused her curiosity even that much.

It really would have been grand fun if she could have counted on Larry to help her pay back Peter. It wasn't that Larry didn't have a sense of humor. His picture ought to be next to "mordant" in the dictionary. He and Peter were somewhat alike in this trait — except that Larry did know when to quit, usually. The trouble was, he was just too practical to want to begin. A sharp quip, that was his forte; but turning around a gag — no way. Besides, she still didn't know for certain if he was a supporting player in Peter's little joke. Given Larry's probity, though, that didn't seem likely.

One prank that had especially stuck in Jess's mind was how, as a child, Peter had saved for six months to buy a cardboard skeleton that he hid in a closet and told his sister was a damned soul come to get her. He'd even melted two red crayons and scared his sister by telling her it was the blood of the soul's last victim. Smiling, Jessica reflected that Peter's obsession with grandiose put-ons had prompted Liz to comment more than once that she might not contemplate divorce but homicide had definitely crossed her mind.

Jessica poured her tea, thinking about the fellow who had left the package. He had a rather intriguing face, would have made a good Byronic hero, an excellent professional brooder. Would she run into him again? It all depended on how far Peter planned to carry his plot. She had to hand it to her mystery man; he was convincing. An attenuated meow interrupted Jessica's reverie.

"Can't I even have a few thoughts to myself?"

Dusty rubbed against Jessica's leg, sat down, and gazed up at her human with a look that could have wrung tears from Basil Rathbone at his most icily villainous.

"You've been fed," Jess replied, knowing that as long as she was eating she would have a furry companion. A glance out the window, then at her watch. In a way she almost hoped her sister would not show. Elizabeth was coming over to instruct her on working culinary miracles with the limited ingredients available during the war. A gourmet cook under any circumstances, Liz Hennessey was determined to develop the same talent in her younger sister. Jess had never been averse to that idea — or any idea, for that matter, connected with food.

Still, it was such a beautiful day; without a short walk outside it would seem an awful waste. Tonight's jitterbugging and fraternizing at the Canteen wouldn't leave her in any condition tomorrow to drag herself much further than the distance between her bedroom and her study. And she would have to recuperate enough to go out dining and dancing again, with Larry and Liz and Peter in the evening. After being cooped up in the theater with rehearsals all week, Jess felt positively claustrophobic. What she wouldn't give to be reading in her favorite secret, secluded spot in Central Park — safe from being confronted by Peter or any of his partners in crime.

The doorbell rang. A quick sip of tea, and Jess was on her feet and into the small foyer by the front door. The doorbell rang again, this time with a suggestion of impatience.

Jess opened the door, greeting her sister with, "Fifteen minutes late, Liz. That's almost punctual — for you, anyway."

Elizabeth Hennessey lifted her chin, narrowed her eyes in her trademark sign of displeasure, and returned, "You have an interesting way of showing your gratitude to the person who taught you how to make something other than tomato casserole seven nights a week."

"C'mon in," said Jess, pretending to be abashed.

"Always respect your elder sister, especially if you want a nice Christmas present," Elizabeth advised, sailing in.

Elizabeth only slightly resembled Jessica. Both had dark hair; both had faces that could be described as patrician, with a glint of the impish in their eyes and smiles. However, the similarities ended there. Elizabeth stood a good three inches taller; her features were longer, thinner, with a touch of the sardonic. Her dark hair was fashionably upswept on either side of her head and complemented with a bun at the nape of her neck. All in all, there was a bit more worldliness in her appearance and her almost husky voice. At first glance, she appeared the experienced sophisticate to her sister's younger skeptic. Jess knew how deceptive that was, though. As only a sister could, she understood that the amused glint in Liz's eye was just her way of laughing up her sleeve at all the people she had fooled into thinking a Martha Raye was actually a Rosalind Russell.

Elizabeth's eyes swept the room, taking in the tea service, pausing imperceptibly during her survey of the den, before returning to Jess.

"I see you have some tea, Jess. After a long walk down here I'd love some."

"Just get another cup from the kitchen," Jess replied amenably.

Elizabeth hesitated a moment before saying, "It was a long walk. How about letting me sit down a minute? You wouldn't mind getting some tea for your weary sister, would you, Jess?"

"Wait a minute. Are you trying to tell me you walked here from the apartment? That's nineteen blocks. When did you leave, yesterday?"

"Now, Jessica, that suspicious expression just doesn't become you."

Jessica's expression didn't change.

Elizabeth reluctantly admitted, "Actually, I did walk part way. The cab left me off at the top of the street. It was a long walk down that street in this heat. So why don't you be your wonderful, generous self and do me this little favor? After all, you want me to be fresh and strong when we get to work."

"Elizabeth," Jessica queried, folding her arms, "how 'fresh and strong' do you have to be to cook? I'm not asking you to haul away a few tons of truck tires."

"You came pretty close the other weekend when we cleaned out your cellar for the rubber drive."

"It was our part for the war effort," Jess defended herself with mock innocence.

"Then I put out more 'effort' than you did, kiddo. I carried four boxes, to your two, into the school."

"Well... you *are* taller and stronger than I am."

"Giraffes are taller than Clydesdales," Elizabeth calmly pointed out.

"Am I being compared to an over-sized horse with hairy legs?" Jessica raised her eyebrows.

"The answer to that depends on whether or not I get my tea."

"Okay, you win," Jessica laughed.

Strolling into the kitchen, Jess left her sister slipping out of a brown linen blazer that matched a pencil skirt and complemented her pale yellow blouse. Even when she was just helping her kid sister to do some cooking, Elizabeth always looked as if she had the MGM wardrobe department dressing her. More likely, Liz must have just come from an earlier appointment, probably a visit with Peter. Working for the government during the war meant a lot of weekend overtime for Peter and Larry.

It was only when Jessica returned to the dining-room table a little too quietly that she realized her sister had been interested in getting more than a cup of tea out of her. Jessica's sophisticated sister was standing in the den, shaking the brown paper-wrapped package with all the poise of Shemp Howard from the Three Stooges. Her back to Jessica, Elizabeth wasn't even aware of her sister's return.

Jessica placed the cup and saucer on the table quietly but observed loudly, "I see you've recovered from your exhaustion, Elizabeth."

Liz Hennessey fairly jumped, fumbling to hold onto the package. Jess said not a word, watching with a bland curiosity that did not quite mask her amusement. Elizabeth turned, first embarrassed, then annoyed, as Jessica pressed her lips together to keep from laughing.

Forcing herself to return the package casually to the couch, Liz asserted, "I wasn't doing anything wrong."

"Of *course* not."

Elizabeth folded her arms, narrowed her eyes, and replied, "All right, Jessica, don't kill it." Shifting emotional gears, Elizabeth calmly ascended the three stairs to join her sister, continuing, "Besides, you can hardly blame me for being curious about the package. You were so mysterious about it."

Now it was Jessica's turn to be startled, puzzled. "Mysterious? With whom was I mysterious? How *did* you know about the package, anyway?"

With an eloquently simple shrug and a conspiratorial tone Elizabeth explained, "Well, I promised not to say, but I went to see Peter this morning. We were supposed to meet in the coffee shop, as usual, but he was so busy that he sent Larry down to ask me to wait. Larry and I started talking, and naturally you came up — and your odd behavior last night . . ."

"Odd behavior?" Jessica interrupted. "I don't see why Larry always has to be talking to *you* about me. I don't know why he forever seems to think I have a problem when I don't."

"Now you're exaggerating," pronounced Elizabeth in her best knowing-older-sister tone. "Anyway, Jess, there are no secrets between sisters."

"Apparently not," Jessica dryly agreed, glancing down at the bundle she had caught her sister examining. "But I would like to know what Mr. Sanders thinks *I* have a problem with."

Elizabeth chided, "It's nothing to get your ears in an uproar about. Larry just told me there was some funny business about a criminal type in Shaftner's who had you acting screwy, and that Harry said you were kind of secretive about covering this brown-paper package you'd carried out of the drugstore. When Larry saw you in the dressing room last night, he saw the package hidden in a shopping bag. But when he asked a reasonable question about what was in the bag, you implied there was something else in there. From you're covering up, he put two and two together that there was something fishy about the package. He's just concerned."

"About what?" Jessica wasn't sure if she was more annoyed or amused. "That I might be smuggling state secrets in a Macy's bag? That's one for the books." Larry could be obsessively discreet, but only in matters *he* considered important. Even if he was a great guy, it really got her goat when he arbitrarily decided that she was in trouble and needed him to take her in hand. Did his conversation with Liz mean that Larry was working with Peter to pull a fast one on both sisters? Knowing Larry, it was almost easier to believe that she was caught in the middle of a spy plot!

"So, what *is* in the package, Jess?" Liz broke into her sister's thoughts. "I couldn't tell by rattling it. It's packed pretty solid. You've got me stumped — and you know that takes some doing."

"You said it. Has anyone been able to hide a Christmas present from you since 1909?"

"That's before I was born, dear. You know that."

Jessica folded her arms and fastened her sister with a skeptical smile.

"All right, the *end* of 1909! Anyway, are you going to tell me what's in the package?"

Here was a point certainly worth considering. Liz would be a divine ally against Peter; she had plenty of axes to grind after suffering through so many of his pranks. Unfortunately, Jessica wasn't sure what would hex their alliance against Peter first: Liz's hair-trigger temper or tendency to blab. Better to keep her sister out of this deal.

"No, Liz, I'm not going to tell you. It's a present for someone — not you. And we both know that you can't be trusted to keep mum once you find out who's getting what. So there. Tea?"

Liz was not about to allow her sister the last word, however. "Jess, I lived with you for seventeen years of your life. I can remember when you painted a peanut-butter mural on the hall wall in front of Mum and swore to her you didn't do a thing. Don't try to pull the virtuous act on me."

"I never said I was virtuous, just that I can keep a secret better than you."

"Be a sport, Jess. Can't I take a little peek? Just let me accidentally slit the side with a knife so I can look inside."

"Elizabeth, it's time to hit the kitchen and start cooking."

Her sister's stare could have raised icicles in Tahiti.

"Cheer up, Liz, maybe I'll impale myself on a mixing spoon."

"Jessica, people don't impale themselves on mixing spoons. It can't be done."

"You also said no one could stick pancakes to the ceiling the way they do in the movies — until I made breakfast for you that morning after your second-to-last fight with Peter."

"You go to the kitchen. I'll be there in a minute."

"Where are you going?"

"To get your first aid kit."

It was a few hours later. Jessica and Elizabeth sat relaxing over their tea. Luckily, tea drinking was practically a mania with the Minton family, since coffee was in such short supply now. Elizabeth wore an over-sized Band-Aid on one finger.

"We finished earlier than I expected," Jess ventured.

"There's still the dishes," Elizabeth pointed out, graciously remaining silent on the topic of her injured finger. "Remember, we left them to soak a little while."

Jess nodded and sighed almost imperceptibly. However, little escaped Elizabeth. The older sister paused over her tea a moment before asking, "Something wrong, kid?"

"Oh no, nothing," Jess replied quickly, shaking her head. Funny how you could simultaneously hope that someone would and wouldn't press you further.

"Are you annoyed that I stepped on the cat?"

Jess smiled and answered, "No, it wasn't your fault. I realize that the minute Dusty scents food, she's all over you like a Marine who hadn't had leave in six months."

"Are you feeling guilty about..."

"Er, no, well, I mean I *am* sorry about your finger." But more than being embarrassed about her sister's injured finger, Jessica wanted to talk.

"I was just thinking, Liz. After last week, I've been dying to get out of the house and away from everything for a little while. I certainly won't have much opportunity for the rest of this week. I'm stuck with a schedule that only lets me out long enough to run from rehearsals to the Canteen and back again. You wouldn't care to let the dishes go and take a little stroll with me?"

Elizabeth shuddered slightly and said, "I don't let dishes go unwashed."

"Even mine?"

"It's the principle of the thing," Elizabeth replied evenly. Then she added, "But, if you really would like to get out of the house, Jess, I'll do the dishes for you, battle wound and all."

"I can't let you do my work."

"You never had that problem when we were kids."

"Did you offer to do me a favor just so you could use that line on me?"

"Don't be silly. You could use some time off. Why don't you just take a book, go out to the park, and do some reading. What about that out-of-the-way place you like to sneak off to?"

Jess paused for a moment, beginning to smile as temptation seduced her. She ventured, "You really wouldn't mind?" A hesitation, then, "Even after what I did to you with the spoon? I really didn't mean to hurt you, Liz."

"Oh, in that case I'd better send you off, if I want to live. There are knives in that sink."

Jess hugged her sister, then started for the study to get her book. Elizabeth offered, "I know you get headaches from too much sun, Jess. I'll get you that broad-brimmed felt hat you like."

"I'm not that much of an invalid," Jess called lightly over her shoulder as she walked down into the den. She was just thinking of what a generous sister Elizabeth could be when she inadvertently caught sight of the package on the couch. Jess turned back to her sister — who was looking at the package. With a cool smile, Jess scooped it up and proceeded to the study, her bundle securely nestled in the crook of her arm.

"Ah, Jess, what are you doing?"

Jessica turned at the study doors with a cheery, "Oh, I thought I'd just put the package away."

"In the study?"

"In the safe in the study," Jess corrected pleasantly before she turned and disappeared into the next room.

"My sister," concluded Elizabeth Hennessey, "is a rat."

* * * * * *

Jessica put down her book, resting it on her lap. Legs neatly tucked under her, she felt cozy and comfortable on the stone steps, obscured and shaded by a row of hedges and a copse of trees. Every once in awhile, the leaves and lighter branches would sway with the late summer breeze. A delicious hideaway.

Starlings and grackles were whistling their intricate incantations, interspersed by the abrupt chirps of sparrow. Was that a catbird querying, "Sharon?" Jess liked to think of this place as her private set of ruins. Indeed, hidden within the copse, the steps, as well as a little wall barely rising even with the topmost stair, almost appeared to be the remains of some lost edifice overgrown by the limited wilderness of the urban park. Only the fact that the steps were located in a small alcove in the greenery seemed to indicate that this had been planned as no more than a place to retire from one of the many paths crisscrossing Central Park.

The entrance to Jessica's right was gradually being obscured by growing branches. Not many people took advantage of this place any more, which suited her just fine. There had been plenty of times over the past few years when the pressures of trying to make her career work had made this isolated spot a godsend.

Lately though, even this hideaway wasn't isolated enough. There was no refuge from thinking about what had happened to the world. Jess instinctively refused to believe that America, itself, could be invaded, but she hadn't expected Pearl Harbor, either. What about British Prime Minister Neville Chamberlain and all the supposedly reasonable appeasement that had handed Hitler most of Europe on a silver platter? It shouldn't have worked out that way. It shouldn't have worked out with most of the world ripped apart. So much had changed, changed faster than Jessica could keep up with.

Jess leaned back and closed her eyes. What was she doing to make things better? Collecting rubber, aluminum — not hoarding — any fool could do that. Tripping the light fantastic with soldiers at the Canteen. Talking to guys in the service there. Some of them needed someone to talk to. Some of them needed a good right hook. She'd faced off a few too many pawings and pinches of late. Still, did she do enough? She wasn't exactly fighting in a trench, not even working in a munitions factory. Those thoughts put her troubles with Peter in perspective.

The branches rattled. Funny, she hadn't felt any breeze just now. Jess opened her eyes and nearly jumped out of her skin. Settled neatly on one knee on the grass next to her was the gentleman who had left her with that darned package. His hand swiftly over her mouth, as well as his serious dark eyes, muffled her instinctive outcry. But Jessica Minton was a girl who recovered fast. With lethal calm she freed herself and warned, "If you ever put your hand over my mouth like that again I'll bite it."

"Touché, Miss Minton." His hazel eyes and expression glinted humor, but only briefly. The lean-faced man's tone was serious as he informed Jess, "I want my package."

"You think I wander around Central Park toting a 'Lost and Found' from Schaftner's? Get serious, fella."

This opportunity to strike back at her rat-for-a-brother-in-law, even if only through his hireling, left Jessica inwardly chuckling.

However, there was no humor in her uninvited companion's insistence, "It's imperative I get the package. You must bring it to me."

"So imperative that you have to ruin the one chance I get in over a week for a little peace and quiet? To be perfectly frank, I think you're nuts. Tell you what, bub, if you want the package you can just go around to Harry Shaftner, leave a message with him, and pick up the darned thing after I've had a chance to drop it off."

"That's out of the question. They'll be expecting me there. I can't be seen with it. I can't even be seen at your flat."

"Believe me; you're not going to be invited."

"I won't be seen there. It's too dangerous. You know there are fifth columnists, infiltrators, everywhere. You'll have to meet me someplace isolated, alone."

"You? Alone? You sneak up on me and give me all these lines about 'danger' and 'secret meetings' like some kind of paranoid maniac, and you think I'm going to meet you alone?"

"You're alone with me now."

"Not for long, buddy," Jess retorted, slapping the dark felt hat on her head, grabbing her book, and getting up.

Surprised by her sudden movement, the man instinctively pulled back to let her pass. But he wasn't surprised for long. In a jiffy he was on his feet, grasping Jess's elbow and swinging her around to face him.

"I can't let you go now, Miss Minton."

"If you don't let me go," Jessica threatened, "I am going to beat you to death with my annotated anthology of British literature."

"The fewer who know you have the package the better. The quicker I get the package, the less chance anyone has of knowing you had it."

For a moment, an image of the fire plug at Shaftner's muscled its way menacingly into her thoughts. Wait a minute, what was she getting jumpy about? He was part of the gag, too! Darn, these guys were good. Peter's little pal here almost had her there for a minute. Almost, but not quite. Two could play this game. Maybe she could have some fun stringing along her brother-in-law and his pawn.

"What if someone already knows I have the package?" she questioned slowly.

"Then you'd best give it me as soon as possible."

His quiet intensity was unnerving. Only the fact that stuff like this just didn't happen in real life saved her from falling for Peter's little plot. Hoping to unsettle her antagonist by calling his bluff, Jess calmly informed him, "I don't want to get any deeper into this. Maybe I'd better turn the package over to the police."

His fingers tightened on her arm as he insisted, "No! Don't you remember, last night I warned you that this is bigger than anything the metropolitan authorities are prepared to handle!"

In spite of her determination to play it cool, Jessica instinctively took a step backward. But she caught herself. What was she thinking? She just wished Peter hadn't come up with such a convincing actor.

Seeing her reaction, her companion dropped Jessica's arm and explained, "I know I've proceeded mysteriously. I realize this entire chain of events must seem more than a little queer, Miss Minton, but the less you know the less involved you are. Considering the position that having the package puts you in, I can understand why you feel you have the right to know what's going on. Let me say that . . ."

Something caught his attention. He halted, gazing beyond Jess toward the overgrown aperture behind her. She didn't like to admit that she was almost reluctant to turn around; but being Elizabeth's sister, curiosity got the better of her. Unfortunately, as she was six inches shorter than her man of mystery, Jessica couldn't see what had captured his attention.

Apparently his own vantage point wasn't quite good enough, for he moved away from her toward the opening to get a better view, careful to keep himself out of the sight of anyone outside.

Recovering herself, Jess demanded, "What is it? What am I supposed to think is wrong?"

He didn't reply immediately. Instead, he turned, looking strained, uncertain, then glanced back over his shoulder toward the overgrown opening.

"Well, what is it?" Jess demanded, annoyed she'd automatically lowered her voice to a cautious whisper.

"I have to go."

"Oh, really? Goebbels and Goering strolling hand in hand out there?"

"If I were you, Miss Minton, I'd cut out being flip. You're in danger if anyone knows you have the package. I expected more sense from you."

"Why? You don't know me. Or do you?"

"I wish I could explain everything right now, but I can't. For your sake as well as mine, I have to go before we're seen together. I can't even afford to try to get the package from you at the Canteen."

"Oh, *must* you go *so* soon? We were just getting to know each other."

The man looked at her as if he were playing from Lillian Hellman's sober *Watch on the Rhine*, and she'd responded with some squirrelly lines from *Arsenic and Old Lace*, but he soldiered on, "I'll get in touch with you. We'll work something out about the package. Just stay here long enough that no passerby might suspect we've been here together."

About to nail her companion with a snappy rejoinder, Jessica was silenced as much by his unexpectedly gentle touch on her shoulder as by his words, "I can see I've unsettled you. I'm very sorry, Miss Minton. Truly. You don't deserve this; but believe me, I'll keep an eye on you."

He was off, leaving Jess uncertain how to react to his appearing so concerned for her. Well, her brother-in-law had certainly hired himself a darned good actor! Lost in those thoughts, Jessica approached the entrance to her no longer secure retreat, then abruptly stopped. Outside, a short distance down the path, was a husky figure in a familiar trench coat and hat, his back to her. A man shaped like a fire plug. He looked about, shifted his stance, waiting. Waiting for her so he could drag out this gag even further? Peter just did not know when to quit! Her annoyance forcefully supplanted any thoughts about the first fellow's seeming sincerity. Darned if she would indulge her brother-in-law or his cohorts in any more fun at her expense. Come hell or high water, she was going to sit down, pick up her book, and relax. Damn it!

Returning to the stone steps, Jess shot one fierce glance back toward the aperture as she smoothed her skirt beneath her before sitting down. Heaven help Mr. Fire Plug, if that were him, should he dare invade her little retreat. *Calm yourself, kiddo,* Jess silently soothed herself. *Just let the book open where it will, so some delicious Romantic poetry wafts you away on its viewless wings to serenity.* The book opened on "Rime of the Ancient Mariner." *Swell, just what I need, a poem about a good-natured cluck who ends up pulled out of his happy life by the crazy yarn of a hypnotic, charismatic, wild-eyed nutcase.*

Except, unlike Coleridge's Mariner, the English guy hadn't been wild-eyed or seemed nuts. Just playing sincere and concerned for all he was worth. Jessica gritted her teeth. Peter knew that she'd been a sucker in the past when a guy appealed to her tender side, her idealistic side, too. Wasn't Larry's big draw for her that he didn't take advantage of her trust? Yeah, Peter could have told his good-looking henchman to play on her ideals while treating her as if her feelings mattered. He knew that she'd been taken in before by a guy or two with the right words but the wrong actions. What he apparently didn't know was that those experiences had wised her up.

Jessica walked boldly toward the aperture and peeked out.

No one.

The young woman stepped out into the sunshine of the path. Greenery, blue skies, a few squirrels — but none of the nuts she had been expecting. Yup (to quote Gary Cooper), this was too much like a bad melodrama, right down to the timing and dialogue. Well, she'd take good care of her mystery man and her brother-in-law. By the time she finished with them they'd wish the Axis had gotten its hooks into them instead of her!

CHAPTER THREE

"Jessica, I believe Peter asked you a question."

Staring confusedly across the table at Elizabeth, Jess took a fraction of a second to get her bearings.

Elizabeth took advantage of Jessica's daze to continue, "I know even Peter's *questions* are enough to put anyone to sleep but try to humor him this once, Jess. I do, occasionally."

From next to Elizabeth, Peter Hennessey, a wicked Irish glint in his blue eyes, countered with deadly casualness, "While every show of good manners from you, Liz, prompts someone to faint."

Elizabeth sharply tapped the ashes from her cigarette into a silver ashtray. Her eyes narrowed when Larry, who sat between her and Jessica at the round, richly appointed table, quirked a smile at Peter's remark. He seldom encouraged Peter's jibes at Liz, but he was amused this time.

Before Elizabeth could launch any clever rejoinders at either man, Jessica had the wisdom to interrupt, "I'm sorry, Peter. This has been a long week. I guess I've just been thinking about the play — and how, ah, troublesome it's been. I'm not looking forward to tomorrow when we go back to work. Our director is spending the entire weekend rewriting like a madman with the author. He isn't exactly a sweetheart under the best circumstances — after a God-awful weekend — brother, look out!"

Had she rattled on too much? The last thing she wanted to do was give Peter the idea that his little plot was unnerving her. Well, at least appearing to brood over the play's problems offered a believable alternative for her disquiet. Let Peter smart in doubt over what the score really was. Thinking to better establish that only work was eating at her, Jess nodded at the fish her brother-in-law's flashing cutlery had reduced to neat pieces and mused, "That's what will happen to us tomorrow."

Chin resting on her upturned palm, Jessica fleetingly considered that one didn't put one's elbows on a table in this hotel's elegant dining room. She continued to defy decorum, more interested in what Peter's next move would be.

Peter regarded his sister-in-law with amusement, inquiring, "Is Vane really so terrible?"

"He makes SS officers look jolly."

"Really?"

The blue eyes glanced at her for a moment, amused. Then Peter disappointed Jess's hopes to unsettle him by continuing to eat, pausing only when Larry initiated a discussion of one of his favorite topics, the brilliance of the British in their victorious North African campaign. Larry took more than a little umbrage when Peter suggested that Montgomery's victories over Rommel were not so much due to the British general's being a better tactician but to his being better equipped and better supported. Germany had spread herself too thin over too many fronts to support herself adequately in any one area — according to General Peter Hennessey.

Despite her annoyance with Peter's rib, Jessica couldn't help smiling when Elizabeth glanced from the animated conversation of their two male companions back to her and pointedly stifled a yawn. Neither Peter nor Larry noticed; they were too busy re-campaigning their way across North Africa. Jess sometimes wondered if Peter and Larry might not run the war better than Eisenhower or Montgomery.

Well, maybe she could forgive Peter a little since he and Larry were under so much pressure working for the government, though neither of them was in on anything very confidential. To be honest, she still wasn't sure exactly what they did. Peter had tried to explain his job to her once. It must have been complicated, because to this day she had no idea what he had been talking about except that it had something to do with transportation. She hadn't been game enough for another try. Elizabeth had made her feel a little less of a dope by pointing out that it was hard to understand an explanation that put you to sleep by the third sentence. When he wanted to torment her, Larry would answer Jess's questions about his work with a straight-faced, "It's the same as Peter's. Why don't I have him explain it to you?" Consequently, Jessica had resolved *never again* to be curious about Larry's work. Anyway, how interesting could a civil service office job be?

Jess suspected that the real reason for Larry's fascination with the private strategy games he played with Peter stemmed from his inability to join the actual fighting. She had learned Larry's life story from him over the time they'd been dating, as well as from Liz and Peter. Her boyfriend had come to America from England a little over ten years ago and was now an American citizen, but his ties with his mother country were still strong. When England had first gone to war, Larry had tried to go to Canada to volunteer for service, but the lingering result of a childhood injury had nixed that plan. With the war, his and Peter's work in city transportation had caused them to be frozen in their positions — the type of job that wasn't glamorous but was still vital to the bigger war effort. Jess always knew that this was not enough for Larry; so perhaps his mock battles with Peter were a vicarious attempt to be involved in the world's struggle against the Fascists.

"You look so fascinated by the discussion, Jess. You don't mind my distracting you for a minute, do you?" Elizabeth broke into Jessica's thoughts.

Jess smiled briefly in response. Elizabeth studied Jessica a moment before carefully resting her cigarette on the ashtray and saying, "You look a little drawn, kid."

Jessica paused before explaining, "As I told Peter, it's been a long week. And last night at the Canteen just about did me in. There was this one sergeant from Cleveland, looked as if someone had cut his hair with a lawn mower. The best I can say about his dancing was that at least he wasn't wearing combat boots. He danced with me all night!"

"At least you know you're popular."

"He did say that I was a 'swell dame,'" Jess agreed with an amused nod.

"All danced out after last night?" Liz surmised.

"I hope you saved a few dances for me. I'd hate to let this dance floor go to waste," Larry joined in with casual gallantry.

"For you, Larry, I'll always have dances," Jessica promised airily.

"Shall we, then?"

Jessica accepted Larry's arm, and they moved out onto the dance floor encircled by the dining area.

As the two swirled into the crowd of dancers, Peter started to return to his dinner. Then, catching his wife frowning at Jessica's nearly full plate, he paused. A neatly lacquered fingernail tapping her cheek further betrayed Liz's preoccupation.

"Liz? Something wrong?"

"Oh, I... Peter, did you notice that Jess didn't finish her dinner?"

Peter glanced at the dish in question and agreed, "You're right. Do you think she'll want the rest of it?"

"Peter, you have enough in your own dish." Elizabeth glanced back at her sister's plate, dissatisfied, thinking out loud, "It's so unlike Jess not to eat. She's almost as bad as you, when it comes to food. There's something wrong."

"Liz, you're Jessica's older sister not her mother. The girl is twenty-eight years old. She can look after herself," Peter pointed out reasonably.

Elizabeth considered her husband's words. They made sense, but she still wasn't satisfied. She glanced at Jessica's plate again, then mused, "I wonder if this has to do with the package."

"What package?" Peter inquired, taking a moment off from his rice pilaf.

"Someone left behind a mysterious package. Didn't Larry tell you anything about all this?" Elizabeth asked, genuinely surprised.

"No. Maybe Larry wanted to respect someone else's privacy. Wait a minute, how did you know about this package?"

"Oh, I was just talking to Larry before I saw you yesterday, and he seemed preoccupied so I just . . ."

"...ferreted the story out of him? Elizabeth, have you ever considered doing intelligence work? It's a good thing you're on our side."

"I resent being compared to a rodent," Elizabeth shot back, additionally annoyed by her husband's obvious enjoyment of his successful needling. She picked up her cigarette again.

Realizing his wife was genuinely concerned, Peter wisely let pass a golden opportunity to crack wise about Liz confusing ferrets with rodents. Instead, he took a conciliatory tone and apologized, "I'm sorry, Liz. You're worried, but Jess is a big girl — a smart girl. I've never seen her get in over her head. Don't worry."

"Oh, maybe you're right," Elizabeth conceded, more resigned than convinced.

Seeing the topic settled, Peter studied his wife a minute before inquiring, "Tell me, Liz, I see you're smoking. Does that mean you've finished eating?"

"Oh, here!"

Elizabeth irritably passed across the remains of her Chicken Kiev, glanced at her husband, then turned away. Peter nonchalantly proceeded with his dining, musing aloud that he hoped they had his favorite, banana-cream pie, on the menu for dessert.

Jessica and Larry glided through the swirl of dancers as the band lazed through "Skylark." The dance floor, like the dining room, was romantically lit: just dusky enough to be dreamy but not so dark that you might get the idea the kitchen was afraid to let you see what you were eating.

Larry was a marvelous dancer. Foxtrotting across the floor, never hindered by other couples, Jess relaxed. Poor Liz. Her sister loved to dance as much as she. Unfortunately, Peter didn't share his spouse's enthusiasm. Occasionally, Elizabeth would manage to steal Larry for a dance. Not tonight, though! In Larry's comfortable hold, Jessica had no intention of switching partners with anyone.

"So, young lady, have you given my proposal any more thought?'

"To get married? Larry, I thought we'd agreed to give that more time. You know I'm not ready to settle down completely, the way you want."

"I thought I did give you time, Jess."

"One week to decide to retire from the stage and accept a lifetime engagement as Jessica Sanders?"

"Oh, I don't know, as Mrs. Larry Sanders you'll always have star billing."

"Just not my own first name."

"What?"

"Never mind. Just a personal quirk. But, Larry, I'm in the middle of rehearsals for a play. I can't just quit . . ."

"I thought the play was making you miserable. Don't you want me to take you away from all that? The timing seems perfect to me. Besides, what's there to wait for? We're both good dancers, we're both reasonably attractive, and I think we bump along rather well together, don't you?"

"Couldn't you make it sound a little more romantic than that, Larry?" Jessica smiled, though still serious.

"Jessica, you know that despite my dashing good looks and superlative dancing skills, I am a practical chap."

The urge to say, "Practical doesn't have to be pedestrian" came to mind, but that seemed a little too flip. Why wasn't she dancing on air rather than on this shiny floor? Larry was crazy about her, wanted to spend the rest of his life with her. Far and away better than most of the fellas she'd dealt with, he wasn't going to break her heart like Terry from college or Eric from summer stock. The compliments and attentions weren't just a sheep's pinstripe over wolfish intentions. So what more did she want? What was missing?

"Never mind," Larry said, accurately reading her silence. "If you have to think that hard, you're not ready. But don't worry. I know you'll change your mind eventually. You'll come around and I'll be right here."

"I don't want you to feel led on, Larry . . ."

"I know what I'm doing, even if you don't — yet." He smiled knowingly at Jessica. "It will be worth the wait when you come to your senses."

"Larry," Jessica corrected patiently, "being on the stage isn't some kind of fever dream. I've worked very hard, for a long time, to get where I am."

"Of course, Jessica. I understand. That's why I can wait. A girl like you is worth it."

The dance ended, and Jessica wasn't sure how to feel. Somehow the whole Peter deal seemed unimportant by comparison. Every girl wanted to get married, have a family. But why did it have to be a choice between vocation and domesticity? Even though she cared for Larry, something she just couldn't put her finger on kept telling her to say no, but she wasn't sure many people would understand how she felt. The one advantage to dating heels was that they were never serious enough to make this kind of demand on her.

She could really do with a minute alone to get herself back on an even keel.

"Larry, you go back to Liz and Peter. I have to, shall we say, 'powder my nose'? I'll be back in a minute or two."

Larry seemed ready to say more, but Jess slipped away as quickly as she could through the crowd of gowns and tuxedos.

The ladies' room was beyond the dance floor, further across the dining area, and down a little corridor near the entrance where a perpetually smiling *maître d'* stood. This restaurant specialized in seafood, a blessing for the proprietors during these meatless war years. At any rate, considering the house specialty, Jessica was not terribly surprised to see the ladies' room designated by a lobster in a skirt. Jess shook her head. The lengths to which people would go to be clever!

Entering, Jess smiled at a bored maid seated by the table under the wall mirror. As she sat down before the mirror a stranger entered and required the maid's attention for some adjustments to her dress. A good look at herself in the mirror left Jess comparing herself to her sister. She'd thought her gown of white muslin with flatteringly fitted bodice and short, slightly puffed sleeves attractive, but the yellow-chiffon strapless number that positively molded itself to her sister's torso put her in the shade. That matching chiffon scarf must have been a personal gift from MGM's Adrian to Liz. If she and Elizabeth ever both became nuns, her sister would still find some way to look more glamorous.

With a resigned sigh, Jess fished through her little white evening bag (handy enough to palm on the dance floor) for her lipstick. Maybe she should talk to Liz about how to deal with Larry. Her sister had fixed them up in the first place. Still, Liz had never worked the way Jess had. Could she understand her sister's predicament? Some of the girls Jess had gone to school with would, some of the girls she worked with, too. But almost everyone else would tell her she was crazy if she let a great catch like Larry get away. Well, she wasn't going to come up with an answer tonight.

Last minute adjustments finished, Jess took her purse and exited the room. Walking up the little corridor, Jess passed the maitre d' — and stopped dead in her tracks. Neatly uniformed as a waiter, serving a meal several tables away, was a familiar fire-plug shaped man. He started to look up. In *her* direction. Jess didn't wait to see whether he'd spotted her. One hasty step backward and she was in silent, single-minded retreat to the room of the be-skirted lobster.

The maid was still sitting there, still bored, but Jess didn't smile this time. She vaguely wondered what the maid might think of her unusually quick return, before her mind raced onto more pressing worries.

What in Sam Hill was one of Peter's flunkies doing at this place on her night out? Was it a coincidence, his working here? But a luxury hotel like this certainly would be above employing this third-rate William Bendix type. No, Mr. Fire Plug could only have gotten in here if Peter had pulled some strings to get him hired for the evening — and hadn't this restaurant been Peter's choice in the first place? It was all falling pat into place. Peter must have decided that he had to pull out all the stops to break her. She hadn't been sufficiently rattled in the park by Mr. Mustached, Mystery Man; she didn't believe she'd said anything that would make Liz tell Peter something was eating her kid sister. So Peter was hoping she'd make a scene right here in the restaurant. Well, she'd fix his little red wagon; she'd go right back out there and act as if nothing were up. He couldn't catch a fish if it didn't chomp on the bait.

But Jessica hesitated. Peter was cagey. He wouldn't go to all the trouble of getting some mug hired in this place for the night, then take a chance she wouldn't see him or react to him. No, Jessica knew Peter Hennessey too well to think for one minute that if he were setting her up for a confrontation, he would let her ease her way out. If she stayed, Peter would find a way to force her hand. So, how to forestall Peter before he put that big palooka in a dress and sent him in here after her?

"Jessica Minton, what makes you turn tail and run the minute you see your big sister coming?"

Jessica nearly jumped. Instead, she turned to face Elizabeth, who stood with an eyebrow raised in inquiry.

"Say, kid, what is wrong?" Elizabeth's amusement melted into concern. Liz sat down next to her sister, worrying, "You look as if you'd seen a ghost."

Jess turned away before replying, "Nothing. I'm okay — Well, maybe a little overtired."

Liz leaned back, regarding her sister speculatively.

"You don't look tired, Jessica. You look damn jumpy."

Jess shook her head, "Really, I'm fine."

Elizabeth wasn't buying. "Look, Jess, did it occur to you that I might be able to help you?"

Jessica hesitated, for although the maid was going through her sewing kit, her expression no longer looked quite so bored. Jess shot a look meaningfully at Liz, then back at the maid. Elizabeth glanced back, smiled, then rose from her chair, purse in hand, saying as she turned to the maid, "Dear, you look as if you could use a change of scenery."

The girl protested, "But what if somebody wants me here?"

"We'll hold down the fort while you're gone. We want to talk in private. Here, go buy us a couple of post cards from your trip."

A bill dropped into her sewing kit. The maid was no dope. She left.

After a quick check to establish that they were alone, Elizabeth pressed, only slightly more curious than concerned, "All right, Jess, what gives?"

Jessica did some rapid calculating. True, she was breaking her word to herself about keeping things quiet, and Liz did like to spread news. However, Elizabeth could sometimes be persuaded to keep her mouth shut if convinced that the circumstances were serious enough. Then, there was the blunt fact that Jess needed a way out, *now*. She had to escape undetected, and if anyone could help her surreptitiously slip away it was her sister, the Michelangelo of stealth.

Relating all the craziness of the past three days, from the little performances in Shaftner's to the sudden appearance of the suspect waiter (who probably had seen her), Jessica finished, "Once I figure out a way to turn the tables on your husband, I am going to kill him."

"No, you won't, Jess; he hasn't accumulated a decent pension for his widow yet. I don't know what that husband of mine was thinking, to come up this particular little plot with the F.B.I. and the police frothing at the mouth looking for fivers. Doesn't that bonehead realize that he could end up getting himself arrested if he got involved in something that even hinted at espionage — especially when he works for the government?"

"You can say that again, Liz. Somehow I don't think Hoover or

LaGuardia would have much of a sense of humor if they ever got wind of this gag. That's just one more reason to play it cool, not let him make a big scene," Jessica worried.

"Even so," Liz reflected, "I have to say, the effort he put into this plot is impressive. It's a doozy. The rube with the mustache probably had no problem following you. Peter could easily have told him where you live, and I did mention to him when he came home for late lunch Friday that you had called to tell me not to see you after rehearsals — you'd be working late. He must have been planning this for some time and decided then that his moment had come."

"That's what I thought. He did go to a great deal of trouble to play a practical joke, though, didn't he?"

"Jessica," Elizabeth countered, "you seem to have forgotten what Peter did to me with shaving cream and yak hair after we saw *The Wolf Man*. Remember, he even took pictures with the Brownie to prove he carried that one off? And don't forget that clever little number he pulled on his sister with the devil costume."

Jessica nodded, remarking, "There's another rat around here besides the one in your upsweep."

Liz patted her styled, dark hair, giving her reflection a little smile before agreeing, "And I had to marry the rodent."

"I'm still not sure what set him off, Liz. I know he gets a little sore with me when I defend you during some of your quarrels, but he's never pulled anything like this before on me."

"Maybe you've been living on borrowed time. Jessica, you were *way* overdue."

"I guess that makes sense. So, what do we do now, Liz? I don't particularly feel like running into that gorilla outside — I might be charged with homicide afterward. Anyway, I'm too tired to be clever now, and I do want my vengeance to be just as elaborate as your husband's hoax."

"We certainly will have to work on this," Liz concurred.

"So, you'll help me?" Jess asked, pleased.

"What are older sisters for?" Liz grinned, wickedly conspiratorial. "Anyway, I never did get even for the yak hair."

"So, where do we start?"

Liz considered, "We don't have time to plan anything complicated now."

"We ought to meet and have a nice long conference," Jess concurred. "I'm afraid, though, that I'm going to be pretty busy with rehearsals, till Saturday at least. I don't know when, or for how long, I'll be free."

"I can telephone you during the week. But just to throw Peter and his playmates off balance, why don't you change your schedule and routes a little? I'll try to feed Peter some false information — mix up his routine."

"There's just one problem, Liz."

Liz looked at her sister quizzically.

"If I stay, I think that Peter will try to force my hand tonight, before we're ready to turn the tables on him. We want to come up with a plan that will give him a dose of his own medicine, so maybe he'll think twice before pulling one of these stunts on some other poor soul. And, let's face it; wouldn't it be grand to outfox Peter tonight? However, the point will be moot if I can't give that mug out there the slip."

Liz rose, paced pensively then halted. Her face lit up with a deliciously demonic smile as she explained, "It's a cinch. Peter's flunky saw you when you came in here, so he'll be looking for a brunette in a white gown, right?"

"Okay. So?"

"So, he won't be looking for a woman in yellow chiffon —" she whipped off her scarf "— and matching turban."

Jess looked at Liz and smiled, "Liz, you really ought to be with the Underground, smuggling people out of France."

"True," Elizabeth agreed. "True."

A few minutes later, Jessica surveyed herself in the mirror. Strategically placed tissue made up for some of nature's insufficient endowments. Liz's shoes were absolutely murdering Jessica's feet, a killer combination of a size too small and heels two inches too high. But, shorter than Elizabeth, Jess found the extra height indispensable for navigating in her sister's dress. She'd tripped three times on the hem of the gown just trying to make it to the door in her own shoes — not exactly conducive to a subtle escape.

Finally, Jess turned to her sister and grinned, "Wish me luck."

Liz nodded, shook her sister's hand with mock solemnity, then sent Jess on her way. But Jessica stopped suddenly at the door and turned to her sister. "I just thought of something. How will you explain my unorthodox disappearance to Larry and Peter?"

Liz thought for a moment then brightened with a "eureka" expression and explained, "This is perfect. Earlier this evening we were talking about your friend Iris Rossetti and how every month she has a new boyfriend breaking her heart. We can tell the guys that you ran into her in here. She was in throes of misery again, and you had to take her home because she had just found out her latest was two-timing her. You had to get her out fast because she was going to go back into the restaurant and make a scene."

"You think they'll buy it?"

"Of course. Larry will think you're sweet — probably call you up later, so be sure to go right home and keep your story straight."

"Good, but how will you explain that I suddenly had to take Iris home in your dress?"

Elizabeth had to think before suggesting, "Okay, okay. I've got it. When we were in here, you asked me to let you try on my dress to see how you would look — they've both already heard you admire it several times, so they could buy that. I'll say we were in such a hurry to get Iris safely home we didn't waste time changing back. Good enough?"

Jessica pondered the possibilities hard, "I don't know. You sure they'll buy it?"

Elizabeth nodded, "Now, don't worry. Peter's too busy indulging his addiction to banana cream pie to think about details. And as for Larry, I'll take care of him."

"Well, it's a cockeyed story, but knowing everyone involved, I think it just might fly. If anyone could stretch a few glimmers of possibility into gospel, you're the one."

"Good luck, kiddo," Liz saluted smartly. With a crooked smile, Jess marched off.

For a moment, Jessica stopped just outside the ladies' room. She'd better locate the fire plug if she expected to escape before he could see or stop her. He was there — darn! — serving a meal, just now starting to look up. Still moving, Jess snapped open her purse, obscuring her face as she pretended to search it for some elusive object and promptly walked into the *maitre d'*. His smile didn't look quite so perpetual.

"I, er, sorry."

A quick glance in the direction of danger — somehow the commotion seemed to have escaped the fire plug. The *maitre d'*, however, regarded her icily.

"Excuse me."

Jess would have much preferred to counter the man's frigid stare with a crack that it looked as if someone had dashed off his mustache with an eyebrow pencil. Under the circumstances, though, all she could do was glide off as inconspicuously as humiliation would allow and silently grouse, "I just hope Peter's little pal gets stiffed when he looks for his tips."

* * * * * *

The fire-plug-cum-"waiter" who had given Jessica such a turn leaned against the rough brick wall at the rear of the restaurant. The alley was dark, only slightly illuminated by a vague glare from the main street, giving his outline a hazy glow. Impatiently, he watched the smoke from his cigarette curl up and away.

He tensed slightly at a sound more sensed than heard. Abruptly, he put a barrel between himself and the dark end of the alley. Both wary and weary, he peered into the blackness beyond. Then he relaxed, or at least seemed less ready to strike as he recognized the tall, wiry form of his confederate. He stepped forward into the darkness, knowing he had nothing good to report, but more irritated at his companion than at himself over the circumstances. He wasn't used to working this way, and he didn't like his new partner on this mission.

"I take it she saw you?"

The accent was British, hints of the industrial North almost buried under a university education.

"Yeah, she saw me all right. That was your plan, wasn't it?"

"That was part of it," the dark man with the mustache replied. "Did you contact her?"

"What do you think, buddy?"

"I don't think you talked to her any more than you think I'm your buddy."

"She slipped out before I could." It killed him to admit it, so his tone was almost belligerent, daring his partner to claim he could have done better. "You didn't lose her, did you?"

"A girl tottering out in someone else's high heels and a dress a size or so too big isn't easy to miss. I've got to give her high marks for imagination, though."

"Of course you saw her. You were keeping your eyes peeled for her in the hotel bar across the street, while I was working under cover, getting calluses on my bunions."

The younger man's mouth tightened. He could have commented that his companion shouldn't have let an amateur, no matter how creative she was, give him the slip. Instead, he dryly observed, "At least you can keep the tips."

"You know, sonny, I didn't ask to work with you."

Again the younger man was politic and didn't correct "with" to "for."

"Neither of us had much of a choice, so we'd better make the best of this bad bargain. At least she saw you and responded."

"Yeah, I shook her up. She bought in, and she snuck out."

He didn't include, "when I wasn't looking."

The younger man shook his head, disagreeing, "Her nerve's not cracked. She gave as good as she got when I cornered her yesterday. I had a devil of a time trying to convince her she's in danger. And tonight, you didn't scare her. She just wasn't about to let you put her on the ropes. Don't underestimate this one."

"She's a two-bit actress."

"No, she's not. Not at all. I spent a great deal of time researching her, researching all of them. I know her, and she'll be tough to break. She's passionate, but she's sharp. I was here some years ago and saw her do an inestimable Rosalind once. She was especially deft in the scene where Rosalind turns her uncle's charge of treason back on him without appearing anything but respectful."

"Just because you're upper crust doesn't mean you should be going all hoity-toity, intellectual on me, buddy."

Under other circumstances, the misapprehension about his class background would have prompted sardonic amusement from the younger man. He only said, "My point is that Jessica Minton is like that character. She may feel for others' 'wounds,' which works well into our plans. But she also thinks about nuances, and if we want to stay ahead of her we'd better never underestimate her or we are sunk — and you know that lives, including our own, depend on this plan working."

"Yeah sure. I got you — just don't go asking her for her autograph or nothing like that."

"I'll try to restrain myself. Right then, let's see about implementing the next step. She still isn't convinced, but she's thinking. It's time to soften up Miss Minton some more, before we really move in on her."

CHAPTER FOUR

On break from dress rehearsal, Jessica sat in her dressing room trying her darnedest to mend a pair of silk stockings with inconspicuous stitches. Lack of money didn't keep her from replacing them; you just couldn't purchase what was no longer on the market. As it was, she'd spent two hours in line waiting to get these at the last auction of confiscated black market hose. Absently plucking at the light black crêpe bodice of the costume she'd dubbed her "floozy dress," Jess reflected that today things hadn't gone nearly as badly as she'd expected. Not exactly Dunkirk, more like trying to pitch a no-hitter to Ted Williams. Anyway, back to the stockings.

Unfortunately, a decisive knock forestalled her intentions.

"Come in," Jessica called, stowing the hose in one of her dressing table drawers.

The door opened and Frederick Bromfield peered inside just as Jess was reaching for a small bottle of milk on her dressing table.

"Ah, excuse me, Miss Minton. I know you have little time to eat, but I wonder if you could spare a moment? I would not take up too much of your time."

"No problem. Come right in, Mr. Bromfield. Here, let me clear this chair. Sit down. Please."

Bromfield put up a hand, protesting, "No, I do not intend to stay long. You are entitled to have your lunch in peace. I just hope this is not too much of an intrusion for you."

"Why no. Not at all. I was just finishing my milk, anyway. Believe me, you aren't a bother."

In spite of her welcoming words, Jessica felt something of a heel because she never could quite buy Frederick Bromfield's old-world charm. She really admired his work, but no one could be this naturally polite. Maybe she'd lived in New York too long. Maybe she figured that his flawless decorum had to mask a core of German decadence. Or was he German? He'd built a formidable reputation from his work in that country, but no one could ever pin him down on his native land.

Bromfield's glance fell on the framed picture Jess kept by her mirror. In the photograph she and a young man were emoting in Restoration dress.

"Is that you, Miss Minton?"

Jessica nodded. "My first important role in college — *The Way of the World*."

"Ah, the classics. You are an exceptional young lady. Congreve is wonderful."

"Yes, Congreve is, but I, unfortunately, wasn't," Jess remarked wryly. "I like to have that around, just so I never take myself too seriously. But, I thank you for the compliment, Mr. Bromfield."

She also briefly reflected that the young man with her, though good on stage, was an even better actor off — but that was another soap opera altogether.

Frederick Bromfield sighed, making a sad gesture with his hands before saying, "I wish charm were wisdom, Miss Minton. Perhaps then I could persuade my niece to tell me what is bothering her."

Now, why would a man who never joined the rest of the cast for their late night confabs suddenly decide to be sociable, no personal, with her? Even though Jess had worked with Bromfield once before, she was no closer to him than anyone else around here.

Reading Jessica's expression, Bromfield shook his head and chided himself, "Here, I get ahead of myself, again. I haven't told you why I want to talk about my niece."

Jessica leaned forward, interested. Frederick Bromfield actually discussing his personal life was almost like Garbo dropping by for a chat.

"Miss Minton, do you remember last Friday night, when I was waiting to see someone?"

"You had to talk to someone," Jessica concurred.

"The person with whom I wanted to speak was you."

"Me?" That *was* some unexpected revelation. "Why didn't you talk to me *then*, Mr. Bromfield?"

The older man shook his head, explaining, "I'm sure your friend is nice and dependable; but this is personal, Miss Minton, about my niece."

"Are you sure you want to tell me anything, Mr. Bromfield? I'd like to help, but I honestly don't know if I have anything worthwhile to say."

Not that she wasn't darned curious, but Jessica never felt comfortable digging into people's privacy. Well, almost never.

"Miss Minton, you are a young lady; my niece is a young lady. Now, who understands a young lady better, another young lady or an old man?"

"You're not so old, Mr. Bromfield, but go on. I'll try to help if I can."

"You see, Miss Minton, my niece, Fritzi, she has this boyfriend. They break up quite a bit, but now they are together. No matter what, she's unhappy, with or without him. She always seems afraid. Sometimes I think she is ready to tell me what's bothering her, but she never can. Now, Miss Minton, what could frighten her? What would make her afraid to talk to her uncle? What should I say to her?"

What on earth had prompted these sudden personal revelations from Frederick Bromfield?

Bromfield went on in her silence, "Maybe I'm an old man who has spent too much time in the theater. Perhaps I worry too much. Perhaps I'm overprotective."

"Mr. Bromfield, I don't know the situation well enough. All I can say is, let your niece know you care, that you know something is bothering her; and then, if she needs to talk, you're there. If you honestly think there is something wrong with this boyfriend, check him out. That way, if you do have to discourage her, you'll at least have something concrete to back you up — although, let's face it, love is generally not only blind but deaf, dumb, and slightly deranged."

The older man's tired face appeared a little less seamed with concern. He nodded thoughtfully. "I think you are right, Miss Minton. Poor Fritzi is alone. Her parents are still in the old country. I try to look after her. Young ladies should not be alone. Perhaps, yes, I think I can help her best by doing as you say."

"Remember, Mr. Bromfield, I'm hardly a professional sob sister. You should do what you think best."

Bromfield nodded, finally saying, "You are a good person to take the time to listen to the problem of a man you hardly know. I could tell you would be so kind from the way you stuck your neck out for me over that juvenile's 'behavior problem.' Now, if you ever need someone to talk to, you can come to me. You will allow me to repay you that way, will you not, Miss Minton?"

"Of course," Jess agreed. But behind her smile, she silently pondered how odd that this man, with whom she had yet to reach a first-name basis, should propose trading personal secrets. Still, a troublesome niece went a long way to explaining why he'd seemed distracted during rehearsals.

Bromfield hesitated, smiled, then said, "Well, then, Miss Minton, enjoy your lunch."

He smiled briefly again and left Jessica, closing the door behind him.

Jess compressed her lips into a crooked line of dissatisfaction. Had she said the right thing? God forbid that kid should be tangled up in something serious! Another rap on her door and a summons back to work abruptly ended that train of thought.

"Yes, yes. All right!" Jess answered, distracted, quickly stowing her sewing things.

Aside from an irrefragable determination to get things done right, there was another reason Jess was anxious to hit the boards. Harold Vane had offered the added incentive of an entire Saturday free if the rest of rehearsal went well. What a grand deal that would be for her! An avid "improver of the breed," Jessica was not about to miss this Saturday's Saratoga Handicap at Belmont Park. The Saratoga racing schedule was usually held all the way out at Saratoga Springs, but with long-distance pleasure driving banned since last year, the meet had been moved to Long Island. All of which suited the city-bound Jessica Minton just fine.

* * * * * *

Jess not only found out she'd have Saturday free, but was lucky enough to squeeze in a late lunch at Shaftner's with Elizabeth on Thursday afternoon. It wasn't that Harold Vane had gone soft. He just didn't want any unnecessary personnel in his hair when he was busy whipping a few less fortunate performers into line. At last, the sisters could confab on tackling Peter.

What a pleasure to slip out of costume and into brown slacks and a short-sleeved silk blouse swirling with tropical avocado, olive, and old-gold blossoms. What a God-send trousers for women were — a big-time improvement over having to deal with crooked seams on silk stockings, when you could find them.

Just outside the theater, Jess squinted against the brightness of the sun before sprinting across the street. She was as light-hearted as a kid on Field Day, racing downtown to see the parade after school let out early. As much as she loved her work, the sun was just too warm on her skin and the breeze too delectable for her to relish toiling inside a dark, stuffy building. And what a treat it was to settle into the delightful business of tying cans to the tails of Peter and his pals.

Entering Shaftner's, Jessica immediately spied at the lunch counter a dark-haired woman in a perfect apple-green summer suit, the brim of her matching hat elegantly curving over her brow. Hmm, why hadn't the usually alert Liz noticed her entrance? Aha, Elizabeth was determinedly re-cleaning the counter in front of her with Harry's own washcloth. Harry looked on in sour silence, for him a colossal show of restraint.

Sighting Jessica, Harry almost burst with relief — in a deadpan, jaded, New York fashion. Jess smiled, silently acknowledging that the only reason Harry hadn't locked horns with Elizabeth was that he knew her to be Jess's sister. Otherwise, there would have been a battle that made Midway look like a cake bake.

"So you finally come in," Harry said.

Elizabeth dropped the cloth.

"Oh good, you're here, Jess. Sit down." Turning to Harry as Jess sat down, Liz instructed, "I'll have my lunch now, with Jess."

"Just a root beer and a turkey sandwich," Jess requested.

"Oh, here's a shock. Three days in a row you eat like a normal person." Harry turned to Elizabeth. "Do you know this sister of yours, last Friday, for supper, orders cheese Danish? Do you think I gave her that?"

"I hope not," Elizabeth concurred.

Harry gave an abrupt little nod, now willing to leave the two sisters to talk.

Elizabeth fairly pounced on Jessica, eyes gleaming with devilish delight,

"I know the best way to drive Peter and his buddies crazy. I guess the only reason I didn't think of this before is that it's so simple — but it's perfection!"

"Well, give!"

"What did Peter's friend tell you that you absolutely could *not* do?"

"Um, a lot of things. Could you be a tad more specific, Elizabeth?"

"Well, what would be the most credible, sensible thing to do under the circumstances?"

"Leave town. Oh, for heaven's sake, Liz, stop playing *Information Please*! What do you have in mind?"

"You have no imagination, Jessica. Now listen, all you'll have to say is that you've turned the package over to the police. . ."

"I told the guy I was considering . . ."

"Don't interrupt. I didn't finish. Next time Peter's stooge pops up, tell him that you've *already* turned the package over and they've put a *guard* on you. Tell that joker that the police are watching you when he's talking to you, and they'll be wanting a few words with him. You could even throw in something about the F.B.I. being interested. I'm sure it wouldn't be hard for him to buy the police calling in the Feds over something connected with 'the war effort.'"

"The bit about the G-Men is a nice touch, Liz. Not only would he sweat it out, but I'm sure he'd go running to Peter with a mouthful. You *are* evil, Liz — and to your own husband!"

"Listen, Jess, Peter dishes it out often enough; he can take it for a change." A pause, then an ominous, "Besides, as mentioned before, I still owe him for the yak hair."

Harry brought their lunches. After they'd both thanked him, and he'd left to restock some shelves, Jessica took up where she and Liz had left off, "So, what do you think we ought to do with the package, Liz?"

"If you ask me, we should open it and see what's inside," Liz suggested eagerly.

"Why waste our time? It's all part of Peter's gag, so there couldn't possibly be anything worth looking at. Besides, Liz, I don't want to give your husband the slightest excuse to claim that he got me curious enough to take a peek. No, what we really ought to do is work up a clever ploy to fix him and his pals but good."

"You could always give it to me. After your friend has had enough time to get back to Peter and throw a scare into him, I can leave it in the house where Peter can see it and realize the jig is up. Yes, I do think turning the package over to me is a clever idea."

"And let it end up where Peter can get his paws on it? I don't think so. He's just smart enough to find it, hide it on you, and then try to start the whole megillah all over again. No, Elizabeth, the package is staying put, where I can keep an eye on it."

Elizabeth started to argue, but she could see that her sister meant business. Well, she could always work on the kid later. Catch her off guard. Liz switched gears with the query, "So, you and Larry are planning to go to the races Saturday?"

"Yes, if rehearsals run, well, I hesitate to use the word 'smoothly' in connection with this play. But, when did you talk to Larry about this? We only made our plans Monday evening."

"Peter was too busy to meet me for lunch yesterday, so Larry volunteered to take me out."

Jess shook her head, teasing, "Peter and I had better watch you two. Next thing I know you'll be running off to Reno together."

"Not much chance of that with the transportation shortage these days," Elizabeth quipped.

"You could always disguise yourselves as soldiers."

"Hardly. Olive drab is definitely not my color."

* * * * * *

By Jiminy waltzed home first in the Grand Union Hotel Stakes. It was some time before Jessica counted Tudor King, her pick — and the ninth horse under the wire. Leaning back, nearer to Larry, Jess admitted lightly, "All right, all right, I was wrong about one race."

"One race?"

"A couple of races, then."

"Try three races."

"I wasn't wrong about the last race before this one."

"We didn't bet that race because you said no one can predict the outcome of a steeplechase," Larry noted, certain he'd finally topped her.

"And did we lose any money? No. I was right then, too."

Larry shook his head doubtfully, still not sure how Jess had managed to turn the tables on him. Sometimes he thought she could win an argument with Chico Marx.

"Now, let me look at the program," Jess playfully commanded. "Oh, here we go. Unchallenged."

"Hmm," Larry responded critically, studying the past performance form under the horse's name. Jess followed his gaze and wished she hadn't shown him how to read the chart.

"According to what you've taught me, this horse doesn't appear to be a very likely prospect."

"He's due to win."

"He appears to be about ten races overdue." Larry rejoined. "At least he's consistent."

"Okay, Larry, since you're the great handicapper, you pick the winner."

"Agreed."

Larry furrowed his brow, concentrating over the racing form, then announced, "With Regards."

"With Regards? That horse is lugging one hundred and thirty pounds. He'll need a crane to drag him down the track!"

"As I recall, you once informed me that the best horse carries the most weight. Apparently the man who assigns the weights must also think this the best horse. I respect a professional's judgment."

Jessica started to explain that the track handicapper had also assigned the other horses less weight to make it easier for them to finish even with the high-weight. Instead she merely smiled: "Fine, cook your own goose. I'll place the bets; we'll see who knows horse racing."

"That's all right with me. However, *I'll* go. There's no reason for you to wander about."

"Larry, I can get to the two-dollar window and back without a guide — I promise not to 'wander.' Besides, I'd like to stretch my legs a little."

As Jessica rose, Larry agreed, "All right, Jess — and those are nice legs to stretch."

Jess gave her best cat-that-feasted-on-cream smile, as Larry stepped aside for her to reach the passage leading to the exit. A warm, strong breeze sprang up from the track below, whipping Jess's dark hair and imperiling her white turban. Her glance turned to the infield tote board. Hmm, those odds were pretty high against her choice.

Jess followed a crush of people down the passageway — no picnic, especially on such a hot day. She sighed with the heat, glad she'd elected to wear this light dress, with its pale raspberry swirls on white. It was so cool, she almost felt unclothed. Hmm, now could a naked woman distract the crowd enough so she could slip through to the pari-mutuel window? Nope, Rita Hayworth, Betty Grable, and Dorothy Lamour in the buff couldn't shake up this logjam of hardened handicappers, unless one of them had a sure-fire tip on the next race. The herd moved forward, but not far. Jess considered herself lucky when she was finally able to sight the two-dollar window, a feat achieved only by craning her neck and leaning to the side like an inebriated flamingo.

A voice cut into Jessica's thoughts, "Say, lady, who da ya like in the foith race?"

Instinctively, Jess turned, but her reply froze in her mouth as she recognized the package's owner.

"You'll excuse the accent. I had to get your attention without prompting you to cause a stir," he whispered.

To Jessica's surprise, he took her arm and began to draw her out of line. Recovering herself, Jess planted her white-sandaled feet firmly on the ground, nearly dislodging the man's hold, and snapped in a low voice, "No!"

A few heads turned, causing annoyance to sharpen the mustached man's features even more. It was a good thing she knew this was all part of a joke because that expression of his could have given a girl the creeps. And how was he able to speak so quietly, yet project such steeliness, as he demanded, "You mean to say that placing a bet on a horse is more important to you than helping your country?"

"But the odds on this horse are great," Jessica countered. Elizabeth would have loved that comeback.

The compelling blend of disbelief and fury clouding the man's face left Jessica admiring his emoting, but that didn't stop her from further needling him, "Okay, buster, shoot. This line's moving slower than my pick in the last race. Tell me your yarn."

"Not here. Some place less conspicuous, by the statue of Man O' War."

He had actually carefully looked around before speaking.

So Jessica did, too, before calmly disagreeing, "No. I'm not about to lose my place in line."

"Look here, Miss Minton, it's time to stop playing games. This is serious business. Come with me."

He wrapped an arm around Jessica and steered her out of line, warning, "If you fight me it will create a scene that will be embarrassing, to say the least. I'll be gone before you can get track security, and you'll look foolish, possibly even drawing the attention of just the devils from whom I'm trying to protect you."

Giving Peter the satisfaction of reducing her to a public spectacle was not an option. Fine. Two could play this game. She'd pretend to string along before nailing this clown with the little plot she and Liz had cooked up. Let him go running to Peter with his tail between his legs.

Far enough from the crowds, he swung her around to halt beneath the shade of a tree near Man O' War's statue, but not so abruptly as to attract attention. Quietly, yet still forcefully, Jessica's "captor" warned, "Listen to me. Snap out of it. I'm trying to get both of us out of this alive. I will tell you where to deliver the package..."

"What package?"

Jess had to ward off an attack of the snickers when he stared at her, most likely bewildered that anyone could be so flippant when he was so *deadly* serious.

"Is there something wrong with you? Can't you see the precarious situation we're both in? It's imperative I get the package away from you before it's too late for you, for me, and the war effort. That package cannot, must not, fall into the wrong hands. Hasn't any of my urgency sunk in? Do you think I sneak around like this after women for the fun of it?"

"Really, Mr. Whoever-you-are, I'm not interested in your, ah, aberrations."

Gleefully, Jessica concluded that being beaten at his own game was driving her companion daffy; his expression after the last quip was twice as threatening as the hurricane of '38. He turned away, as if to find the means to contain his temper — or was he hiding a flash of amusement at her quip? Score one for the Minton girl!

Well, his eyes were far from jolly now that he faced her again.

Bravo! Good effect, Jess thought to herself.

Suddenly, he stiffened, as if alarmed by something behind her. Jessica barely had time to catch his expression before he grabbed her and hid their faces in a kiss.

Completely taken off-guard, Jess couldn't even think of struggling, at first, but when she did she found herself pinned so tightly she could barely squirm.

Just my luck, I get the strong, wiry type, she silently fumed, unable to free herself.

Just as suddenly, her companion released Jessica and explained, "Sorry, I didn't want that chap going by to recognize us together. I'm afraid that was the only way I could hide..."

"Why, you fourteen-karat wolf!" Jessica exploded in a low voice. Her anger grew as she bit out every word, "A joke is a joke, but this going too far! Nobody paws me!"

"Don't you think you're over-reacting?"

Where did he get off being *amused* at her furious discombobulation?!

"That sinks it," Jessica snarled before she hauled off and let him have it, right on the jaw.

"Aiee!"

The shriek was Jessica's.

Unbelievably aching waves of pain roiled up her arm. Never having been angry enough to slug anyone before, Jessica had had no conception that a well-connected blow could be almost as painful for the puncher as for his, or in this case her, victim. No wonder even Joe Louis wore gloves. Good thing there were no real enemy agents around. With a pain threshold this low, Jess concluded, all they'd need to do was threaten to make *her* hit *them*, and she'd not only spill everything she knew, but cook up a few things to boot.

Aware of nothing but her excruciating pain, Jess didn't immediately notice that an arm had encircled her shoulders and guided her to a nearby water fountain. She stared at her former tormentor in surprise. He quickly, gently, expertly inspected her injured hand while remarking wryly, "No bones protruding. Can you move your fingers?"

"Of course I can move... argh... well, I can move them, but I don't enjoy it. No thanks to you."

"My jaw," he winced, shifting it, "returns the compliment. Give me back that hand. Come along now. Yes, let's just run some of this cold water over your knuckles, kill the swelling."

Jess started to crack he'd gotten what he deserved, but the water on her knuckles sent a wave of nausea through her mid-section that made her sway like a suspension bridge in an earthquake — until her companion steadied her. She caught herself wishing that maybe he weren't trying to play her for a sap. As if the alternative would be an improvement.

He broke the silence with, "You said something odd before, about thinking all this was some kind of a joke. Do you really believe that? A rather dangerous joke in these times, isn't it? Unbelievably elaborate too, wouldn't you say?"

"Peter Hennessey hired you and plotted this out with you. So, you should know that nothing's too far out for my brother-in-law. I don't suppose he told you about my sister-in-law, the yak hair, and Lon Chaney, Jr. in *The Wolf Man*?"

"Yak hair? No, never mind that." He had an odd expression, as if remembering something then recalculating. How to trick her? A better prospect than his needing to figure out how to save her from fifth columnists. Finally he said, as if almost relieved, "You've connected me with your brother-in-law. That's why you won't help me, won't even believe me?"

"Why, Mr., ah . . ?"

"Crawford."

"Mr. Crawford, do I need to answer? I thought your kind had ways of 'knowing things.' Slip up?"

"Touché," he admitted with a crooked smile. And she was surprised at how mischievously sweet his eyes seemed when he smiled like that.

Then Mr. Crawford took out a handkerchief. Dry amusement lingered in his eyes as he explained, "I'll wrap this around your knuckles. It's wet and cold; that should numb the ache. Move your fingers again."

Jessica complied, a bit less painfully, remarking ruefully as she regarded her hand, "Battered but unbroken."

He moved his jaw again, winced, and pronounced, "Same here."

Jessica couldn't suppress a smile. While Crawford, as he called himself, finished wrapping the cloth, she watched his hands thoughtfully. She'd hardly have expected any stooge of Peter's to minister to her so kindly; he was blessedly gentle with her aching hand. Here she went again, being a sucker for a good turn. Still, there was something in his face that drove her to level with him.

"Crawford, I was going to try to throw a scare into you and Peter by saying I'd turned the package over to the police, and they were tailing me in order to catch you. I'd wanted to see the two of you terrified at the prospect of your scheme backfiring."

He took a moment to think before asking, "But you didn't turn the package over?"

Jessica shook her head.

"It's a good thing. They'd probably never buy your story — and I'm afraid you can't afford to let anyone know you have that package. Even if the local authorities took the package, I can't see how I'd be able to claim it before they opened it, which cannot be allowed. You'd have us both in a nice mess."

"Why should I believe you? You still haven't proven to me that you aren't some flunky of my brother-in-law."

Jessica's tone wasn't hostile, but it was indisputably firm.

He seemed to weigh his options carefully before answering, "If I can prove I am what I claim to be, that this isn't a joke, will you return me the package — and keep mum about it?"

"I'll need some convincing, Mr. Crawford."

Crawford considered this, then looked Jessica square in the eye. "Right, then. I'm going to let you in on some intelligence to which my connections make me privy. It's still sensitive information, so I expect you to keep this quiet, even though it's not directly related to the package. Within a few days, we'll allow the *New York Times* to release the story of this summer's capture of Nazi saboteurs who landed this June on Amagansett and at Jacksonville, Ponte Vedra Beach..."

"Saboteurs!"

"I believe I mentioned something about keeping this quiet?"

Collecting herself, Jessica argued, "I don't understand why this has been on the q.t. so long."

"If you want to catch spies, you don't announce that you know they are skulking about. Alerting the quarry has a tendency to diminish your chance to catch it."

"All right, all right," Jessica relented, doubtfully. He made sense, but then Peter's middle name could have been plausibility. It killed her not to know where the truth lay when the stakes were this high. But all Jess could come up with was, "So, how do you know all this?"

"I am in intelligence, Miss Minton, What do you think I'm doing with this package in the first place? — all conjectures about your brother-in-law's penchant for overdone pranks aside."

"For all I know you're just feeding me another tall story."

"Read the *Times*. You'll see for yourself."

Jessica countered, "Even if you are on the level, why should I play ball with you? Wouldn't I be smarter to turn the package over to the F.B.I.?"

"You could do that, Miss Minton; however, that would bring you out into the open. The wrong people would find out you have the package. When they do, you will be in grave danger — they can't chance your knowing what's in it, that you might tell someone what you discovered."

"Let me get this straight. You're telling me the Feds can't protect me?"

"I told you before that I am dealing with some kind of a mole, an infiltrator. That's why we're flying without a net until I can get this package out of town to *my* superiors. At least according to my plan, no one will know the package was out of my hands, so there will certainly be no reason for you to come under suspicion. For all they know, my rambling about is just a ruse to shake them."

His answers really were good. Maybe too well thought out even for Peter. Good God, was she really in danger?

Seeming to read her thoughts, Crawford offered, convincingly sincere, "I assure you that the safest, wisest course is to do as I suggest. It's imperative that no one know you have the package."

He almost had her. Then she remembered another player in her brother-in-law's scenario. What a relief to slip back into seeing all this as a hoax. She honestly could have killed Peter for almost getting her.

"What about the man outside in the trench coat? The one who was around the night you left me the package. He showed up again in the park. He must be in on our little secret by now. I even saw him at the restaurant where I had dinner last weekend."

"He's one of my contacts. His appearance was a signal that I needed to stash the package and bolt. I wish I could have left it for him to pick up, but we were both being followed. So, you can see why the package was actually safer with you, a woman no one suspected. No one would have a reason to trail you. This was one time he couldn't run interference for me."

"Oh really? Too bad he didn't 'run interference' when you decided we had to hide from your mysterious man a few minutes ago," Jessica glowered.

"He can't be everywhere, Miss Minton," Crawford quipped; but seeing the sparks in Jessica's blue eyes, he instinctively passed a defensive hand before his bruised jaw.

"You will promise not to say anything more?"

"Sorry, but I'm still not entirely sure I'm ready to buy what you're selling. After all, if your story about keeping everything on the q.t. between you, me, and your buddy were true, then it seems to me you're playing pretty fast and loose with Allied security. Your superiors must be Grade-A dopes to give you two butterfingers such a free rein. Makes me a bit nervous to think a crew like yours stands between me and the Axis."

He wasn't rattled by her sarcasm. Strangely enough, Jessica had the feeling he was rather enjoying it as he explained smoothly, "There's less chance of anyone betraying me if I'm given a free rein, as you put it. And you do seem to forget I want to keep my loss of the package secret. I can't chance a security leak, not when I don't have the package, myself. Not with some of the problems we've had lately."

Jess stared speculatively at the man, giving nothing away to his dark, probing eyes. Let *him* wonder what lurked within her clever little head. They weren't happy thoughts. With a sudden twinge of disappointment, she wondered: if he were merely Peter's accomplice, was the consideration he'd shown for her injured hand just a trick to gain her trust?

"Will you keep this quiet, Miss Minton?"

"Let me put it this way, Mr. Crawford: I'll be just as much on the level with you as you are with me."

Let him stew over that for awhile. The discomfort tightening his features as he tried to interpret her disconcertingly amiable smile satisfied Jessica.

A sudden cheer from the stands turned them abruptly toward the track. The race was over, and it wasn't long before the loudspeaker announced the finish. All Jessica needed was to hear With Regard the winner, Unchallenged second. Not only had Larry been right about the race, he'd been right about her not making it to the two-dollar window. Oh, and of course she could just tell Larry the real reason for the gaffe, injured mitt and all — he'd just love that. But the worst part was that none of this was her fault! It was all Mr. Crawford's. She turned on him, her eyes lancing him with anger.

"Right, I expect I'd better be moving along now. Remember what I said about the newspaper and about not repeating this information. Good-bye, Miss Minton."

He melted into the crowd before she could give him what for.

Suddenly alone, Jessica felt her anger collapse into an uneasy mix of annoyance and concern. So now where was she? All her life, hunches coupled with some good old horse sense had saved her skin. True, she had been buffaloed a few times, yet in her heart of hearts she'd always known when someone wasn't really on the level. This Crawford case was something else entirely. Unlike those others, *he* rang true, even if his story was screwy. And it wasn't as if there were no Nazi infiltrators around. Less than two years ago a spy ring of *thirty-two* had been put on trial after one of their own had snitched on them. Only this June, two air raid wardens, for crying out loud, had been tried and convicted for sending secret messages in invisible ink to Germans hiding out in Spain and Portugal.

So was Crawford working for the Allies or her brother-in-law? *Big* difference.

No, Crawford's espionage story was just too incredible! That conclusion brought Jessica little relief. If this were really Peter's game, he had her, at least until Crawford's news story about the spies came out. There was no way she would risk the war effort, heck, even her life, just to avoid embarrassment. She was stuck waiting it out. That was when Jessica realized that she had been circling Man O' War, mumbling to herself, and evoking the fish eye from some of even the more hardened pony players. Not a good idea.

She couldn't let Larry see her like this. He'd be worried about her, bless him. Granted, it would be swell to toss all this onto someone else's shoulders, but she was a big girl now and she had to take care of her own responsibilities. Jess was not about to complicate Larry's life by dragging him into this mess, just to make things easier on herself.

Well, she was an actress; so act! God, she hated not leveling with Larry, even if she could tell herself it was in everyone's best interest. Yes, performing was her game; but, until Crawford had popped into her life, lying hadn't been — short of her answers to Liz's "Do I look fat?" or Peter's "Am I losing my hair?"

It also niggled at her conscience that if this were Peter's little game, one reason she didn't want to tell Larry was that he'd chide her for being too gullible. Anyway, there was little that rankled her more than lying, except maybe waiting — the other "delightful" aspect of her situation. And that was really the only option left to her right now. Wouldn't that make the party at Peter and Liz's tomorrow just ducky? Jess could say one thing, though: if Peter and Crawford were in cahoots, what Hamlet did to two-thirds of Denmark would look like a Shirley Temple movie compared to the vengeance she   planned   to   exact!

CHAPTER FIVE

If Elizabeth and Peter's apartment hadn't been the size of North Dakota, the party would have been a crowded affair. Voices with various accents floated through the high-rise apartment, for many of the friends that Elizabeth and Peter had made on their pre-War European excursions were now refugees from the Nazis.

In the Hennessey home, with Peter nearby, Jessica couldn't help stewing over the nerve of her brother-in-law's plot against her — or was it that Mr. Crawford's information just might be on the level? Jess restlessly crossed one leg over the other, smoothing the skirt of her black, crêpe dress, the gold brocade on the bodice ascending in chevron point to a v-neckline. An older man chatted on at her, but she was only half listening. No, it just had to be that Peter was running a Jim Dandy scam. So why did she still have a vague case of the jitters?

"I don't mean to interrupt," Larry had appeared out of nowhere, pausing to nod a greeting to her companion before offering her the appetizing news, "but I knew you'd be happy to hear the buffet is served, Jessica."

Smoothing her hair, which was gently pulled back into a coil at the nape of her neck, Jess made her excuses to the other gentleman and followed Larry. They approached the two long tables laden with an array of food that could have rivaled a starving man's mirage. When Jess cracked to Larry that her sister must have spent an afternoon knocking over little old ladies for their food coupons to come up with this spread, he set her straight with the low down on office politics. Since several supervisors from work were here, Peter had been able to finagle a little something extra as a business expense.

Jessica silently considered turning the tables on Peter by snitching on him to the Truman Commission's government fraud investigations. No, not big time enough for the senator from Missouri to pursue.

A few tables were set up on an outdoor terrace running the length of the apartment. Luckily for Elizabeth, this apartment was below the fifteen-story blackout requirement, so she didn't need to draw the curtains on the glass doors leading to the terrace. Larry and Jess settled comfortably at one of the white-painted, wrought-iron tables. Even with a partial blackout on, Jessica could still luxuriate in the ambiance of late summer in the city. A pristine, lemon August moon fantastically transformed the buildings, while nearer edifices overshadowing streets and distant buildings hid what lay beneath in velvet darkness. Traffic sounds wafted up, deliciously haunting, from below. Jess let the conversation with Larry lapse, to settle back in catlike contentment by moonlight. Strains of one of the Dorsey Brothers' "Contrasts" drifted

58

through the terrace doors. The voices inside were no more than amiable murmurs. Good. No distraction from this happy mixture of anticipation and fulfillment — a nifty parole from worry.

"I know you love it here."

Jessica looked away, over the balustrade, into the night. Why should Larry's breaking into her reverie give her a frisson of awkwardness?

"Every time I come here I marvel at how Peter, a poor civil servant like myself, can afford such a magnificent apartment," he continued.

"You know what an expert Peter is with investments, Larry. Remember how he's helped me?"

"Hmm. Takes quite a bit of capital to make an investment that would pay sufficient dividends to maintain this way of life."

"I think you mean Elizabeth's way of life," Jessica playfully corrected. "Lucky for Peter he's acquiescent."

"That sounds a trifle catty, madame."

"Guess I've been living with Dusty too long."

Jess sliced herself an appetizing sliver of turkey. After a bite she queried, "Didn't I tell you the story about the painting Elizabeth bought for a song but resold for a bundle?"

"I don't think so. Do tell. I could use some pointers on how to accumulate enough to retire early."

"Oh, Peter can't retire on their investments. Liz sees to that."

"I think I see claws."

"The better to needle my sister with!" Jessica grinned. "Anyway, I will grant that coming up with a spread like this in the middle of all this rationing qualifies as a major-league miracle."

"All right, I retract my wisecrack," Larry smiled. "So, go on. Finish your story."

"It's actually pretty simple. On one of their prewar European jaunts, Elizabeth came across a painting in some old antique shop in, gee, Austria? Anyway, she knew what it was and the proprietor didn't. I guess it was done by some obscure American expatriate artist who died young and became famous only over here."

Larry smiled and commented, "You sister must have had Fortune sitting on her shoulder, to wander into the right shop at the right time."

"Fortune nothing!" Jessica laughed. "Elizabeth loves good art, and she has a real sixth sense about bargains — she could out-haggle John L. Lewis during a coal miners' strike."

"Does that instinct for scenting out a deal run in the family?"

"No, I'm just good at playing the ponies — when I can make it to the two-dollar window. I was right about Prinçequillo."

"But somewhat less perspicacious when it came to With Regards and

Unchallenged," Larry teased, before adding considerately, "How is your hand, anyway? That was unbelievably bad luck, Jessica. First you're held up in the queue; then the cashier accidentally slams the grill on your knuckles when he closes his window. Could that happen more than once in a million years?"

"At least I'm safe for another nine-hundred-thousand, nine-hundred and ninety-nine," Jess quipped brightly, changing the subject, "But what's this about you being a 'poor civil servant'? That's not exactly a tar-paper shack you hang your hat in out in the suburbs."

"I'm being paid under the table by a foreign government," Larry deadpanned.

"Oh? So, just what do you do that attracts high-paying, surreptitious interest?"

"Let me call Peter in here to explain it to you."

Jessica couldn't help laughing at the old joke, and Larry joined her. She looked out into the cool darkness beyond the terrace, smiling. Such a lovely night it was! Well, Larry was a good sport, when all was said and done. Maybe she should give him more credit. After all, he was one of the few guys gentleman enough not to need a sock in the jaw to keep him from making like an octopus — generally. Jessica turned back to Larry, her expression revealing her content. He reached across the table and took her hand.

"So this is where you two have been hiding?"

Jessica and Larry both started back in their chairs, turning to see Elizabeth join them in a swirl of white, ribbed chiffon. Liz's hair may have waved dark and loose past her shoulders, but its resistance to the gentle breeze suggested that even when she assayed the natural look, Nature had better not get too familiar.

Impeccably urbane, Elizabeth captured Larry's elbow and guided him to his feet, leading him inside with, "Now, Larry, you really ought to go in. Herr Brenner, or is it Monsieur Heroux, no, I think it's Peter, after all — they all sound alike when they get into war and politics — anyway, Larry, one of them wants to continue the discussion of the Sicily invasion with you. You'd better go right in. I'll take care of Jess."

Jess stood up, once more impressed with her sister's talent to be as aggressive as she pleased without losing a whit of her charm. Hmm, had the right sibling taken up acting?

Elizabeth re-entered the terrace, her flared white skirt gave her the appearance of gliding, while her eager expression uncomfortably reminded Jessica of a vampire opening the doors for a Red Cross blood drive.

"So now, Jess, what's new with our plot to put my darling husband behind the eight ball?"

How to answer? Life would certainly be much easier without having to play it close to the vest with Liz and Larry at the same time. She didn't think she had enough vest for both of them.

"I ran into Peter's accomplice, Mr. Crawford, at the race track. That's how I got this."

Jess held up her healing but battered knuckles.

"Did that so-and-so hurt you?!" Liz was as incredulous as she was furious.

Heartened by her sister's support, Jessica shook her head, relaxing into a devilish smile. "Oh, no. I took a poke at him."

Liz's smile was pure ice as she commented, "Sounds like the beginning of a beautiful relationship."

Jessica teasingly reproved, "Elizabeth, just because you and Peter model your marriage after the Joe Louis/Buddy Baer fight doesn't mean everyone else should."

"Let's get back to the real topic, little sister. Why on earth did you hit the rube?"

Not quite able to face Liz, Jessica mumbled, "He, ah, kissed me."

"Oh well, Peter's really gone too far now! And what would Larry say?! How could Peter do this to his friend..."

"Liz, Crawford didn't kiss *Larry*. I'm the put-upon one here."

"Yes, but, what did Larry say?"

"Nothing. I didn't tell him. I'm not going to tell him — and neither are you. Don't give me that look. No sense in sending Larry on the war path, even if it might get your rat of a husband in Dutch. I'm not making Larry a patsy, too."

"Okay. All right. For Larry's sake. So, go on. What else happened? I assume he didn't enchant you into submission with his romantic assault."

"Hardly. Anyway, Liz, it's something of a long story."

"So give me the *Reader's Digest* version."

Summarizing events she wasn't even sure she fully understood would be about as much fun as wrestling for the last pair of hose at Macy's, but Jessica plunged forward, "Mr. Crawford, at least that's what he claims is his name, grabbed my attention; plucked me out of line at the two-dollar window; put on a most convincing indignant act when I didn't buy his 'this is your chance to save your country' speech; kissed me, allegedly to keep some enemy agent from seeing our faces; took it on the jaw from me; and, well, this is the hairy part, told me, to prove he was on the level, that sometime this week the newspapers would print this just-released story about Nazi agents recently captured around Amagansett and Florida. Liz, that enemy agent yarn one-upped me but good when I tried to rattle him with the story you and I cooked up. I didn't know what to say then."

Liz studied her sister carefully, her first finger tapping her cheek, then questioned, "So, you buy his story?"

"Well, common sense tells me he can't be on the level. It's just that, Liz, you've followed the news. You heard about the Duquesne case last year and those two air raid wardens arrested this June. He did sound convincing."

"No, no, Jess, this has Peter Hennessey's lovely paw prints all over it! It would be just like him to cash in on recent events to be convincing, and would you expect anything but an Oscar winning performance from someone he'd hire? No, I don't buy this little fairy tale for one moment. After all, *have* you seen that saboteur story in the papers?"

"Well, no. Not yet. But this was only a day ago."

"Day, week, year — I doubt you ever will. The two of them are probably laughing up their sleeves at keeping you on tenterhooks this long. I vote we nail them tonight."

"Elizabeth," Jessica began, "this isn't a democracy. I'll admit Crawford's story sounds screwy, but, frankly, I don't want to take any chances while we're waiting to find out if it's the real deal or the bunk. And, well, I hate scenes, which is exactly what you have in mind, isn't it? Nature isn't the only thing red in tooth and claw right now. You have that 'can't wait to taste blood' look in your eyes. Listen to me, Liz, you know the kind of a scene you have in mind is just what Peter is looking for. That's the whole point of his little pranks. If we come on all emotional now, we'll be giving him *exactly* what he wants. No, if we really want to get to him, we've got to play it cool. Mark my words, it will drive your dear little spouse nuts if we act as if nothing is happening. And just think, if Crawford claims that he rattled me at the track, our calmness will completely undercut him. We might even set those two knuckleheads against each other, if Peter thinks one of his minions is making a sap out of him and said minion can't get Peter to believe him. Trust me, Liz, playing it cool for now will be our sweetest revenge."

Frowning, Elizabeth argued, "No. That's not what I want to do. I think..."

"Elizabeth," Jessica interrupted firmly, "we're talking about my life. It's my decision. I appreciate your help, really I do, but the final decision is mine."

Elizabeth started to argue but thought better, finally saying, "Suit yourself, dear. Far be it from me to violate a sister's personal sovereignty."

Jessica folded her arms, tapping a finger speculatively as she observed, "Why is it, Liz, that I have the funniest feeling I oughtn't to trust you, hmm?"

"Now, Jessica, when have I ever... Ah, perhaps that's not the best tack."

"Perhaps not. C'mon. Let's get back to the party. Peter and Larry may put everyone to sleep if we don't get the coffee started soon."

Elizabeth nodded agreement, relaxing as her sister slipped an arm through hers, and they turned to go inside. Jessica was smiling, but she had an unsettling suspicion that she'd only won the first round with Liz over confronting Peter. How to be sure? Tie up and gag her sister? Maybe push her off the balcony? No, that would only slow her down.

* * * * * *

The party had broken up some time before. Behind the bar, just right of the balcony, Peter was keeping company with a bourbon. A cloth lay sprawled a few inches from the ring of moisture left by his drink. He was not particularly interested in Elizabeth's instructions to clean up.

"Jessica, you've straightened those cushions on the couch three times," he pointed out. "Liz couldn't make it any neater. Sit down, kid. Relax."

But Jess just stared distractedly at the pristine white couch.

"I promise I won't let Liz thrash you if the couch isn't up to her idea of scratch," Peter persisted, leaning comfortably forward on the bar.

"What? Oh. Peter? Did you say something?"

She looked straight at her brother-in-law, preoccupied.

Peter frowned at this. He actually looked sincere.

"Jess, what is it? Nothing wrong, is there?"

Had Peter perceived her stiffening at his question? Forcing herself to smile, she crossed slowly to the bar and replied casually, "No, I'm just a little tuckered out. It's late, and I've really been pushing myself quite a bit over the play. I like my work, but it takes a lot out of a girl."

She sat at the bar and gave Peter a weary smile, hoping no suspicion flickered in her eyes.

"Like a drink? I always take one to pep me up."

"Peter, since when have you ever waited till you needed to be pepped up to take a drink?"

Peter smiled, finished his glass, and pronounced, "I'm anemic."

"Another one of those and you'll be positively flammable."

Unperturbed, Peter poured himself another shot. Jess was on the verge of commenting, but held back. If Elizabeth didn't keep her implied promise to play it cool, he'd be better off somewhat anesthetized. Maybe Peter had downed sufficient firewater for her to pump him unobtrusively about his little plot. Then again, were all his concerned queries about her welfare *his* attempt to pump *her*?

"Nice of you to leave Larry and me to do all the work."

Elizabeth and Larry sauntered in from the kitchen, to the left. Planning, conducting, and wrapping up this soirée had taken their toll on Liz's cool elegance, especially since high-paying war work had made temporary domestic help scarce — not that many could live up to Liz's standards. Larry looked tired as well. He'd probably want to go home as soon as possible. Good. The sooner they left, the less opportunity Elizabeth would have to do something that would oblige Jessica to kill her.

"Elizabeth," Peter responded, "I wisely chose to let each of us do what he does best. I don't want to get in trouble again for mixing dirty dishes with the glasses under the bar — and you and Larry *are* inspired dishwashers."

"While you and Jessica are gifted at drinking and sleeping, respectively, of course," Larry interjected.

Peter toasted Larry before polishing off his drink.

Larry addressed Jessica, "I think I'll get your wrap now. Liz, you don't mind?"

"Heavens, no. You look asleep on your feet, Larry."

Jessica was almost ready to sigh her relief. Maybe her sister *would* keep her word.

As Larry started across the living room for the bedroom and Jess's wrap, Elizabeth suddenly called, "Oh, Larry, I hung it up in my closet. The walk-in one; it's by the bath."

Larry turned and nodded. Her motives not entirely altruistic, Jessica slid from her bar stool and swiftly started after him, calling, "Maybe I'd better help you, Larry."

"Don't be silly, Jessica, Larry's a big boy," Elizabeth countered, deftly turning her sister around to sweep her back toward Peter. "Let's just relax with your favorite brother-in-law."

"What's the big idea?" Jessica muttered, pinching the inside of Elizabeth's arm.

"Ooh," Elizabeth squealed, tightening her hold on Jessica's arm, forcing her back to the bar and Peter. "Darling, the most bizarre things have been happening to Jessica."

Jessica's mouth dropped like a hammer from the top of a twenty-story building as Liz brightly continued, "Did you know this strange man has been following Jessica around, bothering her about some package he claims he left with her in that drugstore across from her theater?"

Before Jessica could remind Elizabeth what had happened to Lavinia in *Titus Andronicus*, Peter straightened up and questioned, "Jess, is that right? Is Liz serious? Have you called the police?"

"I . . ."

"Yes, Peter," Liz interrupted, sweetly triumphant, "that's exactly what she did. I wouldn't be surprised if the police were tracking down that rube named Crawford, and whoever his accomplices are, this very minute."

"Ah, well, that's a relief. You girls were right on the money."

"Yes, of course, Peter, we're... wait a minute. You're glad that the cops are going to nab this guy? Aren't you worried about what's going to happen when they get their hands on him and his pals?" Elizabeth pressed, growing increasingly disconcerted as her plan fell apart.

"Why the heck should I be worried?" Peter stared her down, puzzled. "Jess, do you know what's gotten into your sister?"

Jessica refrained from commenting she'd wished it were arsenic. Everything was playing out exactly as she'd warned Liz it would. Glancing a warning at her steamed sister, Jessica made a gallant attempt at damage control. "You know Elizabeth; she's such a worrier. Don't fret, Peter. Everything is just fine. Just fine."

"But this story? Liz's not kidding? You've been followed by some screwy guy? Are you okay?"

"Sure. Of course, the authorities seem to, um, think it's all some kind of, well practical joke," Jessica, temporized. She shot a lethal look at her sister for corroboration.

"And Liz took it seriously?" Peter chuckled.

That did it. Her lips fairly curling, Elizabeth shot back, "If anyone around here would know about practical jokes . . ."

"Elizabeth, you think... me? You think I'm responsible?"

"If the squirting carnation fits . . ."

Peter actually tried to think about the mangled metaphor a moment before giving up. Leaning forward on the bar, unable to contain his laughter, he choked out, "This is great! Somebody else plays Liz for a sap, and I get the credit! I got your goat without even trying!"

"Look, buster, don't think playing dumb is going to get you off the hook. I've known you too long not to recognize when you're trying to kill a joke. We're wise to you, and we can let the police in on what we know, too!"

Peter hesitated, regarding first Elizabeth and then Jessica quizzically. The corner of his mouth turned up infuriatingly, before he taunted, "Oh, will you? And I suppose you'll be able to prove I'm guilty?"

For a fraction of a second, Jessica had the cold, hollow suspicion that Peter's apparent ignorance meant she really had spilled some dangerous beans. But that nasty, triumphant smile — Peter seemed to be enjoying himself too much not to have a hand in this.

Elizabeth had come to a similar conclusion, but her temper prompted her to voice her anger. "Don't waste our time with that innocent act, Peter Patrick Hennessey. Of course you're in on it. Who else would be able to spice up the plot with a little 'not to be repeated,' confidential information about spies picked up around Amagansett and Jacksonville?"

"Jeepers Crow, Liz!" Jessica snapped, flinging up her hands in anger. Where was a blunt object when she needed one?

"You stinker, Peter Hennessey, are you or are you not going to admit that this is all your tasteless brainchild!?" Elizabeth pressed, leaning forward on the bar.

"Better watch it, Liz," Peter dryly warned. "You're going to gouge the wood with those fire-engine red claws of yours."

"Argh!" Elizabeth's fists pounded the bar. "That's it! I hope you and your little pal Crawford live happily ever after! Good-bye!"

Jessica started to reach after her sister but turned back to her brother-in-law to insist, "Peter, she's going to walk out on you again. You've got to apologize."

"Apologize? For what?"

"For... what? Peter, stop being such a weasel. A joke's a joke, but this is going too far."

"Look, Jessica, your sister should not blow her top over a little joke. Liz is a big girl."

"She's hurt. Hurt enough to walk if you don't calm her down."

"And if I apologize now, it'll just make her think she's right. Let her go and cool down. I'm not going to encourage her to throw tantrums by giving in to her."

"Peter," Jessica coldly measured out her words, "if you'd been negotiating the coal miners' strike last year, I swear we'd all be burning peat moss for the next forty winters."

"Works in Ireland," he returned affably.

Jessica allowed herself an unladylike snort, before turning on her heel to find Liz and try cleaning up this mess. Almost bumping into Larry, she grimaced her annoyance with the other couple. Larry nodded his comprehension and suggested, "I'll talk to Peter while you work on Elizabeth."

Jessica nodded, starting for the bedroom, but Larry's voice stopped her, "Jessica, I have to tell you that I heard enough of the argument to know something fishy is going on over that package. When the air clears, *we* must talk."

Larry turned away and went to Peter, leaving Jessica to mutter to herself, "Swell."

Reaching the closed door of Elizabeth and Peter's bedroom, Jessica knocked but didn't wait for a response before entering. The room was elegant, though masculine enough to suit its male occupant. Liz could merge any styles without the hint of a clash. The white chiffon of her evening gown was spread out neatly across the bed. Elizabeth's back was to her sister as she zipped up the dusky-rose street dress into which she'd changed. Without turning, Liz breezily requested, "Help me out and hang up my gown, won't you, Jessica?"

"I ought to hang you," Jessica returned coolly.

Elizabeth glanced back at her sister, briefly, then moved across the room to her vanity and mirror, art deco black and gold. Sweeping her hair off the sides of her face with clips, Elizabeth grudgingly allowed, "I suppose I didn't keep my word very well."

"I suppose you didn't."

Jessica went over to the walk-in closet near her sister and scouted a hanger.

"I suppose you expect me to apologize," Elizabeth posited, not quite as confidently as she'd intended. Then she blurted, "Honestly, Jessica, I thought I was doing the right thing, calling that heel on what he was doing to you. No one picks on my sister."

Jessica turned from the closet, hanger in hand and warned, "Two things: first, you don't critique how I hang this damn dress for you; second, if you ever open your mouth like that when I tell you not to, you can just get used to being called Philomele — and I don't mean because you sing like a nightingale."

Elizabeth dropped a protesting hand as her sister turned away to hang the chiffon gown in the closet. Maybe making a snappy comeback wouldn't be just the thing right now. When Jessica emerged from the closet still looking mighty troubled, Liz said, "You realize I can't stay in the same house as that stinker another minute. I really do appreciate your putting me up."

"Don't you mean putting up with you?"

Arms akimbo, Liz pointed out, "He wasn't exactly Prince Charming to you, Jessica. None of this would have even happened if he hadn't decided to play wise guy with you. I'm burnt up for your sake, too, you know!"

Jessica started to protest. Instead, she sat down on the bed and said, "All right, look, Elizabeth, I realize your intentions were good, but I'd rather keep the both of us off the road to hell. Listen to me from now on, okay?"

It killed her, but Elizabeth conceded, "Yes, well, all right. I guess you were right."

"Oooh!" Jessica collapsed on the bed, an arm extended over her forehead, "Can this be? Elizabeth Hennessey admits she's wrong? Will Hitler be dancing with Mrs. Roosevelt next?"

"Don't get wise," Elizabeth grumped, tossing some underwear at her sister. "Here, make yourself useful."

"What's this?" Jessica sat up, clutching the lingerie Elizabeth had flung her.

"A change of... heart. Here, here's my overnight bag, start packing."

"Hmm, *not* three suitcases. Could this be merely a short stay?"

"You sound relieved?" Elizabeth paused, hose dangling in her hands.

"Let's just say not many people would relish having a guest who inspects their housekeeping like a top sergeant going through the barracks," Jess sweetly smiled.

"Another crack like that, Jessica, and I'll never go back to Peter."

* * * * * *

Jessica Minton leaned back against the front door she had just shut, closed her eyes, and sighed into the soft, salmon glow of the Chinese-lady table lamp to her right. Whatever else might be wrong with them as a couple, Larry's good-night kiss was usually pretty nifty. But tonight, once he'd made sure Liz was out of earshot in the kitchen, Larry had let her know he was sore at her for not having leveled with him. He'd been reasonable and rational to the nth degree, never raised his voice, but he'd still been mighty sore.

Shoving herself away from the door, Jessica slipped her wrap from her shoulders and tossed it over the nearby dining-room chair. Larry'd given her what for, for not confiding in him or giving him the package for safekeeping. He'd really been annoyed when, instead of being contrite, she'd insisted she didn't need to be protected from Peter's practical jokes. What really took the cake was that he'd been a little concerned this actually *might* be more than one of Mr. Hennessey's pranks. Funny thing, though, Jess had the distinct impression that her suggesting that *his* imagination was hyperactive had gotten under his skin as much as her keeping something from him had.

The cellar door was suddenly thrust open before her, and Jess had to choke down a startled cry.

"Raow!"

Dusty stood in the doorway looking woebegone. So much for Larry being the hysterical one.

"Of course, I am a brute abandoning you for an entire evening," Jessica agreed, taking the cat up in her arms, fur on her gown be damned. Dusty succumbed to Jessica's blandishments and closed her eyes with the pleasure of having her neck rubbed. The corners of her mouth seemed to curl up slightly. Jessica, herself, was not averse to the comfort offered by her feline, whose free paw stretched across her chest in a gesture of alliance. But eventually Jess had to break the spell.

"There we go, pet." She lowered the cat gently. "I'm bushed, and I've got to turn in."

Dusty strolled after Jessica to the bathroom, settling into a seated position by the bathtub, wrapping her tail around herself with stately grace. How Jess envied her cat's cozy calm. Elizabeth and Peter's fights took more out of her than them, and that little chat with Larry hadn't been a trip through the park, either. Feeling one-hundred years old, Jessica removed her shiny clip earrings, then pulled the door closed to get the hanger for her dress.

"Huh?" Jessica smiled her surprise to see her nightgown, filmy ice-blue, hanging there. Before turning in, Elizabeth had set it out for her.

In spite of everything, Liz was a good kid. Her heart was in the right place, even if her head wasn't always. Undressing, Jessica recalled how on the drive over Elizabeth had immediately gone to bat for her when Larry had been a little snippy. It was nice to know that she had someone else in her corner. Dusty blinked approval.

"Okay, then, Dusty. You're both in my corner. As for who has the sharper claws...?"

Still, why couldn't Larry give in to her as quickly as he did to Elizabeth?

Teeth brushed, face washed, the rest of her nightgowned and slippered,

Jessica pondered the quiet in her room. Maybe Elizabeth was already asleep? That would suit Jessica just fine. At this time of night — a glance at the watch on the edge of her sink — eek! — Morning, Jessica was in no mood to discuss marital problems, or anything, for that matter.

"After you, madam," Jessica instructed Dusty with a gracious wave of her hand, and Dusty trotted out in the lead.

The bedroom was amber under the lamp light on Jessica's bed-side table. Elizabeth was conked out on her cot. Eyes half-closed, Dusty was kneading the covers at the foot of Jessica's bed. But Jessica was too antsy to sleep, exhausted and antsy. Settling into bed, she decided she had plenty of time to do some reading. What was that book she'd started, now? Her glance fell on the copy of *Hard Times* on the bed-side table. Brother, you said it!

* * * * * *

Jess blinked irritably, trying to pull the covers over her head. What had disturbed her blessed forty winks? Ah, that was it! Some fiend had invaded her dreamy haven by drawing the curtains and raising the blackout shades.

"Rise and shine, Jess. You can't sleep forever."

The fiend had Elizabeth's voice.

"Don't bet on it," Jessica muttered, burrowing deeper beneath the covers.

"Come on; it's time to get up. You can make like a mole some other morning," Elizabeth quipped, as she strolled down to the end of the bed, deftly whipping back the covers behind her.

Defiantly, Jessica took refuge beneath one of her pillows, only to be foiled when her sister snatched that away, hit her with it, then stepped back, quite pleased with herself.

Abruptly, Jessica sat up, blinking against the morning light and mumbling, "I dreamed... I could have sworn... Elizabeth Pamela Hennessey, did you just hit me with a pillow?"

"Dreams can be so realistic," Liz dead panned innocently.

Jessica eyed her sister suspiciously, before questioning, "Just what prompted you to come in and torture me, Elizabeth?"

"I had to see you before I left."

As she attempted to push her hair into some kind of order, Jessica noticed that her sister was smartly turned out in dark skirt, brown and yellow checked blazer, and pale yellow blouse. The perennial upsweep and bun at the nape of her neck, the perfectly applied make-up showed Elizabeth was ready to go.

"Where are you off to now, Liz? How can anyone be so organized this early?"

"Some of us roll out of bed before the crack of noon, dear. Anyway, I'll meander home, after I run up an enormous charge at Bergdorf Goodman."

"Just to keep Peter in line?"

"Mmm, hmm."

Leaning forward, arms around her knees, Jessica queried, "Elizabeth, don't you think you're playing a little fast and loose with your marriage?"

"Relax, Jess, after having to fend for himself at breakfast, lunch, *and* dinner, Peter will be begging me to come back. He always does."

"And they say romance has gone out of modern marriage."

"Don't be such a cynic," Liz chided. "You know as well as I that the big lunk is miserable over being a stinker. He always regrets it."

"We'd all regret it less if he, if you both, thought about what you said before it slipped out," Jessica warned wryly.

"Marital advice from the woman who's afraid to get married?" Elizabeth queried.

Jessica straightened, "I'm not afraid. I'm just not ready. Besides, Larry and I have a lot to work out first. I don't want to end up with us fighting all the time."

"Come on now, Jess. You know we don't fight *all* the time. I'll tell you, though, making up is worth it. And you can't afford to wait for Mr. Perfect. There ain't no such animal. If we're going to speculate over who would be the perfect catch, we might as well fret about how much better I could do with Cary Grant."

"Oh, in that case, let's worry about how much better *I* could do with Cary Grant. Shouldn't sisters share?"

"I'll keep that in mind should Mr. Grant and I cross paths over a head of lettuce at the market. In the meantime, I have your breakfast ready. Be back in a minute."

Elizabeth left, and Jessica plumped her pillows before leaning back against them. *Mmm, nice and comfy*, she purred to herself. *Now luxuriously roll your shoulders and stretch. Mmm, hmm, even better.* The only thing missing was Dusty's good-morning greeting, which could consist of anything from nuzzling to head butting.

Newspaper tucked under her arm, Liz strolled back into the room with a breakfast tray, remarking, "I had quite some time getting in here without your cat. She followed me everywhere once I hit the kitchen. Why is Dusty only sociable when there's food around?"

"She's a cat." Jessica shrugged. "What else do you expect?"

Delivering the tray to her sister, Elizabeth merely raised an eyebrow. Jessica smiled as she settled down to her breakfast of poached egg, muffins, and coffee. Elizabeth left the folded newspaper at her sister's side, querying, "Enough to hold you?"

"Beats the heck out of corn flakes! I think I can handle it. Will you stay and chat?"

"I have a few dishes to do. Don't worry. I'll be back in no time. In the meanwhile, why don't you put your college degree to work and read the paper?"

"I can do without the sarcasm."

Liz paused at the door for, "Oh, by the way, when I come back, remember to tell me how wonderful the muffins are."

"Homemade?"

"How could you guess?"

Alone, Jessica shook her head in amusement at her sister. For a moment, she wondered if Liz had used up too much of her monthly rations for the meal. Well, it was near the end of the month anyway. One bite of muffin convinced her today's culinary delight would balance out any scrimping for flour and sugar to come.

Jess shook out the newspaper. While she sipped her coffee, her attention was caught by a headline on Russian advances through Bryansk. Any story detailing the Axis's set back nabbed her hopeful attention. Putting down her cup, Jessica raced through the portion on page one, then excitedly skipped several pages into Section A for the end of the story. But she never finished it. Right below it her eye caught "Amagansett" and "saboteur." Fingers actually trembling, Jessica flipped back to find the beginning of an article she hadn't expected, wanted, to find. An icy wave rolled through her as the details hit with sickening familiarity.

"I forgot to ask you... Jessica, what's wrong? You look as if you'd just won a vacation in Bayonne, New Jersey."

Dropping the newspaper, Jess was overcome by a jumble of excruciating emotions. But always a trooper, she pulled herself together and coolly hit her sister with the horrifying spot they were in. "Elizabeth, this Crawford thing is no gag."

"Gag? Peter's joke? What are you talking about?"

Picking up the paper, Liz looked for an explanation. As she read on, she slowly sank down on the side of the bed, with a long, rueful "Oh."

The paper slipped to the floor.

"Jess," Elizabeth began tentatively, "what are you going to do?"

"I — I don't know. Liz, what have I, what have we, done?"

"What do you mean?"

"Liz, he told me to keep this on the q.t. — it was imperative — and now look! You, Peter, and Larry know everything. What a mess!"

"Maybe they won't find out about Crawford's story being true," Elizabeth lamely suggested.

"Oh, right, Liz, maybe starting today Peter and Larry will both suddenly decide never to read another newspaper or listen to the radio — or talk to anyone who does."

"I get your point."

"Jeepers Crow, how could I do this? How could I put us in such danger?"

"Danger? Jessica, what do you mean by danger?"

"Remember, Liz, Crawford warned me not to tell anything to anyone. He said even calling in the F. B.I. wasn't safe. There's some kind of leak." Jessica's words trailed off into a shudder, before she continued, "And I got us into this jam."

"Don't forget, you had some help from your know-it-all sister."

Jessica smiled wanly. Elizabeth folded her arms, saying, "Of course, placing the blame doesn't get us out of this fix."

They brooded silently, painfully for several minutes, and then Jessica began to consider out loud, "You know, Elizabeth, this is only a devastating problem if Peter and Larry talk, right?"

"Sure, otherwise it's just a horrible problem. That's still a mighty tremendous 'if,' little sister."

"But, Liz, I think I can convince them to forget everything. Now, listen, what if we tell them it *was* a practical joke . . .?"

"That we played on them? No dice. Not after that *battle royale* my darling husband and I had last night."

"Not by us, then. I'm thinking of something better. There was this juvenile lead whom Harold Vane let go. It's a long story, but the kid blamed me because I'd defended Frederick Bromfield against him. He even made a stink and 'darkly hinted' about getting even."

"You want to tell the fellas that *he's* the trickster?" Liz considered slowly. "But what about the *New York Times*? This guy would need a heck of a lot of pull to get the *Times* in on his joke."

"We-e-ll... we could say he had a contact there, so he heard about the story before it broke in the news. Peter and Larry would have no way of knowing otherwise. They don't even know the kid, so there'd be no way to check up on our story. You have Larry lean on Peter, to make sure he drops the whole issue. Larry listens to you. Better yet, if Larry feels that he has to smooth everything out, he'll be too busy to ask embarrassing questions."

"You think it will work, Jessica?"

"Elizabeth, it's going to have to."

CHAPTER SIX

A dark chamber. Lying peacefully beneath the coverlet, her eyes closed, Jessica alone was illuminated. A hand moved into view, gripping a vicious knife. Its blade descended swiftly and Jessica's eyes snapped open. The few deft slashing movements drove her to laughter.

Still laughing, Jessica pulled herself up to lean back on her elbows.

"I knew you were sneaking up. You didn't buffalo me, Mr. Bromfield."

"Ah, but how was my imitation of Douglas Fairbanks?"

"Senior or junior?"

"Is there a junior?" Her companion shook his head.

"Sure there is. He was in *Prisoner of Zenda* with Ronald Colman and Raymond Massey. Had a short run as one of Joan Crawford's husbands, too."

"I don't know much about the talkies. Senior, then, of course, as Zorro," Bromfield explained in as light a mood as Jessica.

"The 'Z' of Zorro?" Jessica inquired dryly, glancing at the knife. She chided, "I'm afraid you don't look like Doug, Sr..."

"Ah, but I did not say I would imitate Fairbanks' looks. I only said I would imitate *him*. And was not my 'Z' a perfect imitation?"

"No difference," Jessica agreed, then, reaching out to tap the blade, continued, "Though there isn't much chance of your slashing anyone with that, is there?"

Bromfield nodded before he drove the knife into his palm, the pressure forcing the blade of the prop to retract into the hilt.

"Just make sure you always get the prop, Mr. Bromfield!"

"Rest easy, Miss Minton. I always test this prop out before I use it. You're safe in my hands."

"I'll have to remember to stay on your good side!"

Jess shaded her eyes over the footlights in an attempt to view the empty seats beyond, finally wondering aloud, "Isn't Harold ready, yet? I thought he was in a hurry to finish this run-through."

"Harold Vane is Harold Vane. He'll get back to us when he gets back to us," Frederick Bromfield replied, his calm reflecting years of experience with testy directors.

"All right, you two up there. Down to business. This isn't a relief project!"

The voice that growled out of the darkness was Harold Vane's.

After Vane had imparted key instructions, and Jessica asked him some questions, the players commenced their scene. Broderick, Bromfield's character, had finally discovered the duplicity of the woman played by Jessica. Furious that she'd been making time with his son, as well as with him, he pulled a knife and stabbed the woman to death. End scene.

Unfortunately, the scene did not run smoothly, but through no fault of the actors. An unruly bunch of wasps, having nested somewhere backstage, decided to join the performance. Vane must have gone soft-hearted, or the closest he'd ever get, for he allowed the two to break for the day after Frederick Bromfield took a sting and Jess suffered several near misses. The wasps did not fare so well; Vane decided to bring in an exterminator before the insects disrupted any more work. The last thing he needed was his two leading actors to be wasp-swollen beyond recognition with the play opening in two days, on September ninth.

As the two actors exited into the wings and started along the scenery-clogged corridor to their dressing rooms, Bromfield began, "Miss Minton, I must tell you that your advice about my niece worked. Things are going much better now."

"Your niece? Oh, oh, yes. Great. I'm glad everything turned out fine. So, you found out what was troubling her?"

"Ah, yes. That's all settled. We talked everything out," he assured her as they stopped at his dressing-room door. He continued avuncularly, "I appreciate your help, Miss Minton. Remember, any time you have a problem I will return the favor and listen to you."

Jess thought, *If only you knew what you were offering!* However, she only said, "Of course. I'm just happy I could help."

Thoughts of Crawford's package now reawakened, Jessica was no longer happy as she made her way back to her own dressing room. Wasps and Harold Vane notwithstanding, the hours on stage today, the discipline of submerging herself in her role, had blessedly driven everything else right out of her head. Now the battle between her desire to get the package and Mr. Crawford out of her life and the dread of having to participate in this spy story come true troubled her anew — and unlike Madeline Carroll in *The Thirty-Nine Steps*, she couldn't rely on sympathetic screen writers to get her out of a jam.

Jess pushed on into her dressing room. No sooner had she closed the door than movement behind her floor-length screen startled her backwards. Crawford!? Who else? She had expected him all along, but now that he was here, Jessica couldn't roll back the anxiety surging up and congealing into an unpleasant lump in her throat.

"Damn! No ash trays!" cursed Elizabeth from behind the screen.

Jess put a hand to her chest and sighed her relief that it was only Liz. She didn't have to face James Crawford after putting the hoodoo on his case with her big mouth, not for the moment, anyway. Her voice, not as steady as she'd have liked, called, "Please don't sneak around here, Liz."

Stepping into view, Elizabeth hesitated the briefest of moments to assess her sister's expression. What she read there sent Liz striding across the room, saying, "This deal with the package really has upset you, kiddo. You'd better sit down."

Jessica nodded, "Yeah, I guess I'd better."

"Has anything else gone wrong, I mean, happened?" Elizabeth pressed as Jessica sat down at her dressing table.

Elizabeth was dressed to the nines: cream colored silk box-jacket over a beige jersey dress sparkling with iridescent threads, the peaked crown of her broad-brimmed hat matching the brown-gold of her fitted gloves. But she clutched her enormous square leather bag too tightly for someone who'd just enjoyed a social luncheon at the Waldorf — unless she'd gotten stuck with the check.

"Liz, has anything happened to *you?*"

"No, no. But that's what's worrying me. Nothing's happened yet. Doesn't it get to you?"

Jessica smiled ruefully, "I guess we're both giving new meaning to 'war nerves.'"

"Hmph," Elizabeth groused, "What's this Crawford rube waiting for anyway? MacArthur to go back to the Philippines? Doesn't he think we have lives?"

Jess wanted to point out that his actively fighting the Nazis might have something of a higher priority. Then again, it would be far less trouble just to change the subject. Kicking off her mules, Jess queried, "So what *does* bring you here, Liz?"

Elizabeth brightened. "I have good news. Peter bought the story. He waffled at first. He thought no kid could organize such an elaborate gag, but I catalogued a few of his own more adventurous pranks, and he wound up believing me. I think he was even a little jealous that someone out-plotted him. I just hope this hasn't given him any ideas."

Jess smiled, but only halfheartedly.

"Look, Jess, if holding the package makes you so uneasy why don't you let me take it?"

Jessica shook her head, "No, that won't do at all, Liz. You just finished convincing Peter this was all a practical joke. What would he think if you showed up with the package? Anyway, this is my responsibility. You're not even supposed to know about it. Thanks, but there's no other way."

Elizabeth shrugged, "I guess you're right. So what will you do?"

"What else can I do? I'll just have to wait for the mysterious Mr. Crawford to make the next move. I guess I shouldn't worry; he did say as long as I kept things quiet there would be no danger," Jess concluded wearily.

"We kept things quiet. Fairly quiet. Well, they should be quiet now."

"So, we'll have to stop worrying. That won't solve anything," Jess pronounced, abruptly getting up. "I'm going to change, and maybe we can go part way home together. Who knows, we may even be able to get a cab."

"Maybe," Liz allowed, taking the chair her sister had vacated.

Jessica snatched up a short, fitted yellow jacket and her dark brown slacks from a little closet to the right of the door and disappeared behind the screen.

Liz continued, "I guess we really shouldn't worry. You said he assured you everything would work out fine. Besides, kid, playing this kind of role must be old hat to you by now, after some of those melodramas you've been in."

Poking her head around the corner of the screen, Jess quipped, "I wish you wouldn't say that, Liz. I get killed in this one."

Liz grimaced, "Oops. Sorry about that, kiddo. But, well, there don't seem to be any snags. Peter believed me and... Larry did believe you, didn't he?"

Jessica's response came after a momentary hesitation, "I think so."

"You *think* so?"

Jessica stepped around the screen, buttoning her jacket as she explained, "He seemed to ponder what I was saying just a shade too much for my comfort. But he didn't argue with me, either."

"You know Larry, Jess," Elizabeth came back, shaking her head as she rose. "He ponders if you tell him to wear a gray suit instead of a black one."

Jessica smiled wearily. "Yep. Guess you're right, Liz. I just wish that I didn't have to lie to him. It goes against my grain."

"Sometimes you really are a Girl Scout, Jessica. You're going to have to get over that, especially in this situation."

"That's the trouble," Jessica worried. "I think I'm starting to get over it a little *too* well."

"Jessica, if I were 100% on the level with Peter, we'd have been on the road to Reno years ago."

"'Road to Reno'? That sounds as if you should be heading off with Hope, Crosby, and Lamour."

"Just as long as I get to wear the sarong. C'mon, let's go see if we can shanghai ourselves a taxi."

Jessica took her sister's arm, and they strolled out of the dressing room.

But Liz stopped them short to say, "Oh. Before I forget, I hope you're not going to be upset. Peter and I can't make your opening night. Peter has to go to Rhode Island for a convention of that Hibernian organization he belongs to. I really would rather wait for him so we can go together. Sorry, Jess."

"That should be the least of my worries. With my luck, Crawford will show up to get his package as a spear-carrier in the middle of Act Two. Just come second week. It'll give us a chance to work out some of the bugs."

The sinisterly distended shapes of the wasps hovering around one of the overhead lights sent a shiver through Jessica and inspired her sister to crinkle her nose and remark, "I hope you work *those* bugs out, too, before I spend two hours here."

"You and I both. They've had too much opportunity for target practice already," agreed Jessica, ushering her sister out into the autumn gold of late afternoon.

* * * * * *

Through the open door, sounds of clinking glasses, swing music, and a jumble of delight and laughter spilled into the night from the party inside Iris Rossetti's apartment. Taking her leave in that doorway's square of light, Jessica Minton felt disquietingly set off against the blue-gray gauze of the New-York-City late night. Wearing this gleaming white gown, the jeweled epaulets of her matching jacket glinting in the street lamps' tepid illumination, Jess had the disquieting sensation of standing out conspicuously to lurking Axis agents. But Jess would *not* give in to the jitters. So she put her acting chops to the test, playing a scene of lighthearted parting from Iris, the play's willowy ingénue.

Momentarily, Jessica wondered if her chum might prove more of a standout target, towering above her, tricked out in a blond upsweep and a long dress of green, blue, and white floral splashes, its plunging neckline and bare midriff no less flashy than the colors. But Jessica only voiced their shared relief on surviving opening night — and their delight that, miracle of miracles, they had a success! The women briefly batted back and forth the theory that all the pre-production jitters had created just the right aura of anxiety for their taut little drama. Jess could see Harold Vane inside, a cheroot clamped in a toothy grin, as he contemplated a scotch and ignored the admiration of well-wishers. It had been a great party, and reveling in creating something wonderful with an ensemble had driven all her anxieties about dealing with Crawford clean out of town — that and three Singapore Slings — until a moment ago.

From behind them, Larry cleared his throat a little *too* emphatically. Iris tried to catch her eye, expecting a quip from her friend, but Jessica wasn't about to play. Still, she did take her time turning around before answering neutrally, "I'll be down in a minute, Larry."

"The master calls?" Iris whispered with a wink.

Jessica's retort was a tart but smooth, "You really think he is?"

"Not unless he can pull a gun on you," Iris giggled. "But he is a keeper." One hand squeezed Jessica's arm in camaraderie and Iris left her with, "Got to get back. This crew drinks like fish; I have to check the liquor!"

Jess smiled, girded herself... for what? Turning, she called, "Let's go, Larry."

Larry nodded quickly and opened the taxi's door for her. His face was just as pensive and strained as it had been all evening — and he was awfully anxious to go. Something more than letting the cabbie's meter run was eating him. The package?

Jess nearly stumbled on her long skirts as she entered the cab. Maybe she could have done with one or two fewer Singapore Slings. She really ought to have all her wits about her to handle Larry tonight, more accurately, this morning. Whatever he had in mind, it had to be a doozy. He'd merengued rather than fox-trotted through "Begin the Beguine." That was a bad sign. Larry always picked the less complicated step when he had something IMPORTANT on his mind.

Masking her uneasiness Jess gave the cabbie her address, managing not to plead, "And step on it!"

"Jessica, it's imperative we have a talk," Larry began.

"Oh?"

"Yes, Jessica. I blame myself, somewhat. I haven't been entirely fair to you. I haven't trusted you, but I want you to know I trust you now. And that you can trust me. I realized everything tonight, during your performance."

"Everything?"

Oh God, did that mean Larry hadn't bought the story Liz and I cooked up?

The cab bumped them roughly over something in the road. Larry reached to steady Jessica. Still holding her hands in his own, he pressed on, "If you want to stay on the stage, I'll go along with that. I'm willing to let you keep acting until you're ready to settle down, outgrow it. There's no reason we can't marry."

"Oh, goodness," Jessica elaborately sighed, in spite of herself. "Is that it? We've been over this a thousand times before. I thought we agreed the other night that we'd give it all a rest for a while."

Larry's face darkened like Heathcliff on the moor, and Jessica's heart tore a little. It wasn't the same old game tonight. Larry really was serious this time, and she'd hurt him — not what she wanted at all.

"Jessica," Larry pressed, "I just told you that I'd changed my mind about your career. It's not like a 'thousand times before.' Anyway, what did you mean by 'that's what I'm upset over'? What else would I be upset over?"

"Oh, well, I meant that... well, you know how much has been on my mind with the play and all... I just, thought, you looked so intense, that something important was bothering you. Wait a minute, '*let* me keep acting'? 'Outgrow' it?"

But Larry seized on her slip of the tongue.

"'Important,'" he repeated coolly, staring her down as he considered the word. "I see. My decision to have a complete change of heart; my sacrifice to accommodate you so that we can spend the rest of our lives together isn't important? I'd like to know what *is*."

Jessica shot Larry a sharp look, determined that he not discover her deeper concern — a concern important to his well-being, too, according to

Crawford's warnings. She spoke carefully, "Now, Larry, you know that was just a poor word choice, a slip."

"We both know what Freud said about slips."

"Yes, they shouldn't hang below your skirt," Jessica deadpanned, hoping to defuse a tense moment. No dice.

"Flippancy, Jessica? That just shows how much you need me to help you to settle down. But my decision about us ought to have cleared that path. There's something else bothering you, isn't there?"

"Well, Larry, I did tell you the play . . ."

"Jessica, you've been anxious over your work before, but I've never seen you insensitive. You're not still stewing about what you thought was Peter's practical joke, are you?"

"Of course not." Had she snapped that answer? This was a scent she had to throw Larry off but fast. "We settled that. It was that young actor, with his newspaper contact. I thought you believed me."

Good grief! Had she actually used a loaded word like "believed"? Would Larry interpret that word as implying she and Liz had tried to convince him of a falsehood rather than just provide a true explanation? Or was she turning paranoid, expecting Larry to dig for hidden significance in her every word?

Larry thought for a moment, then patiently persisted, "You haven't quite been yourself for some time, and tonight..."

"Look, Larry," Jessica attempted to head him off, "it's now the a.m. This is *not* the best time for a girl to make a momentous decision, not this girl anyway. We can talk this out later, like two adults, when neither one of us is all tuckered out. You want a serious discussion, don't you?"

"You still haven't answered my question about your behavior, Jessica."

"Larry, I didn't know I was on trial here." Jess was sympathetic, but she was tired and worried and losing patience. "You shouldn't expect me to explain every facet of my behavior. I'm not a gangster and you're not Thomas E. Dewey prosecuting a criminal."

"Hey, hey, you kids," the driver startled them both by cutting in. "Two people together like you shouldn't be fightin.' Aaah, the war has everyone crabby, these days — what with no rubber, no sugar, no coffee, no silk stockin's for youse dames, no gas. A war gets under everybody's skin."

"Especially the soldiers,'" came Larry's clipped rejoinder.

Jessica clasped and unclasped her hands in her lap. Larry was on the money in nailing the cabbie, but she had the distinct impression he was also losing patience with her for not immediately falling into concordance with his plan. And maybe their relationship *was* all he had on his mind. Maybe Crawford had made her so screwy she was seeing connections to Axis plots everywhere she turned.

And she was, indeed, missing the big picture. Larry had made a notable concession to her about her career — which led her to a different problem. Why wasn't she jumping for joy at her beau's change of heart? Maybe because she was in the middle of a spy plot that might be the end of them all. If only she felt she could turn to Larry for advice. No, that thought made her seize up inside. She had to protect him from getting mixed up in Crawford's horrible SNAFU. But Larry could be a regular bulldog when he chose, so keeping him off the trail called for extraordinary measures.

As if on cue, the cabbie popped in, "You folks is smart to take a hack, save you the worry of trying to stretch out those gas coupons."

Snapping up the opportunity to distract Larry, Jess leaned forward to tell their cabbie, "You don't know the half of it. My boyfriend's ration tickets were lost at the O.P.A. office. But they're so afraid that handing out extra tickets might make it easier for the originals to wind up on the black market, they won't issue him any new ones. Unless they find them, we have to call cabs or hitch rides until next month."

"That's a shame, a real shame."

Before Jess could go on, Larry put a hand on her arm and questioned sternly, "Jessica, what is this runaround about?"

"You say runaround, Mac? Yeah, it is frustratin,' ain't it to need some juice for the old engine an' not be able to get it? Some folks even go to black market gas stations."

Hoping to capitalize on this diversion, Jess encouraged the cabbie, "But how do the stations get away with it? How do they know whom to sell to? People can't just walk in off the street."

"Naw, no one wanders in off the street. They have ways of checking."

"Must be expensive, the gas I mean," Jess mused, heading off Larry's attempt to cut in.

"Yeah, well, an extra fee or so, but ain't it worth a little extra dough to have your peace a' mind?" the driver queried philosophically. "But like I was sayin', lady, you has ta know someone who'll take you to that kinda place; I mean, like I says, you can't just waltz in off the street. You can get in a lot of hot water for playing the black market game. My brotha tells me this stuff."

"Don't you think the authorities should crack down, though? After all, it's a lot less dangerous to run out of gas in the city than it is to run out in Italy or the South Pacific."

"Yeah, lady, that's true, but I bet them big wigs in Washington have their extra share, an' we're still doing fine overseas. So why can't the little guy like you or me get the extra stuff, too? Look at your boyfriend here; he's not a gouger or anything. It ain't his fault they lost his coupons. Just one of them things. But the poor slob's stuck."

They turned onto her street, and Larry took charge of the conversation. "Jessica, I've stood more than I deserved. You need to terminate this conversation and explain what you are up to."

"Say, lady, what's your boyfriend so steamed about?" asked the driver as they pulled up to Jessica's door. "Hey, there's no reason some gas shortage should mess up a nice little romance. It ain't fair for a war acrosst the world and some screw ups at the O.P.A. to break up a nice couple like you two. I think I can get you outta this jam."

"Once and for all," Larry now growled, "the gas shortage is not breaking up our... Wait a minute, why am I conversing with this man?"

"You got me, Larry. Doesn't this tell you that maybe you need to catch some serious shut-eye before taking on a serious talk about us?"

Against all Jessica's expectations, Larry's features melted into a speculative smile before he said, "My dear, there's more going on here than meets the eye. After I deal with the driver, we're going inside for a talk. Whatever the mysterious problem is, we'd best settle it."

Larry then briskly turned on the cabbie and informed him, "You are quite correct, 'Mac,' I do need quite a bit of petrol. You see I have to do a great deal of traveling for my work, and you know how the government never adequately reimburses its people."

"You work for the, uh, government, bub?"

"Yes. The rationing board as a matter of fact."

The cabbie's mouth dropped open. Larry, flashing a disarming smile, popped out of the cab, gallantly standing aside to allow Jessica to follow him.

"Suddenly so reticent, sir? Aren't you forgetting the bill?" Larry queried.

The driver managed to mumble the fare, staring at Larry, stupefied.

Larry paid him off, saying, "Do keep the change. And if I were you, I'd find a new side business, one that isn't going to siphon the lifeblood out of the chaps who are dying for you. Just remember. I've got your number."

The cabbie gulped and stared vaguely at the money in his hand, then shifted gears and floored his vehicle away from Larry.

Her past concerns lost in the moment, Jessica smiled with gentle warmth, "Larry, I'm proud of you. Maybe there'll be a few more guys alive because you scared some low-down chiseler away from preying on the war shortages. Good show, old chap! I don't think he'll stop long enough to be caught, though."

"I was rather amazed by the speed at which he departed," Larry deadpanned. "Who would expect a machine that old to have so much pickup?"

In spite of, or maybe because of, the earlier tension between them, Jessica couldn't help cracking up at Larry's delivery, having to lean against him, coughing with laughter. As he helped her straighten, himself grinning, Jessica, pulled away, bursting into another fit with, "You should be even more surprised, Larry. That was your ride home!"

"But of course I can ring up a cab from your apartment. That will give us more time to talk."

That sobered Jessica up. With a mildly rueful expression she allowed, "Well, I guess you got me there, but it's against my better judgment."

It was Larry's turn to smile impishly. Jessica took his arm. She really did owe him more than just ducking out until the pressure was off, even if she was trying to protect him. Mr. Crawford sure had complicated her life.

Jessica led Larry to her door, saying, "C'mon. But you know, you are a rat. That poor guy. He thought he was going to make a tidy killing, and you come up with that line about the rationing board." They reached the landing before her door and Jess shot Larry a questioning look with, "I didn't think you worked in that department."

"I don't," Larry was deliciously devilish, "but the driver doesn't know that. Perhaps I should have made a point of examining his I.D. card, not saying anything of course — just smiling significantly."

"You are evil," Jessica, chuckled. "Because of you, he'll probably be afraid to carry on his 'charity' work in black marketeering. That poor 'altruistic' man." As she bent her head and rummaged through her purse for the apartment key, she offered, "C'mon in and call that cab. We can talk while you're waiting."

"Thanks."

After Jessica had unlocked the front door, they entered the darkened foyer. Jess fumbled and softly cursed her way to the Chinese-lady lamp. With a tendency to trip over things, she had never liked walking into a darkened room, and this business concerning the package did not exactly ameliorate her uneasiness. Still in darkness, Larry closed the door behind a shade too abruptly.

"Aiee!" Jessica jumped, whirling to hiss at him, "Don't do that!"

"All right," Larry returned irritably, adding, "but why are we whispering?"

"I'm not [raising her voice] whispering."

Jessica flicked on the soft light.

"See, Larry, nothing to worry about."

"I wasn't worried."

"Oh, don't argue."

Jessica turned and led Larry across the dining area, pausing before descending to the living room to flip on the wall switch for more light. She forced herself not to glance and see if Larry had perceived her relief when the lights dispelled the shadows that might hide... what?

"You know the phone's over by the couch," Jessica forced casualness into her voice. She was just beginning to wonder why Dusty hadn't greeted them at the door, when Larry paused and queried, "Did you change this couch?"

Jessica relaxed at this distraction, "Sure did. I put a floor-length cover on. Now when Liz lifts the rug to look for dirt, I can outsmart her and sweep everything under the couch."

But Larry didn't laugh.

"Larry, what's wrong?"

"I'm just a little tired. I was thinking about all we need to discuss tonight."

"Oh, you poor kid, Larry. You do look beat. We really should hold off any serious conversations tonight. After all, it's past one o'clock, and you have to work and I have a performance..."

"Jessica, this is important. It's our future. We have to set aside the time to work things out, don't you think?"

Jessica started to protest that setting aside the wee hours of the morning wasn't going to lead to a coherent heart-to-heart, but she knew that look in Larry's eye. To him, a disagreement now would say their relationship was not as important to her as it was to him. That was not the case at all. And she didn't want to hurt Larry by making him think it was. But she needed to figure out how to get him to back off until she really was up for such a serious conversation — because with the play, the package, and the late hour, all Jessica was up for right now was a snoring contest with Dusty.

"Okay, Larry. Sit down, make yourself comfortable. Would you like a drink?"

"Yes," he considered the prospect and even smiled, "that would be lovely, Jessica. Thank you."

"Fine. I'll just pop into the study and whip you up a scotch and soda."

"Jessica, you're one in a million."

"Um, hmm," Jessica smiled, but she turned away before Larry could see her face fall. He wasn't getting a drink because she was hospitable but because she wanted time to think.

Proceeding wearily toward the study doors, Jess tried to kid herself that if she plied Larry with enough drinks he'd pass out, and she could leave him to sleep it off on the couch. No good, he and the discussion would still be there in the morning. Was it guilt, exhaustion, or both that was smothering her sense of humor? *So stop fooling around,* she told herself, *and come up with a brilliant dodge, Einstein!* It wouldn't take that long to fix a drink, and she needed to figure out how to deal with Larry when she went back to him.

Jess opened the study's double doors just enough to reach in and flip on the light before she entered — but *only* because she didn't want to chance tripping over Dusty.

As the dark room brightened, Jess froze. Almost directly in front of her sat Dusty, blinking in the new light, offering her typical cat greeting. She leaped to the floor — from the footstool at the feet of the smiling Mr. Crawford, who sat comfortably in the Queen Anne chair before the blackout-shaded bay window.

Before he could translate the affable glint of his eyes into words, Jessica whirled, closed the doors behind her, and leaned dazedly against them.

Larry turned, leaning over the back of the couch, his forehead furrowing with amused perplexity, "That was quick... but, my drink?"

Jess recovered herself enough to push off from the doors and answer, "Oh, yes... I... forgot... something... in here."

"Oh, what?"

"I... ah... forgot."

To Larry's raised eyebrow, Jessica smiled swiftly and queried, "Call that cab, yet, Larry?"

"No, Jess. Remember, we were going to talk first?"

"Ah, yes," Jessica smiled, but inwardly cursed, *Damn.*

"One scotch and soda coming right up," Jessica promised and backed into the study, still smiling — until she closed the heavy double doors and whirled on Crawford, hissing, "What are you doing here?! My boyfriend's out there, for Pete's Sake!"

Standing now, Crawford surmised, "You don't seem terribly happy to see me."

"No kidding!"

Striding right up to him, she demanded, but not loud enough for Larry to hear, "Why on earth did you come here? You told me it was dangerous."

"My partner is running interference for me this evening." He glanced at his watch, "But you've been rather late. I'm afraid you've kept me a long time just to check on you and the package."

"Oh, excuse me, next time I'll have my social secretary contact your secretary — what do you mean 'check' on the package? Don't you mean 'take,' as in 'back'?"

"Hardly. Not at this point. I need a safe house to hide in with the package until arrangements have been made for me to deliver it to... well, the less you know, the better off you'll be."

"Oh, please. Do tell me. I'd hate to think of enemy agents torturing me for nothing."

Crawford's features relaxed into a wry smile. "I wouldn't fret too terribly over being tortured, Miss Minton. I have everything under control."

"Coming from you, that's not reassuring."

Jessica turned away and walked toward the study doors, straining for any indication that Larry could hear their interchange. Meanwhile, Dusty viewed them from her refuge beneath the loveseat, rotating her head to follow the volleys.

"So, I take it my evidence convinced you?" Crawford prodded.

Jessica hesitated, thinking that the evidence had also convinced Elizabeth. She hadn't exactly kept things top secret. Turning slowly, she answered,

"Yes."

Luckily he seemed not to recognize her concern, for he nodded, "Well then, all I need do is check the package and I can be on my way."

"Oh? Really? How? You can't hop out the window behind you. It's too dark for you to clear the spike fence. Or do you intend to just waltz nonchalantly past Larry out in the parlor? He's a little too intelligent to buy you as Clem my kissing cousin from the Ozarks. Larry's suspicious enough as it is."

Crawford's expression hardened and he crossed to her, demanding, "Suspicious of what? Have you told him about the package?"

Another step, two, backward and Jessica was near the door. Crawford wasn't far behind. She shook her head, insisting, "I... no, not really... no, don't give me that look. He saw it in my shopping bag that first night, but I haven't told him anything about you."

Crawford halted a few disquieting inches away. Jessica stared back at him, mustering defiance to stave off intimidation. Why couldn't Dusty leap out and savage Crawford's ankle? The cat dropped her eyes at Jessica's glance. When she turned back to Crawford, he conceded, "I suppose you couldn't help that. I'd just feel better . . ."

"Jessica? What's taking so long to make a single scotch and soda?"

Larry's voice was clearly not far from the door. In desperation, Jessica shoved Crawford into the wedge of space between the door to her right and the mahogany secretary. Larry almost fell into the room as Jessica flung the doors open inward, hiding Crawford, and inadvertently smacking him in the face with the door.

"What was that thump?" Larry queried, viewing the door curiously.

Jess turned him to face her with, "Oh, there's a stack of books back there. I'm always catching them on the door. One of these days I'll have to put them away. When do I ever have the time?"

"I could have sworn I heard you talking in here. Is something wrong, Jess?"

"Well, you know Larry. Yes, yes there is." Her eyes fell on the bay window across the room. "I just can't get that darned window open. It seemed so stuffy in here. I was talking to myself, cursing a blue streak trying to open it. I just wanted a little air. It's so stuffy in here . . ."

"Is it?

"Well, yes. I'd have had your drink by now, but when I tried to open the window . . ."

"Because it's stuffy?"

"Yes. Of course. I just wanted a little air, and the window's stuck. The handles won't turn."

"All right then, Jessica. I'll give it a go."

"Good. I'll put out the light."

"What?"

"Well, Larry, you'll have to get in under the blackout shade if you want to work on those windows; and even if we are below the fifteen story limit, we can't take a chance on any light escaping."

"Jessica, honestly, do you think any U-boats will be cruising the side streets above the Village?"

"Go ahead, be a wise guy. But just remember my black-out warden is a fanatic *and* an insomniac. I don't think I should get stuck paying a fine just because you're..."

"All right, all right, Jessica. Put out the light. Put it out. I just want to go back, sit down, talk things out..."

"And have your scotch."

"I need a scotch."

Jessica trotted over to the switch. Crawford should be able to figure out what she was up to, she hoped. Spies were devious that way, right? She switched off the lights, leaving them in the faint glow from the living room. As Larry went over to the window, Jess slowly closed the door by the switch, leaving the other open for Crawford to slip out.

Raow!

"Damn cat!"

"Larry!"

"She's the one who's supposed to be able to see in the dark, not me!"

Jessica moved swiftly forward and took Larry's arm to guide him to the window, silently apologizing to Dusty. Poor Larry. Of course he'd never get the window open; of course she'd flicked the levers that locked the handles. It might have been summer, but since getting the package she'd tried to lock the house up tight. So, how *had* Crawford gotten in?

Straining under the blackout shade, Larry grumbled, "Are you sure these aren't locked? What was that?"

He started to turn around, under the heavy shade, as a door creaked behind him. Jessica held him back with a hand on his arm and a playful, "Oh, Larry, no ghosts. It's just Dusty playing with the doors. If I were you, I wouldn't bother her until her tail stops smarting. Let's worry about this window. I can't spend the rest of the summer sweltering in this room."

They pushed together. No luck, of course.

"Jessica, this is obviously stuck solid. What did you do to it?"

"I... well, nothing I can think of. Should I complain to the landlord? Oh, let's give it one more try."

Jessica could more feel than see Larry's skeptical regard beneath the blackout shade. She tensed until he agreed, "All right then. Once more."

They'd started to lean into their task again, when a heart-stopping crash outside the study sent Larry whipping from under the shade, "What the blazes!? It came from outside the room."

"That darn cat," Jessica fudged desperately. "Probably knocked over the telephone, again. I'll check it out. You look over the edges of the sill. Now that I think of it, the landlord painted it not too long ago. Maybe it's sealed. I'll be right back."

Jessica sailed from the room before Larry could argue, decidedly closing both double doors behind her.

Not three steps into the room, she halted in her tracks. There was Mr. Crawford having a devil of a time trying to get back on his feet while entangled in the telephone cord and an end table. Shaking off her annoyance, Jessica charged forward, growling *sotto voce*, "What are you doing!? I nearly destroy every vertebra in my back to cover your getaway, and you take a flyer in the middle of my living room! Can't you even manage to walk across a room and out a door? If you're what's standing between me and the Axis, maybe I'd better start learning German."

Despite his embarrassing attempts at extrication, Crawford tried his best to sound cool. "I'm perfectly capable of crossing a room, Miss Minton. I would have been gone by now if you had trained your cat not to get underfoot."

"Don't you pick on a poor dumb animal."

"'Dumb' can be interpreted in more than one way."

"How dare you insult my cat!" Jessica hesitated, her forehead wrinkling as she reflected on what she'd just said. With a shake of her head, she temporized, "Well, you know what I mean."

"Yes. I do. That's what's beginning to frighten me."

Crawford was free, but Larry's voice suddenly carried through the study doors, "Jessica, I've discovered the reason your window is stuck. You left it locked!"

"Oh," Jess scanned the room anxiously. "Damn, you'll never get to the door... you've got to hide... oh, the couch... quick, under the couch!"

"I don't see how I could fit."

"Try!" she hissed. "There's nowhere else. Move!"

Jessica's expression, and an even more expressive shove, convinced Crawford to hit the floor and roll out of sight a fraction of a second before Larry entered, chastising, "The next time you tell me a window is unlocked, make sure it is. For heaven's sake, Jessica, you've got to be more observant. We could have hurt ourselves."

"There's a lot of dirt under here," Crawford groused, loudly enough for only Jessica to hear.

She fought back the urge to retort and concentrated on Larry, meeting him halfway, explaining, "Gee, sorry, Larry, but the catches sealing the window were off last time I looked. Liz *was* over the other day. She might have flipped them shut. You know how meticulous she is."

"Did you think to look first?"

"Why? The last I knew, the windows were unlocked," Jess insisted serenely. "Anyway, don't you want to talk about us? Let's sit in the kitchen. If you don't want your scotch, I'll make some coffee . . ."

Larry shook his head, then drew Jess down on the couch beside him.

"You'll sit here and talk, Jessica." Larry's arm encircled her. "I want to know why you're so desperate to avoid the subject. This is serious, dear. I never expected you to be *this* flighty. What are you so afraid of? Aren't you serious about us?"

Jessica studied her knees uncomfortably. She and Larry could talk about a lot, have a lot of fun, but when had baring her soul to Larry ever been easy? Having an audience beneath her didn't exactly make the situation a breeze, either.

"Larry," she still didn't look up, "marriage is so important, so permanent. I just can't say 'yes' at the drop of a hat."

"Jessica," his tone was gentle and not commanding, so she responded when he said, "Jessica, look at me. You know this isn't any dropped hat. I've changed my tune for you. I've said, go ahead, keep on acting until you're ready to quit. Don't you believe me? I love you."

"Well, it's just that 'men are April when they woo, December when they wed,' Larry."

"Where does that come from?"

"*As You Like It*. Rosalind. Act three, scene..."

"No, no, Jessica. Why are you throwing Shakespeare at me? What does it mean?"

"It means we've had versions of this conversation before, and something always changes your mind, or my work gets in your way. It's not your fault, but..."

"Don't you think I can be patient? You need someone like me to take care of you, Jessica, and I'm here now."

"Well, Larry, I care about you," she protested, partly squirming over Larry's making his plea when he had more audience than he knew. But it was just as disconcerting not being able to put her finger on what didn't seem right about Larry's concession.

"Couldn't you say 'love,' Jessica?"

He didn't sound angry or reproachful, just gently intense. Perhaps that silenced the protest forming on Jessica's lips. She looked down, considering. They'd seemed so simpatico when they'd first met. It was just that the closer they'd become, the more her acting seemed to get in the way of Larry's plans for them, big and small. She could always trust Larry. If he left, there'd be a hole in her life. So why was it that when she looked at him again and thought about saying "yes," something tightened in her stomach?

Larry smiled ruefully, his arm slipping from Jessica's shoulders to clasp her hands. He finally spoke, "We're neither of us getting any younger, Jessica. We've been seeing each other almost a year now. It's time to make things permanent."

"Larry, I'm twenty-eight and you're thirty-five. Neither of us is exactly ready for the rocking chair and knitted shawl. We've both still got all our teeth."

Larry shook his head. "There you go exaggerating again, Jessica. Do you really think either one of us is going to find someone better suited? One would think you were looking for a gallant to sweep you off on his steed."

"Why can't we each have our own steed and ride off together?" Jessica queried with a touch of lightness.

"That flippancy shows just why you need me. I'm the serious, steadying influence you need, and you're the bright light for me."

"Larry, if you steady me too much, my light might flicker out."

They both had to take a minute to ponder why that metaphor didn't work.

"I must be spending too much time with my sister, Mrs. Malaprop. Give me a minute, Larry. I can come up with something better than that. It *is* way past one o'clock."

"If you thought it through, dear, you'd realize that the better metaphor is that a steady influence might make your light shine in a more mature direction. No, wait. That doesn't make much sense, either." Jessica nodded and Larry continued, "You're right. It is a little late for that sort of thing. So, I'll cut straight to the heart of the matter, Jessica. You're acting is an important part of your life right now. All right, but that doesn't mean we can't still marry soon. You may keep at it until you grow beyond it and we start our family."

"Whoa! Can we put the parking brake on here a minute? We're not even engaged and you have me pushing a baby stroller."

"You can't tell me that you don't want children, Jessica?"

"Well, I... Why can't I have both, children and the stage? Now don't give me that look, Larry. There are plenty of other actresses who have both..."

"I'll wager their husbands and children aren't too pleased with the arrangement. You have to realize, Jessica, that you can't live like this forever. You don't want to wake up one morning, your youth gone, your career with it, and you all alone."

"All you left out were the lugubrious violins."

"Be serious, Jessica. Face facts. You must realize that I know what's best for you; what's right for both of us. I thought that you trusted me."

"Larry, a lot of what you said makes sense — except for me ending up without even a cat — but marriage... something just doesn't feel right..."

"That's why you need me so much, darling. You rely too much on your feelings. You need someone who's logical."

"It seems to me, Larry, that I couldn't have built myself a reasonably successful career, supported myself, without a smidge of logic. Your comment did not score you any points," Jess responded levelly.

Larry thought a moment before conceding. "All right, Jessica. I can be patient. But I'm not giving up. I want you for myself."

Jessica knew what was coming next. As Larry leaned forward to kiss her, she used one arm to hold him at bay while she deadpanned, "Larry, not in front of the cat."

Dusty curled her tail around herself, settling into an imperial crouch as if to remind them that they were chaperoned.

Larry sat back to decide how to take Jessica's attempt at lightening the situation, but stopped suddenly, "I kicked something under the couch. What have you got...?"

"An old rug," Jess retorted quickly, drawing Larry to his feet and rushing him back to their heart-to-heart, "I just need to be sure you won't change your mind, about my career — that's where I was going with the Shakespeare thing. You can understand that, can't you? You know I'd never deliberately hurt you, Larry. When the play's settled we can talk. You've come around this far. Maybe I can get you to see that I need to be more than only someone's wife."

Larry studied her thoughtfully before finally saying, "You're sure that's all that's troubling you, the play? Nothing more?"

"Of course there's nothing more," Jessica forced herself to laugh lightly. "Here, let me call you that taxi. It's late, and we both ought to be asleep... alone... at home."

"Right."

He hesitated before Jess, but didn't kiss her. Instead he finally said, "I'll flag a taxi out on the street."

"At this time of night?"

"I'd like to walk, to think, Jessica."

"Maybe you ought to think about muggers," Jessica warned.

Larry patted her shoulder and observed more cheerfully, "At least you're concerned."

"Here's a real thrill," Jessica teased, "I'll even see you to the door."

Larry made a quip about shocking the cat when they kissed good night. Jess was just relieved that they were far enough from the couch to avoid further entertaining her hidden guest.

It wasn't until Larry had left that Jessica leaned back against the closed door and uttered a sigh that set Dusty's ears flicking.

That was Crawford's cue to pull himself out from under the couch, stretch, then sneeze into his handkerchief. Jess winced at his attempts to uncramp his limbs, even if she did want to crack him one for putting her through what seemed like hours of anxiety.

Pushing away from the door and crossing the apartment, Jess began, "It isn't terribly comfortable under there, is it?"

"Speaking from experience, Miss Minton?" Crawford queried as he finished dusting off his jacket, "Luckily, I've had plenty of related experience hiding from Nazis."

"I'm sorry Larry kicked you."

"But not for your having slammed me with the door?" came his wry response. He tucked the handkerchief back in his pocket.

"I, um, guess I forgot about that."

Maybe he had reason to be irritated with her, too. So, if *he* wasn't holding a grudge...

Crawford rubbed his face, allowing, "I don't think there'll be permanent scarring. But may I suggest you and your friend find some common ground other than inflicting physical abuse on me? Shall we look in on the package, now?"

"Oh, yes. All right. It's in the safe. In my study. Please follow me," Jess replied, deciding not to respond to his gibe about her and Larry. As if she needed romantic advice from him!

She just barely suppressed a smile when Crawford glanced warily at Dusty before following her to the study. Funny, but there was something inviting in the humor lurking within the sharp angles of Crawford's features. She must really have been through the wringer with Larry tonight if the guy who'd SNAFUed her life now almost seemed like a relief.

The safe was embedded in the right wall, behind a pull-down drawer in the built-in bookcases. Jess hesitated just briefly before starting on the combination, noticing Crawford's scrutiny. Subtly, she shifted her position so he couldn't see the numbers, then felt silly. Would he really come back to steal her hidden heirlooms?

"How many people know about the safe?"

Without turning, Jessica answered, "Just my immediate family, my sister and brother-in-law, Larry."

"And the combination?"

Jess turned, puzzled, a little unsettled, by his inquisitiveness.

"Why would I give out the combination?"

"Don't you trust your family, Miss Minton?"

Jess blinked at the question, but he didn't persist, "Never mind. Never mind. Just open the safe. Yes, there it is. All right then. Sorry to call it a night, but I'd better be going before it's too late."

"Just like that?"

"Were you expecting dinner and dancing?"

Jessica shook her head, irked at his amusement. Irked that she didn't want to feel irked but to smile at his quip.

"I really think you should take this package, now, Mr. Crawford, and get out of my life. I don't feel safe, and I don't like lying to my boyfriend, putting my family in danger, not knowing who's spying on me."

Crawford appraised Jess before saying almost gently, "You can't lose your nerve. I promise I'll wrap this up for you as soon as I can."

"When?"

"Next week. I should have a safe house secured where I can keep the package with me until I can leave the city. I'll arrange a meeting for you to hand over the package to me."

"Next week? Why that long? And I have to bring it to you?! I'd have to have my head examined to do that. No, you need to take this thing away yourself."

"I told you I can't, Miss Minton; not until I have a secured hideout where I can keep the package until it's safe for me to leave the city with it."

"Did it ever occur to you, Mr. Crawford, that I'm scared?"

That seemed to give him pause. Crawford slowly leaned against the bookshelf near her, then quietly assured, "Of course you're nerved up. There are times when it even gets to me."

His eyes dropped. Pondering, remembering? He caught himself and looked back at her, resolute, "But I know what I'm doing. I won't make any more mistakes. We need to confuse the others, Miss Minton."

"And, I suppose the theory is: if I'm in the middle of this and I can't figure out what in God's name is going on, how will someone on the outside be able to figure out?"

"Roughly. Yes."

Jess flipped up her hands and walked past Crawford, turning before the doors and concluding, "Do I have a choice in this? No, I didn't think so. I'm not happy with the situation, Mr. Crawford."

Crawford shifted away from the bookcase, replying, "I never promised you happiness, Miss Minton. However, I can promise you relief, eventually. In fact, do you have a city map?"

"A map?"

"It's simple. I'm going to trace out the route I want you to take to get to me. It's going to be a bit round about, to throw off anyone who might follow you. . ."

"Follow me?"

"*Might*. A highly unlikely 'might.' I just want to play it safe, for you and my package."

"You've been doing such a grand job so far."

He ignored her crack and pressed, "Where's the map?"

Jess glanced behind her, into the living room, thinking out loud, "Let's see, a city map. Okay, I was looking at one this morning, on the coffee table, in front of the couch. You do remember the couch?"

"I still hold the sweet scent of dust in my nostrils."

"I'm supposed to trust myself to a man who's intimidated by a few dust kitties?"

"Don't kid yourself, Miss Minton. These are more like dust saber tooths."

"I'll relay your complaints to the maid," Jess tried to sound sour, but darn it, even after all he'd done to her, he could be funny.

Jessica left the room, and Crawford was on her heels in a few long strides, saying, "I'm afraid I'm still pressed for time, Miss Minton. Would you check the alleyway and rear window by the kitchen? I'd rather leave here as inconspicuously as possible. It would certainly be less suspicious for someone to see you peer outside than to see a strange man."

"Would you like me to carry you to your friend?"

"Could you, Miss Minton?"

"You know, Mr. Crawford, I really don't like you at all." Not that that was really true.

"Such a pity. I really am a likeable fellow, if you get to know me."

"Let's hope the acquaintance doesn't drag out long enough for me to invite you to my wedding," Jessica shot back.

Now why did Crawford eye her strangely at that rejoinder? Then he turned to the map on the coffee table to say, "Please check my escape route for me. There's some place I have to be shortly."

Jess regarded him, baffled, then forced herself off to the kitchen. She did want to get rid of him, right? A thump behind her was a reminder that anyone's journey to the kitchen intrigued Dusty.

The window above the sink overlooked the little yard space between Jessica's home and the house behind her. In the night gloom, barely illuminated by one of the few still operating street lights, all she could make out were a tangle of rose bushes and gardening gone awry since Mrs. Wharton had left; but it was empty. Dusty nearly made her jump out of her skin, affectionately rubbing against Jess's legs in hopes of a little tuna surprise.

"We've had enough treats for the evening, Dusty," Jess pointed out, reaching down to run a comforting hand from the cat's head to tail. Whom was she comforting, really? The cat's purr rumbled up and sputtered. A little lick of her hand let Jessica know she had one ally, anyway.

Jessica hesitated at the kitchen door. There oughtn't to be any one out there, she reassured herself.

Jess pulled open the door. Slowly her head edged out. Up the alley, down the alley. She could make out no one lurking in the shadows or exposed by the swath of faint kitchen light.

The evening (no, morning!) catching up with her, Jessica sank against the door frame, saying, "Dusty, is this ever going to be over? And then there's still Larry."

Sensing someone behind her, Jessica whirled, sending Dusty scurrying under the table. It was only Crawford, standing quietly in the kitchen doorway, watching her. And his expression, it was, well, regretful. Regretful and tired. The war catching up with him?

He spoke first. "Would it matter to you, if I said I was sorry? I'm not happy about bringing you into all this."

Jessica looked down, not about to let him see that his words had softened her reserve — but that was simply because she was so tired. Jess only said, "Coast is clear."

Crawford turned to Dusty and queried, "Truce?"

Jess couldn't help remarking dryly, "Just don't come between her and her food dish."

"I'll do my best."

Crawford crossed the room, glanced up and down the alley for himself, then turned back to Jessica, "All right then. I've marked the map and jotted down some instructions for signaling me when you get to my door. Everything depends on your not letting anyone else see what I've written. Can you handle that?"

"Yes, sure. But how will you let me know when?"

"I've given that some thought. I noticed quite a bit of Browning in your library while I was waiting for you this evening. So what I'll do is post you a volume of Victorian poetry from one of the Village bookshops. I'll disguise the information as part of an inscription in the fly leaf, the first number will be the time, definitely evening, and the second number will be the day of the week."

"You really think that will work? No one will intercept it or know it's from you?"

"Why should they be suspicious of your getting books? And I'm not exactly going to sign my own name. When my partner's available to run interference, I'll slip into a shop and make the arrangements. You'll be all right. Just don't let your nerve crack. That's when things fall apart."

Jessica's mien softened, for she read something painfully personal to him in those words.

"And don't let that young man of yours railroad you into anything. I know what happens when two people try to build something expecting the other chap will change. Make sure he really does take you for who you are — and you him. If he gets too high-handed, just remind him that 'men have died from time to time and worms have eaten them but not for love.'"

"I don't really see how that's any of your business. How dare you?"

What really infuriated Jess was that Crawford seemed to have put his finger on something she'd been grasping at all night.

"Just a little friendly advice. And here's some more." He dropped a key on a leather thong into her hand. "Don't leave your spare key outside, even if it is hidden by the shrubbery next to your front step. If I could find it and use it to get in, so could someone much less a fan of yours. I know I won't have to tell you not to worry about me."

Jessica's hands curled, but he was gone — with the last word. She turned to Dusty, ready to order, "Kill!" Dusty, however, was too busy slurping down her milky nightcap to heed commands. Come to think of it, Dusty was always too busy to heed commands.

Heck, the only thing Jess had going for her this night was that at least Larry hadn't gotten wise to this miserable plot.

CHAPTER SEVEN

It was a cold, gray, rainy Monday afternoon, and Jessica Minton was semi-conked out on her bed: too exhausted to move, too wound up to be 100% asleep. Last week's opening combined with waiting for Crawford's latest delivery had taken their toll. She hadn't even bothered to change out of her chocolate blouse and green and buff plaid skirt when she'd collapsed on the bed. At least she'd kicked off her pumps.

Cuddled next to her, cheek and paw on the pillow, was Dusty. A little below Dusty rested an old volume of Christina Rossetti's *Goblin Market*. How had he known she liked Rossetti almost as much as the Brownings? That she had been looking all over for a suitable edition of this long poem? Having the run of her library while he waited for her last Friday night probably hadn't hurt.

After fretting for two days, keeping an eagle eye out for the book (even though she knew better than to expect a delivery on Sunday), Jessica had practically collapsed in relief when Crawford's volume arrived this morning. But talk about short notice! Telling her to meet him on Tuesday in a book delivered on Monday! Well, it did make sense, Crawford's not wanting to wait. The less time he left himself open to being caught at his safe house, the better.

How about that inscription, too? It made sense on more than one level, one of which only the two of them would get:

Dear Miss Minton,

What a sterling performance Friday night. Not everyone realizes just how talented you are. My other favorite is *As You Like It*. It made me feel like an eight year old, escaping with you into the forest of Arden. Please accept this volume, number three of the set, as a token of my esteem. I've heard that you love the Victorians. I thought the title would make you think of me.

Kindest Regards,
Your Greatest Fan

So which Friday performance did he mean: the one on stage or the one she'd put on for Larry to hide her inconvenient guest? In spite of herself, Crawford's quip evoked a sleepy smile. Anyway, the message itself wouldn't have provoked suspicion from a nosy spy, or even Liz. It was *clearly* from some admirer trying to butter her up. Had he really seen her in *As You Like It*?

Had he really liked her Rosalind so much? Funny he should have picked one of the parts that she'd most loved playing, had most felt at home in.

Dusty jumped up, as startled as Jess by the ringing front door bell.

"Don't give me an accusing look, Dusty. I'm not expecting anyone. Are you?"

But the flippancy died away quickly. Swinging her legs off the bed, scootching her feet into her shoes, Jess knew that she couldn't ignore the summons. What if it announced a change in plans? Or was someone out there checking to see if she were home before breaking in to look for the package or the message in her book? She'd better at least take a surreptitious gander through the window near the door. Before she left the room, Jessica hesitated over hiding the book. Well, it was supposed to look like an ordinary volume, so why not leave it on her end table? It had worked in Poe's "The Purloined Letter." She tried not to dwell on the fact that Poe had far more control over his writing than she did over her life.

Rubbing sleepers from her eyes, Jessica trotted down the corridor, stowed Dusty out of harm's way in the cellar, and, reaching the alcove, came to a stop. No more ringing? Her visitor had given up? Was a break-in in progress now that she appeared to be out? Or maybe Crawford's plottings had made her paranoid. The only way to know for sure was to take a peek out the window, see who, if anyone, was skulking around.

Jessica teased the curtain back and found herself confronting a view of her visitor leaning away from her, over the rail of her porch, obviously (to Jessica, anyway) searching for the key that Crawford had convinced her was not safe to hide there.

"I'd know that derrière anywhere!" Jessica laughed to herself.

Jessica flung open the door and demanded, "Elizabeth Hennessey, what the dickens are you doing?"

Liz almost flipped over the rail, then straightened herself with a little too much dignity and turned on her sister, "If I want to be scared out of ten years growth, I'll look at the meat prices. Where have you been? I thought I'd be ringing that bell until my hand fell off."

"Sorry, Liz. Just catching forty winks. I didn't quite hear you at first."

"Well, aren't you going to invite me in? I'm three-quarters mildewed from waiting for you. And, say, the spare key isn't where you usually hide it."

As Liz came in, Jessica temporized, "You really don't think I'd be leaving the spare hanging outside, you know," lowering her voice, "under the circumstances. Anyway, why didn't you just use the new key I had made for you after I changed the front lock?"

Slipping out of her damp raincoat and handing it to her sister to hang, Liz admitted, "I forgot it at home. I haven't put it in my purse, yet."

Jessica gave Liz a hard look. "But you haven't lost it?"

"No, no. Of course not. It's safe. I put it just where I'll be able to find it, but no one else will. In my cold cream jar."

"The point is for you to use it, not make sure it has 'the metal you love to touch.'"

"Anyway, changing the locks and doing away with that key was good thinking, Jess. I'm proud of you. You should make more decisions like that."

"Thanks." Jess wondered how Liz would feel if she knew that she had unknowingly handed Mr. Crawford a compliment. "So what brings you by, Liz?"

"I was a little blue with Peter gone and the apartment empty, so I thought a little shopping with you might cheer me up."

"Elizabeth, since when have you ever needed an excuse to go shopping?"

"True, but honestly, with Peter gone I need someone to carry the packages."

"You could knock off shopping until Peter gets back," Jessica teased, closing the closet after hanging Liz's coat.

"Bite your tongue, little sister! He's gone for almost a week!"

"Heavens! I wouldn't want to suggest anything to put B. Altman or Bergdorf Goodman out of business!"

"Don't get wise," Elizabeth shot back, her eyes narrowing.

"You go into the living room, and I'll put on the water for tea. I'm really not up for going out, so why don't we just settle in for the afternoon and relax. While I make the tea, put on a record, browse through a book. You can find some way to entertain yourself till I come back."

"Entertain myself, huh? What should I do? A little dance, tell a few jokes?"

"Go sit down!"

Jess enjoyed setting up the tea things, waiting for the water to boil, bustling around her kitchen to the soothing, rhythmic thrumping of rain on the roof. The kettle's whistle fluttered, then soared into an angry shrill. Pouring the boiling water into her Blue Willow tea pot, Jess contemplated spending the afternoon in a nice, relaxing chat with Liz.

"What the devil is this, Jessica?!"

Boiling water splashed on the tray, and Jessica started back, perplexed as she took in her irate sister flashing something rectangular and shiny.

"I don't know, Elizabeth. What the devil is it?" Jessica shot back, bewildered.

Elizabeth balanced a silver cigarette lighter between her thumb and first finger for Jessica to see, before commenting triumphantly, "It's a lighter."

"Good, Liz," Jess responded as she finished pouring the hot water, "next we'll teach you to identify cigarettes and matches."

Elizabeth visibly restrained herself before pressing on in an ominously measured tone, "I found it on the floor by the end table that has a nick I never noticed before. What's your excuse for that?"

"I'm a lousy housekeeper," Jess quipped, moving past Elizabeth to return the kettle to the stove. Had Crawford damaged the table he'd upset?

The rain was still rhythmically thrumping, but it wasn't soothing any more.

"I know this isn't yours, Jessica," Elizabeth observed, significantly.

"Clever deduction, Elizabeth, considering you know I don't smoke. Did it occur to you that Larry might have dropped that... thing?"

"Larry's initials aren't J. C."

"Larry's not the only friend I have who smokes, Elizabeth. For heaven's sakes, stop being so melodramatic. I swear I should never have told you that Crawford's story was true."

"I never said that there was any connection between this lighter and Crawford," Elizabeth flashed triumphantly.

"No, but that's the only thing important enough to upset you this much, and 'C' is his last initial. I would assume you weren't upset just because I left a lighter on the floor. I know you don't like my housekeeping, but you've never gotten hysterical over it before."

"I'm not hysterical!"

Elizabeth recovered herself swiftly, in spite of Jessica's raised eyebrows. Coolly, she informed her younger sister, "I see you've picked up a few of your brother-in-law's tricks. Well, don't get smart with me, Jessica Minton."

"All, right. All right. I'm sorry, Liz, but I don't like you snapping at me for no good reason."

"Jessica, I don't like being left out in the cold. Larry told me you were acting pretty irrational last Friday . . ."

"Larry always thinks that I'm acting irritation... Wait a minute. You two were talking about me? What did you say to him?"

"Jessica, don't try to change the subject. Crawford was here that night, wasn't he? How could you see Crawford and not tell me?" Elizabeth accused.

"Elizabeth, you make it sound as if I had a party and didn't invite you. I'm sorry if I've made you unhappy, but how can you expect me to drag you in any deeper? This could get dangerous."

"But you could endanger yourself?"

"I don't have any choice. I'm the one with the package, remember?"

"Is that really the reason?"

"Well, why else, Liz?" Jessica returned, growing annoyed with her sister.

"I'm talking about your Errol Flynn complex. Everything's an adventure to you, isn't it? You can't resist a challenge . . ."

"I can, too."

"Oh? Well then, you just tell me you aren't enjoying any of this."

Jess wasn't about to admit to her sister that as much as she'd wanted to crown him, this Crawford could still make her smile. Instead, she redirected her sister's attention, "Liz, how could anyone possibly enjoy having a sword of Damocles dangling over her head?"

"You might have thought about the fact that I'd be worried about you." Elizabeth insisted, no longer angry. "I mean, yes, I do want to know what's going on, but what's more important is that I'm your sister. I can't let anything happen to you."

By design or not, Liz's concern left Jess inwardly wincing with guilt.

"Okay, Liz, you've got me. I have seen Crawford. He's given me instructions to meet him later to turn over the package. Then neither of us will have to worry anymore. All right?"

"Okay. So where and when do we meet him?"

"*We* do nothing. *I*, well, the less you have to know the better," Jessica roundly corrected her sister.

Elizabeth's lips compressed into a tight line, but Jessica cut her off before she could argue.

"Look, Elizabeth, I've already told Mr. Crawford I'd meet him alone. And, anyway, I'm not going to risk putting you in any danger."

"But it's all right for me to worry about you until this mysterious meeting comes off?"

"Liz, it will all be over soon. I'm sorry you're upset, but I'm not about to drag you along and throw a monkey wrench into plans that have already been worked out. Subject closed."

Elizabeth started to protest but appeared to think better of challenging her sister's set mind. She relented, "Then if there's nothing I can do . . ."

"There's nothing you can do," Jessica concurred, circling the table to put an arm around Liz before continuing, "Now, relax. Sit down. Have some tea — and just be glad you can sit back while I do the dangerous work."

"Delivering the package?"

"No, letting Dusty up from the cellar. I think she's trying to claw her way through the door about now."

CHAPTER EIGHT

Drawn shades isolated the bright, warm, cherry-paneled study from the New York darkness. Jessica Minton, her cheek propped absently against her hand, sat reflecting in the same comfortable chair that had held the unsettlingly ubiquitous Mr. Crawford just last Friday. She'd put Debussy on the hi-fi to calm her nerves, but the prescription wasn't really working. No surprise, then, that staring at the blue and white ceramic tiles of her fireplace across the room wasn't any better a distraction from the prospect of the evening's "mission."

Her glance drifted upward, taking in the array of photos on the mantle, assembled under the print of Durand's *Kindred Spirits*: her parents; Lois, Iris, and her at Bar Harbor; Dusty; old chums Rose and David Norquist; Larry (a guiltily swift glance, that); Elizabeth and Peter's wedding portrait; her and Elizabeth.

Jessica's lips slipped into a smile, remembering Liz's extrapolation that the "J" in J. Crawford had to stand for "James," because all mysterious gentlemen were named thusly. Jess had of course commented, "Oh, you mean like James DeWinter in *Rebecca* and James Rochester in *Jane Eyre* and . . ."

Elizabeth had cut her off before she could go any further.

Jessica's smile faded with another glance at the clock. Still not quite time to leave, and so her eyes drifted to the package sitting ominously on a nearby chair. What secret hid within it? When she'd believed the package was just part of a gag, Jess had assumed it held either stuffing or something Peter had dummied up to look "top secret." *Not* opening the package had seemed like a way of one-upping Peter, denying him proof that he'd provoked her curiosity. Now that she knew this *whole* deal was the *real* deal, Jess couldn't shake a burning inquisitiveness. Would she ever know what lurked inside? The package would be out of her hands after tonight.

A glance at the clock warned: time to go! Jess crossed the room to Dusty, who sat imperially on the desk, and took the gray tabby in her arms, cradling her. Surprisingly, rather than object to this abrupt maneuver, Dusty settled in comfortably to scrutinize Jessica, while Jess rubbed her neck.

Wouldn't it be nice not to have to leave?

But that's not the way the world wagged. Jess carefully put down her feline ally, then went back to snatch up the package. Smiling swiftly, she promised Dusty, "I'll be back. Don't wait up for me, cat."

She pulled on a light coat over her white blouse and black slacks. Unlocking the front door, she hesitated, listening to the passing cars, suspicious of their drivers. *C'mon, now, kiddo*, she encouraged herself, *would a fleet of master spies really cruise Damascus Place, just waiting for you to step outside?*

That humor evaporated in a flash at a knock on the door. Who in Sam Hill? The knock came again, impatient now. If someone were after her, he wouldn't be polite enough to knock, would he? Or would he be smart enough not to want to attract any attention?

Jess bit her lower lip. The black-out curtains ought to hide the room's lights from outside snoopers. Perhaps she could sneak out the back way. The alley by the kitchen door also led to the street behind her house. Or was this caller trying to spook her into doing just that?

"Jessica? Are you there?" came through the door.

Larry.

What was Larry doing here? Never mind that, what was she going to do about him? Could she tiptoe out the back way? Of course, she'd be an awful stinker to sneak out on Larry, but there was no denying that her duty to Crawford superseded decorum. Lamming it out the back would also forestall another sticky discussion about marriage. Jessica had no time to debate which factor weighed more heavily with her, for just as she remembered she'd unlocked the front door, it opened.

In walked Larry, who took a moment to register surprise at seeing her before uttering a puzzled, "Didn't you hear me, Jess? I knocked and called several times."

"I was in the kitchen, feeding Dusty. You know I can't stop in the middle of that, not if I want to live. I rushed out as quickly as I could," Jess managed as calmly as possible.

Larry's forehead wrinkled as he regarded her coat.

"Oh, I was, planning to meet Iris at the theater; she's returning a piece of jewelry I lent her. But on my way out I remembered I had to feed Dusty, so I rushed back to the kitchen. I hate to say this to you, Larry, but I really have to dash."

Jessica had expected Larry to be skeptical of her explanation, especially its torrential outburst. What startled her was his scowl. She was sorely tempted to discover what was eating him, but keeping to Crawford's tight schedule precluded that. Hoping to soothe Larry's dark looks and stay on track for her appointment, Jess causally offered, "If you want to wait, Larry, I'll be back in a few hours; but I do have to hustle along now. I don't want to keep Iris waiting."

"Oh, can I give you a lift, then?" His tone and features were calm now, but there was something in his eyes that signaled to Jessica that she'd better proceed carefully.

In spite of herself, uncertainty, almost panic, flickered in Jessica's eyes. There was no way to reach her destination either secretly or on time if Larry were with her. But how could she turn him down without making him suspicious?

"I was afraid of this," he said, unhappily shaking his head at her hesitation, slowly crossing the room to stand in front of her.

"Of what?"

Larry looked straight at her and surmised, "You're going out to meet your Mr. Crawford, aren't you, Jessica?"

Her defensive stiffening was automatic, especially when Larry's eyes fastened on the package incriminatingly in her grasp. And how had Larry gotten Crawford's name?

Forcing herself into one of her best performances, Jess was all casual reasonableness. "This has got to go out to Frederick Bromfield."

Larry extended a hand, tipping the package to face him, and observed matter-of-factly, "There's no address, Jessica."

Jess gripped the package imperceptibly tighter, but answered lightly, "I didn't say I had to mail it to him, Larry. Will you get a load of yourself, acting so suspicious! Liz and I explained some time ago that the big deal over that other package was all a vindictive prank. Honestly, don't I strike you as the last person to get involved in some espionage plot?"

"You could be duped. Jess, that story of a joke is just too pat, and you have been acting damned strangely lately — especially last Friday night. I've done some checking . . ."

"Checking?! What gives you the right to . . .?"

"Actually, Jessica, I'm glad I did do some checking, because I came up with something about your friend."

Trying to bluff Larry about James Crawford was clearly useless. He was on to them both. But how? Jess tilted her head thoughtfully and questioned, "Where did you get this information, Larry? What makes you such an expert on Crawford?"

Larry's admission seemed to go against some hidden internal grain, but he answered her, "Jess, I shouldn't be telling you any of this. I'm sworn not to, but things have gone too far. If I can save you from making a horrible mistake, putting yourself in a terrible jam, it's worth it. It's worth it."

Again Larry hesitated. Jessica hung on this pause.

Abruptly, Larry resumed, "You know Peter and I work for the government. I'm afraid we've never been quite on the up and up with either you or Elizabeth about our duties. That's one reason Peter is so adept at making our work sound confusing. We are provided with a cover story, but Peter can't resist exercising his creativity. I'd prefer to lie outright. It's easier to stay consistent."

"Are you saying you two do some secret work for the government? The F.B.I.? Army Intelligence?"

"No, not exactly."

"Well, what then, exactly?"

"We're a different government branch. I'm afraid I can't give you a name. Do you think I would make up something like this, Jessica?"

"Well, no... I... but..."

"That's why we can't have visitors in our offices, why we always have to meet you or Liz down in the coffee shop."

Jessica gnawed her lower lip. This revelation had knocked her for yet another loop. When Liz had complained about security being way over the top for a department on transportation, Jess had always chided her that any information could be used by the enemy during a war. Apparently, Liz had better instincts than she did about top secrets. Well, she'd better get her bearings, and pronto. Too much depended on her making the right decision about Crawford and this package.

"So, exactly how can your work make you think I'm being played for a sap, Larry?"

"I still can't tell you any more than that we file, process, and, in some cases, judge the veracity and value of information coming in from undercover sources, including B.S.C. — British Security Coordination. So, you see, I would have access to any file on Crawford, and I found something submitted fairly recently. That, Jessica, is how I know this is not merely the prank of a disgruntled actor."

"Okay, then, how do you know we're talking about the same James Crawford? The name's not so unique."

"You tell me, Jessica. According to my intel, early thirties, tall, dark and longish hair, a mustache."

That hit home, but Jess wouldn't let on, instead pressing, "All right, you found something? What?"

"I shouldn't be telling you this, but if it will stop you, save you... You see he worked for the British with the underground in France, the Crawford in my records. There was an incident with one of the cells. The Nazis wiped out everyone but him and another chap. They barely got away, injured, but they got away. There were suspicions that someone was playing both sides against the middle — where Crawford was one of only two survivors..."

Larry had effectively floored her. Jess sat down, hard. She couldn't think, but she had to. Finally she managed, "But he was injured, Larry. If he'd sold out to the Nazis, he didn't make a very good deal, did he? And there was still the other man. He could have been the snitch."

"Or they both could have been. Being shot up is still better than being dead. You can't trust him."

"Apparently his superiors do. If he were guilty, why would he still be free, let alone working for them?"

"That's the queerest part, Jessica. After he was pulled back from France, I can't find any record of him — as if he disappeared from our files. You've got to ask yourself: why has he fallen off the radar screen? There's something fishy about him. *Is* he really working for our side?" Larry gripped Jessica's arms and urged, "Can't you see, darling, this man is using you. He's trying to turn you into a traitor who'll leak information. He might be playing on your closeness to Peter and me."

In spite of Larry's logic, convincing though it seemed, some instinct nagged her not to turn against J. Crawford.

"Oh, Larry, I just don't..." She broke off her reluctant protest and began to smile as Larry's last words made a connection with one of Crawford's warnings. "Larry, Mr. Crawford told me I couldn't safely turn this package over to a government agency because there were some dangerous security leaks. Perhaps his mission is under double-wraps for that reason."

"Crawford could very easily be lying to you, Jessica. How can you even be certain this 'leak' is in our office?" Larry argued. "I've certainly never heard anything about leaks."

"Well, if there was a leak, no one would be stupid enough to mention it to the people under suspicion. Maybe his assignment is so important that it's been covered up until he finishes it, when it would be too late for some infiltrator to scotch everything. Anyway, Larry, you said before you didn't believe Crawford's story because you couldn't find any supporting information. Think: if he were with the Axis, you certainly would have found some file to prove that, right? But you didn't, did you?"

Larry gave her a long look, shook his head, then countered, "Perhaps, Jessica, perhaps. Then again, he might be too clever to let himself be caught. These double agents are damned sly."

"But you could be wrong," Jessica firmly insisted. "Your case isn't airtight. The odds are still that Crawford is on our side."

Larry had to think that one over before he responded, "All right, Jessica, you could be right. I'll grant that much. However, the circumstances of his last mission still leave too much doubt about Crawford's dependability. I can't have you taking a chance. I can't let you go, Jessica."

Jessica resisted the temptation to toss off, "How do you intend to stop me? Tie me to the chair?" Instead, she reasoned with him, "What else can we do, Larry? I have to give him this package."

"No, no, Jess," Larry said, shaking his head, "Listen to me. I have a plan. I haven't said anything about this case to my superiors yet. I knew I had to talk to you first. So you can give me the package, and I'll take care of it, get it to the proper authorities. I'll say it was left with me. No one will know you were in any way involved."

"We can't do that, Larry. Remember what Crawford said about the security leak. You might easily give the package to the wrong people. Then you'd be the unintentional traitor, and our enemies would walk off with something valuable. And, Larry, if I'd be in danger from anyone knowing I had the package, then your turning it in would certainly be just as dangerous for you. I won't let you stick your neck out for me like that. You're not going to be hurt, or... anything, because I can't live up to my responsibilities."

"But you're just a girl. Why should you have to risk your life because you were in the wrong place at the wrong time?"

"Larry, there are just some things that people have to do, girls included," Jess explained gently, wishing a realization that was so important to her wouldn't sound so clichéd. "Look how people said that Poland's being steamrollered by Germany and Asia's being eaten up by Japan were foreign problems, none of our business. It didn't bother people that half the world was sinking out of sight because it wasn't happening here. It took Pearl Harbor to show that if you wait long enough, and it's usually not a long wait, what happens over there eventually ends up over here. I know I sound as if I'm selling bonds, Larry, but it's true. I can't cry, 'it's not my fault,' and walk away. I've got to face up to what I'm stuck with. It's a tough break, but this problem won't go away, even if I do."

Larry tapped the chair's arm impatiently, arguing, "Jess, this isn't a Lillian Hellman play. Your life could be on the line. Don't you understand that?"

"Larry, why shouldn't I understand that? I'm not stupid. Anyway, Mr. Crawford told me I'd be safe. I *can* handle this, and I'll be back before you know it. Believe me; I've no burning desire to be a martyr."

And the circuitous route that Crawford had created for delivering the package was just a precaution, Jessica assured herself, yet again. But she didn't mention this thought to Larry.

Larry studied her carefully, before saying, "Jessica, I know that you were up to something last Friday night. I didn't say anything before because I feared you would tip this Crawford off. Frankly, I think you're in over your head. I think you're infatuated with the adventure of this plan. You're not objective enough to handle the situation."

Jessica's eyes fired but she retorted coldly, "I am not an irresponsible fool." Taking hold of her temper, she pointed out less severely, "If I were so irresponsible, Larry, I *would* let you risk your life for mine."

Larry was not reassured. "Jess, let me deliver the package. You'd be safe."

"No, Larry! For heaven's sake, no! You haven't heard a word I've said. This is my responsibility. And don't you realize Crawford is expecting *me*? If you show up with the package, he'll figure something is wrong. He could take off, and we'd be stuck with that terrible thing for heaven knows how long. What if he thought he had to hurt or even kill you to protect himself? I told you, I won't let anything happen to you because I'm a coward."

"It's not a question of cowardice."

"I have a responsibility. I'm going."

Larry made one last try. "I can't change your mind?"

Getting up, Jessica answered, "No dice, Larry."

He studied her face, searching for some sign of weakness. There was none.

Larry sadly asked, "I guess I've been defeated?"

Jess put her hands on his arms and answered, "Not defeated. We're just in agreement."

It was so easy to slide into his arms, to be held tightly by him, to feel his hand in her hair. He had frightened her, and it felt so good to be allies again. But she was the one who had to go, not him.

Jessica pulled away. Softly, she spoke, "I have to go now, Larry. I'm late as it is."

He touched her face and relented, "Yes, all right."

"Walk me outside," she smiled with a touch of impishness, adding, "I'll walk you to your car."

Larry nodded, then volunteered, "I could wait for you here."

"No, at home, Larry." They were both silent as Jessica took the package, then found a shopping bag in the closet in which to stash it. She turned back to Larry and promised, "I will call you. Don't worry about that. It may be late, but I'll call."

When they reached his car he held her again. This time when they kissed Jess startled herself with her own passion. They'd never seemed to share this much warmth, been this much in sync before.

She pulled away slightly.

"I do have to go. I think the neighbors have had enough of a show tonight," Jess said wryly.

Larry's smile was dry.

"I do want to take care of you, you know."

"I know." Then on reflection Jess added, "Larry, you can't follow me, either."

He responded with an expression of cool amusement, agreeing, "I promise."

"Good."

There was something in the way Larry's eyes dropped that prompted Jessica to add, "Just make sure you're more trustworthy than I've been the past few weeks." A pause before she added, "And I am truly sorry about that."

Turning away swiftly, Jess started up the street before she could see Larry's expression sink into lines of concern.

Jessica would not look back. Already, she trembled as she walked. This time something had clicked between Larry and her as it never had before. She'd been unnerved, confused, keyed up — and there he was. She gripped the package tighter. The thought of meeting Mr. Crawford made her feel abruptly uncomfortable.

Oh please let Larry *be wrong,* Jessica prayed. *Let me be doing the right thing. Let me make intelligent decisions. Let me get out of this jam alive.*

* * * * * *

All was so still at the darkened theater's stage-door. The alley cats seemed to have deserted their surrounding dens. City traffic, muted by the buildings, wafted in, ghostlike. Even the moon seemed to be muffling itself behind the charcoal gauze of clouds. The excruciatingly slow creaking of the stage-door, as if controlled by a sinister hand, invaded the unnatural quiet. A slender figure emerged, hesitated, then shot down the last two steps of the entrance and into the darkness of the alley. Jessica was in too much of a hurry to be frightened now. She was following Crawford's instructions to stop at the theater as part of his roundabout route to throw off the suspicions of anyone who might follow her.

Another stride and she was out of the alley. She hadn't expected to find the street lights such a comfort, dimmed as they were to meet blackout regulations. A few people passed her. Cars were parked against the curb. At least she didn't have to face the unknown alone. Jessica picked up her pace. There were still a couple of blocks to go before she hit Broadway. Then it would be a few more blocks through Times Square and down to the bus terminal. She looked impatiently at her watch. Damn, she'd better sprout wings! Otherwise, she'd never reach Crawford on time following the circuitous route he'd outlined for her. Maybe cutting down one of the alleys off this street would save some time? Except that they *were* awfully dark, awfully forbidding.

The sky rapidly grew more overcast. Rain would not be welcome tonight, not with all this walking. Jess fished in her coat's pockets for her black beret. She was slipping on her hat when an inadvertent glance up the street revealed a taxi parked ahead on the opposite side. Hmm. Yes, that same type of cab with a dented fender had been parked across from the head of her street when she'd left home earlier this evening. How often did you see a cab parked and waiting in New York City? It had also pulled out before she could get to it — well, that was typical. It had to be a coincidence. Obviously a cab company would have more than one taxi cruising the city that had been the victim of a fender bender.

Was there a passenger? She hadn't *seen* anyone. Jess swallowed hard, resuming her walk at a cautious pace, trying to suppress the suspicion that the cab's passenger might have ducked down to hide. Unthinkingly, she edged closer to the buildings on her side of the street.

Just play it cool, kiddo, Jessica told herself. *Ignore the taxi and concentrate on the head of the stre...et!*

The street suddenly disappeared as Jessica found herself yanked into an alley that had opened off to her right. A hand clamped over her mouth and sealed off her desperate shriek. For a moment, Jess was too horrified even to struggle. Then ingenuity took over as she felt herself pulled deeper into the alley. Falling back on an old childhood habit, she bit the hand that gagged her.

"God damn! Lady!"

Jess's back and shoulders ached from being slammed against the wall. Her attacker was a dark hulk in the shadows of the alley.

"I don't care what you say, mister, I'll never give you this package!"

Jess held the bag with Crawford's bundle tighter and tensed, poised to elude her attacker. She wouldn't let Crawford and the Allies down, even if the enemy was onto her.

Looming forward, blotting out the alley's entrance, he informed Jessica unpleasantly, "No one gets away with bitin' me!"

"*She* will!"

The hulk dropped under a swift conk on the head. Blankly, Jessica stared down at the felled body. When she was able to look up, the identity of her rescuer nearly felled *her*. The shopping bag dropped from her hands, precisely on the head of the woozily reviving man on the ground, sending him back to La-La Land.

"That must be some heavy package, Jessica," Elizabeth wryly noted. "Between the two of us I guess your friend will be out of commission for some time."

Jessica cleared her head with an abrupt shake and demanded, "Elizabeth, what in Sam Hill are you doing here?"

"Elementary, Jessica. I resolved to spend every night until Peter came home in a cab near the top of your street, waiting for you to make a suspicious departure. Thanks for only taking two nights."

"You're welcome, but wasn't it rather expensive?"

"I gave up one day of shopping. Anyway, I had a feeling about tonight," Liz preened, "and my sixth sense was right. It usually is."

"Remind me to take you with me to Belmont Park sometime."

"You sound annoyed."

"Sound? Try I *am* annoyed. You deliberately intruded when I expressly forbade you to."

"And if I hadn't, you probably wouldn't be around to snap at your loyal sister now."

Jessica's mouth tightened. She hated it when Liz was right. Still, that didn't change one unfortunate circumstance.

"All right, Liz. Just skip it," Jessica relented, retrieving her bag, "But there's still a chance this man will be able to relay an account of what happened to his superiors. They'll probably put two and two together and figure out that the woman who saved me is you."

"Oh."

"So what do you suggest we do now?" Jessica queried sarcastically.

"You could let me go with you to deliver the package since I'm already in this up to my neck," Elizabeth suggested helpfully.

"Argh!"

"Anyway, if this rube knows about me, I'm going to find out about him," Liz pronounced, crouching over her conquest.

"What are you doing?"

"Going through his pockets. Looking for identification," Elizabeth answered without looking up.

She stopped.

"Jessica, I've found several wallets and a watch, and some rings . . ."

"Oh," Jess uttered, relieved.

"What?"

"He's not a spy. He's just a thief. Liz, we're in the clear."

"I feel so silly," said Liz, straightening up.

"By the way, Liz, what *do* you have in your purse to knock him out so easily?"

"Three copies of *Gone with the Wind*."

"Good heavens, you could have killed the man. Thank God you weren't reading *War and Peace*."

Jess didn't have time to address the obvious question of what exactly Liz was doing with three copies of *Gone with the Wind*; it would bear looking into, though.

"So, shall we go now that everything's all settled?" Elizabeth pressed eagerly.

"Go where? Oh, wait a minute now, Elizabeth. You aren't going anywhere with me. Remember, you're not in this up to your neck anymore."

"True, but if you don't let me come with you, I'll just follow you anyway. You won't be able to escape me, Jessica."

And Larry always said that Elizabeth was the sensible one?

Jess shook her head, then questioned impatiently, "First, what are we going to do with our friend, here?"

"Leave him. We have bigger fish to fry."

"Oh, I don't know, Elizabeth. He's been out quite a while. He may be hurt. We can't just leave him. And if he's all right, we still can't leave him. He might go off and shake down someone else. He *is* violent. You know, about this time there's usually a beat cop having coffee in the diner around the next corner and up the street a little ways. One of us should go get him."

"*One* of us?"

"If both of us go, our pal here could take off. I don't want to be responsible for giving him the opportunity to assault someone else. Believe me, this guy's an ugly sort. He might go off and commit a worse crime. Look at the way he threatened me just because I bit him. You'd better let me go for a policeman."

"Jessica, whoever stays here alone with this mug is going to be sorry. Do you think he's going to buy a bouquet for whomever he wakes up to?"

"Okay, then hide around the corner where he can't see you and keep an eye on him. See which direction he heads if he takes off. Personally, I think he's down for the count."

"Do you? Anyway, why should I be the one to stay? How do I know that you'll come back if I let you go?" Elizabeth's question dripped skepticism.

"You don't trust me?" Jessica retorted indignantly.

Liz's expression clearly answered that question in the negative.

"Okay, Liz. You win. But if you go, you've got to leave your purse so I can hit this rat if he starts to come around again. I don't have a shoulder bag stuffed with lethal novels."

"No, better yet," Liz was digging furiously through her bag, "we'll truss him up like a turkey. I have some heavy-duty jump rope in here."

"You brought rope with you?"

"Jessica, we're playing in the big leagues now. I'm always prepared for an emergency. You could learn from me."

"Apparently."

Liz had their fallen bruiser squared away in no time, leaving Jessica to wonder exactly where Liz had developed this peculiar skill. Summer camp?

"I'll be back in a snap," Elizabeth more threatened than promised.

"You'd better be. I'm on a schedule and I, we're, late already."

Liz nodded. She started up the alley, but Jess stopped her by calling, "Liz, I'm never going to forgive you for this, but don't think because you can come with me you can still stick with me when I hand the package over to Crawford. You're going to have to wait unobtrusively. He's only expecting me, and if you show up, he'll be suspicious."

"That's fair enough," Liz agreed, "but don't try any tricks, Jessica."

"Have I a choice? Just make sure when you come back it's with a cop."

Jessica gave Liz a few minutes to get to a main thoroughfare before peeking around the alley entrance. All clear except for the cabbie her sister had apparently paid to wait for her — the same cabbie Jessica haggled into taking her onto the next leg of her journey. Liz would hit the roof when she got back, policeman in tow; but Jess had no intention of dragging her sister any deeper into this mess. This was her responsibility alone. Better to have Liz mad at her than in danger, no matter what Crawford had promised about safety.

* * * * * *

"Okay, lady. This is it."

The cab had pulled up on a curbless street. Paying the driver, Jessica stepped out. The "fragrance" of fish was too strong to allow her to notice much else. Smart man, Mr. Crawford — no one could track him here and stay conscious long enough to nab him. A glance at her watch reassured Jess that taking the taxi had allowed her to make up the time she'd lost through that little "distraction" in the alley. She just prayed that cutting short the roundabout route Crawford had designed to throw off any possible followers wouldn't be a problem.

Fog drifted in from the river to Jess's right. Though the fog wasn't heavy where she stood, it still wasn't exactly the type of atmosphere she would have ordered for the evening. Looking around, Jess found the area relatively deserted. Liz, whose culinary leanings often led her to the Fulton Fish Market, had once told Jess that from two to nine in the a.m. this place was jumping with business. Now, though, at night, it was almost like being in a graveyard. The East River washed tirelessly against the jetty. Warehouses and docking sheds obscured a good view of the river. Brooklyn loomed somewhere beyond. The fully overcast sky and fifteen-story blackout surrounded Jessica in unwelcoming gloom.

Some distance ahead, the metal skeleton of the Brooklyn Bridge seemed to emerge from a cluster of buildings and disappear into the fog over the river. Mr. Crawford's hotel couldn't be far, then. His directions, which she had been careful to destroy, had indicated it was just beyond the bridge. Well, she'd never get to Crawford by cooling her heels, soaking up the sinister ambience. Jess started off, quickly passing two grizzled night wanderers who appraised her with cynical curiosity. She hardly noticed them, caution keeping her well into the street, away from the cavernous overhangs of seller's stalls.

The sign MEYERS HOTEL BAR brought a flash of anxious anticipation. A landmark Crawford had told her to look for. She was on the right track. Thank God. So, where was Crawford's "associate" hiding? Of course he wouldn't be there for her to spot. If she could see him, so could anyone following her. Penned in by the dark hulks of decrepit buildings, Jessica longed for a hint of her guardian angel, preferably armed.

Instead, the bridge loomed monstrously overhead. Jess gazed up cautiously as she moved beneath. The rumbling traffic gave her the creeps. The possibility of a sharpshooter on the promenade or hanging from the girders, waiting to pick her off, taunted her.

Emerging from under the bridge unscathed, Jess ordered herself to occupy her uncomfortably vivid imagination with locating Hardy Street. That was when she had to leap to her left as a car whizzed past. *Damn!* Maybe she ought to include avoiding traffic in her cogitations. She could start by getting on the sidewalk. Now when had South Street sprouted a sidewalk? And street lamps, too!

People, some pretty shabby, passed her. Bars seemed especially popular around here. Jess tucked the bag holding her precious bundle closer.

An intersecting street came up, and Jess dashed across to the opposite curb, even though there was no traffic to dodge. Force of habit, not uneasiness, that was it. The next street was her destination, praise God! Jess slowed slightly. Across the street was the stocky form of a man preoccupied with viewing the fog sifting over and around the buildings next to the river. Darned if he didn't remind her of Frederick Bromfield, a lot. But this blackout-compliant lamplight was too dim for her to be sure. Jess proceeded uneasily. Bromfield did live not too far from here, and she'd heard him mention enjoying rambles along the river. The last thing she needed now was for someone she knew to see her and wonder what she was doing in this scruffy neck of the woods. Unobtrusively, Jess edged closer to the buildings flanking her left, turning her face away from the opposite side of the street. This way, even if she might never be sure if the man was Bromfield, it would be harder for him to identify her.

There it was, Crawford's street, Hardy. Jessica couldn't help scurrying around the corner. Darkly dilapidated, Hardy was creepy enough to make her forget about the gentleman who seemed disconcertingly similar to Mr. Bromfield. Lamp posts, spaced intermittently, lent a grimy illumination to the worn brick buildings, ancient parked cars, and battered sidewalk. Streets, almost alleys, melted into the murk between buildings. Spidery fire-escapes clung to the faces of buildings packed together down each side of the street. Of the few people visible, some occupied themselves with unclear pursuits on the fire escape landings; others seemed deadened by sleep, or means more sinister. Not exactly a choice location for a late night walk.

But the end was in sight. Right ahead on the left was her destination. The lettering of DAVIDSON'S HOTEL (with a crippled "E") was clear enough. She approached that darkened doorway tentatively. At least no one was lurking. Jess hastily pulled open the door and stepped into the building's dingy interior.

A narrow foyer. Stairs before her, off slightly to the left. She hesitated uncertainly, staring at the grizzled, Hawaiian-shirted man who leaned on the desk-clerk's counter, reading one of the daily tabloids. She looked hopefully up the stairs.

"You want something, sister?"

He still leaned, without looking up.

"I'm, uh, just delivering something to a friend."

Now he looked up, smiled familiarly, and cracked, "An' I bet I can just guess what you're deliverin.'"

"It's this bag, wise guy. Only what's inside may end up broken because it was used for cracking a certain smart-mouth over the head."

He gave her a half smile, half snarl. Jessica never responded. She was too busy striding up the stairs. Out of the clerk's sight, Jessica fairly dashed. She was finally going to clinch this deal! No more anxiety, no more danger, no more lying! It would be a pleasure to see J. Crawford's face — it would mean she'd finally hit the finish line in this unpleasant little handicap. No lead weight packed by a champion race horse was half as heavy a burden as this damned package.

By the time Jessica turned the corner, after reaching the second floor landing, her speed had waned considerably. Jesse Owens she wasn't, and the package wasn't exactly filled with feathers. 30A loomed above her, at the head of the stairs. Two doors down was her goal. For the first time, it occurred to Jess that some of the anxiety and danger would be over for Crawford, too. This SNAFU couldn't have been any picnic for him! With her help, though, he'd have his package back so he could complete his mission. Now that she was almost out of the woods, it seemed safe to empathize with the man, even to be glad things were finally going his way.

Jessica reached the top of the stairs. There was 30C, the "C" hanging crookedly. She even recalled the special knock perfectly. It was a Fatima-grade miracle that she could still remember her own name at this point.

The door opened slightly — and Jessica was yanked into the room by her still upraised hand.

A low-watt, unshaded bulb cast a dismal light from above a lumpy bed against the left wall. Crawford swiftly reconnoitered the hall outside before closing the door and turning to her.

"I know I'm great company, but I didn't think you'd be this anxious to see me," Jess cracked, a touch shakily.

"There's no one out there," he said quickly. Then boring his dark eyes into hers he added, "Change of plans. You'll have to take the package and leave while it's still clear."

Her mouth was still doing a creditable imitation of the Holland Tunnel when Crawford abruptly moved away, concerning himself with partially pulling back the dark curtain from the window to anxiously study what lay outside.

"Wait just one minute, you, you — I don't know what you are!" Jessica raged, stalking Crawford to the window. Gripping the bag holding the package, Jessica gave Crawford what for, "Look here, buster, tonight, in order to deliver this charming little valentine to you, I, first, had an argument with my boyfriend; second, was mugged; and, third, so antagonized my sister that she'll probably hire someone named Leftie to rub me out. I won't even begin to touch on the absolute turmoil you've turned my life into for the past weeks. And now — NOW — you expect me to blithely trot off with your 'bundle of joy'? Well, Mr. Crawford, Mr. J. Crawford, after all this, can you give me one good reason why I should take back your little package?"

"Calm down, Miss Minton," Crawford warned with a coolness that checked Jessica. He smiled bitterly as he informed her, "I'm afraid there's been something of an eleventh-hour twist. I no longer have a partner to run interference for me. He was killed earlier this evening, not far from this building, when you were already on your way here. I chanced staying so I could sneak you, and the package, out of here. The murder was a rather convincing hit and run."

Crawford closed the curtain and walked past Jessica to the bed. He stood a moment, then sank down on the bed's edge, wearily massaging his forehead.

Jessica stared uncomprehendingly at Crawford. Killed. Dead. Her mouth opened, but her brain could supply no words. Crawford's previous assurance and this new revelation just wouldn't jive. It was like going to an Andy Hardy comedy and seeing Andy suddenly take a hatchet to his family in the last reel. Finally, she managed, "But he wasn't supposed to get killed. What went wrong?"

Crawford lashed out bitterly, more at himself than her, "We must have screwed up. Sorry, for... 'Sorry.' There's a damned useless word."

Jessica turned away from him, confused, scared. And then it hit her with a wallop that if Crawford's partner were dead, no one had been around to ensure she hadn't been tailed here. Someone could easily have seen her, even if the package had been tucked inside a shopping bag. Perhaps they'd spared Crawford in hopes of getting the two of them together.

"They could recognize me, Crawford. There could be someone out there who can now recognize me because there was no one around to protect me."

Crawford was on his feet, beside her, his hands on her arms, warning, "Get hold of yourself, Miss Minton. Hysterics are a first class way of setting yourself up for a fall."

"And who has better reason to be hysterical? Believe me, this wonderful news of yours that I may have blundered into a nice, lethal trap is the perfect cap on my evening of misfires. Forgive me, Mr. Crawford, but I think realizing I may not be long for this vale of tears is sufficient grounds for hysteria. Perhaps I'm selfish, but I can't help feeling there must be an easier way to give my understudy a break."

Crawford's expression told Jessica that her words stung him, but he was too professional to let that hamper him. Turning his strained attention back to the window, he offered, "There's no reason to connect you with me or the package. Go now. I can find a way to trail you unobtrusively so you can reach home safely."

Jess was silent, watching him. There was no longer any humor left in the man. That frightened her. She didn't expect him to crack wise constantly, but there had been a reassuring aura of control in his lightness. Now, he seemed off balance with guilt and weariness. So if Crawford wasn't in control, who was? Definitely not his late partner. That left only Jessica Minton. Panic started to rise in her, only to be cut off as she fully grasped that another human being had died, and she had not for a moment considered his terror or his pain. She'd only been concerned about herself.

Then there was Crawford. Dear God, the man who had died was a partner, perhaps even a friend. Was Crawford brooding over another failure, like the one Larry had described in France? And with all that, he'd waited for her, even offered to tail her home. Perhaps she had the excuse of a nerve-wracking night, the excuse of never having had to reckon with murder. Still, she couldn't shake the guilt over being blinded to others' suffering by her fears.

Dropping the package on the bed, she turned to Crawford and confessed, "I can't believe I've been so insensitive, so rotten, to you. A man was killed, and I've been complaining about myself. You must be torn up. I know your profession is dangerous, but to have a person you know killed before your eyes — or don't you want to talk about it? I'm sorry. I'm blundering. I wish I could make this up to you — to your friend. Maybe it's all my fault, anyway. If I'd realized that the mug who came into Shaftner's was your partner, I could have given him the package. Instead, I took it and, well..."

Jess looked away, brooding over her last words. When she finally turned back to her companion, his expression gave her pause. J. Crawford looked decidedly uncomfortable, as if he'd been dealt a hand for poker when he was playing canasta. Yet, Crawford appeared more upset with himself than her. For getting her mixed up in all this?

"Miss Minton," he started carefully, "you most likely saved our bacon that night. You see, I wasn't able to warn my partner immediately that I'd ditched the package. There's a good chance that if you hadn't taken the package, our enemies could have pinched it."

Jessica regarded Crawford skeptically, finally questioning, "How do I know you're not just trying to make me feel better?"

"Miss Minton, in all the time I've known you, when have I ever done anything that made you feel better?"

The corners of Jessica's mouth instinctively turned up.

"Right. Now, as for your unforgivable selfishness," he paused, "I see that I've put you too much on the spot. I hadn't the right to ask you to blithely handle the kinds of pressure people have to be trained to deal with. I wish I could let you off the hook now, but unfortunately . . ."

"I can't let my country down, and I guess that means not letting you down," Jess interrupted him. "I realize I can't run away from jams. I don't want you, or anyone else, hurt because I didn't do my best to make sure the package got to the right people. I won't let anyone be hurt if I can help it."

"Don't be so noble, Jessica," Crawford warned tightly.

"I don't understand."

Crawford inhaled deeply before continuing, "Miss Minton, I don't mean to be harsh with you. Don't be harsh on yourself. People can't always live up to their ideals. Don't be so idealistic; you'll get burned."

"At this point, Mr. Crawford, I'm already a little singed. You may not want to believe this, but I'm not stupid — not completely, anyway."

He took her in with those hooded dark eyes before agreeing, "No, I don't for one minute believe you are."

Jess couldn't put her finger on why, but she had the feeling her acuity was worrying him a little. Before she could consider further, he reassuringly took her hand.

"Now, Miss Minton, all I have to do is come up with a brain wave that will extricate us from this muck-up."

Crawford released Jessica's hand to cross to the window and think.

"It's impossible for me to bring the package in on my own, without someone to run interference. So, until I can find a way to replace my partner without jeopardizing the operation, I'll have to leave the package with you. At least, my enemies don't know you have the package, so they won't be looking for you. I'm the one they have an eye out for, not you."

"I wish I could say I was sorry about that last part, but . . ."

Crawford shrugged, continuing, "We may just pull this off, though. No one followed you here, right?"

He *would* have to have forgotten her catalogue of the night's misadventures. Jess hesitated, looking away as she replied, "No one I didn't know."

"What does that mean?"

He didn't sound terribly pleased. Jessica turned back reluctantly, still not quite facing Crawford, to explain, "Um, you see my sister followed me to the theater. She did stop me from being mugged, though. If I'd lost the package to some nameless thief, you'd never have recovered it."

Jess spoke the last comment in defiance of the dark look hardening Crawford's features.

"Anyone else?"

His tone could have given penguins a chill.

"We-ell. I'm not sure, but I think I saw another actor from my play, down here."

"Who?" he demanded so sharply that Jessica jumped a little.

Darn Crawford for making her feel as if she had been called to the principal's office! Darn herself for answering him almost placatingly, "Frederick Bromfield, or at least someone who looked like Frederick Bromfield. He didn't see me, though. Probably wasn't even him, anyway."

"That's a comfort," Crawford sarcastically concluded. After thinking a moment, he went on, "And I have an unpleasant suspicion, Miss Minton, that the argument with your boyfriend was connected with bringing the package to me."

As he turned away from her to pull back the curtain for another quick reconnaissance of the street, Jessica winced. Crawford might have been ironic but he was not amused. She tried to jest, but a shaky voice undermined her, "How'd you guess?"

Curtain still in hand, Crawford turned back to Jessica and coolly let her have it. "This is no joke, Miss Minton. Hasn't anything I've said about the stakes for which we're playing sunk in? What are you doing taking a chance by involving these people?"

Jess marched over to her antagonist by the window and shot back, "Look, buddy, don't give me that baloney! I didn't issue any invites. People aren't stupid, you know. I didn't tell anyone anything — they guessed. So much for your clever attempts to keep things under your hat!"

Crawford's jaw set. Was he more angered or surprised by her counterattack? She folded her arms defiantly in front of her. That was when he lunged at her, shoving her below the window frame. Jess hadn't hit the floor before a gunshot and the shattering of glass terrified her more than she'd ever imagined possible.

Crawford's annoyed groan pricked Jessica to open the eyes she'd automatically screwed shut. Crouching partly over her, just below the window, Crawford turned his face away from his right arm. His eyes were worried, his features tense.

"Mr. Crawford?" Jessica began anxiously, "Are you all right?"

"It's a graze," he returned, a strained smile controlling his features. "Luckily, my jacket had the worst of it."

Too shaken to do much more than shudder with concern for Crawford's injury, Jessica still managed to ask, "Are you leveling with me? You're absolutely sure it's not serious?"

Crawford rolled away from Jessica and against the wall, pausing before answering, "I've had much worse. Neither of us will be all right if we don't get out of here immediately."

"I don't understand," Jessica began anxiously, starting to get up.

Pulling her down, Crawford warned, "No, stay below the window. He may still be waiting for us."

"What's going on? Who's 'he'?"

"The chap in a room across the street who just took a shot at us. We need to get out of here before he comes over to finish up. Now do as I say. Crawl across the floor without raising yourself higher than the bottom edge of the window. Mind the glass on the floor, but move. We have to get out of this place."

There was no arguing with his expression, so Jessica picked her way as quickly and carefully as she could around the broken glass and across the room to the door. If she hadn't been so terrified, Jess knew she would have felt darned silly crossing this dingy floor on her hands and knees.

Jess started to reach for the door knob, looked back at the window, then down to Crawford, and questioned, "Will he see my hand when I try to open the door? I don't think I can turn the door knob down on the floor like this, can I?"

Crawford shook his head and commanded, "Wait."

He hauled himself over to her as swiftly as a commando bellying up a North African beach, or at least with the alacrity Jessica imagined one would have. Fortunately, that nicked wing of his didn't seem to slow him down much. Leaning on his good arm, Crawford craned his neck for a sharp glance back at the window, then swiftly sat up to pull open the door. Leaning back against the wall, he pulled a small but nasty looking hand gun from inside his jacket. A shoulder holster? Tensely, Jess watched her comrade further crack the door open just enough to peer through the doorway carefully and scan the hall.

"All right, get up and get off," he instructed without turning.

"Stand up? On my feet?"

"Unless you have some other means of locomotion."

Jessica was quickly up and out into the hall. Crawford slipped out after her, taking Jess's arm as she looked questioningly at him.

"Let's go, Miss Minton," he said, guiding her away from the stairs she'd used earlier, after a quick glance in that direction.

"Wait. Where are we going? The stairs are back the other way," Jess protested as she found herself pulled down the corridor.

"There's another set of stairs behind a door at the end of the corridor."

"You think of everything."

"It's part of the job."

"Mmm, too bad you didn't think of a better place to hide the package before you blew out of Shaftner's."

Halting, Crawford demanded, "Speaking of which, where is the package?"

"I... You don't have it? We must have... ah... forgot it."

Crawford scowled, glancing anxiously down the corridor. Turning back to Jessica, he instructed as he moved her to the second staircase, "I'll go back for it. You wait here, on the stairs. Make sure you close the door."

"What? Me? Wait here? In the dark? Alone?"

"Either that or wait out here in the light where you'll be a prime target."

"Meet you behind the door."

Jessica started to close the door, but paused to call softly, "The package is in the shopping bag, and, well, be careful, Mr. Crawford."

"I've no intention of getting myself injured again, or worse," he dryly assured her. "Don't worry. Wait back there where you can't be seen."

Jessica reluctantly closed the door, shutting herself off from Crawford. Immersed in unrelieved blackness, she pressed herself against the paint-peeling door. She found herself praying: for herself, for Crawford, for staying alive. Her hand lightly touched the door. What would she do if he didn't make it back? What if he were seriously hurt? Could she help him? How would she even know? She wanted to growl like Dusty, angry at this helplessness.

The door opened, and Jessica nearly fell into the hallway. Adeptly, Crawford caught her, conveying the seriousness of the situation by foregoing any wisecrack. Handing her the bag with the package, he guided her back into the dark, closing the door behind them, and instructed, "All right now. Let's get out of here. Hold on to that railing."

Instinctively, Jessica tightened her grip on his arm and cracked, "Fine. I'll hold on, but if I slip, I'm taking you with me, buster."

Gripping the rail on his side with one hand, Crawford slowly led his uncharacteristically quiet confederate into the darkness, saying, "Just take it slowly. You'll be fine. Not many people know about these stairs. I pulled the lock off the door myself. We shouldn't be followed. You can relax a bit now."

"I'm fine," Jessica answered quickly, if not convincingly. "But, your arm? Is it bad?"

"I'm all right. It isn't painful. The jacket took most of the punishment. Pity, though. I can always shake a bit of sulfur over my arm, but jackets are hard to replace. Cloth rationing back home and all that."

Jess smiled, but briefly. She hesitated before saying, "It's bizarre, trying to walk when you can't see. I keep expecting to find the river Styx at the bottom of these steps."

"Careful here. We're going to make a turn on this landing. Just think of me as Virgil."

Jess laughed slightly, "If this were Good Friday the setting would be perfect. I didn't know you read Danté."

"There's no requirement that agents be illiterate," he returned easily.

"My, an educated man. So how did a nice boy like you end up in a lousy place like this?"

"Let's just say I was a hard-working lad from a manufacturing town lucky enough to earn a scholarship and dedicate my life to instruction — until the war interrupted my academic pursuits."

"At a British university?"

"Ah, Miss Minton, I never said that. So, what did you decide about what's his name?"

"What's whose name?"

"Your beau."

"Oh, Larry. What did we decide about what? About the package? I talked him into trusting you so that I could deliver it."

Crawford surprised Jessica by not bristling at her indiscretion. "I concluded as much from your presence. No, I was curious about the marriage plans."

If this were a ploy to distract her from her anxiety, it backfired. Jessica answered with ironic politeness, "Do you think that's any of your business?"

"I saved your life, Miss Minton. I feel more than a bit responsible for you."

"My life wouldn't have needed saving if you hadn't fouled up in the first place, friend."

"Hmm, I take it from your touchiness that you're still having some doubts."

"Maybe I like keeping my private life private."

"I'd just hate to see you make a mistake. It's a bad business when two people don't know whom they're marrying."

"What's that supposed to mean?"

"Let's just say I once dodged the bullet I see headed for you and your friend."

"Gee, Mr. Crawford, I didn't know that in spy school they gave lessons in advice to the lovelorn. Let's just get out of this rat trap, okay? As the song says, 'I'm a big girl now.'"

"Suit yourself."

He didn't sound offended, so why did she almost regret snapping at him?

They had reached the bottom stairs, and Crawford, all business now, stopped her at a closed door. Jessica couldn't help a little gulp when he drew the gun again, informing her, "I'll go first. We'll be stepping into an alley. Stick directly behind me; we're going to do a bit of zigzagging till we reach the Brooklyn Bridge. We'll take the promenade across. If I see that no one's followed us by the time we get there, we can relax a bit. After we cross the river, it'll be safe to flag down a taxi to send you home."

"Where will you go?"

"I'll find a place to go to ground and patch up this arm. No, don't look at me like that. A little sulfur over it and I'll be fine."

"You carry around sulfur drugs?" Jessica was impressed.

"Just part of my kit. Never mind that, though. Let's just concentrate on getting out of here, shall we? Whatever you do, don't let go of that package."

Jessica nodded vigorously. Crawford opened the door slowly, leaning cautiously against the wall. His gun was poised. Jess sucked back her breath, feeling like Evelyn Ankers or Anne Gwynne perpetually hiding from monsters in grade-B horror movies. Did Evelyn and Anne also hold their breaths to keep from throwing up?

Crawford edged out into the alleyway, then beckoned Jessica to follow. Cautiously, still slightly queasy, Jess joined Crawford, briefly hesitating to orient herself in the fog that had rolled deeper into the city. Where had it been when that sniper had taken a shot at them?

"This way," called Crawford through the murk.

Jess followed Crawford's vague shadow at a rapid clip into the darker end of the alley. Another turn and, thank God, there was a light ahead.

"Where are we going?" Jess questioned apprehensively.

"The first alley finished in a dead end. We'll move onto South Street, then branch off into another side street and follow these back alleys the remainder of the way," Crawford explained matter-of-factly.

"But when we step out onto South Street, anyone could see us."

"Unless we take South Street, we'll be trapped in that cul-de-sac. That doesn't offer a terribly good chance for escape."

Even in the dim light, Jessica's reservations were written clearly in her features. She turned away from Crawford to stare down the alley then reluctantly agreed, "Okay, Mr. Crawford. Let's go."

As they reached the mouth of the alley, Crawford instructed, "Just act casual. We're not even going to check for the enemy before stepping out. That would raise a red flag to the sniper and any chums he might have, if they're still around. Can you manage?"

"Oh, sure, piece of cake."

Crawford crooked a smile at Jessica's sour tone, before curving his arm around her as they swung onto South Street.

"Let's not get carried away, pal."

"Looks more natural this way, Miss Minton, don't you think?" Crawford replied innocently.

Jessica tilted her head up to him and warned, "Just make sure you keep your mind on the real business at hand."

Crawford casually glanced behind them, then returned his attention to the street ahead.

"Anything?"

"A woman. A heavy-set man."

Jess started to turn, to check if it were Frederick Bromfield, but James's grip firmly held her back. "What did I say about not turning around?"

"I just want to make sure it's not that colleague of mine. I'll rest easier . . ."

"You may 'rest in peace,' if you don't listen to me. Do as I say and don't chance letting him see your face. From this distance, we're just a chap and his girl out for a late night stroll. Submerge yourself in the part. Remember, you only have eyes for me."

"Hmm, I can see that bullet didn't puncture your ego, Mr. Crawford."

* * * * * *

It was late, but some cars still passed below, their taped headlights barely cutting strips of fuzzy light into the fog. The haze was deeper over the river, consigning to a rolling gray limbo anything beyond the steel scaffolding near the Brooklyn Bridge promenade. As soon as Crawford said that they hadn't been followed, that it was safe to stop and rest, Jessica seized the moment to take five. There'd been too much dashing about tonight for anyone not named Seabiscuit. Leaning wearily against the rail, she tried to catch her breath.

Crawford had unobtrusively turned away from her, and before Jessica recognized what he was doing he had slipped part way out of his jacket sleeve, torn open a sulfur packet, and shook it into his wound.

"Your arm? How is it?" Jess questioned, concerned, leaning toward Crawford to check.

But he waved her back with, "It's not pretty, but it's not bad. Don't worry. As I said, I've had far worse. I'm done, anyway. I can bandage it up better when I light somewhere."

His arm back in his jacket sleeve, Crawford leaned against the railing and commented, "I don't mind a bit of a breather myself, now. How about you, any better?"

Jess nodded, trying hard not to shake as her adrenaline drained away. Crawford's mustache quirked into a smile, and she realized he was probably thinking that this was one of the few times she had been at a loss for words. Jess shifted slightly to peer down at the river behind them. Crawford was looking ahead, his attention captured by an irregular series of strange flashes haunting the fog with a distant glow.

"Lightning," Jessica remarked.

Still observing the flashes, Crawford noted, "A bit late in the year for that sort of thing, isn't it?"

Jessica shook her head, adding with a dry smile, "I can remember a few nights back home, in Massachusetts, when we had storms like this."

A vague rumbling interrupted.

"Just like this," Jess continued. "Humph, thunder in autumn. I haven't thought about, well, there's this old saying about the weather there . . ."

"If you don't like it, wait a minute; it will change. Mark Twain, right?"

Jessica's lips turned up mischievously. "Once again, a well-read man, I see."

Crawford smiled quietly, as if he'd let down a barrier. Then he turned back to the flashes over the river, his features suddenly haunted. Under her eyes he remained silent, his expression growing more troubled.

Finally, she ventured, "Does the storm remind you of the blitz?"

Crawford didn't bother to look at her when he answered, "There's nothing, anywhere, like the blitz."

"You were in London?" Jessica questioned quietly.

He pulled a flake of paint from the rail before answering quickly, but with control, "London, Coventry, — or what's left of them."

"I'm sorry, Mr. Crawford. I didn't mean to press you on something painful."

Crawford faced Jessica and explained, with a bitter smile, "It's not actually a matter of pain. You learn to live with certain things, accept them, or at least stop thinking about them. To face seeing your homeland, your people, smashed and battered. You learn to redirect your hate. Channel it into tearing apart your enemy, the way he tries to go after you, so you don't tear yourself apart. Sometimes it works. But I sure as hell hope we end this before all anyone knows is how to destroy. Revenge doesn't really satisfy."

He seemed vaguely surprised and embarrassed for having admitted so much.

Jessica studied the man a few inches from her. His unexpected openness had disconcerted her. At last, she managed, "We're very lucky here, in this country, aren't we — not to have been through what you have. We read about bombings, but I wonder if we ever really think about what we read. People only see names and numbers, but never other human beings dead, unless it's someone close to them."

"I've seen people dead," Crawford noted wearily, his attention returning to the river. "I've seen children dead. That's the hardest part. But I can't afford to be human. And that's no good. I have to do rotten things so that others can't get around to creating even more rottenness. It's one bloody mess."

Jessica's arm had slipped through his, her hand gently touching his sleeve.

"Feeling sorry for me, Miss Minton?"

Jess didn't face her comrade when she answered, "I feel sorry for the whole damn world." Then she turned to Crawford, continuing, "Maybe if I help you this time, then it will be that much easier for you to do the rotten... well, what I mean is the people who do rotten things will be able, won't be able to do as many rotten... well, just pretend that I made a clever parallel to what you said."

Crawford smiled slightly, saying, "Sometimes we're just too full up with feelings, thoughts, to know the right words to string together." Then he added, "You never did tell me if you were going to marry Harry."

"Larry. That's certainly a *non sequitur*. Why *are* you so preoccupied with the two of us, anyway?"

"I told you; I've gotten used to being responsible for your life."

Neither was sure how long they faced each other before they slipped into each other's arms and kissed with a naturalness that made their act seem more inevitable than spontaneous. There really was nothing in the world but the warmth between them at that moment. Jess's beret slipped away. Her hair was soft and gently scented. His cheek felt comfortably rough from a missed shave. They sought each other for a second, hungry kiss. Within the sphere of their arms they had shut out the cold and confusion of the world.

"Oh, Larry!"

As soon as she spoke, Jessica jerked away, but not out of Crawford's hold. He whipped his head around to survey the haze behind him.

A little embarrassed, Jessica tapped her forehead, admitting guiltily, "Not out there, in here."

"Oh, I see," Crawford said, his arms slipping away.

"You do? How can you? Even I don't."

"It seems I've complicated your life in more ways than one."

Jessica smiled ruefully but said nothing.

"Do you think you're right for each other?"

Jessica looked away, then back, and shook her head, saying, "I... I just don't know. There was a moment, tonight, earlier, when I thought I did, or we could be — Before that there was always this, I don't know, this kind of low-grade friction between us. But I can *depend* on him."

"You're sure about that?"

"Of course I am. Why would you ask a thing like that?"

"Just thinking about someone I trusted when I was younger."

"But Larry really is serious. He does want us to marry and have a life together. And look how I've paid him back tonight."

"What do *you* want, Jessica Minton?"

"Well, I, I want to get married, some day. Maybe to him. I certainly can't break up with him just because you and I had a great kiss."

"I thank you for that — I couldn't have done it without you. I guess I want to warn you not to kid yourself. You're better off alone, instead of settling. Look, I know I've got no right to say any of this. The work I do, I have nothing to offer you — but if it had been you six years ago . . ."

"Why? What happened?"

"The short-hand version, the one that doesn't violate security: there was a girl from the same working-class town, born just enough above me that only my working my way up to a lecturer at University got her to see me." Crawford paused and a rueful expression belied that the memory still had some power over him, despite all else he'd seen and experienced. "I thought what I was would be enough for her, but she wanted someone who would take her a few more pegs up the social ladder. It would have been nicer if she'd just let me go rather than hanging on until she found somebody who could take her where she wanted."

"And I'm like her, aren't I? I'm not playing square with Larry? I'm one Grade-A heel."

He put a hand on hers and reassured Jessica, "I didn't say this to make you start beating up yourself. Except where I and the package came into the picture, you've been a lot more on the square with your friend than she ever was with me. Once this package is out of your life, the situation will be much clearer for you." Crawford released her hand and said more harshly to himself than to Jessica, "Anyway, I never should have kissed you. You were vulnerable, upset. There's no place for these feelings on a mission. I never made this kind of mistake before."

"You're not that kind of a fella?"

Crawford shook his head, "I must be getting old. They'll have to retire me soon, before the wrong people do it permanently."

"Don't say that."

He hesitated before responding, "Why not? Do you realize what a mess I've made? I barely pulled through my last mission. A few superiors were afraid that my misgivings about the set up would reflect badly on them, so they sent me on assignment over here to gloss things over. Rather than giving me the rest I deserved, no needed, I was put back in harness too soon to cover their . . ."

"I get the picture."

It all dovetailed with Larry's account of the fatal incident in France.

"So when another agent intercepted plans for a new type of German bomb fuse here in your country, I was supposed to ferry the plans back to England. You see, the Jerries like to whip up little surprises for the boys in UXB Squads."

"UXB?"

"Sorry. Unexploded bombs. We have specially trained units to defuse them."

"So what went wrong?"

Jessica pulled up her coat collar as the river damp began to get to her.

"The other agent, he thought he could shake his pursuers. He couldn't. Or rather, I suspect, I might have been recognized, aroused suspicion. He ended up dead. Now I have two men on my conscience from this mission — not to mention all the fellows who'll buy it if I don't get these plans home. Then I had to make a real dog's dinner of it by dragging you in."

"Don't say that."

"Why? Feeling sorry for me? Or am I beginning to frighten you? Are you worrying that you might be the next victim of my incompetence?"

"Frighten? Try horrify! Look, just consider that if you leave me to run around like a decapitated chicken while you have a comfy wallow in self-pity, then we'll definitely lose all those guys you're trying to save. I'll help any way I can to pull you through. Just remember, though, this is no Knute Rockne speech. You mess up again and I'll nail you to the wall."

Crawford leaned back against the steel girder and observed, "Very persuasive."

Jess moved closer. "Now, are you over your hysterics or will I have to slap you around?"

Crawford didn't try to suppress his smile. Then, he was serious again, saying, "I am sorry for dragging you into this jam. I wish I could have picked someone else to come in and sit next to me in Shaftner's."

"It isn't as if you had a say in the matter," Jess smiled. "Besides, if I hadn't sat next to you, we'd never have had this lovely evening together."

He smiled again and started to reach toward Jessica's arm, but thought better of it and repeated, "I honestly wish there had been another way."

Jess began slowly, "I, uh, hope you don't mind my asking this, but, what is your first name? After everything that's happened tonight, I feel funny calling you 'Mr. Crawford.'"

"Does sound a bit stuffy, doesn't it? It's James."

She looked at him doubtfully.

"You don't approve?" he queried, trying to figure out why.

"Oh, it's not that. Exactly. Actually it's a long story. 'James Crawford' couldn't be a pseudonym, could it?"

"It could be, but wouldn't you rather not be mixed up with a strange man whose name you don't even know?"

"No matter what your name is, you're still a strange man."

He arched an eyebrow, and she knew he wanted to kiss her again. She knew (darn it!) she wanted him to.

But James Crawford only covered her hand with his, and she tried not to let herself think how good that felt, as he began, "We do have a problem with your sister and Larry. Can they be relied on not to give away the show?"

That was a tough one. Finally, Jess decided, "If I say I handed over the package to you, they'd both have to believe everything was settled, finished between you and me. They'd have to drop the subject."

"But you don't like having to lie, do you?"

"No. I don't. I've been lied to too many times to relish deceit."

"Then I'm sorry I have to keep you at it, Jessica. I wish there were another way."

"So do I. But we haven't much of a choice, have we? Everything will be over soon, anyway, so I won't be lying for long, will I?"

"I shouldn't think so."

"I have to tell you something more about Larry, James. You may not like it."

"Go on"

His eyes were not easy to read.

"Larry suspected you. He found out about that incident, that assignment that went wrong, and told me about it. He also said that since you dropped off the radar afterward, your disappearance might mean you were now working for the Axis. I guess what you've told me, everything that's happened tonight, all prove he was wrong. He never heard of you because your work is under double wraps. The only thing is, if I tell him the whole truth, he'll know that this case isn't all safely put to bed. So, to throw him off the scent and keep him safe, I've got to continue lying to him. As I said before, that lying is going to be murder for me."

"I know, Jessica, but there isn't any other way. Tell me though, this is important, how did he know anything about me in the first place?"

"That's the kicker, James. He analyzes and evaluates intelligence data. I guess you're both in essentially the same business."

"You didn't buy his arguments?"

That reaction was unexpected. Not anger, nor alarm, nor panic, but quiet cogitation.

"No. No, I didn't. You had told me that you worked independently. I figured that if this case was a secret, as you'd told me, maybe information on you was too sensitive for even Larry to see. Besides, James, after what you've told me tonight, the things that have happened, I can't help but believe you're on the level."

"Has he told anyone about me or the package?"

"No, no. He told me he hadn't said anything yet, to keep my name out of things, to protect me. I think I can get him to continue to sit on this information. That will keep him out of trouble and let you settle the case, right?"

Crawford nodded thoughtfully, but was silent. Troubled by Larry's knowledge and suspicions? Finally he questioned, "And even with all his concerns, you are still sure that he didn't follow you tonight, Jessica?"

"He promised. Larry's a man of his word."

"Perhaps he might think it was worth breaking his word to keep you safe."

She didn't have an answer for that one. Finally, she said, "All I can say is that I didn't see him following me, and I kept an eye peeled for him or his car. It's not as if he's an agent like you and has all these methods of subterfuge up his sleeve."

"No, it's not," Crawford agreed. "Well then, just pay attention and try *very* hard to deflate any suspicions of his that might arise. Make sure that he knows you only have his best interests at heart. I don't think you have to lie to do that. Now, it's about time we got to Brooklyn. There should be at least one taxi around with your name on it, my comrade-at-arms." He paused, not quite comfortable with his parting bit of advice. "One more thing about Larry; don't make any personal decisions until we've ended this mess."

CHAPTER NINE

Jessica Minton was in torment. Fortunately, she wasn't playing comedy, so the guilt, the uncertainty could be channeled into her stage performance. Big consolation, that. But the performance she'd given Larry over the phone last night — or more accurately, early this morning — had been no walk in the park.

In the end, though, she was pretty sure that he believed Crawford now had the package and she was in the clear. What's more, it was a darned good thing she could depend on Larry's not having followed her. Larry would have gone through the roof if he'd known how dangerous the evening had turned out to be. Or would he have been more upset if he'd known about her romantic lapse with Crawford? Well, that was all it was, a mistake made in the stress of the moment. That was absolutely all — no matter how right it had felt at the time. So why couldn't she stop feeling like a heel? Maybe because Larry would never cheat on her. He would also never trust her again, even if he did forgive her, if he knew. Could she blame him? Had she actually treated Larry just as badly as she'd been treated by former boyfriends? Even if her lapse had happened only that once on the bridge, and under strained circumstances, it shouldn't have happened at all.

It didn't help Jess that she had come to like James Crawford and felt for what he was going through. More disconcerting, his warning to be certain before marrying Larry had given clarity to her misgivings about a future with her boyfriend. Wouldn't it be dreadful for two people gradually to realize they needed different lives but were tied together? Of course there was such a thing as divorce, and she wasn't a practicing Catholic anymore. But for all her inadequacies, Jessica was not about to go into a marriage planning an easy out. Larry wasn't that sort, either — in spades!

Still, Larry had been trying to meet her half way. Was she just not giving him enough credit? Not making enough of an effort, herself? *Would* she really make Larry happy in the end by breaking off with him? She certainly couldn't explain to him how her experiences with Crawford had shaken her commitment to their future together. It would make no sense to him. She didn't quite understand it, herself. Things were way too complicated now for her to make a wise final decision about her relationship with Larry. She couldn't think straight. Wasn't that why Crawford advised her against any such decisions until this gambit was dead and buried — oops! *Really* bad choice of words!

But *would* she have been drawn to Crawford if everything were right enough between her and Larry?

Regardless, Jessica was still pro enough not to let her acting suffer. Strangely enough, she couldn't say the same about Frederick Bromfield. Tonight, Bromfield's performance was off. Worrying about his niece again? At least he'd never said anything to Jess about seeing her on the East Side. Apparently, even if he had been the man she'd seen, he hadn't noticed her.

The curtain fell at last, and the cast made its exit. Lingering backstage to talk with Iris after curtain call, Jessica was slightly disconcerted to see Frederick Bromfield ahead, on the painful end of a discussion with Harold Vane. She was feeling for Bromfield when he looked up and sighted her, giving her a "significant" stare. What was that about? A plea to liberate him from Harold Vane's persecution? The director also turned in her direction, said something abruptly to Mr. Bromfield, and charged off.

Concern in his eyes, Bromfield came up to her and Iris, querying, "Miss Minton, may I have a word with you?"

"Of course, Mr. Bromfield. Iris and I were talking, but we can spare a minute," Jessica returned, sympathetic to her beleaguered colleague.

Bromfield hesitated.

"If you don't mind, Miss Rossetti, I must talk to Miss Minton alone. I hope you are not offended, but this is personal."

"No, 'course not," Iris gave her usual chipper consent. Turning to Jessica, she said, "See you later, kid. Good night, Mr. Bromfield."

Personal? It had to be Fritzi. Jess hated to admit that she felt relieved.

"Let's talk in my dressing room, Mr. Bromfield," Jessica began, starting in that direction. "We can have some privacy there. Having problems with your niece again?"

"I'm not worried about Fritzi any longer. You're my concern."

"Me? Why me?" Jessica laughed without breaking stride, but thinking, *Brother, you don't know the half of it!*

"You are involved with James Crawford. Trust me. That man is trouble."

Jessica halted, staring at Bromfield. His impassive face gave her a really bad feeling. Instinct told her to deny knowing Crawford. Protect him. The older man's expression revealed he didn't want to be harsh, but he was not going to back down.

"I saw you with him last night. I do not know if he has forced himself into your life, or if you are voluntarily connected with him, but you must break off with him. Now. Before he endangers you."

His tone was soft, but his eyes were relentless.

Jessica hesitated, swiftly calculating: Bromfield had seen her with James, so denying that she knew him would look fishy. She'd just have to make everything sound above board.

"Mr. Bromfield, what's so bad about James Crawford? He seemed like an okay guy when I met him, not that I know him all that well."

Bromfield shot an anxious glance up the corridor, then another down it. Finally he asked, "Do you know the Desirée Cafe?

"Uh, yes. Down the street, right?"

"Good. We cannot talk here. I do not think we should even leave together. Meet me at the café in ten minutes."

"That doesn't leave me enough time to change," Jess reflected aloud.

"That is a minor consideration in comparison to what I have to tell you. Remember. Only ten minutes."

Bromfield left Jessica standing there brooding. *What a fine mess!* she grumbled to herself. What could Frederick Bromfield possibly have against James Crawford? Yet, he certainly would have no earthly reason to lie about James, would he? Maybe it was all a mistake. No, too convenient. So had they known each other in Europe? It had to be a mistake.

Jessica made it to her dressing room in a snap. A glance at her watch told her she'd better scoot. No time to wait for Helen, the wardrobe mistress, to help her change. So, she'd better not get caught leaving the building in this get-up. Grabbing up her jet-beaded jacket and the lacquered feather cap she'd worn on stage, Jessica was off. What could Bromfield have to say?

A sign announcing the Desirée Café loomed into sight, just ahead. Not the most exclusive watering hole in town. Jessica pushed open the simulated leather doors and stepped inside. To her left, a densely populated bar curved off into cigarette haze. The rest of the floor was filled with crowded tables. Further in, booths lined the walls to the right. Where the dickens was Frederick Bromfield? She couldn't spot him anywhere in this bar full of people celebrating as if Roosevelt had green lighted liquor production again. Preoccupied, Jessica didn't notice the approach of a somewhat-less-than-sober gent, until he nearly staggered into her.

"Say, honey, haven't I seen you somewhere before?"

Barely glancing at her new acquaintance, Jessica returned, "I certainly hope not."

Unexpectedly, an arm encircled Jess's shoulder as her would-be swain wheedled, "Aw, come on, honey."

"Move it or I'll break it," Jessica threatened pleasantly.

The arm slid away and her admirer melted back into the throng, freeing Jessica to proceed on a table-to-table search for Mr. Bromfield.

Abruptly, a harried host stopped her.

"Sorry, lady, no unescorted women allowed."

He noticeably appraised Jessica's "floozy" costume.

"Oh no, you've made a mistake. I'm meeting somebody here."

His tone was more weary than insulting. "Yeah, well, sister, I've heard that number before."

Jessica had a theory about the mentality of men who addressed her as "sister," but before she could launch into a choice epigram on the subject, she was interrupted.

"Is there a problem here?"

"Mr. Bromfield," Jessica greeted him warmly, then turned a deadly charming smile on the host.

"I've been waiting for this lady. She's a colleague of mine from the play at the Cherry Theater. Perhaps you've heard of our play . . ."

"I don't have time for play acting, gramps. I got other problems."

The host disappeared, and Jessica allowed her companion to take her arm and guide her through the crowd to a banquette. Frederick Bromfield courteously allowed her to slide in before sitting, himself. While a waiter took their orders, Jessica vaguely noted that the walls were adorned with paintings that were more tantrums in oil than abstract art. She hoped that the villainy Bromfield attributed to James Crawford would turn out to be no more authentic than this poor excuse for the *avant garde*.

Her companion waited for the waiter to leave before speaking. "Cigarette? Oh, I'm afraid I forgot that you do not smoke. Do you mind if I...?"

Jessica abruptly shook her head, thinking, *Let's get on with this*! Only a gargantuan exercise of restraint prevented her from blurting out her anxiety.

After lighting his cigarette and taking an initial drag, Bromfield exhaled a stream of smoke and said, "You were late. Perhaps you told someone that you were meeting me?"

"No, no, of course not. I just had trouble getting away. There was quite a crowd at the stage door. And I had to dodge Helen from wardrobe, too."

Bromfield nodded, seeming relieved at her explanation, but Jess still didn't like the way he watched her.

"I'm afraid all this mystery has piqued my curiosity, Mr. Bromfield. Why do you want to warn me against this James Crawford?"

Would he buy her casual air?

"'This' James Crawford. You know him better than that. I saw you all the way down on the lower East Side. I said to myself, 'Why is a nice girl like Jessica Minton going into a flea-bag hotel?' So I waited to make sure you would be all right. And then what did I see, but you walking arm and arm with him. I'm only trying to help you, Miss Minton. Please level with me."

"Well, if you saw us, Mr. Bromfield, why didn't you just say hello? There's no need to make a mystery out of a simple errand."

Bromfield took another drag on his cigarette, exhaled, thinking over how much to reveal, then answered, "I couldn't confront him, not with you there. I'm only trying to help you. What's between you two? What would your young man say?"

"Larry wouldn't say anything. Everything's perfectly innocent," Jessica couldn't help snapping, a guilty conscience triggering her temper. But she couldn't afford to lose control. She had to walk a tightrope of finding out what her well-meaning colleague knew about James Crawford without dragging him into the mess her life had become.

In a calmer tone, she explained, "Really, Mr. Bromfield, as I told you, I hardly know this Crawford. It's a girlfriend who has a romantic interest in him. I was just dropping off a present from her to him. But I agree with you, I wasn't impressed with where he hangs his hat, either. If I hadn't promised to help her out, you'd never have caught me within ten feet of that rat trap. I know he's a starving musician or something, but I didn't realize he was in *that* bad an area until I got there and it was too late to turn back. In for a penny, in for a pound. I know it doesn't look good for this Crawford guy, living down there, but he seemed okay for the brief time I saw him. He even walked me out of the neighborhood. Still, if you have reason to believe he's a shady character, maybe my girlfriend shouldn't get mixed up with him. I think you'd better tell me what you know."

"You don't trust me, Miss Minton?" Bromfield seemed hurt. "Isn't it enough that I should tell you this man is dangerous? Do you think I would lie to you?"

"Oh no," Jess assured Bromfield feelingly, responding to his concerned mien. But James wouldn't lie to her either, would he?

Reasonably, Jessica continued, "You know from your experience with your niece, it isn't easy to talk someone out of a bad romance. You've got to give me something solid to go on. Help me the way I tried to help you with Fritzi."

Jessica watched Bromfield evaluate her words, not taking his eyes from her face. She fought mightily to suppress her eagerness when he came to some conclusion and started to address her. That's when the waiter arrived. To Jessica's excruciating frustration, the interruption seemed to set Frederick Bromfield thinking yet again. Jess stabbed her sloe gin fizz with the plastic swizzle stick as she waited.

"Miss Minton," Bromfield began wearily, "I will tell you what I dare. I will tell you that I saw James Crawford years ago in the old country. He brought me much grief. He is the type of man who mixes himself up in dangerous activities. Illegal activities. Please, do not allow him to mix you up in such things."

Jessica's brow furrowed as she studied the man across from her. Frederick Bromfield had never seemed so jowly, so worn.

Finally, she questioned, "What do you mean by 'illegal activities,' Mr. Bromfield?"

He shook his head violently, asserting, "No, no, I cannot say. It is something I cannot speak of, not even to you, though I am afraid for you. This must be enough."

Jessica Minton sat back slowly. Putting two and two together was giving her an extremely distasteful four. Hadn't Mr. Bromfield fled Europe to escape the Nazis? No! She would not believe James Crawford was mixed up with the Nazis, as Larry suspected. Not after all he'd said to her last night. He certainly wouldn't have saved her from the sniper and given her back the package if he were an enemy agent. Unless the heat was on him, and no one knew that Jessica Minton was the one who really had the package.

"Miss Minton, I see you have been considering what I have said. I hope you've decided to accept what I have told you. The Crawford I knew was always up to no good — something illegal, even dangerous. If he thinks you could get in his way, I wouldn't put it past him to harm you."

"Harm? Me? All I did was deliver a package, Mr. Bromfield."

"And that package you carried, do you know what was in it?"

Jessica blinked at Bromfield. For just one moment, his tone had probed razor-like, sharp and cold. Most likely he hadn't even realized the slip of his mask. Jess sat silently, watching him uncomfortably.

"Miss Minton," he pressed, kindly tone returning, "would you be angry if I suggested that the 'friend' of whom you speak is you?"

The switch back was so fluid. Had she imagined that aberrant steeliness?

Stupidly, Jessica blinked again, then, recovering herself she answered, "I wouldn't be angry, Mr. Bromfield. I know you're concerned about me, but you've got it all wrong. It's my girlfriend who's involved with Crawford. Believe me; I'll be sure to pass on everything you've said. And just so I can really convince my girlfriend, tell me, is there anything else I should know about James Crawford?"

She really wanted to grab him by the shoulders, shake him, and demand, "Is James Crawford with the Nazis?! Is that why you hate him?!" But she couldn't let anyone know how deeply she was involved with Crawford, especially after what had happened to his colleague. And silly as it was, Jess couldn't stop turning over in her mind that brief but unsettling change in Bromfield.

"I have told you all you need to know," he replied quietly, watching Jess.

Jessica put on a pleasant expression, refusing to be stared down.

Bromfield turned his attention to the pocket watch hanging by a chain on his vest. Snapping the watch open, he stated without looking up, "It's late now, Miss Minton. I must return home."

Bromfield called for the check, saying sadly when he paid their bill, "At least you will let me do this for you?"

"I wish you would believe me, Mr. Bromfield. I honestly have listened to you."

He seemed to agree only out of politeness. As Bromfield escorted her through the crush of people, Jess's mind clicked rapidly, trying to make sense of his mysterious warnings about James Crawford. No go.

They finally stepped out onto the street. Ah, what a blessed relief the crisp evening air was from that overstuffed bar. Breathing it felt like quenching your thirst with a cool drink.

Bromfield turned to Jessica and said kindly, "You are a good woman. I hope you will be careful and do nothing foolish."

"I won't. Believe me," Jessica assured him, knowing darned well that at this point she wasn't too sure she'd recognize folly if it jumped up and bit her on the... well, never mind.

Bromfield nodded tiredly and started off. Watching the old man stooped beneath the heavy coat, Jess wondered what she should do now. To her surprise, before he had gone more than a few steps, Mr. Bromfield turned, came back to her, and asked, "Miss Minton, does Crawford still stay in the place where you met him last night?"

Guessing what he had in mind, Jessica warned him anxiously, "Mr. Bromfield, if Crawford's dangerous, you ought to stay away from him, too. Please, don't get yourself into any trouble trying to even old scores."

Bromfield's look seemed to slice right through her defenses. Might he interpret her concern as more for Crawford than for him? *Was* that conclusion far from the truth?

However, the older man smiled and answered, "I will stay out of trouble. I can protect myself."

And she couldn't? But Bromfield turned and continued on his way before she could search his face for an answer. Jessica lingered to watch him, then sharply started back for the theater. Her heels clicked briskly on the pavement as she tried to puzzle out Frederick Bromfield's warning. How could she doubt James Crawford after everything that they'd been through? For God's sake, he'd saved her life! But what did Frederick Bromfield have to gain by lying to her?

That night there had been a connection between James and her, not suddenly springing into existence, but unexpectedly revealed. If Bromfield were telling the truth, couldn't James Crawford have changed since the two last saw each other? Seeing what had happened to Europe, to his home, might have shaken James up, forced him to re-evaluate his life. That happened to people — and not just in that Tyrone Power/Joan Fontaine movie *This Above All.*

And then, Jessica was back in the theater, the past few minutes only a blur of troubled cogitations until she nearly knocked down her fellow player, Greg Ferrell.

"Whoa! You're out in left field, Jess. What's with you?"

"Oh," Jessica forced herself back to reality, "Nothing. Just thinking over some business I have to work out with Frederick Bromfield, in the play."

"Oh, yeah, sure. Say, I'm supposed to meet Iris and Steve in Chinatown for a bite. Want to come?"

"I'd love to, Greg, but I'm bushed. I'm just going to crawl into bed and curl up with some Charlotte Brontë."

"That ought to put you to sleep, pronto."

"You kids today have no sense of aesthetics."

"Yeah, but this kid's got a powerful appetite for Chinese. See you... What a dope!" Greg slapped his forehead with his hand. "I almost forgot. Your sister's waiting for you in your dressing room."

"Liz?"

"Unless you have another one. She came in, just after you stepped out. Iris had her wait in your room."

"Great. Thanks, Greg," Jessica smiled, squeezing his arm. "Have a good time with everybody. I'll see you tomorrow."

Fairly trotting down the corridor to her dressing room, Jessica sighed over Liz's still being involved. However, since a thoroughly steamed Liz had been literally waiting on her doorstep when she'd arrived home last night with the package still clearly sitting in her bag, trying to pull another fast one on her sister had been out of the question — even for her own good. Buffaloing Larry with a mere phone call, that had been so much easier. Larry trusted her more than Liz did. That conclusion left a guilty sting. Anyway, since Liz had tagged Jess for some time that night, there was some chance she'd been seen by the wrong people. So she deserved to know what the score was, so she could keep on her toes. The only thing that made Jessica a little easier about coming clean to Elizabeth was that since the whole caper with the package had proved legit, her sister had developed a startlingly new talent for discretion.

And in spite of her reluctance to share even a chance of danger with Liz, Jess was relieved to have her sister for an ally. She could really use Liz's advice right now. Elizabeth would certainly be frank about letting her know if she was being naïve in thinking that the James Crawford she knew was not the shady character Bromfield had described.

Jessica had just opened the door when, in a filmy whirl of pale shrimp chiffon, Elizabeth yanked her into the room, shoved the door closed, and plunked her in the chair by the dressing table. Barely pausing for a glance in the mirror to deftly adjust the chiffon scarf covering her hair and draping around her neck, Elizabeth demanded, "So shoot. What did you worm out of Bromfield, kid?"

"Iris told you I was meeting him?"

"Yeah, but that's all. She didn't seem to know any more. It wasn't hard for me to put two and two together, though. So how much did you learn from him?"

"Not much," admitted Jess ruefully.

"How much is not much?" Elizabeth demanded, folding her arms.

Jessica smiled sourly, "'Not much' means Mr. Bromfield said he knew James Crawford in 'the old country,' where our friend was 'dangerous' and involved in 'illegal' activities. He thinks Crawford is still up to no good."

"Hmph." Elizabeth's eyes narrowed speculatively. "How would Bromfield know him anyway? They're not even from the same 'old country.' Say, didn't Bromfield come here to get away from the Nazis?"

"The same thought crossed my mind," Jessica observed, looking her sister in the eye.

Liz broke the silence that had descended, "Jess, I don't like to say this, much as I like to say 'I told you so,' but this doesn't sound too good for your pal Crawford. Do you think he's hoodwinking you?"

"The man saved my life, Elizabeth. Why would he do that if he were an Axis spy? Wouldn't it be better to eliminate the loose end? And why would *our* side want me dead, or him, either? Wouldn't he be more valuable as a live prisoner? The Feds didn't bump off those saboteurs at Amagansett, the ones he told us about, or the Duquesne crowd."

Liz considered before agreeing with a nod, "True."

Elizabeth's conceding points in favor of Crawford? That was surprising, even a relief. Jess concluded that there was no need to let Liz know just how relieved she felt. Considering Liz's partiality for Larry, it would be more than awkward should she realize Jess's confused feelings for Crawford.

"You know, Jess," Elizabeth began, leaning back against the makeup table, "maybe we've been looking at this from the wrong angle. Remember, you did say Frederick Bromfield said 'illegal.' That doesn't automatically make Crawford a pal of the Nazis, not by a long shot. Maybe we've become so wrapped up with the package we can't see the forest for the park rangers. We end up thinking everything is connected to it."

"You really think so, Liz?" Jess asked hopefully.

"Don't jump the gun, kid," Elizabeth cautioned. "You're forgetting Mr. Bromfield said Crawford was a shady character. He might be working for the right side and still be a criminal. In fact, I bet that type flourishes in the secret agent profession."

"Mmm, I suppose you're right. But, Liz, the things he said and did, Crawford really seemed on the square. What Mr. Bromfield said didn't feel right to me."

"I know I usually go by feeling, Jess, but why on earth would Bromfield lie? There's no reason for him to try to turn you against Crawford, except for your own good."

Jessica hesitated before venturing sheepishly, as if even she couldn't quite believe what she was saying, "Someone who didn't want me to deliver the package to Crawford might try to drive a wedge between us."

"Jess, you're not trying to tell me you think that courtly old man is with the Nazis? He's just not the type!"

"Well, Liz, what *is* the type? Are you expecting someone with a Heidelberg scar, swastikas tattooed up his arms, and a permanent snarl? A little obvious for undercover work, isn't it?"

"But, Jessica, Mr. Bromfield's always been so nice to you. How can you think such things about him?"

Jessica shook her head, agreeing, "Yes, you're right. It does sound silly once you say it. Paranoid, even. Lord, I'll be glad when this is over."

"So will I. We can go back to normal, and you can forget about everything, including James Crawford, and get back on track with Larry."

Jess didn't say anything. She didn't want to go around this mulberry bush again. Last night, after she'd returned home, Jess had tried to explain her doubts to Liz about her future with Larry. All Liz could do was blame an infatuation with Crawford and adventure. But their problems predated Crawford, even if Liz kept ignoring that fact.

"Jessica, don't get involved with that man. You don't know him. Maybe he is witty; he does gallant things — but this isn't a twenty-five cent romance. Besides, you're better off with Larry."

Jessica shot her sister a sharp look and countered, "Liz, you can stop jumping to conclusions right now. I told you last night and I'll tell you again, just because I sympathize with a man doesn't mean I'm going to run off with him. You're being absurd."

"Sometimes you smile a little when you talk about him."

"I do not. And, anyway, whatever happens between Larry and me isn't Crawford's fault. It's a problem with me and Larry."

"What are you talking about? What problem? What do you mean, 'Whatever happens'? What *is* going to happen? You better not let Larry get away, if you know what's good for you."

"Could we change the subject, please? Get back to the package?"

Elizabeth scowled, "Just don't end up putting too much faith in someone who may be playing you, kid. Be careful. It's damn easy to get caught up in the adventure. Look at me, staking out your apartment. Try to be objective. Bromfield knew Crawford before you did; he didn't like him. Bromfield's never had it in for you, Jess. Now, what does that add up to?

"Liz, even if Mr. Bromfield is telling the truth, I'm not going to turn on a man who saved my life based on one story. Anyway, maybe Mr. Bromfield just *thinks* he's telling the truth. Maybe when Bromfield saw James Crawford doing something that looked shady, he was actually on some kind of mission," Jessica reasoned, facing her sister's concern.

"Or maybe, Jess, because Crawford is crooked, working for the Allies now is the only way he could get out of hot water."

"You make me feel as if I were playing Polly Peachum to his Macheath," Jessica admitted ruefully.

"Don't go literary on me," Elizabeth warned, adding, "I still have the feeling I haven't entirely won you over."

"One must always keep an open mind."

"Hmph, well, one also ought to keep a full stomach. I skipped a late supper with Kathy and Joanne to check up on you, kid. Shall we grab a bite of dinner before we end up grabbing breakfast instead?"

"Suits me fine," Jess agreed, relieved to no longer have to defend Crawford or herself. "Just give me a minute to change."

Jess disappeared behind the screen to slip swiftly into a ginger-brown wool suit and black jersey. While zipping up her skirt, she asked, "Elizabeth, one thing puzzles me. When Iris told you I was meeting Mr. Bromfield at the bar, you sat tight here. When did you suddenly lose that insatiable curiosity of yours?"

"About the time you told me someone took a shot at you."

"Oh, that's reassuring."

"Hey, if it were up to me, you wouldn't be mixed up in this mess at all. But don't worry, little sister, it'll all be over soon."

"That's what I'm afraid of."

Jessica paused at the mirror to angle a black felt beret on her head, then led her sister out, flicking off the lights and closing the dressing-room door behind them.

As the two women proceeded down the corridor, Jess heard an ominous buzzing overhead and remarked, "As if things weren't bad enough, the wasps are back!"

CHAPTER TEN

Dapper in a sharply cut, gray, pin-striped suit, Peter Hennessey was the only one standing in Jessica Minton's dressing room. Years of experience had convinced him this was the most effective position for pontificating. Since his return, Peter had been preoccupied with the fall of Italy. So, rather than percolating with excitement over getting to see his sister-in-law's play for the first time tonight, he was detailing the difference between taking Italy and slogging across Europe into Germany, in excruciating detail, to Jessica and Larry — excruciating to Jessica, anyway. Larry's response was quite different, for he almost immediately got himself into a verbal dustup with Peter over whether Russia was really the Allies' "friend," since that camaraderie had developed only after Germany had turned on Russia. Jessica needed all her self-discipline not to throw them both out. Being a helpless captive to their argument was hardly the most effective way to prep for her performance. She had more than enough mental and emotional distractions to deal with as it was.

Larry was defending the Russians. "Millions starved, frozen, killed, and they not only managed to hold off the Jerries, but shoved them halfway across the country. You've got to admire that kind of strength, Peter."

"And fear it, too."

Larry leaned forward to insist, "It seems to me that there's an island in the North Atlantic that has done a rather commendable job of staving off the Germans. Are you just as afraid of all the Englishman who haven't knuckled under?"

"You're actually asking an Irish boy to say something good about England? Anyway, I think it's time we change the subject before my sister-in-law slips from boredom into a coma." Peter turned to Jessica, snapping his fingers before her and urging, "Wake up, Sleeping Beauty."

Jessica blinked, then quipped, "Watch it, ace, or Elizabeth won't be the only one at home in ill health."

Jess then offered Larry a dry smile. He returned it but seemed to shift his eyes a little too quickly. Had he sensed her recent difficulty facing him? Crawford's assessment of her and Larry was eating at her almost as much as having lied about the package.

Taking up her watch, Jessica rose, forcing herself to sound cheerful. "Sorry, but you two armchair generals will have to scram before you win the war. I need some time to myself to prepare for my performance. Go find your seats and continue the debate out front. Just try to refrain from violence once the play starts."

"No problem, Jess. Larry knows when he's lost the argument."

"And, Peter, I'll be sure to let you know should that ever happen," Larry returned with equal smoothness, getting up.

Jess smiled, linking her arms with her two guests, and walked them to the door, teasing, "I wish Liz had been able to come tonight, just to help referee. I don't think I can handle two of you myself."

"I'll keep Peter in line."

"We'll see about that, Mr. Sanders," Peter returned confidently.

Before the exchange could blossom into a fire fight, Jessica cut in, "I am so sorry Liz had to come down with that headache. She went to all the trouble of waiting for you to come back, Peter, so you could see the play together, and now this."

"I wanted to wait," Peter agreed, "but Liz insisted Larry and I go tonight. She thought you might be disappointed if we didn't. You know Liz. Once she makes up her mind . . ."

"I know," Jess agreed ruefully as they reached the door. She added conversationally, "There must be a run on bad health around me. The theater's doorman was struck by a hit-and-run driver this afternoon. He's not badly injured, but we're out a doorman for the next few evenings."

Larry opened the door and paused, saying to Peter, "Would you mind going on ahead? I'd like to speak to Jessica for a moment."

"Sure — even though I know the two of you will be talking about me behind my back,"

Peter grinned before he left the two.

Jessica didn't see her companion's expression when he turned back to her after Peter had gone. She was too busy trying to look fascinated with adjusting the belt of her olive dressing gown. Larry's request had sent her stomach plummeting like the 1929 stock market, but there was no reason she should let him see that.

"You definitely turned the package over?"

His words came quietly, but Jessica instinctively shot a swift surveying glance up the corridor. She faced Larry again, cautioning tensely, "Don't talk about it here, with all these people around."

"No one could have the foggiest what we're talking about, right?"

Jessica replied carefully, "No. No, I suppose not. I guess it's too soon for me to get completely back on an even keel. Anyway, I've already told you everything that mattered. Let's just forget the whole mess. I want to get back to normal again."

Jessica had briefly looked away, but now she faced Larry. He seemed dissatisfied. How she wished she could have leveled with him.

"Jessica," Larry asked carefully, his eyes very intense, very black, "is everything all right?"

"Of course. Why not?"

Try as she might, she couldn't control the ghost of a flinch when Larry suddenly caught her chin in his hand, tilting her face to his, before he questioned significantly, "There's nothing you want to tell me?"

"I'm sorry, Larry. I feel just terrible. You've always been so good. You're so understanding, and I had to lie to you."

"It's over now. Skip it, Jessica," Larry told her gently.

She looked at him and smiled, only to tense a trifle as his hand slipped down to rest against her neck.

"You *are* on the level now, Jess?"

Jessica could feel the pulse in her jugular beat into his palm. Larry did not take his eyes from her face.

"Well, I'm afraid it's getting late, Larry," Jessica informed him, trying to disguise how uncomfortable his nearness made her by playfully tugging the lapels of his black suit. He didn't move away, though. His thumb pressed just a tad disconcertingly against her lower jaw.

Jessica gently but decidedly moved Larry's hand away, holding it in her own, and saying with a convincing muster of good humor, "I have to get ready. You're going to have to join Peter now, painful as that might be."

Larry's expression didn't change. Finally, he dropped his hand, saying, "We'll talk later."

"Right!" Jessica called with convincing brightness to the back Larry had turned on her.

It wasn't until Larry was gone that Jessica sank back, exhausted, into the doorframe, the sensation of his thumb's pressure against her jaw finally faded. Good grief, in that moment when he'd held her face just a little too tightly, Larry had given her a chill, and not the kind a girl got from Tyrone Power.

For the first time, Jessica noticed Frederick Bromfield and Harold Vane in deep discussion just up the corridor. Bromfield beat a tense rhythm on his palm with the hilt of the stage knife. A shiver twitched across Jessica's shoulders. Why had Bromfield given her that disturbing lowdown on James Crawford?

Closing her dressing room door on the world outside, leaning heavily against it, Jessica brooded over her tête à tête with Bromfield in the bar. She couldn't take his word over what she, herself, had seen in James Crawford. He'd cared for her bruised hand when she'd left his jaw smarting; he'd appreciated what she'd done for him and the Allies; and he'd regretted the dangerous disruption of her life. He'd *saved* her life from the sniper. More than that, there was something in him that made her feel at home, in spite of, no maybe because of, every damned disaster they'd shared. And he'd cut to the heart of her concerns about Larry. But she, like James Crawford, didn't for one minute think that there was any future for the two of them. Not one minute.

Jessica shoved herself away from the door, slowly walking to her dressing table. Twisting herself into knots right now wasn't going to solve anything. It would just distract her into giving a lousy performance.

Interestingly, it was Frederick Bromfield, not Jessica who turned in a distracted performance that evening. But more went wrong with the play than a subpar effort from the lead actor. One of the newly returned wasps had retired beneath the covers of the bed on which Bromfield "murders" Jessica. The ornery insect expressed its dismay at being disturbed by unceremoniously letting Jessica have it on a most embarrassing portion of her hip, driving her to twist violently right before she was "stabbed." Jess comforted herself that she had reacted *before* she was supposed to be dead. It wouldn't quite do to have a corpse flopping about.

At least, being "dead" during the last scene, she'd had time to get the stinger removed and her wound iced before the final curtain. Then, the whole process of final bows became a blur, because she could not wait to get back to that blessed ice pack! But Jessica's curtain-closing thoughts were invaded by another kind of buzz — Frederick Bromfield had missed curtain call. After the hasty reorganization for final bows and the last curtain fall, Jess and Iris fled down the corridor together before Harold Vane could prompt anything odiferous to hit the proverbial fan.

"You know, Iris, Mr. Bromfield isn't the only one playing a vanishing act. I couldn't see Larry or Peter in their seats when we took our bows. Is that a comment on us?"

Iris laughed, "Let's just call your chums a couple of philistines."

"Philistines, huh? Now there's a fifteen-dollar word!"

"Fifteen, nothing! It's at least worth a picture of Andrew Jackson."

"Well, just don't swallow any thesauruses, thesaurusi... oh, heck. You know what I mean."

"Maybe just a few Latin dictionaries. Then I can teach you to spell. See you tomorrow, kid."

Standing in front of her dressing room, Jessica smiled after Iris. The smile faded. What had happened to Peter and Larry? Had they sneaked out to beat the crush? They might even be waiting in her dressing room. No voices in there, though. Jess pushed open her door. Maybe Liz had taken a bad turn and called Larry and Peter home? Their hats and coats would still be in here if they hadn't left — possibly even a message from them.

Something had been left for Jess all right, but it was a far cry from *her* idea of a message from Peter or Larry.

A stocky male body in an overcoat was stretched face down on the floor. She was barely conscious of the smatter of blood around his head and on the nearby couch — or on her dressing gown, soiled and crumpled on the floor.

Jess knew who he was, but some grotesque imp of the perverse pushed her to make sure. Turning him over by the shoulder, Jess found an answer to her inquiry that sent her flying from the room, silent screams tearing inside her skull.

She'd never seen a man shot in the face before, but she could just recognize that mangled mess as having once been Frederick Bromfield. Bromfield was dead after warning her against James Crawford, dead only a few nights after asking where Crawford lived and never quite promising not to even old scores.

Good grief, she was now standing on stage, which the stage hands were busy breaking down. She'd run this far without even realizing it? Then Crawford's features rose in her mind's eye — to decompose into the thing that had been Frederick Bromfield's face. It was a stiff battle to keep her knees from wobbling.

"You okay, Miss Minton?"

Vince Manzi, one of the stage hands, had come over, his words breaking into her thoughts, his eyes regarding her curiously, full of concern.

Automatically, Jess shot back, "Yes, yeah, sure, Vince. Of course."

But she wasn't. Jess was lost at sea, surrounded by a fog of horror, trying to make what she'd found in her dressing room square with the reality she'd known. Sheer instinct that she must hide anything connected with the treason plot was her only guide at the moment. It was all that kept her from screaming, "Good God! He's dead! Shot in my room! What do I do?"

Vince was speaking, but it took a moment for his words to cut through her confusion.

"I thought maybe you were sore at Mr. Bromfield. Looking for him to chew him out for his trick. A dumb trick, if you ask me!"

It took a moment for Jess to connect the subject of Vince's irritation with what she'd found in her dressing room. When she did, Jess automatically fired off in a low voice, "Trick? Bromfield's trick? What do you know about him?"

Immediately, Jessica regretted her intensity, as Vince, taken aback, stammered, "Gee, Miss Minton, take it easy. I mean, I can see Bill the prop guy getting bent out of shape. He's so particular about his gear. But, after all, Mr. Bromfield would never actually stab you. We both know he *didn't*. You're standing right there."

Vince finished with a nervous little laugh, but Jessica didn't much notice, anxiously demanding as her understanding grew into alarm, "What? Vince, what are you talking about? What do you mean 'stab me'?"

As if she didn't have a pretty good, a pretty horrible, idea exactly what Vince meant. Taking it easy was basically beyond her at the moment.

The young man blinked under her unexpectedly fierce questioning, then replied, "The knife, here." Vince hesitantly held up the prop knife in his hands, gloved to protect them while breaking down the set. Except Jessica could see it wasn't the right weapon. The reflective gleam of light on its blade, its sharply honed edge, the care with which Vince held it, all told her that this knife was no prop. It was for real. Wait, hadn't Frederick Bromfield been nervously handling the weapon before tonight's performance? Hadn't he once assured her that she was safe because he always checked to make sure he had the right knife? The *right* knife. The uncharacteristic balefulness of Bromfield's stare when she'd resisted him in the Desirée Cafe lowered in Jessica's thoughts. Why had he been so interested in the contents of the package, anyway?

Vince was going on, "He used a real one. I found it when I was clearing the props after the stabbing scene. Like I said, he, obviously, never would have hurt you. And he was careful not to. He stuck the knife right there, away from you, in the bed. Let's face it, who could think the old gent would hurt a fly?"

Who, indeed? She or James might think so. No, Jessica would *know*, because only she was aware that Frederick Bromfield hadn't intentionally missed her; only she knew that her life had been saved by the sting of a wasp she now blessed! Vince was saying something more to her. Maybe how surprised he was that the old guy had such a devilish streak in him? Jessica wasn't sure, because that rush in her ears was blotting out almost everything around her. *Damn it!* She would not faint! She would not turn all gushy and helpless! But she sure wouldn't mind sitting down on that bed over there. How much death could a girl face in the space of ten minutes — especially when one of those fatalities might have been her!

Jess reached the edge of the bed, with still enough presence of mind to be careful of her wasp injury, and sank down.

"Gee, Miss Minton," Vince apologized. "I didn't mean to get you this upset. I thought you were wise to his gag and just mad at him. Don't be upset. I'm sure that's all this was, just a gag. What else could it be?"

That last question made Jess catch herself. For so many reasons, she *definitely* could not let Vince know that Bromfield hadn't been fooling around with that knife. In fact, she'd better cool his suspicions pronto before he said something to the police, when they came, about the knife that could connect her to Bromfield's murder — and through her, probably to Crawford.

She took a quick look around and spoke quietly, making sure no one overheard her, "Of course it's a gag, Vince. But it's *not* funny. It's darned serious. This is exactly the sort of thing that could get Mr. Bromfield into deep trouble. You know Harold Vane; he could fire Mr. Bromfield, even blackball him." The kid didn't know Bromfield was past worrying about his job prospects now. He didn't know that she did, either. "Just put the knife out of the way and don't breathe a word about it to anyone, especially the stage manager. Don't even mention our conversation. No matter what. We've got to save the guy's reputation, even his career. Do you understand?"

Vince's features were intense when he promised, "You can trust me, Miss Minton. Wild horses couldn't drag it out of me. I won't do anything make Mr. Bromfield look bad, even cost him his job."

"Thanks," Jess agreed, hoping it was a good idea to demand that promise. She was so flummoxed by the horrible revelations of the past minutes that it had slipped out before she'd thought it through. She was starting to think now, though. If Vince should ever crack or just even have second thoughts once Bromfield's murder came out, her requiring that promise would make her look mighty suspicious. *Damn!* She wished she could clear her head; she was certainly in over it! Lord, she could use some professional guidance from James Crawford, but no luck there. Maybe, though, she was a little glad of that: if he weren't here, then he wasn't Bromfield's murderer. Still, to whom could she turn for help? She knew she had to call in the police, but she needed time to pull herself together. She didn't want to be alone in this right now.

"Jessica?"

The anxious eyes she raised made Larry Sanders demand from the wings "What's wrong?"

"Oh, oh, you don't know the half of it," Jessica returned shakily.

Larry swiftly crossed to her and began, "I was on my way back to meet you at the dressing room when I saw you fairly hurtling back on stage. What happened, Jess?"

Jessica gave the concerned Vince a quick glance and then assured the young man, "I'm fine, Vince. You hit the nail on the head. I had one heck of a mad on, that's all. It's just as well I didn't find our friend out here on the stage. But my temper's all spent now. Whew! Being furious really takes it out of a girl. I know you're busy. You go back to breaking down the set. Don't let me get in your way. Just remember what you promised."

Vince smiled at her. Maybe he was convinced. Maybe he just had too much to do to worry about a contretemps between temperamental actors, but thank God he let it go. The stage manager was giving Vince the evil eye for goldbricking, so the young guy moved off to finish his work. Jessica turned back to Larry, wishing she had seen exactly what Vince did with the knife. But further worries in that direction were driven from her as she saw the depth of concern for her in Larry's dark eyes. Right now she was darned glad that he was Mr. Dependable. Her only qualm, and it was a doozy, was: could she keep him from asking too many dangerous questions?

"Okay, Jessica, are you going to tell me what this is all about? Are you all right?"

Jess took a deep breath and laid her cards on the table, in a voice only loud enough for him to hear, "Larry, I know this sounds incredible, but, please believe me; Frederick Bromfield's murdered body is in my dressing room."

Larry's sympathetic expression stiffened into displeasure. Not the response she'd been looking for, though she wasn't exactly surprised.

"Jessica, I don't find this particularly humorous, especially considering what has been going on lately."

"I am absolutely serious. You've got to believe me, Larry. You ought to know me well enough to realize that this isn't something I'd joke about. I'm *not* Peter. He's clearly been shot dead. Please, come to my dressing room and see for yourself," Jessica urged intently.

Her sincerity struck a chord with Larry, and he ran a hand pensively through his wavy dark hair. Then he began with more than a hint of irritation, though not directed at her, "Do you think Peter could have planned this as one of his little jokes?"

Jessica shook her head, briefly closing her eyes to force out the memory of what was left of Frederick Bromfield's face, before answering, "I only wish it were. This is no gag, Larry."

"And what about James Crawford?" Larry questioned tightly. "He's been a bit of a dark horse all along, hasn't he? I've warned you he's dangerous."

Jessica shot Larry a sharp, indignant look. Still, she couldn't deny that he was echoing her own, earlier suspicion. Except Larry's suspicion was filled with condemnation. He wasn't seeing the possibility that James might have saved her from the man who had tried to murder her. Then how could Larry? Only she knew that Frederick Bromfield had been trying to murder her — only she and Bromfield.

Jess finally said, "You know of no concrete reason to connect the two of them." *She* did, but Larry didn't. "Don't go jumping to conclusions. Don't go jeopardizing his mission. Let's deal with the matter at hand. We need to call in the police, don't we?"

It occurred to Jessica that she might have further reassured Larry by repeating what she'd told him earlier: she'd delivered the package; she was all done with Crawford. But Jess couldn't. The earlier lie still stuck in her craw. The best she could do was skirt the truth and hope that Larry wouldn't ask any more questions.

Larry folded his arms in front of him, mulling things over and not regarding her happily while he did so. Jessica tried not to let on how tensely she waited to see if he'd bought her temporizing. At last Larry dropped his arms and said, "All right. Where's the nearest telephone?"

Logic and patriotism had gotten to him. He knew that the next reasonable step was to call the police, as well as that he couldn't chance calling attention to Crawford's mission. Jess just wished her dishonesty hadn't been part of the mix as well, good intentions or no.

"Well, there are a few phones around here. The nearest one is in... Oh, wait!" A truly disturbing possibility struck her and she worried anxiously,

"Larry, I've been out of my dressing room some time now. And I blew out of there so fast, I left it unlocked. What if... Oh, my goodness... Larry, could someone have sneaked in and moved the body? We've got to see before we call the police in."

"Really, Jessica," Larry seemed to lose patience. "Move a body out of a crowded backstage without anyone noticing?"

But Jessica had experienced far too much impossible intrigue over the past few weeks to share his skepticism. She told Larry decisively, "I'm going. You can follow me or not. We need to go back anyway to lock the door and make sure no one wanders in and disturbs the, ah, crime scene."

Jess saw Larry quirk his mouth in agreement, realizing the wisdom of her last sentence, but she didn't wait for him to voice his thoughts, moving determinedly past him backstage, down the corridor to her dressing room. She sensed Larry close behind her, though she didn't turn to him. At the back of her mind flared a brief hope that she might unexpectedly discover that this actually *had* been one of Peter's awful gags. The image of what had met her eyes when she'd turned over the remains doused that thought immediately.

They neared the dressing room. Vaguely, Jessica noted two prop men straining to carry a poorly rolled rug through the stage door. A small gathering alternately watched and offered the two men help. Iris happened to turn, recognize Jess and Larry, and grin, "Oh, you found one of them, anyway."

Jessica smiled wanly, replying, "He found me."

Iris grinned again, waved briefly to Jessica and Larry, then went off to her dressing room. At least the usually inquisitive Iris hadn't noticed her forced humor. However, Iris's query did bring an earlier question to Jessica's mind: "Larry, where *were* you and Peter at the end of the performance, anyway?"

"Jessica, this is hardly the time to start playing twenty questions."

"Yes, of course. I guess I'm trying to avoid the inevitable. All right. Let's, let's go in."

Jessica pushed past Larry, but her hand hesitated over the doorknob.

"You're sure he's dead?" Larry's voice came quietly, intently, so close to her ear that it seemed the world held only her, Larry, and the corpse.

Jessica fought down the shiver, and turned her head to face Larry with a heartfelt, "*Too* sure, Larry."

Jess's hand lingered on the doorknob. What if the body were gone? No! You couldn't just stroll into the dressing room and out again with a dead body, or a living one, for that matter. Of course there was that neat little trick Cleopatra had supposedly used to smuggle herself in to see Caesar.

Jessica whirled toward the stage door through which the stagehands had exited with their "burden." Moving instinctively toward the outside, Jess was vaguely aware of Larry pushing into her dressing room. Fine, let him think she was crazy, but she had to know if she'd been outmaneuvered.

"Jessica, I wish you'd step in here a moment."

Larry's voice halted her. No one else picked up on the overly controlled tone, but she read its command: "Get into the dressing room, pronto."

Larry stood in the middle of the floor, his back to her. It was only then that Jessica realized she was back in the room, the door closed behind her.

When Larry turned to face her, his altered stance revealed the body. Jessica tried not to cringe at seeing it again, but focusing her attention on Larry was even less comforting, his eyes shiny black stones set fathoms deep. He swiftly turned away, and she could barely detect the huskiness in his voice when he questioned: "What happened here, Jessica?"

Slowly approaching Larry, Jessica halted as he bent over the body. She started to speak. There was blood spattered on the couch. The couch she'd slept on yesterday. Right where she'd slept yesterday.

Larry abruptly crouched down by the body, and Jess snapped to in time to shift away as Larry turned it up by the shoulder. Jess heard the vague thud of the body falling back on what was left of its face. Larry looked down at the corpse, then piercingly back at Jessica.

"What's going on, Jessica?"

She'd have given her right arm to be able to confide in Larry now that death was right in the room with them, but how could she tell Larry something that might leave him just as dead?

"Going on? Larry, how on earth should I know?!" she lied, though not happily. "I just found him here. All I know is that, that is, was, Frederick Bromfield, and he's dead."

Larry's eyes probed resolutely at the strained mask she'd thrown over her features. She turned away, and her glance fell on her blood-stained dressing gown, on the floor by the couch.

Before Larry could press her further, Jessica asked, "Larry, can't we cover this up with something? I have a couple of blankets in the closet."

Larry hesitated, then observed, "We have to notify the police, first. I don't think they'd want us disturbing the remains. Though I wish I hadn't forgotten myself by turning him over just now. I'm afraid the Doubting Thomas got the better of me. Damn Peter's influence."

The police had slipped Jess's mind, but James Crawford's warnings about the dangers of involving them came back with a vengeance. Would she have to lie to them to protect him? What about protecting herself? Frederick Bromfield had wanted her dead. His using a real knife instead of a prop in the play's murder scene proved it. Had he told anyone else about her? Had James done this to Bromfield to save her?

"All right, Jessica?"

"Oh, yes," Jessica shot back, then ruefully added, "Right as anyone can be under the circumstances."

"He was a friend of yours."

Jessica dropped her eyes under Larry's unexpected sympathy, under her own realizations about Frederick Bromfield's "friendship."

"Say, what are you two up to?" came Peter's cheery inquiry from the doorway, his eyes on his sister-in-law.

Preoccupied with fathoming Larry's contemplations, Jessica returned absently, "Covering a dead body, Peter."

"No. Really. What are you doing?" Peter good-naturedly insisted, not looking into the room as he turned and closed the door behind him.

"We've just covered a dead body," Larry tiredly informed Peter.

"Okay. I can take a joke. Come off it now, guys . . ." Peter stopped in mid saunter when Larry stepped aside to reveal that this was no joke. It took Peter barely a moment to exclaim, "That's a dead body!"

"There's no buffaloing you, Peter," Jessica remarked wearily.

Peter ignored her to continue staring at the still form on the floor. Larry was the one to speak, with a bit of asperity, "As I was saying, we have to contact the authorities, Jessica."

"Contact the authorities," Peter agreed decisively, never removing his eyes from the object under discussion.

Jess surveyed Peter before concluding, "Peter, you look worse than I feel. Better step out of the room for a minute. In fact, maybe you should go for the police."

"Right, get the police," Peter agreed, his tone was businesslike but he seemed dazed.

Jessica turned back to Larry, "You didn't touch anything, did you, Larry? You don't want to have destroyed evidence."

"No, no, of course not. You saw that I only turned over... Peter, are you still here?"

"Right. I'm still here," Peter concurred, still staring at the corpse.

"Weren't you going for the police?" Jessica gently prodded.

"Yes, yes, I was."

But Peter didn't move.

Jessica headed off Larry's impatience with Peter by saying, "I'll make the call, Larry. In fact, come to think of it, there's usually an officer on the premises. I'll get him. You splash some cold water on Peter's face. Try to snap him out of it."

As she passed Peter, Jessica put a hand on her brother-in-law's arm and reassured him, "It's okay, Peter. Larry will take care of you."

It was less than ten minutes later, though it seemed an eternity, that Jessica returned to her dressing room, Officer Max Gate in tow. When she pushed open the door, Larry and Peter were, oddly enough, checking out something above the couch. They turned around abruptly as Jessica and the policeman entered, their expressions definitely troubled by what they seemed to have discovered in Jessica's absence.

"Mmph," was Gate's eloquent assessment of the tableau. He began an examination of the room. Jess was aware that after exchanging glances, Larry and Peter looked at her. What was *that* about?

Unexpectedly, Larry encircled Jessica with his arm and turned her away from viewing the remains of Frederick Bromfield.

Seeing his sister-in-law's pallor, Peter seemed to conclude that she needed to get out of the room, never mind just not face the corpse. He suggested, "Jess, would you like to get out of here?"

Jessica briefly closed her eyes before wearily replying, "You know it, Peter."

"Officer, would you mind if we removed to another room? Miss Minton is a little off just now," Larry requested.

Max Gate had to translate "removed" to "went," but his response was quick enough, "Yeah, all right, but," he turned to Jessica, "have you people moved anything around since the murder?"

"I don't remember," Jessica answered. "I don't think so. Larry? Peter?"

They shook their heads, and Jess turned back to Officer Gate, "No, not that I can think of. But I guess our fingerprints should be all over. The three of us were in here before the play. I'm also afraid that both Larry and I turned over, the um, remains. But we barely touched... him. I'm sorry."

"Mmph. Okay, you in the gray suit, take her out of here, but stay in the building. I want to speak to this other guy, here. Neither of you say anything to anybody else until I give you the okay."

Jessica and Peter nodded. Jessica hesitated uneasily. Why detain Larry? Before she could ask, Peter ushered her out.

They leaned against the wall outside the room, relieved that almost everyone had gone home by now, although that probably wouldn't please the police. Peter finally broke the taut silence with, "Jessica, why would anyone want to kill that guy?"

Jess shook her head. "I hadn't exactly expected it."

"No, I guess you wouldn't have? You're just part of a harmless little theater group, right? Who would picture any of *you* getting mixed up with criminals, murderers? People take these sorts of things for granted when they see them in the *Times* — then, when something happens under their noses, it knocks the pins right out from under them. That's what shakes up the average Joe, when crime comes knocking on *his* door. Your friend really seemed like a nice old gentleman to me, what I saw of him, what I remember you saying about him. Who'd have expected any crooks to have it in for him? Let me tell you, no matter how much I see, I'm always knocked for a loop when it hits this close to home. Think about it: we get all het up worrying about the Axis wiping us out and forget that there are plenty of dangerous lowlifes ready to do the job right here at home. It just gives me the creeps to realize how unsafe any of us really is."

Jess looked at her bewildered brother-in-law, bleakly amused. Imagine if he knew the whole story! She couldn't let him stand there and stew, though. She couldn't let herself, either, so she asked, "Peter, what happened to you and Larry at the end of . . ."

The policeman and Larry joined them. Jess clammed up, seeing Larry so strained and preoccupied. He smiled tiredly at her before explaining, "I'm afraid I've been elected to help take measures to ensure no one else leaves here before the detectives arrive. Why don't you see if your friend Iris will let you stay in her dressing room until this is over?"

"Good idea, Larry," Jessica agreed. "Do you think, though, that I could get my suit out of there, so I can change out of this floozy outfit? It's hanging in the closet, by the door. Getting it shouldn't disturb the room."

"I'll see, Jessica."

Larry moved toward the policeman, who was instructing some of the stagehands and performers. The two conversed for a moment. Then the policeman seemed to agree reluctantly, but only after checking the suit to make sure it had no bearing on the murder. When Larry handed Jessica her outfit, his eyes sought to steady her, and for a moment she gratefully relaxed. But only for a moment. Making her way to Iris's dressing room, Jess pondered how she could be heel enough to deceive such a good scout. Well, she had to protect him, protect him and Crawford. And she knew feeling like a heel had more to do with deceiving Larry about what happened on the Brooklyn Bridge than about everything else that had occurred over the whole past few weeks combined.

After the policeman had spoken to her, Iris was percolating with questions while Jessica changed into her pin-striped, russet suit. Here she went again, stonewalling yet another friend. What she wouldn't give to just pour out everything troubling her, the way she and Iris used to do in their late-night, diner girl-talks. But Jessica Minton wasn't going to risk drawing Iris into this mess, too. At last, Iris decided to slip out, having finally realized that pressing her friend on this gruesome subject was only torturing Jess.

Peter had retired to the men's room to gather strength, and now Jessica found standing alone in front of Iris's mirror a mixed blessing. No one plagued her into reliving the horrible experience. She even had a crackerjack opportunity to put together a convincing cover story for the police, though she didn't relish lying to them. Until the package had dropped into her life, she'd always challenged adversity openly and taken her lumps right up front. So, she wasn't happy that the best plan she could come up with was no lies, only omissions — even for a good cause, even to help save Allied lives.

And what if Larry put two and two together? Jess frowned darkly into the mirror, without thinking, picking up Iris's brush and tapping it impatiently on her palm. A murder in her dressing room wasn't exactly a ringing endorsement of her claim she'd put all danger behind her by getting rid of the package. Had she told Larry much about the niece and the boyfriend story? Would he assume Bromfield's death was connected to that situation?

"Damn!"

In her frustration, she'd snapped the handle off Iris's brush. She wanted to be out of here. But where? Where was she going, period? She needed to talk to Crawford. Was that what galled her the most, needing his advice to make her next move? Or was it more frightening to consider that if Frederick Bromfield had been on to her, others might be as well? She wanted control of her life back, but how could she take control when she didn't know the facts?

"Jessica?"

It was only Larry. Jess raised a hand to her chest and briefly closed her eyes with relief before pointing out, "Larry, this is not the sort of evening for sneaking up on a girl."

He shifted, clearly more uncomfortable than amused by her joke. Jessica's brow wrinkled as Larry turned away to close the door behind him before facing her again.

"Jessica, there are a few things we need to set straight between us before the police start their inquiries."

"I don't understand," Jessica temporized cautiously, understanding very well.

"Jessica, I never once heard you mention any regret or anger at the murder of a man you worked with. Someone you told me sought you out when he was distant with the others. One would think a stranger had died."

"Shock," Jessica countered calmly.

"Possibly, but the timing of this unfortunate incident is rather significant, don't you agree?"

With cool indignation, Jessica retorted, "To hear you talk, anyone would think that *I* killed the man."

"Don't be ridiculous, Jessica," Larry snapped, "and don't try to cloud the issue with exaggerations. It seems a strange coincidence that this fellow should be murdered right after you became involved with Crawford."

"I told you that's finished!" Jessica shot back. "Now that that mess is over and done, I hope you won't be indiscreet in front of the police and undo all the hard work we put into carrying out our mission. It would be a fine kettle of fish if you made all our worry go for nothing."

Larry regarded Jessica speculatively, finally saying, "I don't want to see you fall into a trap you can't get out of."

"I'm not as naive as you think," Jessica replied quietly. She turned away from her companion, only to grimace painfully as her wasp wound made unanticipated contact with the dressing table.

Her expression had been reflected in the mirror and Larry softened, "Jess, what's wrong?"

"Nothing, nothing," she answered, leaning carefully against the dressing table. Rubbing her hand against her forehead, she continued, "I was stung by a wasp in an inauspicious location."

"Sorry, Jess," Larry offered, "I didn't mean to ride you so hard. You know how I feel about you. I'm just worried."

"That's okay. Worse things can happen to a girl."

"I'm back," Peter offered somewhat less than cheerfully as he pushed open the door and rejoined them.

Jess kindly suggested, "Peter, sit down. You look terrible."

Sitting heavily in a chair across the room, Peter worried, "I just wish I could have called Liz. I imagine the cop has good reasons for not letting us get in touch with anyone until after the detectives arrive, but I'd rather not have Liz fret about our being late."

"Cheer up, Peter," Jess teased. "We'll tell Elizabeth the names of everyone who held us here and kept her in the dark. I wouldn't want to be in their shoes."

A peremptory knock riveted all three.

"Detective Winston," an abrupt voice from the other side of the door announced.

Larry, closest to the door, quickly opened it with, "Come in."

The man who entered was exceedingly short. An overworked overcoat hung heavily on him, and a fedora was pulled down on thick black hair. His wearily lived-in face caused Jessica to blink with recognition.

"You look exactly like . . ." she began incredulously before the detective cut her off.

"Save it, lady. I've heard it before."

And he clearly hadn't enjoyed it, and certainly wouldn't enjoy it again at this time of night, especially so close to going off shift.

Peter, however, seemed to have left his perception and tact in the men's room, "He does! You're the image of him!"

"Who? What are you two talking about?" Larry interjected, glancing from one friend to the other.

"What's the matter, buddy? Don't you like comedy?"

There was weariness, and warning, in Winston's tone — unfortunately, Peter didn't heed the latter.

"I'll be, but I've never seen anyone who looked so much like Moe Howard of the Three Stooges. Say, you don't know any of the routines do you?"

"Yeah, I'm a laugh a minute down at the station."

The cold stare accompanying that crack struck home at last.

Trying to weasel out the embarrassing situation, Peter attempted to change the subject nonchalantly, "So, ah, you're one of the detectives?"

"Smart one, ain't you?"

Seeing that Winston was not appeased, Jessica tried to smooth things over with, "I guess we got off on the wrong foot, Detective. I'm sorry."

"Both my feet are pretty sore this time of night lady," he answered wearily, but a touch less sourly.

"Hence the term 'flat foot,'" Peter deadpanned.

The sour look returned, focused squarely on Peter.

"Er, I think I'll be quiet, Captain."

"Sergeant." Turning to Jessica he surmised, "You're Jessica Minton?"

She nodded, hoping Peter really would clam up before she had to gag him.

Winston faced the men, and Larry volunteered, "I'm Laurence Sanders."

"And Milton Berle over there?"

"Peter Hennessey," Peter admitted sheepishly.

Facing Jessica again, Winston calmly fished a notebook and pen from the depths of his coat pocket and queried, "You're the one who found the body?"

A quick glance to Larry, and Jessica answered, "Yes, just after the performance."

Winston nodded, "Suppose you tell me exactly how you found the body and what happened afterwards. Try to tell me everything you remember."

Jessica hesitated uncomfortably. Winston noticed. "Sorry to drag up lousy memories, Miss Minton, but I have to know all the facts. You want us to get the murderer, don't you?"

"You're absolutely sure he didn't kill himself?" Larry interrupted, something definitely on his mind.

"There's a man shot point blank in the face and no gun in the room. If it's a suicide, that means the weapon must have strolled out on its own. What do you think?"

Larry pressed his lips together, but didn't say anything.

Jess wondered whether he was annoyed at Winston's sarcasm or worried that Bromfield's death was linked to Crawford. From espionage to murder wasn't such a big leap, and nothing dangerous or mysterious had ever happened to her until she'd gotten involved with James Crawford. Well, she was worried enough for both of them tonight.

"Go ahead, Miss Minton."

"Yes," Jess began slowly. "Well, I went to my dressing room, after we all took our bows — Oh, did anyone tell you, Detective Winston, that Mr. Bromfield missed curtain call? We were all wondering what happened to him.

I guess we know now." She shook her head, "I'm sorry, this isn't very pleasant to rehash. Anyway, I went in, saw the body, went to it, turned it over — he was face down — and when I saw that face I'm afraid I just couldn't... I just, just ran out of the room. I didn't stop until I hit the stage. I couldn't think."

"That's true," Larry concurred. "She ran right past me. It took me a minute to get my bearings and follow her."

Winston studied Larry briefly then nodded to Jessica, "Go on."

"I told Larry what happened, and he came back to the dressing room with me. He looked at... the body. We decided I should contact the police. Officer Gate can tell you the rest."

"Mmm." Thinking before continuing, he looked squarely at her for, "What about the room? Anything out of the ordinary?"

"No, not that I can think of. Oh, well, I did see my dressing gown bloodied up. I didn't look around much, though. I wasn't exactly in the best frame of mind for sight-seeing."

Winston didn't say anything, but he didn't seem all that satisfied with her answer. He looked up at Larry, who had moved to stand supportively behind Jessica. "What happened with you?"

Jessica exerted a mighty effort not to warn Larry with a sharp glance to keep quiet about Crawford and the package.

"Everything happened as Miss Minton said. I saw her race past me down the corridor. . ."

"You were coming from your seat?"

"Not exactly. I'd received a telephone call near the close of the play. An usher contacted me. It was about a report I'd misfiled at work. I'm afraid Miss Minton was off-stage when I left to take the call, though I rather imagine she'd have been too focused performing to notice my absence. I'm afraid I'm not as much of an expert on the workings of an actress's mind as I'd like to be."

Was that a dig? Jess caught Detective Winston almost imperceptibly checking out her reaction. This was one of those rare moments when Jessica wished she smoked.

"Where did you take the call?" the detective inquired, preoccupied with fishing through one of his overcoat pockets.

"In an alcove off the lobby," Larry answered, slightly craning his neck with curiosity while Winston searched his pockets.

"Mmm, I suppose there were some other people around when you were on the phone?" the detective queried as he finally pulled out a battered pack of Lucky Strikes.

"Yes, especially after I got off the phone."

Winston expressed a silent inquiry as he lit up.

"You see, Detective, by the time I got off the phone the play was over, and I was somewhat overwhelmed by people leaving through the lobby. I had rather a difficult time getting through them to return to my seat. I wanted to get back to Peter. I thought he might be back in his seat by then."

"You left early, too?" Winston queried of Peter, after flicking his cigarette ash in Iris's scallop-shaped, Miami Beach souvenir ashtray.

"Well, yes, I guess so. It's a little embarrassing, Detective. You see, I had Brussels sprouts at dinner, and, shall we say, they were trying to wend their way torturously to release? Common courtesy suggested I visit the men's room — and, I'm afraid I was too painfully preoccupied to notice anyone who could alibi me."

"Wait a minute! You mean neither of you saw the end of our performance?"

Three gazes fastened on Jessica. Maybe these were not the circumstances to stand on professional pride.

"Sounds as if the two of you have worse jobs than I do, what with misfiled reports and chronic indigestion," Winston mused agreeably over his cigarette.

"We both work for the government," Peter agreed.

"Oh?" This with amiable interest. "What department?"

Larry and Peter exchanged hesitant glances, and Larry shot back, "Transportation, but we're not at liberty to discuss it. The war and all; everything is considered sensitive now."

Jess's glance swept the three men. This conversation had taken an odd turn. Winston surprised her further by seeming to consider their answer but then switching the subject.

"So, after you went back to look for your friend at Miss Minton's dressing room?"

"I went backstage and everything happened just as Miss Minton stated. I'm afraid I can't add anything to what she has said."

"You didn't notice anything unusual about the room?"

"Actually, now that you mention it, I did," Larry recollected with a quick collaborative glance to Peter. "Both Mr. Hennessey and I noticed it."

Jessica perked up, studying Larry with intense curiosity.

"What'd you notice, Sanders?"

"The window, over the divan, was pulled somewhat out of its frame and cracked, as if it had been pressured open and slammed back into place in a hurry."

Peter nodded.

Jessica protested, "No, I don't understand. I remember staring up at the window just after seeing that face. The image of the window and... that face sort of merged in my mind, but the window wasn't cracked. I remember that. It wasn't cracked."

"Maybe he climbed up on the couch to get out and got careless when he left, slammed the window behind him," Peter conjectured. "If he cracked the window that way, he must have snuck out after Jess found the body. That's probably why he was in such a hurry when he left."

"Wait a minute, just a minute," Jessica cut in, her voice trembling. "Are you trying to tell me the murderer was hiding, still in the room, when I saw the body?"

Larry placed a hand on her shoulder and said, "But you're still here."

"He could have killed . . ."

Winston took over. "But he didn't. That danger's past. You're not expecting to be running into this guy again, are you?"

How could she tell Winston that the rest of her life might be comprised of similar circumstances if Frederick Bromfield were a Nazi and had talked to his fifth columnist pals about her? But was she appearing too anxious in front of Larry? He could connect this to Crawford and the package. No, that was jumping to conclusions. She'd just found a corpse in her dressing room; she had every right to be rattled.

Oblivious to Jessica's distress, Peter advised, "You'd better go out and dust for prints, Detective. Check the alley outside the window for clues."

"Thanks, Sherlock, but Detective Hodiak and I have already outguessed you," Winston calmly quashed Peter. Turning to Jessica, he asked, "Did you know Bromfield very well, Miss Minton?"

Jessica made a weary gesture with her hand before replying, "We worked together once before. Working together usually makes a cast like a family, not always a happy family, but a family. However, Mr. Bromfield was pretty reserved. Not unfriendly; he just valued his privacy. None of us knew much about his private life. Just recently, though, he did start talking to me about it."

Winston nodded, "So with his new urge to gab, did he ever tell you about anyone bothering him? Threatening him? Did he seem worried or upset lately?"

Bromfield had certainly mentioned a mutual enmity with James Crawford, but Jess wasn't about to give that away.

"I'm not exactly certain Mr. Bromfield had enemies. The closest I can remember to his having an enemy was some fellow seeing his niece. I guess he was giving the girl a hard time. This was a few weeks back, and he had told me not too long ago that the problem was settled. I don't know if it's important. I'm afraid I don't know the gentleman's name, and I only know the niece's first name, Fritzi. He never mentioned a last name, address, anything. I just hope I'm not dragging in an innocent party."

Winston pointed out so matter-of-factly that he didn't look up from writing in his notebook, "No one's going to be dragged in to take a bum rap, least not during my investigation."

He turned abruptly to Larry, who was watching Jessica speculatively.

"What about you, Sanders? Did you know Frederick Bromfield or anyone who wanted to harm him?"

Jessica watched Larry with studied calm. Her hand tightened on the back of her chair, but no other sign of tension escaped her.

"I'm afraid I didn't know Mr. Bromfield very well, just enough to say hello." Larry hesitated, briefly glancing at Jessica, then, "As for knowing anyone who would want to kill him," here a brief pause, "I'll have to say no. As I said, we talked, but never concerning anything so personal."

Jessica looked down, her expression masking her relief. Had even her quiet reaction been noticed? Apparently not, for Winston turned his attention to Peter.

"How well did you know Bromfield, Hennessey?"

"I could identify his name on the program, but that's about the size of it."

"You wouldn't know of anyone threatening him — or any reason someone might want him dead?"

Peter shook his head. "No, I'm afraid not. Sorry."

Winston nodded, then crushed out his cigarette in Iris's souvenir ashtray, right next to Jessica. She started.

He addressed them all thoughtfully, "Now, think about this, all of you. Did you hear anything like a gunshot at any time during the evening? Even a car backfiring?"

Peter and Larry shook their heads.

Larry added, "I wouldn't really notice that sort of thing, I don't think. I didn't hear anything out of the ordinary, at any rate."

"Isn't that odd?" Jessica interjected. "I mean, shouldn't we have heard something? How can a gun be silent?"

"Maybe the murderer used a silencer," Peter suggested knowingly.

"I think you've been watching too many Alfred Hitchcock movies," Larry cut in.

Winston's only response to the dig was a faint smile before he went on, "Did any of you notice anyone different backstage? Anybody you aren't used to seeing?"

Larry pointed out, "Peter and I wouldn't recognize most of the people who are supposed to be here."

Winston faced Jessica.

She shook her head.

"I can't remember noticing anyone unusual, but I wasn't looking, either. When I think about it, though, I did see two fellows carrying off a rug after I found... Mr. Bromfield. I only saw them from the back."

Jessica was in the midst of complying with Winston's request for a description when a knock on the door interrupted. A plainclothes man almost as night-wearied as Winston opened the door and trudged in. He nodded to

Jessica and her companions, before remarking with leisurely black humor to Winston, "Yeah, he's dead, Jim, all righty."

"Finished already, Joe?"

"Yep. The boys from the lab are still at it. I went through the coats in there. Nothin'."

"You went through our coats?" Peter flared.

"Yeah. Relax, mister. I just said you were clean, didn't I?" Hodiak shot back, before turning back to Winston. "How 'bout you, Jim? Finished yet?"

"Just about. You don't have to wait in here for me."

"Okay. I gotta make a call anyways. See you in a few minutes."

Hodiak left.

Winston turned back to Jessica, "Now, for the rest of your description?"

Jessica complied, and Detective Winston glanced over his notes before querying, "Anything else?"

"Actually, yes," Jessica added. "Did anybody tell you that the stage-door watchman was out tonight? Without him, anyone could wander in or out. When the play's on, nobody has time to pay attention to anything but his job."

"Mmmph." Winston paused to consider, but then only said, "Okeydokey, that about covers everything."

Snapping up her purse and almost bouncing to her feet, Jessica startled all three men.

Embarrassed by her over eagerness, she asked in a subdued voice, "Oh, may we go now?"

"Sure. Just give me your addresses and numbers, so I can contact you when I need you."

The three complied, but Jess couldn't help stewing over the "*when*," not "*if*, I need you." It wasn't over. Not by a long shot.

CHAPTER ELEVEN

What a relief to push open the front door, close and lock it behind her, then flip on the dim entranceway light in the safety of her own home, Jessica thought. After everything that had happened tonight, she wished that she *could* find James Crawford behind or under something. It was rough enough to discover a murder victim in her dressing room, but to realize that she had nearly been a victim, herself — brrrr! On top of that was an unnerving ride home. Since she lived closer to the theater Larry had to drop her off first. But for the entire drive, he had repeatedly shot her speculative glances out of the corner of his eye. Cogitating on what she wasn't telling him? Luckily for her, Peter's anxiety to get home to Liz, *tout de suite*, had reprieved Jess from being pressed for information she was in no position to give right now.

A familiar thumpety-thumpety-thump snapped Jess from her brooding, as Dusty galloped up from the living room like a miniature wild pony. The gray tabby skidded to a stop with a peremptory "Braow!" Before Jessica could speak, the cat made an impatient little circle or two, closing with a flick of her tail.

"Dusty? What is it? What's wrong?"

Dusty gave an insistent cry, anxiously circled again, then beckoned once more with her tail.

"Don't tell me you want me to follow you?"

Dusty stared back hard and now snapped her tail as much to wisecrack, "No, I want you to dance with me! Will you come on, stupid?!" before trotting into the living room.

Something was wrong here. Still, Dusty would be the last creature in sight if there were danger.

"Rrraow!"

Dusty had returned to the top of the steps leading into the living room, her disapproval intimidating.

"All right, already. I'm coming. This better be good."

Tail sailing high, Dusty descended into the less well-illumined living room. What if some Nazis had slipped Dusty a little Polish-ham bribe?

"Raow! Aow!"

"Sorry, Dusty. I know you're no quisling," Jessica replied, feeling silly that she was whispering. She'd be more at ease once she'd flicked on the Chinese-lady lamp, so she could see better. All she had to do was get down these . . .

"Argh!"

"Aaow!"

"Shoot! Damn that hurts!"

Stairs.

Jessica sat nursing her aching shin. Dusty had finally stopped hissing and growling. Cats really did get underfoot way too easily. A feline nuzzle and head-butt assured Jess that she and Dusty were still pals. She put her head down against Dusty's. That was when she heard the faint groan.

Trembling with adrenalin, Jessica scrambled over to the lamp — on foot or hands and knees, she wasn't certain. Dusty had fairly galloped across the room to make antsy figure eights before the closed study doors. Now she was scratching at the door, glaring back at Jessica, and scratching some more. The groaning belonged to a woman, and Jess knew of only one woman who would poke around her apartment when she was out at night.

As soon as Jessica had pushed open the study doors, Dusty shot in.

The faint moonlight coming through the broken window wasn't quite strong enough to reveal anyone right away, but Dusty's anxious signal helpfully called her human's attention to the left.

"Oh my God," Jessica breathed at the sight of that vague heap at whom Dusty tentatively pawed.

The young woman dashed across the room. Before she reached the figure, it had stirred just enough to push Dusty weakly away and mutter irritably. Jess would know that grumble anywhere.

"Elizabeth, my God!

Jessica knelt by her sister's side, tentatively touching Liz's shoulder. Muttering something about swearing off Stingers, Elizabeth groggily forced herself up, Jess gingerly helping. Dusty had finally relaxed, convinced the humans, at last, had the situation well in paw.

"Liz, are you all right? What happened? Who did this to you? Are you okay?"

"Oh, I'm fine — except for having been hit over the head with a barn door. Oow."

Jess winced with her sister as Liz put a cautious hand to her head and muttered, "Maybe if I'd worn the pompadour it would've just bounced off."

"Maybe," came Jessica's quiet voice.

Elizabeth steadied herself enough to grasp her sister's arm and say, "Just get me over to a chair, so I can sit on something aside from this floor, okay, kid? Then, um, get me a stiff one."

While Dusty supervised, Jessica tenderly helped her woozy sister over to the love seat, quipping, "Look at the window over there. It figures *your* assailant would be a neatness nut and clean up the glass after he broke in."

"Fingerprints. Must have been afraid of leaving fingerprints," Elizabeth grumped.

Even in the moonlight, Liz looked direly pale. Blaming herself, Jessica couldn't bring herself to say anything more.

Dusty leaped up on the love seat to keep an eye on Elizabeth, while Jessica hurried to get her sister some liquid fortification. She flipped on a light before shakily pouring out a shot of brandy. Turning around, Jess set the glass heavily down on the bar at what she saw, bursting out, "No, oh, no!"

Elizabeth peered at her sister warily through the long fingers supporting her forehead, and slowly said, "Jessica, don't tell me there's someone behind me."

"The safe, Liz. The door's hanging open. Someone cracked it."

Elizabeth started to turn abruptly, and immediately regretted her curiosity. Dizzily leaning back, Liz demanded, "The package? They got it?"

"No," Jess replied slowly, still studying the open safe. "No. I anticipated this might happen and hid it elsewhere."

Elizabeth's mouth twisted, "Jessica, you may not have noticed, but I'm not exactly in the mood for melodrama right now, especially with Gene Krupa doing a drum solo inside my head."

"I'm sorry, Elizabeth. Here, drink this. It'll revive you a bit. Thank God you're all right."

After a few sips, Liz recovered enough to ask, "So where *is* the package, Jess?"

"In a good hiding place. Don't worry," she answered, with a preoccupied glance at the violated wall safe. Jess drew a chair nearer to Elizabeth and sat down, giving her sister some time before pressing, "What happened, Liz?"

Elizabeth recovered enough to smooth out the full skirt of her black voile dress, then pushed on, "I know this sounds crazy, Jess, but you know how I get my funny feelings? All day I sensed something was wrong. Something was going to happen tonight. It started in the morning and just grew worse and worse. I couldn't go to the play. I lied to Peter, sort of — told him I wasn't up to sitting still through a play, not the way I was feeling. I didn't tell him my brainstorm to come here and protect the package. Anyway, I'd just hung my coat and stepped down into the living room to turn on the light there, when I heard something behind me. I was so stupid. Why didn't I turn on the lights when I came in? Anyway, the minute I turned the lamp on, bam! Someone let me have it good on the back of the head. That's all I remember."

"That's it?"

"That's not enough?"

"Yeah," Jessica agreed, wearily unbuttoning her jacket. "It's more than enough. I guess he dragged you in here, the creep who knocked you out."

"I certainly didn't stroll in on my own. The creep must've figured that if anyone else came in before he was done, he didn't want a body in the middle of your living room subtly hinting something was wrong. Never mind that, Jess, are you certain the package is safe? Maybe you'd better check it."

"Maybe," Jessica replied, rising slowly.

Elizabeth got up with surprising sprightliness for someone who'd been conked on the noggin, although she swayed slightly. "Shall we look?"

"*We* shall do nothing," Jessica apprised her sister sternly. "Wasn't that love tap enough to cool your ardor for mystery?"

"There's no harm in just seeing the package. Besides, Jess, there might be no connection between this break in and your package. Maybe this was just your average Joe-Schmoe burglar. He only knocked me out. He didn't kill me. I don't think those people after the package would be that careless with a loose end."

"Yes," Jess agreed painfully, recalling the knife that had nearly silenced her and the successful, brutal elimination of Frederick Bromfield.

"Jess, why don't you go into the bedroom and check your jewelry box, see if anything's missing? I'll check the safe. I know you keep your financial documents in there, the stocks and certificates Peter manages for you. Then we can see if I played hostess to a *real* burglar. Hey, why are you looking at my necklace like that?"

"I was thinking, Liz. If the guy who broke in here were only a thief, would he have left you with those pearls or your ring or your watch, for that matter?"

Elizabeth's hand went to her necklace. "Oh, I guess he... well, it was dark. He might not have seen them, or he might have been after bigger game."

"I suppose . . ."

"Go ahead, Jess. Go to the bedroom and check."

Jessica hesitated.

"Go ahead, Jess. I'll check the safe. See if they took any valuables."

"Okay, all right," Jessica sighed, adding to Dusty, "Come along, cat."

Cat and human exited the room. Jess couldn't put her finger on it, but Liz's suggestion that this was only a burglary seemed dubious. Too good to be true, too much of a coincidence. Jess didn't spare the lights on her way to the bedroom.

When she did return to the study, Jessica had a cold, damp cloth in hand. Dusty was staring down Elizabeth, who was still peering into the safe.

"Looking for my Christmas list, Liz?"

"Good grief! Don't sneak up on me! Not tonight! I can't figure out half of what these papers mean. How can I tell if anything's missing? If I hadn't gotten sapped, I'd have figured this better and switched with you. Jewelry I know about." Before Jessica could relate what she'd found in the bedroom, Liz cut her off with, "Hey, what's that in your hand?"

"A compress, for your head. How are you feeling? You look awfully pale, still. Maybe you ought to sit down."

Elizabeth nodded, but very gently. "Thanks, kid."

She took the cloth, frowning at doing further damage to her coiffure, but applied the compress where it would do the most good and sat down.

"Liz, I think I'd better call you a doctor," Jessica began, concerned.

"No!"

"But your head . . ."

"I'm okay, now."

"Elizabeth, you were knocked out. That could be serious."

"Jessica, I'm okay. I just don't want to make a big deal. I'd rather Peter not know . . ."

"But if you're hurt . . ."

"I'm okay. I promise. Besides, you're the one who wants to keep everything quiet."

"Liz, if it's just a burglary . . ."

"It is, then? You did find something was missing? You've been robbed?"

"Don't sound so pleased, Liz... but yes. My jewelry box was lying on the floor, and some pieces were missing," Jess answered, sitting down across from her sister — troubled by more than her wasp sting.

"Great. I mean, at least this could be just a run-of-the-mill robbery. But you don't look so good, Jessica. What's wrong, kid? Oh! They got some of our grandmother's stuff, is that it?"

"I, I don't know. I'm not sure. It's difficult to think straight after what happened at the theater tonight, Elizabeth. Frederick Bromfield, I found him in my dressing room — shot in the face."

Liz's mouth dropped open.

"My sentiments exactly," Jessica wearily joked. She rose and restlessly paced away from Elizabeth, then turned back, "It's worse than that. Frederick Bromfield replaced the prop knife with a real one for the stabbing scene in the play. He tried to kill me tonight, Liz. He would have, too, if a wasp hadn't stung me and made me twist out of the way."

"What?! How could Bromfield possibly think he could get away with killing you? Didn't he realize sticking a knife in you might make people a little suspicious of him?"

Jessica shook her head, puzzling, "I know. I don't get that, either. Unless, well, maybe he had a plan to frame someone. Make it seem as if someone else had switched the knives."

"Someone like Crawford?"

"Maybe. It's just that I'm not sure how he'd work the frame."

"Well, Eleanor Queen, you won't have much chance of getting an answer out of him now, will you? And why would someone kill him in your room and just leave him there? Anyway, Bromfield wouldn't shoot *himself* in the face just to make sure the frame would stick."

"I do have an answer for your first question, Liz, and it's not pretty. The detective seems to think the murderer didn't have time to dispose of the body. So, the guy was, um, actually hiding in the room when I came in."

"So whoever did in Bromfield, could have done you . . ."

"But he didn't," Jessica shot back.

"Hmm. Why not?"

"What are you thinking, Liz?"

"Maybe Mr. Bromfield had a good reason for trying to frame Crawford tonight, kiddo. Maybe he knew Crawford was going to be in the theater and . . ."

"You think James Crawford murdered Frederick Bromfield!"

"Jess, he might have thought he was protecting you."

Jessica paused. That was the closest Elizabeth had ever come to defending James Crawford. "But killing someone, Liz?"

"Well, little sister, that is what war is all about."

Jessica sank down, gingerly, on a chair, protesting, "I didn't see him anywhere."

"Would you, if he didn't want you to?"

Jessica shot her sister a sharp look, the probability of Liz's conjecture striking home. And with the stage door manager out, who would notice Crawford slipping in?

Elizabeth began carefully, "Look, I just want you to be okay. Are you sure you won't grab the package and come stay with us?"

"No." Suddenly resolute, Jessica faced her sister, "No. This is my responsibility, Elizabeth. Now, don't look at me like that. I'll be safe for the time being. One murder is showy enough. A second, right on top of it, of someone close to the first victim, would make people start asking the kind of questions that would make any infiltrator awfully jumpy these days. Think about it: the F.B.I.'s arrested scores of fifth columnists over the past year or so. That makes fear of exposure a mighty big concern. And with fewer fellow quislings around, a traitor's going to be under extra pressure not to get caught, to keep up all the spying and sabotage. No, whoever's after the package will have to lay off me for a little while, anyway, if he wants to 'serve the Fatherland' over the long haul. That gives Crawford a chance to help me. He's supposed to contact me soon. Between the two of us, we'll work something out. I trust him, Elizabeth."

Elizabeth regarded her sister doubtfully.

Jess insisted, "Look, Elizabeth. This break-in really seems to be just that. Bromfield could even have been working alone. I know Crawford said he usually did, himself."

"That's a mighty big 'if,' kid sister."

"I know. But the point is we can't panic. So, do as I do. Sit tight."

"I don't like it," Elizabeth grumbled.

"It's not exactly my first choice, either, Liz."

* * * * * *

Jessica stared at her distracted features in her bathroom mirror. They'd phoned Peter, and he had shown up in a jiffy to protectively sweep Elizabeth off. A call to the police had been made about the burglary, and now Jess was fretting because it turned out she shouldn't have sent her sister home after all. Well, they'd just have to talk to Liz later. As of now, she was waiting for someone to show up, and would probably keep waiting for quite some time. So here she stood, killing time by experimenting with her hair. Several bobby pins and an awkward French roll later, it seemed she'd have been better off just pacing and brooding.

"Aow!" Dusty's interruption brought Jessica back to earth.

"Oh, Dusty, haven't you led me on enough chases this evening?"

The cat stood her ground, blinked, then offered a silent meow.

"All right. All right," Jessica agreed. Dusty uttered a joyous cat cry and ecstatically trotted into the corridor. Jessica smiled wearily at that reaction. She must be hungry. But Dusty headed away from the kitchen and parked herself before the cellar door — the gateway to her litter box.

"Ah, I see a different need is calling."

Funny how flip you could be when your entire world had degenerated into huge, jagged fragments.

Jessica reached the cellar door, her hand tightened on the knob, but she didn't turn it. Could someone be lurking down there? Dusty pawed impatiently at the door. Although she wasn't terribly enthusiastic about Dusty's leaving any little "bouquets" around, Jess was even less thrilled about leaving any dead bodies around — especially her own.

Dusty was cupping her paw under the door in an attempt to pull it open.

"Dusty, it won't work. You can't pull that door open. I have it... bolted," Jessica's voice trailed off sheepishly.

Not much chance of anyone having crept into the cellar to hide, then bolting the door *behind* him. Jessica slid back the bolt and opened the door on the darkness beyond. After Dusty trotted blithely down the stairs, Jess switched on the light by the door and followed, just to prove she had at least as much nerve as a ten-pound tabby.

The cellar still held its share of shadows, the bare bulb providing only murkiness. Jessica forced herself not to look at the grill-locked doorway in the partition separating her section of the cellar from the other tenant's. The dark, deserted area beyond would not cow her. She simply wouldn't look at it.

As she followed Dusty off to the right of the stairs, the boiler and furnace loomed ahead, almost obscuring two cellar windows. Jessica forced her attention on Dusty, who now seemed more concerned with ingestion than with the end result of digestion. The cat stood by her dishes of water and cat food by the far wall, to the left of the furnace.

"Okay, I'm here. Let's see what the problem is," Jessica said as she joined her cat. "I swear, Dusty, you lead a life of luxury. How many cats have an upstairs and downstairs dining room? Isn't the water in the kitchen good enough for you?"

Jess crouched to check out her cat's empty water dish. Picking it up, she started to rise, saying, "I wish I had someone to wait on me hand and paw . . ."

A subdued rattling halted Jess. Still crouching, she put down the dish and turned toward the window beyond the furnace and the boiler: the source of the sound. Someone trying to break in through the cellar this time? Somehow she hadn't thought of that possibility when she'd taken such comfort in the bolt on the cellar door a few moments ago.

Jess shot a quick glance to the stairs. No, by the time she reached them she'd be in plain sight, and if this intruder were armed... Frederick Bromfield's knife switch made her leery of leaving herself an easy target.

She was safe only for the moment, obscured by the furnace. So what on earth to do? She'd been lucky twice tonight. It was too damn unfair to spare her twice, only so she could die now.

Then Jessica's eyes lit on the toolbox near Dusty's dish. There was a nice, big, heavy, claw hammer. She glanced back at the window, now clearly being jimmied. Defiantly, Jess grabbed for the hammer, only to hesitate. There was also a stack of two by fours. Not many, but one was all she needed.

Quietly, careful not to give herself away, Jessica pulled one of the boards toward her. She wanted a weapon that would let her deal a surprise blow from more of a distance than the hammer would, especially important if this invader was armed.

Nerves silently screaming, Jessica poised herself behind the boiler with board in hand. What in Sam Hill was she doing?! What did she know about incapacitating assailants? The window's screen fell away, followed by the sound of an intruder landing on the cellar floor. To her horror, Dusty dashed past her into plain sight, blaring a feline greeting.

"Ah, hello there, puss."

Jessica dropped the board, shocked by the elation sweeping through her. She fairly flew across the short distance separating her from James Crawford and wrapped her arms around him, breathing a heartfelt, "Thank God you're here!"

She could feel him instinctively tighten his arms around her, his cheek against her hair. But then he was on the job again, holding her away, but not too far, and still gentle, saying, "Jessica, it's all right. We weathered the shooting just fine. You needn't worry like this."

Jessica let herself take comfort from his concern, at first. But her fears flooded back as she realized from his failure to mention any of tonight's horrors that James Crawford hadn't the faintest idea about the deep trouble they were in.

"You don't know about Frederick Bromfield. Someone murdered him, but not before he tried to kill me."

Crawford stepped back abruptly, his hands still gripping her arms, now a little too tightly. Dusty, miffed at being excluded, backed swiftly off, spitting irritably. Jessica wasn't much more pleased to see James looking at her as if she'd hit him with a frying pan. But he recovered and questioned carefully, "What happened with Bromfield, Jessica?"

Jessica had to steady herself to face his disquietingly intent stare and answer, "He was shot. In my dressing room. I discovered him. And... he'd tried to kill me earlier, by substituting a real knife for a prop in the scene where his character is supposed to stab mine."

"Jesus," James Crawford muttered, his face white and his hands tightening so much it almost hurt. "Why would he try to kill you?"

"Well, it turns out that he did see us that night. Later, he warned me about you. He even asked about the package."

"Jesus," Crawford hissed again.

"James, why do you have this expression of Columbus sailing off a flat earth? You're really making me little nervous here. I thought you had things under control. Is this your subtle way of telling me that a race horse with three broken legs has better odds than I do? I'm joking. You're not laughing."

Crawford seemed to be struggling with something, before he began carefully, "I'm sorry, Jessica. This completely violates everything... well... never mind. This is important. Exactly how much did Bromfield know about me, the package, and you? What did he *think* you knew?"

Jess swallowed then answered, "I don't think it's good. As I said, he'd seen us together that night in the fog. I pretended I had to drop in on you as a favor for a friend, but that I didn't really know you. I'm not sure he bought it. But, well, when he asked about what was in the package, I couldn't help myself. I hesitated. Maybe, maybe he thought I knew and was trying to cover up my tracks."

"Damn," James muttered, loosening his hold on Jess and shaking his head. "I don't like this. This is all wrong. I planned so carefully. I'd never have conceived that Bromfield would be allowed to threaten your life — unless something spooked him into acting on his own, and murdering him doubled as punishment and damage control."

"James, what are you talking about? What did you plan? You're not making any sense."

Crawford looked at her tiredly and agreed, "No, I don't imagine I am. But none of this makes any sense to me, either."

Why was James Crawford studying her so strangely? He seemed touched by her compassion, but there was something else in his expression. Something unnerving. He seemed, well, guilty. What the devil was going on?

James reached out and squeezed her shoulder. He seemed to be searching for elusive words that would make some blow easier for her. Finally he began, "Jessica, I'm afraid I haven't been totally on the level with you."

"I don't get you, James."

He paused again, thinking, before he continued, "Jessica, you've been grand through all this. That makes it so much more difficult to tell you something that will probably, no definitely, upset you. You must promise that no matter what I say, you will hear me out to the end. No interrupting, no passing judgment until I finish."

"Oh, of course, James. Go ahead. I'm with you."

"Right then," James agreed resignedly. "The package, just about everything I've told you in connection with it, is a hoax."

"A hoax?!"

In that moment, Jessica's whole world seemed to swirl around and down into darkness. Vaguely, she felt Crawford's hand on her arm, steadying her. But she came back to herself, bitterly tasting cruel truth and shook that betrayer's hand away with, "Do you mean that you have put Larry, my sister, and me through, through hell as part of a damn joke? Did my brother-in-law put you up to this? Do tell. I need to know whether I should plan a double funeral."

"No, no," James hastily assured Jessica, calming as he continued, "I see I used an unfortunate choice of words. I *am* an agent from England. I was assigned to work with your government after I was shot up in France and couldn't handle the kind of field work I'd been doing. What I mean to say is that there are no *genuine* secret documents in the package. I'm not trying to deliver it anywhere. The package and the story surrounding it — all the mysterious goings on — are a lure for an agent of the *Abwehr*, the Jerries' military spies. He's been passing classified information to them. Our engineers mocked up a plan, just close enough to the real thing to fool someone who isn't an engineer. We tightly packed two books in a container, then hid the documents in the books so that they could be found — but not so easily that our quarry would be suspicious.

"We've had strong suspicions about the identity of the traitor, but we needed solid evidence on which to pin our case and a gambit that would distract him from pursuing other real intelligence. I was chosen to draw up this plan and put it into action because of my past success at flushing out infiltrators. The reason I've seemed sloppy was to make our suspect think that he had an easy target suffering battle fatigue. A case of a 'play's the thing to catch the conscience of a king.'"

Jessica was so stunned, she couldn't manage a peep until James had finished. Had she been falling for someone who had only been using her, who had set her up? She pulled herself together and accused with chilling control, "You've done nothing but deceive me."

"I know, Jessica. But I had to. The plan never would have worked if you hadn't believed in it yourself. I wish I could have done this another way, especially since I've come to know you. I had misgivings about this part from the beginning, but there *was* no other way. Catching a traitor and saving lives trumps everything."

Almost numb, Jessica found herself grasping for some reality, "The man who shot at us, when you saved my life. That was real, wasn't it?"

James shook his head, reluctantly admitting, "That was all planned. My partner did the shooting. He deliberately missed you and grazed me." He paused and added, "I'm doing much better now, in case you're interested."

Jess resentfully quashed his attempt at humor with a sarcastic, "This is the same partner you told me had been murdered? That was a lie, too?"

"Yes, I'm afraid so. At the time you were so skeptical, Jessica, I had to use whatever means I could to convince you. You know how dearly every win for the Axis costs us. I felt that tricking — persuading — you to sympathize with me over a friend's death and throwing a fright into you so I could seem to protect you were the only ways open to me. I'm sorry for that. You don't know how much. But you have to consider that the stakes are so bloody high. I just wish I understood what went wrong."

Stiffly, Jessica looked away to stare at the brick wall in front of her. Had everything that had happened on the bridge only been part of a plan to nab a fiver? She'd be — no, he'd be — damned before she'd ask and let on how much that intimacy had meant to her. And she now realized just how much it had meant. It was a major battle to keep the tears from pricking through her lashes. He had to trick her by any means into helping him, huh? She'd love to help him to a fat lip! — which didn't change the fact she'd been the perfect sucker. And that was about the time she started to lose the battle with her tears.

"Look, Jessica, don't..."

Once again, she thrust away James Crawford's seemingly comforting hand.

"Okay, okay. Just can the sympathy act, Mr. Crawford. I've had more than enough of it."

He actually looked pained over what he'd done to her. She didn't need that.

"So, I was part of your bait, then? That's flattering. I suppose you were no more concerned with the fact I might be killed than you would be over the fate of a worm on your hook?"

"That's not fair, Jessica."

"I don't think *you* are in any position to talk about fair, do you?"

He raised an eyebrow.

She thought to herself, *Good, a palpable hit.*

Crawford answered her jibe quietly, "No. You have me. But my plan really wasn't like that at all. I've never made this sort of mistake before. Even in France, that time, it wasn't my plan that went awry. I researched all of you thoroughly, inside and out. You have no idea, Jessica, how conscientiously I worked out my scenario to draw him in and distract him from doing any more damage. I knew that my subject was clever, damned clever. We couldn't get enough on him to bring him in for questioning, and he'd never nip at just any bait unless it came to him through someone he trusted: you. And I set up this so that you wouldn't be hurt. I know my man and, bad as he is, there was no way in bloody hell he should have wanted you dead."

At the end, he couldn't completely choke down the guilt and anger at himself.

Too hurt and furious to hear between the lines, Jessica shot back, "*I* recognized there was something wrong about Frederick Bromfield when his mask slipped only for a moment. *I* didn't need ages of research to see the man wasn't all he pretended. All I needed was one chat."

Crawford hesitated, but both his words and his sympathetic tone revealed it wasn't her jibe that had given him pause, "Bromfield was only a lackey in a two-man cell. I'm sorry, Jessica, but the man I'm after is Larry Sanders."

Jessica had no words. She could only tighten her mouth into a shocked, angry line.

"I'm sorry for being so blunt, Jessica. I'm not always as strong on tact as I should be, and I am used to my plans working. But there's something very wrong here..."

"You better believe it, buster! Of all the contemptible, low-down, dirty lies. How dare you slander Larry Sanders! That man is loyal, good, decent! He's always been completely on the level with me, while you've done nothing but play me for a sap. Oh, you just take the cake. You think you're so clever, but, buddy, you aren't even half the man Larry is. He's the type of fellow a woman can respect, care about, rely on in a pinch. So, if you think for one minute that I'm going to let a heel like you smear..."

"Jessica, I know how fantastic all this must seem to you. How difficult it is to accept that the man you thought you might marry could be a fifth columnist. But you have to understand that these kinds of plans are not set in motion on a whim. The F.B.I. wouldn't have called on me for this assignment if they didn't have strong suspicions about Sanders. And I wouldn't have accepted this assignment without good reason. I'm not a hasty or an unjust man."

"Mr. Crawford, if you are so thorough and efficient, can you explain why you are accusing a man who volunteered to fight for England, even when he was an American citizen, in '39? Surely, your research showed that Larry has been bitter about not being able to join up ever since. That hardly sounds like the profile of a fifth columnist."

"It would if he were an agent with a clever cover," was Crawford's quiet answer. "It's just the kind of rum trick the *Abwehr* loves."

"For the love of Mike! I've had enough of your lousy insinuations! I'm going to put an end to them and you! I'm calling Larry and tipping him off to this frame up right now!"

He grabbed Jessica's arms, warning, "Jessica, you can't do that. This is bigger than you or me. Thousands of lives are at stake if we don't stop the security leak. Hate me. All right. Maybe I deserve it, maybe not. But don't sacrifice the people fighting for all our lives because I hurt you."

That struck home. He had her and she knew it. At least he didn't gloat.

"All right, Mr. Crawford. You can take your hands off me now. I'm not going anywhere. But just remember, even if I don't blow the whistle on you, it's not going to make any difference. Larry Sanders is on the square. You can't hang anything on him — and don't try to frame him, either."

"I won't need to."

He answered Jessica levelly, but she could see she'd gotten under his skin with her loyalty to Larry.

Before Jessica could say anything more, Crawford was thinking aloud, "I just have to figure out how to get you out of this."

"Can't be too soon for me."

"It's no joke, Miss Minton. I got you into this and I will get you out, but I have to protect you from Sanders. He may have liquidated Bromfield for acting on his own against you, or he may have given Bromfield the kill order."

"Don't be absurd. Larry? Never! I'm not afraid of him, but I am afraid of what you might do to him, an innocent man."

"I don't want you involved in any more of this. I'm not going to risk your life further. . ."

"Nice sentiments, Crawford, if I were in the market for them. Whatever you're up to, I want in, just so I can keep an eye on you and make sure you stay honest."

"I can't endanger . . ."

"You've already put me behind the eight ball, and I know I won't be safe until you back off Larry and find the real traitor. So, don't argue. I won't tip off Larry as long as you agree. If you don't agree, you'll be the one endangering thousands of lives."

"You're being foolish, Jessica."

"Trusting you again would be foolish. What's your plan this time, or do I go to Larry and put him wise to you?"

For a moment, Jess thought Crawford's dismay at being checkmated by her was tinged with wry admiration. But she knew better than to trust herself, or him, in the emotions department.

He began reluctantly, "I have someone who can tail Sanders, in case he tries to run, but I don't think he will. I think he'll try to brazen it out. Clearly, my mistake wasn't underestimating his boldness. Yes, my partner and I have to get into Sanders' house. Do a thorough search, strategically plant some bugs. We didn't do this earlier for fear of tipping our hand to him, but it's evident after what's happened tonight, we have to take that chance. Anyway, whatever mistakes I've made, I think I've got my man pegged well enough to know I can find sufficient evidence to snare him for good and all. So we'll have to play the odds that he's too confident of his ability to outsmart me to destroy any evidence he has hidden there. Otherwise, he would have disappeared rather than try to... tie up loose ends."

"And when you don't find anything there, when Larry's vindicated, you'll turn your attention to finding the real quisling?"

"I'll find what I'm looking for, Jessica." His voice was level, unintimidated by her scoffing, "The catch is that he has a new alarm system . . ."

"Larry doesn't have an alarm system."

"Perhaps you know much less about Sanders than you think. His housekeeper doesn't even have a duplicate key."

He wasn't insulting, but Jess still wanted to kick him.

"Go on, Crawford."

"The system is attuned to his key. If I can get that key or a copy of it, I can get in there with my assistant.

Jessica resisted the urge to ask, "The assistant you pretended was dead?" She only queried, "You expect me to just waltz off with his keys?"

"The tough part will be keeping Sanders from knowing what you're up to. I can give you a kit that will let you make the mold easily enough. Just a small metal box with clay inside; simple to carry and to conceal. Close the box and the pressure of sealing it forces an impression into the clay. Once I have that mold, I can take it from there."

"You aren't taking anything anywhere without me. Get that straight. I do think I know how I can get the key without much fuss, though. Larry's planning a dinner party for Sunday, but he has some business traveling that morning. I could tell him it would be so much easier to have Mrs. Hayward and I set up for him when he was out, and if he gave me a key to let her in . . ."

"Outright let him know you have access to a key? I'm not going make him even more suspicious of you . . ."

"There's already been one attempt on my life. *If* Larry were guilty, which he is *not*, he couldn't be any more suspicious than he is already. Besides, if you do your job right, no one will be the wiser about my making the copy and your snooping around. Anyway, you've got it all wrong. Larry is innocent, and the sooner I prove that to you, the sooner you'll start looking for the real traitor. *That's* the way to save my skin. And just to make sure you don't double-cross me, after *I* copy the key, I'll meet you there and let you in — to keep my eye on you every step of the way."

"That's too dangerous."

"And you've done *such* a bang-up job of keeping me out of danger."

Crawford's expression showed she'd struck home, but he agreed, "All right. That's what we'll do. It goes against my better judgment, but we're running out of time, and there's too much at stake. Whether you believe me or not, I don't want anything to happen to you."

"You'll forgive me if I take that line with a truckload of salt. Plain and simple, I don't like manipulators. And that's all you've been to me."

That seemed to push him over the edge. Crawford's words were biting, "Sometimes people have to play fast and loose with the truth when the outcome's so vital. *You* ought to realize that. You've been exceptional at it, yourself, of late."

Jessica reminded him coldly, "Whose dishonesty forced me into playing fast and loose in the first place? I had a deservedly good reputation as a straight shooter until I got tangled up with you. If I hadn't learned my lesson at the track, I'd let you have it on the chops again."

Crawford passed a thoughtful hand over his jaw and smiled, briefly. When he spoke, though, it was back to business, "I'd rather the visit could be arranged sooner, but this will have to do. I think you're relatively safe for now. Killing another member of the same theater company right after Bromfield's death and the attempt on you would draw too much attention from too many people."

"That's a big concern for you, I'm sure. You don't have anyone else to use as bait. Just explain one thing to me. Why this crazy, Rube Goldberg plot? Wasn't there a simpler way to ferret out your traitor without making a hash of everyone's life?"

"I wish there were, Jessica, but our quarry has proved himself too sharp for any conventional method of entrapment. We had to blindside him. Have the only person he would never suspect 'accidentally' put in his path a temptation too valuable to resist."

"I'm his Achilles heel."

"I'm sorry to say, yes. Look, I know you think you have no reason to trust me, but I never meant to bring all this down on you, Jessica. Even though this mission is everything to me, I don't want anything to happen to you. That was part of the deal for my taking the assignment."

She could almost believe those dark eyes. Her instincts... Instincts be damned! Jessica Minton wasn't going to be anybody's chump any more.

Folding her arms, she said coldly, "I think you'd better go now. There's nothing more to say, except to arrange our meeting at Larry's."

"Right."

Now his tone was pure professionalism. Jessica stamped down a flicker of disappointment. They made their plans, and he was gone. Only then did she let herself sink down on the cellar steps and have a good cry. Dusty pulled out all the stops to bring her back around: blinking, nuzzling, head butting. With that feline comfort, Jess pulled herself together. She had to if she was going to save Larry's skin — and her own!

CHAPTER TWELVE

Tuesday was one of those drizzly, raw days of early fall that left people almost wishing for the predictability of winter's ice or summer's swelter. Perhaps that was why Jessica and Liz trudged silently up the walkway to Jessica's flat. The more likely explanation was that they'd just come from a funeral — Frederick Bromfield's. It certainly explained why both were decked out in black, Jessica wearing a felt tam, a veil framing her face and pinned to her suit jacket; Liz in a straw boater and a Bergdorf Goodman gabardine ensemble.

The funeral had been a low key affair, arranged by a relative of Bromfield whom no one in the theater group knew, seemingly the last of the family. Had he known that Bromfield was a Nazi? Was he one himself? No Fritzi, either. Apparently, Bromfield had conjured her up to schnooker Jessica into sharing confidences about her own troubles, namely with the package. Well, now Jess had her answer as to why, out of the blue, Bromfield had palled up to her. Boy, was she ever tired of being everybody's patsy.

Those weren't the only bleak thoughts haunting Jessica during the service in that endless stretch of tombstones, interrupted only by the jagged line of Manhattan rising across the river. One particular suspicion had tortured her ever since the shock had worn off from Bromfield's murder and her own near miss. If Larry wasn't the quisling, who was? Only one other person closely associated with her worked in the same department as Larry: Peter Hennessey. *NO!* Peter might be able to fool her, but Elizabeth Hennessey certainly would never be able to stay with, to love, a Nazi fellow traveler. Impossible! Thank you, James Crawford, for turning me into the kind of a nut case who would even fleetingly entertain such a thought!

All she could be grateful for was the realization that the murderer couldn't have gone from the theater to her home to K.O. Liz. That cleared Larry and Peter of burglary and assault. Big fat deal. That also left them in the theater when Bromfield was murdered. Or perhaps some underling had broken into her house. Just how many people were after her, anyway?

Unlocking her door, Jess commented, "Liz, every time I come home I wonder what I'm going to find next. It's nice not to be alone this time."

"Thanks, I think."

But the two entered the apartment and made their way to the kitchen without suffering any assaults, the quiet unnerving them both. Elizabeth broke the silence by querying, "Jessica, where's Dusty? Doesn't she usually come to greet you?"

"Oh!" Jessica responded, suddenly remembering. "I can't believe that I forgot to let her up from down cellar this morning! Am I ever going to be in trouble. Ah, Liz, my warm, witty, beautiful sister..."

"No."

"I haven't asked you yet. It's not as if Dusty were a Siberian tiger. She's not going to take your leg off."

"Only going to give me a little gouge?"

Jessica's unimpressed stare persuaded Elizabeth to concede the argument.

Alone, after Liz grudgingly left to release the mini-tiger, Jessica took off her hat and veil and jacket so she could get down to the serious business of making tea and putting out cookies. As she considered which china to take down for their "funeral meats," a furious barrage of meows reached her. Jess quickly sought the liverwurst in the refrigerator to appease her feline roomie.

Dusty marched ahead of Liz into the kitchen. Preparing to unleash her anger on Jessica, the tabby was arrested by the scent of liverwurst. First things first. Dusty dived into the deli treat.

"That's what I admire about your cat, her integrity. She can't be bought for love or money. Food, that's another matter," Elizabeth observed, taking a chair at the table.

As Jess put on the kettle, Elizabeth noted, "You must have been doing quite a bit of thinking today, kid, judging from those expressions of yours during the funeral."

"Considering everything that's happened, you can't exactly blame me for having a lot on my mind," Jessica replied with forced casualness, turning from her sister to get the cups and saucers.

"Jess, are you sure you don't want to talk? Maybe I can help you."

Jessica paused before facing Liz and answering, "There's really nothing you can do. Everything's... as fine as can be under the circumstances. Try not to worry."

"Look, you're my sister and someone tried to kill you. Even if you say this Crawford character has you squared away, you still must be upset. Talking usually helps you feel better when something's under your skin."

"Liz, I've told you everything," Jess answered. And she could have just kicked Crawford for once again putting her in position where she had to lie. As she went back to the refrigerator, Liz caught her off guard with, "I know you don't trust that Crawford anymore. I just thought I might be able to fill the gap."

Jessica guardedly asked, "What makes you think I dislike Crawford?"

"I didn't say *dislike,* I said *distrust.* But skip that. It's in your attitude. When you talk about him there's just that hint of the seven-year-old eating canned spinach. What happened, Jess?"

The doorbell rang propitiously.

"Oh, would you get that, Liz? I have to measure out the tea. Thanks for being such a doll."

Elizabeth narrowed her eyes, but she left the kitchen. Winning that round didn't make Jess feel any better. Liz would just bide her time and re-launch her interrogation once the unknown caller was out of the way.

After a minute or so, Jessica realized that the bell was still ringing. What the dickens was Liz up to?

It didn't take long for Jessica to reach the foyer and find her sister leaning against the door mumbling, "I swear I'm losing my mind. That's it, I'm losing my mind."

Unnerved, Jessica questioned, "Elizabeth, what's wrong?"

Liz's eyes widened as her sister's presence brought her back to the real world. She stammered, "Oh, Jessica, you won't believe who I saw out there. You just can't imagine."

"Who? Who's out there, Liz?"

"Oh, Jessica, you just won't believe it. I can't believe it. But, Jess, this guy outside is a dead ringer for, no, it has to be..."

The phrase "dead ringer" connected.

"Oh my God! Detective Winston!"

"No, neither of them," Liz corrected.

Jessica wasn't paying attention to her sister; she was too busy shoving her aside and flinging open the door.

"Detective Winston," Jessica greeted, transforming her flurry into cordiality.

Sourly glancing behind Jessica to Elizabeth, he questioned, "Are you trying to hide something from me?"

Shooting a glare at Elizabeth, Jessica thought, *I wish I could, but you've already seen her.* Instead, she said, "Please, come in."

Winston gave a barely perceptible nod and did just that.

Immediately, Elizabeth leaped forward, punctuating her words with an accusing finger: "I know you. You're . . ."

"Detective Winston," Jessica cut in with finality.

Unfortunately, Elizabeth wasn't close enough to kick in the shins.

Liz turned to her sister with a confused, "But he looks just like . . ."

"Look-alikes do exist," Jess interrupted. "Remember how everyone thinks you look like Rosalind Russell."

"That's true, although she's older," Liz conceded serenely.

Detective Winston visibly forced himself not to roll his eyes.

"Would you like some coffee, Detective Winston?" Jessica took over as graciously as possible. Maybe sharing such a precious commodity with Winston would soothe any irritation Liz had provoked.

"Yeah. Looks like I'm going to need it."

Winston looked hard at Elizabeth, and Jess knew she was on the money about getting him that java.

Elizabeth just turned to Jessica to point out, "We can't give him coffee. You didn't put on the percolator. It'll take some time."

"I'm sure the detective won't mind. He probably has more than a few things to talk about, since he made the trip all the way over here. Don't you think so?"

Elizabeth hesitated.

Jess added, "Liz, your coffee really is tops. Would you make it? You make it so much better than I do."

"That's true."

As Elizabeth left, Jessica, a trifle sheepishly, offered Winston a seat at the table. Sitting, the detective remarked with a jerk of his head after Elizabeth, "And they mistake *me* for one of the Stooges."

Jessica sat down, reining in a natural tendency to defend her sister against outsiders. Antagonizing the man investigating Bromfield's murder was the last thing she wanted.

"Have you discovered anything about the murder, yet, Detective?"

"We're pretty sure the killing was done by someone who knew Bromfield well, real well. Someone he trusted," Winston returned matter-of-factly. "Mind if I smoke?"

Jessica shook her head, hoping Winston couldn't see that his information had disquieted her. She reached over to the windowsill for an ashtray. Handing it to her guest, Jessica asked curiously, "How do you know that?"

"Bromfield was shot at close range; that's why his face was so messed up. He wouldn't have let anyone he didn't trust get that close." Winston lit up, took a drag and exhaled away from Jessica before continuing, "I bet he must have gotten some kind of surprise when that gun went off."

"I'll bet," Jess concurred, preoccupied.

Someone Bromfield trusted. A close friend? Winston hadn't said anything specific, but Jessica felt vaguely under suspicion. Maybe Winston would only construe her uneasiness as natural aversion to a gruesome death. She changed the subject. "Was there something you wanted to talk to me about, Detective?"

The detective surprised Jessica by smiling and revealing, "I think I have something for you."

Jessica perked up as he began fishing through his coat pocket, saying offhandedly, "Sammy Trendler had it. He someone you know?"

"Never heard of him. Who is he?"

Jessica stopped short as Winston removed an envelope from his pocket and pulled from it a photo of a garnet ring with an unusual setting.

"My garnet! Where did you find it?"

"On Sammy Trendler's body."

Jess stared at the implacable Winston. She repeated softly, "You found it on his *body?*"

"*I* didn't find it. You can thank my pal Mick Fine. See, Trendler was fished out of the East River with this on him. Mick Fine, who did the report on your break-in, saw that the ring was on the list of stolen jewelry. He'd been ribbing me about having a case in show biz. When he noticed your name on the robbery report, he let me know we had you in common. So, here I am to have you make an i.d. on the ring. I guess you're pretty unlucky, Miss Minton, running into murder and robbery the same night. Sorry I can't let you come down to the station and get the ring yet. Mick needs it for evidence. But I thought you might like to know we recovered something of yours. Funny, though, he should take one last swim without the rest of the loot. Maybe he had a partner who wanted to get rid of him."

"Yes, maybe," Jessica agreed uneasily. She looked at the photo suspiciously. Considering all she knew, this Trendler could have been a hireling of Bromfield's murderer sent to search her apartment for the package.

Jess suddenly became aware that despite his apparent interest in flicking cigarette ashes into the ashtray, Detective Winston was observing her carefully.

"Cookies!" Elizabeth announced, abruptly rejoining them bearing a plate of various baked delicacies.

"What?"

It was Winston, disoriented by Elizabeth's intrusion.

"I asked you if you'd like some cookies," Elizabeth patiently explained.

The glint in Elizabeth's eyes tipped off Jess to her sister's determination to find out exactly what was going on.

Elizabeth proceeded easily, "I'm sorry they're not homemade. My sister is a career girl and doesn't have time to do much baking, like I do."

Jessica resisted the urge to suggest Liz go home and whip up a batch of something right now, and Detective Winston regarded Liz morosely as he declined, "No thanks, I'm on a low-sugar diet."

As she sat down at the table and Liz continued easily, "Now, don't let me get in the way. I won't say another word. You just go right ahead and continue your crime busting."

Winston smiled thinly at Liz and queried, "Weren't you going to get some coffee?"

"Oh, it'll take a little time to perc. I thought you'd like me to keep you company until it's ready... My heaven! That photo. It's our grandmother's gold and garnet ring, Jess!"

"The ring was found on the body of some character dredged out of the East River," Jessica informed her sister.

Elizabeth tensed, but commented dryly, "At least he had good taste. Why would someone commit suicide after making a valuable haul? Or are we talking *murder?*"

"That's what they pay us to find out, lady," Winston noted blandly. He gave Liz a resigned appraisal, as if deciding he might as well try to work around her, then turned back to Jessica, "There was something else I wanted to ask you about, Miss Minton."

"About the robbery?"

Winston shook his head before pulling something wrapped in cloth from his pocket. It was a familiar knife, tagged as evidence. Jessica clenched her hands in her lap under the table, struggling to maintain her composure. Did Winston know Bromfield had tried to kill her? Had Vince been unable to keep his promise and revealed their exchange over Bromfield and the knife? Dared she come clean with Winston and try to convince him she'd kept quiet out of concern for Bromfield's reputation? Or maybe she could claim she'd been too flummoxed by the evening's horrors to remember about the knife? Would he buy either story? Jess suspected *she* wouldn't. Then again, maybe he *didn't* know anything. Maybe her best bet was to brazen it out. *Damn!* All she knew was that she could not afford to blow open James's plans by letting Winston delve too deeply.

"Recognize this?" he queried casually.

"Of course," Jess answered with equal calm. "That's the prop knife we use in the play. But why show it to me? I don't understand?"

"You said 'prop' knife?"

"Yes," Jess agreed, pretending she couldn't conceive why he should have brought it, despite the knot tightening in her stomach. "Any pressure on the blade will cause it to retract into the hilt."

"When's it used?"

His tone was perfectly conversational.

"In the play. Richards stabs my character."

"'Richards,' that'd be Bromfield?"

"Yes, but what are you getting at? What does the prop knife have to do with the robbery or Mr. Bromfield's murder?" Jessica questioned, feigning puzzlement.

Winston pressed the blade's tip against the plate on which the cookies resided. As Jessica anticipated, the blade didn't retract. Pretending astonishment, she protested, "Well, that can't be the same knife. Frederick Bromfield used a prop with a retracting blade."

"Here's a funny thing about this knife."

Except Jessica knew it wasn't going to be Jack Benny funny.

"In all the confusion of the murder, what with the questioning and everything, and the show being temporarily shut down, your stage manager and prop master didn't catch that the fake knife was missing so quick. So, when they picked up on it, they went looking, and guess what they found? This baby here, kind of tucked away where it wouldn't be noticed. Funny, isn't it? Even funnier, they never did find the real prop knife. What do you think of that, Miss Minton?" the detective asked quietly.

Jessica inwardly berated herself for being too distraught that night to realize before now that she should have grabbed the real knife from Vince. She could have even promised to hide it for him. If Bill and Leo, their prop master and stage manager, hadn't found *any* knife, they'd have been on the war path; but a missing prop would certainly have raised fewer eyebrows than finding a real one, instead. The only break she'd caught was that it sounded as if no one had seen or connected Vince with the knife. Maybe Bill and Frank had been too knocked for a loop at what they'd found to ask the stage hands anything. Thank God Vince had been one of the hands wearing heavy gloves when breaking down the set. Now, if the kid could just keep quiet, maybe weather some police questioning—and she could act naturally—then maybe she'd get out of this fix. Maybe.

So, Jessica turned an appropriately confused glance to her sister. Liz's expression matched hers perfectly. Her sister was a better actress than she'd guessed.

"I still don't understand what you're getting at," Jessica insisted.

"I'm looking for some answers, Miss Minton. It looks like this real knife was the one Bromfield used during the show."

He wanted to rattle her into giving away what she knew — or what he thought she knew, Jessica realized. Perhaps, Winston had read her jumpiness the night of the murder as more than a natural horror at finding a colleague shot in the face. Had he misinterpreted her reaction to indicate she was involved in that murder? Did he now hope that she might be unsettled into admitting her complicity? A lot of people seemed to be underestimating her recently. Well, Jessica Minton wasn't an actress for nothing.

Carefully, Jessica ventured, "You aren't saying Mr. Bromfield would deliberately, ah, try to hurt me?"

Winston's answer was cagey. "He wouldn't have any reason, would he?"

"I should say not," Jessica returned indignantly. "He was always nice to me. And for heaven's sakes, the poor man is dead. How can you talk about him this way?"

Elizabeth, who had remained discreetly (for once) silent, watching and listening, finally interjected, "This is ridiculous. I mean, couldn't the prop knife have gotten mixed up with a real one somehow? We should all be praising God that a wasp stung Jessica so that she jerked out of harm's way. And if, crazy as it sounds, Mr. Bromfield had wanted Jessica dead, he certainly wouldn't have tried to kill her in front of a theater full of witnesses, would he?"

"Unless he intended to claim someone had switched knives on him," Winston calmly pointed out.

"I'm sorry but I can't believe Frederick Bromfield would try to harm my sister. She always spoke so well of him. That's just crazy talk, what you're conjecturing," Elizabeth protested.

Jessica wondered if Winston knew that the prop knife definitely had a different heft than a real one. But Winston only shrugged, returning the knife to the depths of his overcoat pocket, and agreed, "Maybe so. He must have been awfully careless with his knife. Doesn't say much for the prop department."

"Don't let the union hear you say that," Jess warned him.

He looked at her thoughtfully.

Had she been too much of a smart aleck?

"Mmm," Winston uttered noncommittally, finally saying, "So, your sister says you're still here because you moved suddenly. Why *did* you, Miss Minton?"

"A wasp stung me," she returned coldly.

"If you want to take a look at the mark, you'll have to get a policewoman to do it!" Liz added for good measure.

"Or you can ask most of the cast, who saw me limping around once I got off the stage," Jessica explained, more pleasantly. No sense antagonizing Winston too much. She'd exhibited sufficient righteous indignation; now it was time to make nice. "One of the actresses, Iris Rossetti, applied an ice pack. You can ask her."

Winston tapped out his cigarette's ashes, then answered, "If I have to, I will. But your story sounds jake. You understand; I have to ask these questions."

Liz looked ready to detail just how much she did *not* understand, but Jessica beat her to the punch with, "I can't say it's not disturbing, but I guess I can't squawk. We all want to get to the bottom of this tragedy."

Winston wearily got up, saying, "Well, I'd better get going." Apparently this was shaping up as a long day for him. He added laconically, "Other things to look into."

Jess refrained from exchanging a relieved glance with her sister. Instead, she followed the detective to the door, Liz trailing at a slight distance. With an appropriate touch of trepidation, Jessica managed, "Detective Winston, what you said about the knife being real, what you implied was, well, Frederick Bromfield might have made the switch deliberately. I'm in no danger, am I?"

"The guy's dead, isn't he?" Winston replied matter-of-factly. He opened the door behind him and said, "Though I did find out both he and Trendler shared some acquaintances from the wrong side of the tracks. Could be they double-crossed the wrong guy and he caught up to them. It's just the switcheroo on the knife that puzzles me. Why you? You sure you don't know any of his pals?"

"I think I'd remember knowing a gangster type who wanted me dead, Detective Winston."

"Yeah, I would too. His enemy is some smart cookie. Put something on the handle to keep any prints from taking. So, I wouldn't put it past him to think taking you out with the knife would make a nice frame up. You were just in the right place at the wrong time."

At those words, Jess couldn't help shooting an anxious glance from her sister to the detective. He had the right game plan, only his players were wrong.

"You don't think anyone will be coming after my sister again, do you?" Liz demanded with the protectiveness of a cougar mommy.

"Naagh. Like the lady said: she doesn't know anything about Bromfield's playmates. Be seeing you around."

"Nice to meet you, Detective," Elizabeth returned wanly. Jess was silent.

"Likewise, I'm sure."

The moment Jessica closed the door behind Winston, Elizabeth whirled around her startled sister and blurted out, "That flat foot's on to us. He's going to send us up the river — or maybe burn us in the chair."

"Look, Georgette Raft," Jessica began, extricating herself from her sister's slightly maniacal grip, "I'm the one he's suspicious of. You aren't involved. But he's not going to pin anything on me. He has no real proof, and it will take some time to collect any evidence that might be planted against me. Crawford should have this mission completed before that, so it's going to be all right."

"Are you sure, Jessica?"

"Look, Elizabeth, if I'm not acting upset, you shouldn't, either."

"Fine. But what if Winston turns up some information about Mr. Bromfield being a Nazi or about your Crawford and his mission?"

Jessica frowned. "Leave it to you, Elizabeth, to pull a cloud out of a silver lining."

* * * * * *

Waiting for Larry to pick her up for his dinner party seemed to stretch on forever. For the millionth time, Jess stood before her mirror and smoothed her blue, yellow-dotted silk trousers, then patted the lapels of the matching jacket she wore over a yellow blouse. The week had been unendurably long, but today she had the mold of Larry's key tucked away in her apartment. After too many fatal SNAFUs, unbelievably, everything had come off without a hitch. Larry had confirmed her confidence in him by pronouncing her suggestion a capital idea that he give her a key to let in Mrs. Hayward early and help her set up. Not that she'd needed any extra assurance of her beau's innocence. Once he'd left her, she'd made the copy as easily as Crawford had promised. Then she'd been oh so careful to make sure no traces of clay had lodged in the key's grooves. This morning, before the matinée, she'd popped into Larry's house as planned and helped Mrs. Hayward, giving her the key to guard until Larry came back. Even today's Sunday performance had gone like clockwork. So why did she feel as if she were waiting for the other shoe, no, the other anvil, to drop?

"Riaow!"

Dusty wrapped herself around Jessica's legs, as always laying on the pathetic loneliness with a trowel whenever her human prepared to go out.

"I think the wrong one of us went on the stage," Jessica quipped.

"Aow!" Dusty sniped, her eyes baleful.

"Believe me, Dusty, you have the better deal. I'd much rather you were going out, and I could stay home and nestle up in a comfy chair."

Dusty flipped her tail and marched off in disgust.

"I'm in nobody's good books tonight. Not even my own."

Jess couldn't wisecrack herself out of her gloominess over duty to country and Crawford. She sank down on her bed. Playing Mata Hari was not her forte. Playing fast and loose with Larry's trust was even more distasteful — even if she was doing it to clear him. He would never understand if he knew what she was up to, and she couldn't blame him.

How could she? Rather, she blamed herself for being dishonest with him yet again. But she had to protect him from taking a bum rap. She cared too much about Larry to let that happen to him. But what exactly *did* she feel for him? After Larry was cleared, where would their relationship go? If she felt she couldn't entirely trust Crawford, why did a future with Larry seem hazier than ever? And did it mean anything that Crawford had never definitely said that what had happened between them on the bridge was part of the act? As if she really should care, knowing, now, that she had been only a pawn in Crawford's little plot!

The doorbell rang, and Dusty shot from the bedroom to the door, in search of another patsy from whom to finagle a treat. To the impatient jangles of the doorbell, Jessica dashed down the corridor, scooping up a slightly miffed cat to prevent her from making a break from the "big house" into traffic. Jess opened the door on Larry Sanders, handsome in the jet suit and crimson tie she had always loved, in his hand a bouquet of blue and gold flowers. Her face softened.

He held out the flowers a bit awkwardly.

"Oh, Larry..." They did a bit of a juggling act, with Larry trying to hand her the flowers while her arms were full of disgruntled tabby. "They're beautiful. I... Come in. Come in and close the door so Houdini here doesn't pull an escape act. I'll get a vase."

"Certainly."

When Jess turned back to Larry, he had closed the door and was watching her closely. She thought of the key mold hidden in her home and wanted to blush.

"Larry, you'll need to give me those if I'm going to put them in a vase. I have just the right one in the kitchen."

"Jessica, is everything all right?" He held onto the flowers. "I haven't had much chance to talk to you since Bromfield died. That's why I came to pick you up, so we could have some time alone before the party. I've been worried, especially since someone broke into your house the same night and assaulted Liz. I don't like the thought that this Crawford may see you as a loose end that he needs to tie up."

That pretty much floored Jessica. Finally she managed, "Larry, I don't know what to say. I told you that was done with. Believe me, I'm not happy with Bromfield's knife trick." That was no lie! "But he's dead. If someone wanted me dead, he wouldn't bump off a guy for doing the job, would he?"

"But for failing to do the job?"

"Larry, you're getting morbid! It's over." Why did she have to lie to a man who cared enough to worry about her? Would that she *could* tell Larry everything, let him help her and prove himself innocent. But that was her job, to save *his* skin. "Honestly, if for one minute I thought there was a connection I'd be high-tailing it to the G-Men. I don't want to get killed. And I certainly wouldn't take a chance on you or anyone else I care about getting caught in the crossfire."

Larry shook his head, tossed the flowers on the table, and put his hands on Jessica's arms. "I wish I could believe that, Jessica. But I don't think you're seeing straight. It's that imagination of yours. It makes you exciting, vivacious, but it will be the death of you. You've got to put your feet on the ground, or let me do it for you."

Fleetingly, Jessica had a vision of herself floating heavenward, with Larry desperately gripping her tootsies. No, this was serious!

"Jessica, you need me to protect you — and I will — but I can't do it unless you come clean with me, completely. If you don't, it will be a disaster. Tell me what's going on and then let me do the thinking for both of us."

Larry had definitely not scored any points with his last words, but Jessica held back and, instead, tried to calm him, "You're really good, to be so concerned, Larry, but you've got to give me some breathing room. You've also got to give me more credit. It's sweet of you to want to take everything that you *think* I'm carrying off my shoulders, but, Larry, calm down. First of all, stop worrying. Let Detective Winston do his work. He did some pretty sharp probing when he talked to Liz and me the other day."

"He did?"

"Yes, he did. You sound surprised. Liz didn't tell you about Winston's supposition that Bromfield had some connections with the underworld through the burglar? They probably did him in. See, no Crawford involved."

"But why would Bromfield want you dead, Jessica? You haven't answered that question. I should think it would be gnawing at you. It is at me."

"Winston suggested the knife switch might have been part of a frame up. When it didn't work out, thank God, his enemies went for a more direct approach."

"And you're still not frightened?"

"I didn't say it's not scary. Like surviving a car crash. But I did survive, and that's what I have to focus on. I don't need to be reminded how close I came to not surviving. It's over. There's no reason for a bunch of goons to come after me, personally. Let me put this behind me, Larry."

Frustrated, Larry protested, "Is that all you have to say, Jessica? Is that all you have to tell me? Can't I help you?"

At last an opportunity to be completely honest! "You have helped me, Larry. The flowers are lovely. The thought is lovelier. It's wonderful to talk to a guy who cares about what happens to me, who wants to help me."

"A guy who wants to take care of you and save you from the scrapes you always get yourself into," Larry added tenderly.

"Being helpful is just fine, Larry," Jessica insisted firmly. Before he could push the discussion back to dangerous ground, she brightly insisted, "Now, I'm going to help you — to a party that would make Elsa Maxwell green with envy. So, let's get a wiggle on. We've got to put these flowers away. The gold and yellow marigolds with the delphiniums and bachelor buttons are lovely . . ."

"Liz told me they're your favorites for this time of year."

"God bless her pointed little upsweep! Let's feed the cat, vase the flowers, and hit the road!

Jessica spent the entire dinner being gracious, while pondering exactly who of Larry's guests from the office was guilty of espionage, who had plotted her death. It was no piece of cake to play perfect hostess when she might be sitting down to sup with the person who had planned a grisly attempt on her life. How *did* she manage not to steal surreptitious probing glances at each person at the table? The interminable meal finally concluded, and Jessica displayed her best smile as she tried not to rush the guests into the parlor for their after-dinner drinks and conversation. As for herself, it was time to take a break. As soon as she had Larry's guests settled, Jess made an exit under the pretext of fixing her lipstick. It was comforting to leave Larry happily scoring big points with his superiors. Not so comforting was the touch of skepticism in Liz's features at her perfectly normal excuse for stepping out of the room.

Jessica slipped into the library. At last alone. She heaved a sigh heavy enough to sink all four of the Japanese carriers that went down at Midway. Jess wearily crossed the room to Larry's desk and pulled out the chair where her bag sat. For once her compact was easy to find. Flipping it open, she almost jumped out of her skin when the creak of the door behind her revealed she wasn't alone.

"Oh, Peter, you startled me. What are you doing here?"

For a fraction of a second, Peter seemed to cast about for an answer, then blurted, "Oh, I, um, forgot something in here. I, ah, came in to look for it."

Jessica forced herself to smile, but Peter's uneasiness was contagious.

"Oh, well, maybe it's over here," he conjectured before uncertainly proceeding across the room to study the volumes on the bookcases to his right.

Why should Peter be so jumpy about being alone with her? Why had he almost seemed to sneak up on her? Jess didn't like the wild conjectures to which the events of the last few weeks were leading her, but Peter did work in the same office as Larry. Still, Peter was hardly exhibiting the *sangfroid* one expected of a master spy.

Turning sharply back to his sister-in-law, Peter said, "Jessica, I lied to you. I didn't leave anything in here. I followed you. I was looking for you. I saw you slip in here . . ."

"Peter, why do you want to see me?" Jessica questioned carefully.

Peter's gaze fastened on the floor. He shook his head slowly before explaining, "I just don't know where to begin, Jess."

"Is it about your job?" Jessica ventured cautiously.

Peter blinked, startled. "My job?"

"Yes, you know, that little past time occupying you from nine to five so you have the money to pay your bills," she nudged, trying to disarm him. "Well, what's bothering you, Peter?"

"It's Elizabeth."

"Elizabeth?"

Peter nodded vigorously and admitted unhappily, "I think she's seeing another man."

Jessica almost slid down the back of the chair.

"Are you nuts, Peter?" she finally choked out after a few inarticulate stammers.

"You don't think she is?" Peter queried hopefully.

"Not at all," Jessica assured confidently. "Where on earth did you get such a half-baked idea?"

Peter answered sheepishly, "It's just that lately she's been so distant and preoccupied. And, over the last two years or so, we've argued quite a bit more than even you know. Now, the way she always changes the subject when I ask what's bothering her... she's definitely keeping something from me. When I was away on my trip, she was out almost every time I called. Then, there was the night of the murder. She said she didn't feel well, but she ended up at your flat, knocked out. I could only imagine she'd set up an assignation there and run into the burglar instead of her boyfriend. What else could come between people who've been married this long?"

"Peter! How on earth could you think that of Elizabeth?!"

Her brother-in-law cringed under her reproof, and Jess tried to soften her rebuke with humor, "Peter, an affair, in her own sister's apartment, yet? How could you think such a thing?"

He looked at the floor.

"Peter, there's a simple explanation for all this nonsense. Liz has been spending a lot of time with me." That wasn't exactly a lie. "As for her winding up in my apartment that night, you know as well as I do how Liz gets those premonitions of hers. That's what brought her over. And she was right to worry. I was burglarized. She was just a little too early for her own good. Really, Peter, if I don't know my own sister, I don't know anybody — and you should know her pretty darned well, too!"

"You're so right, Jessica. I feel like such a heel! How can I explain myself? I guess we've been under so much pressure at work lately. Maybe I was just projecting all my worries onto Liz. I guess, I guess I just needed to talk to someone — to make me see what a fourteen-karat moose I'm being. I *was* imagining things?"

"You bet," Jessica assured Peter, coming forward to take his arm. Part of her wanted to clobber him for making such horrid insinuations about her sister, but she had far too many worries now to muster the energy for righteous indignation. Instead, she bit her tongue and cheered her brother-in-law with, "Now come on. It's time we went back and joined the herd. By the way, how's Larry faring?"

"Oh, not bad at all." Peter elaborated as they strolled from the room, "Who knows? With any luck, he might be head of our department one of these days."

Hmm, wouldn't that prospect give James Crawford a coronary?

So Jessica smiled and listened as Peter went on, but inwardly she was none too pleased with herself. She'd never realized that Crawford's plottings would put a strain on Peter and Elizabeth's marriage. Sure, Peter seemed reassured, now; but given a little more mysterious behavior from Liz, given a little more time and pressure, Peter could easily start stewing again — with disastrous results.

CHAPTER THIRTEEN

The flagstone walk to Larry's house loomed in the brilliance of a fall mid-afternoon. In spite of her concerns, Jessica Minton admired the perfectly trimmed flame-bush crimsoning in Larry's small front yard. Her dark rust-colored skirt swished as she walked purposefully toward the door with its new lock and alarm. One gloved hand clutched the key, the other gripped her bag clamped under her arm. At the bottom step, Jess made a quick survey up and down the street. The rare person in sight didn't stop to regard her curiously; no one peered suspiciously out a window. Only the key to worry about. After giving her fawn jacket a little tug and adjusting the imagined tilt of her rust toque hat for confidence, Jessica trotted up the three granite steps to the front door. The key came up to the new lock — but Jessica hesitated.

The right key *should* deactivate the alarm when it unlocked the door. Any kind of tampering with the lock, or any of the house's ingresses, would make a racket here and send an alarm to a private security company. And if her key weren't an exact enough duplicate?

Crawford had assured her the plan would work. Then again, lately his assurances and a nickel probably wouldn't buy a cup of coffee. Jessica's hand lowered. What she wouldn't give to march down the steps and back up the street. The key went into the lock, turned. The door opened with a push, and Jessica was inside the house.

No klaxons or flashing lights. No sirens. Just the gloom of the foyer. The curtains on the window next to the door, as well as those in the rooms off the foyer, were all securely drawn, protecting the fabrics against fading from the sun — or keeping out prying eyes? Larry's house had never felt like this. Forbidding. Then again, the rare times she'd been here before had been by invitation, not for breaking and entering.

Impatiently, Jessica rolled back her glove to check her watch. Two o' clock. Crawford should be here any time now. She headed for the kitchen door where she was to admit him. Crawford had decided that although Jessica might be able to get in without attracting much attention, too many people waltzing through the front door would probably pique someone's suspicion. A delivery truck around the rear of the house was decidedly less conspicuous.

Entering the kitchen, Jessica glanced out the window into the alleyway that ran between the rows of houses on parallel streets. No one. Another glance at her watch. Time to wonder if Larry's sending his alarm to a private firm, not directly to the police, was as fishy as Crawford insisted. Why wouldn't an innocent man want the police's help?

Sitting down, Jessica sank inwardly. She'd been doing a lot of thinking the past few days, especially since making the key mold. It killed her to admit it, but hating Crawford wasn't making her any happier or saner, even if he had hurt her. Maybe the job he had to do was more important than her feelings. She still wasn't about to give the guy a medal for what he'd done to her. Well, maybe making him earn a Purple Heart would be nice.

Could she really hate Crawford for doing his job? Didn't she even have herself to blame for her own mixed up emotions? He had discouraged her somewhat. Maybe she could forgive Crawford, after a fashion. Forgive but not trust him. Anyway, what was important now was clearing Larry and nabbing the real traitor.

A rap at the kitchen-door window snapped Jessica out of her one-woman heart to heart. A familiar, dark-eyed face appeared on the other side of the window. Jess hopped up, suppressing an instinctive warm feeling. Businesslike, she crossed to the door, opening it with a tight, "You're late. I was getting nervous."

Crawford was inside immediately, the fireplug right behind him.

"What's he doing here?" Jessica demanded, suspicion taking command.

"We have a limited amount of time, Miss Minton. I can't cover this whole house by myself..."

"I could help . . ."

"Yeah, sure, sister," cut in Crawford's accomplice. "You could also conveniently hide or destroy whatever you found —"

"Hey! Just who do you think you are?"

"Both of you," James Crawford warned levelly, looming between them, "knock it off. We're not here to fight. We're here to close a case."

"Crawford, you really think we should trust Sanders' girlfriend?"

"I wouldn't go out with a guy if he were a Nazi, you gorilla."

"Yeah? Is that something you ask a guy on the first date?" he asked, bristling over the "gorilla" crack.

"No, I make him tell me on the application to *get* a first date."

Before Mr. Fireplug could launch a rejoinder, James shut down the squabble by squaring off against his associate. "You. Stand down. Remember, you're the professional here. You should know better than to let her push your buttons. Channel that energy into searching the upstairs. I'll cover down here."

"What?" Jessica interjected. "I'm not letting him roam around this house alone. How do I know he won't plant evidence?"

Before Crawford's associate could lace into Jessica, James put a hand on her arm and assured her, "I don't believe *you* scoured the house to remove any incriminating evidence to protect Sanders."

He didn't seem all that comfortable saying that. Why?

"I still don't think she should be here," the fireplug challenged. "You didn't make the right call on Frederick Bromfield, either."

"As I recall," Crawford coolly corrected his companion, "no one did any better at seeing that one coming. And you've never heard of me being off my game before that, have you?"

"No."

Jessica was tempted to point out that James Crawford was dead wrong about Larry, but then supporting Mr. Fireplug's hostile suspicions of her wasn't exactly in her best interest. At least Crawford's dour companion went away. He went away grumbling, but he went.

It wasn't easy to mask her relief when the kitchen door swung shut behind that squat little ray of sunshine, but Jess managed. She couldn't hide her surprise, though, when she turned back to Crawford and found him studying her with a strained expression. Part of her wanted to know what was eating him, but Jess forced herself to give Crawford only a quick, uneasy glance and say, "The sooner we start, the sooner it will be over."

Jess was at the kitchen door, when Crawford's voice stopped her. "Wait, Jessica."

Jess did stop, but she wouldn't turn back right away. There was something about James Crawford's tone that left her feeling vulnerable. She finally made herself face him and neutrally respond, "Yes?"

His features were hard to read when he questioned, "You've been all right, then? I've been keeping an eye on you, but there's nothing you have to tell me, is there?"

"Like . . .?"

Why did she have the feeling that there was something he wanted to tell her but couldn't? Only her own wishful thinking?

"No one has said or done anything odd? Sanders, especially, hasn't acted suspicious of you?"

"I'd say an innocent man wouldn't have anything to suspect, but that wouldn't hold much water with you." Now why had she turned antagonistic? Hadn't she intended at least to act neutral? Was she afraid that Crawford would draw the wrong conclusions about Larry's probing questions or Peter's suspicions about Liz?

"I see."

"Well, I'm glad one of us does," Jessica said wearily, pushing through the doorway and into the corridor.

James caught up to her and questioned, "Do you mind telling me what that's supposed to mean?"

Jessica halted, looked James in the eye and returned, "I'm just tired of lying. I don't want to lie to anyone, anymore. I don't want anyone to lie to me, anymore. I know what's at stake. I'll do my duty. But I still want all this dishonesty to be over and done with. It's not the way I live. I'm sure this all just rolls off your back. It's your job. It's your life. It means nothing to you, but that's not me."

James Crawford was *very* quiet. Finally, he said, "Is that the way you see me? That's what you think of me?"

It was as if they were back on the bridge again. Except that his voice wasn't passionate but thoughtful, seriously troubled over something he had to hold back. What Jessica felt in response scared her. She couldn't trust herself. All Jess could say was, "Why do you care what I think? Will that change your mission, your plans, what you do next?"

Crawford's expression was strained, but Jessica could almost have sworn that hope flickered in his eyes. Then he abruptly straightened and answered her question, "We both know what will happen if I don't do my job right. There's no question this mission comes first."

"Fine. Then why don't you get started. The sooner you see for yourself that Larry is innocent, the sooner you can get on the trail of the real quisling."

"You're rather loyal to this Sanders character, aren't you?"

"Not in the sense that I'd cover for him if he were guilty, if that's what you're getting at. And he isn't a 'character.'"

"Guilty or not, he's lucky to have someone stick by him so tenaciously."

"Even if I do it by sneaking around behind his back?" The bitterness in her words was aimed at herself.

James surprised her by touching her shoulder and saying, "Don't punish yourself. It doesn't solve anything. Believe me; I know. Come on, now. There's work to be done."

James Crawford was as good as his advice, setting assiduously to task. Jessica had expected him to head straight for Larry's safe in the study, but she was wrong. Perhaps a safe was such an obvious hiding place, Crawford deemed it the least likely place a guilty man would hide incriminating evidence. The dexterity with which he tore apart and then reconstituted the items in one room after another, neglecting to explore neither the obvious nor the subtle, convinced Jessica that her companion knew his business. Although for a man so good at his work, James Crawford didn't seem all that happy to be doing it. What *was* eating him? A guilty conscience over stringing her along earlier or over just plain drawing her into this mess? Maybe pawing through an innocent man's private life wasn't his cup of tea, after all.

They were in the study at last. A thump overhead drew their attention upward. The fireplug. Only then, Jess realized exactly how relieved she was to be down here with Crawford rather than alone with Mr. Personality.

"Your minion lacks your delicate touch." Jess screwed up her courage to add, "Maybe I should go upstairs and keep an eye on him."

James, who had resumed his work, looked up from a stack of envelopes he had extracted from a desk drawer to ask, "*Would* you like to be alone with him?"

"That's beside the point," Jessica couldn't help shifting uneasily at the prospect, though. "I can't have him making a wreck . . ."

"If we 'wrecked' the house it would rather defeat the point of coming here undercover, wouldn't it?" A quick glance at his watch accompanied the words.

Jessica didn't have a comeback, not a good enough one, anyway. So she settled for honesty. "Larry's been through enough because of me. I just . . ."

"My associate knows his business. And no one is stepping out of line on my watch. Regardless of the methods I've had to use, I still want the truth. It doesn't do me any good to frame the wrong man; the quisling would still be free to devil our chances of winning this war. And whether you believe me or not, I still have to worry about what happens to you."

Jessica's instinct was to believe James Crawford, but she was afraid to. She was afraid he'd see that she did care how much he worried about what happened to her. So, Jess wouldn't let his eyes hold hers, and she turned to walk off to her left.

She had other, less romantic concerns eating at her, as well. Even if James were honest at this moment, what did it matter when he was wrong about Larry? She was still in danger, and he didn't seem to have any other suspects up his sleeve. Jessica wanted some answers on exactly where things stood concerning Larry's innocence and her safety, and so she began by facing James and questioning, "You haven't found anything the least incriminating here, have you?"

"I haven't finished." But James Crawford didn't seem comfortable with his words.

"Do you really expect to find something after all this? From the sound of things, your friend doesn't seem to have had any better luck."

"There's still the safe."

"You honestly think Larry's squirreling away secret documents in there?"

"I may have a degree of independence; but, ultimately, I have my orders. I have to look where I'm told. I have to do what I'm told."

"That doesn't answer my question. Maybe you'd better sign up with Arthur Murray to improve your tap dancing."

"Hey, lady, lay off him." Crawford's suave partner had returned. "He doesn't answer to you. There's something bigger going on than your piddling worries."

"Look, bub, I'm worried about the wrong guy getting railroaded," Jessica retorted. "I'm worried about the right guy getting away with murder, literally — and not just mine, but the service men he'll continue to betray if you master spies don't nail him. Maybe *you'd* better look at the big picture."

"Just who do you think you are, you smart-talking —"

Crawford was between them, again, guiding Jess to the other side of the room with, "All right, down, Tiger," to Jessica and, over the shoulder to his partner, "If you couldn't find anything, don't take it out on her."

Having separated the two opponents, James turned to his partner, "Perhaps you'd better remember that she's one of the people we're fighting to save. From where I'm standing, she's done more than her share."

Jessica didn't turn to face James after he spoke. She didn't want him to see the appreciation and respect in her eyes that his words had stirred.

The fireplug's grumble wasn't exactly what she'd expected. "Awright. Maybe I was a little out of line. Maybe you better just go on and finish the job, like you were told."

Crawford's only response was a tight, "Right. The safe. Can't buck orders, can we?"

Now, Jessica turned back, expecting to find James Crawford at work on the safe and the fire plug watching expectantly. It wasn't so. James was facing her, and Jessica knew he was reading her heart in her expression.

"The safe..." Jessica threw out, as if distracting him could shield her vulnerability.

"There is nothing in that safe. I've searched it already," James Crawford admitted, as if unleashing a floodgate.

"Son, this isn't according to our orders," his partner warned.

"We've followed the spirit," James returned. "And we've kept her in the dark long enough. I've done everything I promised. I've done my bloody duty. She deserves to know the truth. You know as well as I do that we've proved her trustworthy."

"What in Sam Hill are you two going on about?" Jessica demanded, coming forward and relegating her tenderness to the back burner.

James stopped her, a hand on her shoulder and admitted, "Here's some more ammunition to turn you against me. It'll be your choice. I want you at least to have a choice. I had to lie to you again. When we reported in on Bromfield, my superiors didn't trust you not to inform Sanders. They overrode the plan I'd arranged with you. They ordered us to get a copy of the key from the locksmith and search the house before today. I'm sorry, but we had our orders — and they did prove you right about Sanders' house."

Her head swam. Jess was hearing something about there being nothing to pin on Larry. But they'd already searched the house before meeting her here today? Then why was she here now? Why have her make a copy of the key, risk exposure?

"How could you do this to me, *again*?! What am I, a toy to you people? Do you know, Crawford, I was this close to not wanting to push you off a cliff, but now . . ."

"For cryin' out loud, lady, give the guy a break," Mr. Fireplug cut in, startling both Jess and James. "Look, he's not my buddy by a long shot, but fair's fair. He didn't want to do this. He went to bat for you when our bosses started to suspect that you were Sanders' partner, stringing us along."

That nearly knocked Jessica off her feet. She recovered to retort, "After all I've done to help..."

"Help?" the fireplug cut in. "You think it looks that way, with Sanders staying one step ahead of us?"

"Maybe he's innocent. Did anyone ever think of that possibility?" Jessica insisted, looking from one man to the other. "So you found nothing here before, and you still haven't figured out that Larry Sanders is innocent? So, why am I here, anyway?"

"It was part of the cover," James said quietly, uncomfortably, "The theory was that if Sanders were guilty, his attempt on your life through Bromfield indicated that he now saw you as his betrayer, his main threat. He'd concentrate on watching you and be too preoccupied to pay attention to us when we really came here."

"You dreamed that up all by yourself, I suppose?"

"That's what I've been trying to straighten you out on, sister," the fireplug cut in. "He was against all this. Went on about refusing to risk you any further. He wasn't going to set you up. So they made him follow through on this plan just to make him prove he wouldn't sell out our countries because he'd gotten hornswoggled by some dame. You know, they think he's a real pain in the patoot because of you. He's not exactly in line for a promotion."

Jessica appraised James, then sharply questioned, "Is he on the level?"

"That I'm considered a pain in the patoot?" James returned wearily.

"Oh, I already know the answer to that one. I want to know if you really stepped up to the plate for me."

"Would you believe me if I said yes?"

His tone was a little defiant, but Jessica realized it wasn't really with her but with having been forced to play her yet again. Crawford's uneasiness since coming here made a lot more sense once she acknowledged that he didn't want to scam her any more. It scared her a little, but she really did believe them this time. Still, it didn't seem right to give in too soon.

"Why *should* I believe the two of you after everything that's happened?"

After a pessimistic snort, James Crawford said, "You shouldn't. You don't have any reason to. I haven't the right to ask you to."

He moved off to lean back broodingly against the wall, arms folded.

That wasn't exactly helpful. But he wasn't spinning another likely scenario now. Couldn't that be a good sign?

"Sheesh. Will you two stop fiddling around here? Look, I'm gonna go out and sit in the truck and let you have a little heart to heart. But make it snappy. Eventually, someone's going to notice how long the delivery truck has been parked there."

James straightened, shooting his partner a "what-the-hell-are-you-talking-about" look. Jessica stood bewildered. The fireplug finished, "Hell, Crawford, you're no good to anyone all guilt-wracked and everything. Don't get me wrong, I'm not about to offer you a shoulder to cry on. But you're starting to slip, boy, and she looks as if she's had about all she can take before she lets pop what she knows to the wrong person. The way I see it, maybe the brass don't know everything. So maybe you two better settle your scores. We need you back on the beam, Crawford. Much as I hate to admit it, you've been doing a good job up to this point. We can't afford to lose a good man, even if he is a pain in the patoot." Facing Jessica, he ordered, "Do your bit for the war, lady. Give the slob a break." To James he said as he was leaving, "See you in ten, Crawford — fifteen tops."

His tone was wry, but Jessica sensed the depth of feeling underneath as James asked, "So, will you give the slob a break?"

"Where do you want it, the arm or the leg?"

But her heart wasn't quite in the crack, and Jessica couldn't bring herself to meet James Crawford's eyes or let him see into hers.

"All right, Jessica." He crossed to her as he spoke, stopping right in front of her. "You can believe me or not. It's your choice. But I want you at least to hear the way it is. I wish I hadn't had to muck up your life, but none of this was for fun — well, maybe except for a moment or two at the racetrack and in your apartment. But I didn't set out to ruin your life. I was sure we'd catch our quisling, and the Allies would be one step closer to ending this bloody war. I guess on some level I even thought I was doing you a favor, getting you away from a dangerous enemy agent. Can you accept that much?"

"Maybe," Jessica relented slowly. Reining in her hopes was like trying to keep War Admiral under wraps at the start of a race.

"All right then." He hesitated, and Jess saw that what came next was going to cost James Crawford. He was, however, determined to press on. "I might as well make a clean breast of all of it."

"*All* of it?" Jessica repeated with trepidation. How much worse could this get?

"That night on the Brooklyn Bridge . . ."

Damn, she thought. *Here it comes, where he tells me he was trying to snow me with romance. I really don't want to hear this.*

"I was wrong, Jessica. I'd been kidding myself all along up to that point. Holding you, talking to you, being with you, woke me up to something I thought had died and been buried by all I've lived through the past several years. God help me, the both of us, it's the wrong time, the wrong place, but I love you."

Jess caught herself in a double-take. Why did the words she wanted to hear have to hit like an anvil at the end of a ten-story drop? *Could* she trust him this time?

"Aren't you going to say anything, Jessica? I guess I can't blame you if you think this is just one more slick line. But, damn it, I wanted you to know the truth." James walked away, shaking his head, "Not that it matters much, does it? You can have a life with Larry now, if that's what you want, and I have my work. It's not the kind of work that allows much leeway for anything between us, even if you, well, that's all irrelevant now." He turned back to her. "But what I said before about your marrying Sanders. That has nothing to do with me. Just make sure you don't make a mistake. I don't want you to be trapped."

Jessica looked James in the eyes and said, "I believe you."

He blinked, almost grinned in disbelief, then asked, "Why?"

"I, I don't know, exactly. Little things, I guess. You're the first guy to come to the house whom Dusty actually liked. When you didn't know I was watching you, you put back all the quarters you found in Larry's sofa. He'd never have known if they were missing. You leveled with me about this latest bit when you could have gotten away with me none the wiser. Even when I had my doubts about your stories, I had this feeling that you, yourself, were essentially a square guy. Now that feeling makes sense."

"Dusty doesn't like Larry?"

"You *don't* have to look so pleased."

"I've always thought that cats were especially intelligent creatures." James came back toward her. He was standing before Jessica, taking her hands in his to ask, "So, is Dusty the only one in your apartment who doesn't have her claws out for me?"

Jessica lowered her eyes, but her hands squeezed James's as tightly as his did hers. She didn't look up when she ventured, "You said it's the wrong time, the wrong place, James, but what if I feel the same way you do? If what happened on the bridge, what's happening now, means the same for both of us? Could we have just this moment, right now, for us? Is that too much for either of us to ask in the middle of this war?"

James didn't say anything. One hand released hers and tipped her chin up so they faced each other. For the first time, Jess saw the green flecks in the brown of James's eyes, his sweet eyes that were so profoundly happy now. Jessica let her own features reveal the depth of her feelings, feelings James shared with her.

His arms slipped around Jess in a hug that might have crushed her, except that the tenderness of his hold would not hurt her. Jessica returned his embrace with a passion that she'd held in check, only now realizing its depth. He bumped his head on her hat and they both chuckled.

"This is quite a contraption," James remarked, as they pulled back just enough to see each other's faces.

Jess whipped out the hat pins and tossed them, inside the hat, on a nearby chair, quipping, "Fortunately it's detachable."

James's grin widened. His hand caressed away the thick black curls framing Jessica's face, before his eyes smiled into hers and they slipped into a kiss of delicious passion. He held her close too briefly for either of them, before finally pulling back and returning them to reality with, "I can only offer a moment, Jessica. I still have work to do."

Jessica nodded, coming back to the stark reality of murder, espionage, and betrayal. Yet James and she were tightly holding hands.

"Jessica, you have to realize that letting Larry Sanders off the hook doesn't bode well for you. We still don't know for certain who's after you if it isn't Sanders."

"I know. I guess I just don't know whom to... Don't know for *certain*? You have an idea?"

James nodded, reluctant to administer more bad news.

"Someone I know, isn't it? Someone connected to Larry or to Bromfield? Someone in the theater, maybe?"

"Not the theater, Jessica. This is hard to break to you. Because of his proximity to our first suspect, the likeliest candidate is your brother-in-law, Peter Hennessey."

Jessica sharply protested, "James, that's absurd! Peter? Are you crazy? Peter's such a, a..."

"Twerp?"

"That wasn't exactly the word I was thinking, but he is more than a little on the Mortimer Snerd side when it comes to high pressure. You should have seen how pathetic he was when we found Frederick Bromfield murdered. Practical jokes are about as high stakes as he can go. Him? A master spy for the Axis? We should only hope!"

"Where was Hennessey when Bromfield was murdered?"

"In the men's room at the theater — at war with the green vegetables he'd had for dinner."

"Any witnesses?"

"What do *you* think?"

James allowed himself a brief smile at her wisecrack before he pointed out, "Jessica, you have to remember that the person we're talking about is clever. A front of ineptitude is a first-class way to deflect suspicion. Did Hennessey have access to Bromfield's knife the night you were almost murdered?"

"Both Peter and Larry had been backstage talking to me, but I can't believe... not Peter. I'm sorry, James, this is just too hard for me to swallow."

"If not Peter Hennessey, who else in your circle, Jessica? He has had more than enough opportunity to spy, murder, and redirect evidence to Larry. Can you suggest a better suspect?"

Jess faced James, flustered. Slowly, she recounted to James thoughts that tightened the noose around Peter's neck. "It makes sense of something else. The night someone broke in and conked Liz, the window in the study was broken, but there was no glass on the floor. I honestly doubt that I was lucky enough to have the neatest burglar on record. The glass must have fallen outside. Someone broke the window to make it look like a break in because that someone wanted to hide the fact he had the key. He just didn't quite get it right, about which way the glass would fall. Peter ought to hire better help; it would save him bumping off all the incompetents."

"Exactly how does this scenario make Peter Hennessey look guilty?" James questioned.

"Oh, you'll love this. A little dramatic irony aimed at both of us. You see, I paid attention to your warning not to leave the spare key outside. The only spare one belongs to Liz and Peter, and she said theirs was lost. Not so lost after all, I guess. Peter must have just taken the key, lied to Liz, and passed it on to Trendler. Poor Liz."

James hugged her close with one arm, then offered, "At least if it is Peter Hennessey we know whom to go after. If it isn't..."

"What's your next step, James?"

Crawford shook his head before relenting, "We did search Hennessey's office. Nothing. We've wanted to search his apartment for a few days now..."

"But Elizabeth's been home with a cold," Jessica completed.

"Right. Otherwise, I'd have been in there while he was at work, and she was on one of her lengthy shopping expeditions."

"You really *do* do your homework."

"Your sister's shopping addiction is hard to miss, Jessica."

She nodded.

"As soon as you sister is well, I'm going in..."

"Not joined by your little playmate?"

"He was here mainly to keep an eye on you and me. To see if I followed orders — or if you acted as if you were wise to us or plotting something with your brother-in-law against Sanders. Planting something on him."

"Boy, I got slammed from both sides. I was either hiding evidence to protect Larry the Nazi or planting it to frame him and help Peter the Nazi. Your superiors must think I'm quite a Mata Hari."

"I tried to set the record straight, but in the middle of a war no one man's word is going to be convincing without concrete evidence. At least after this, I'll have some corroboration from my partner."

"I'll be relieved when you finally get the real fifth columnist, but good God, if it is Peter ... Poor Liz."

James squeezed her hands and promised, "I will get you out of this, Jessica. Above anything else that's happened, that is the truth."

"I can get you into their apartment."

"What?"

"You probably know that Peter's going away to his Hibernian Society's lodge, upstate, in two days, right? He got stuck being the one to get it ready for the hunting season."

"Yes. Right. We got that information from tapping their line, before the phone broke down."

"I'm willing to bet Peter and Liz were able to get a repairman as soon as this Friday because you and your secret service pals wanted to keep track of their conversations."

James gave a "you-got-me" shrug.

"Well, here's something you don't know. Liz is climbing the walls from being stuck inside with a cold. Friday, she wants me to wait at the apartment for the repairman, so she can go out for lunch and shopping with some friends. There's a sale at Bergdorf's, and she's going if she has to be carried on a litter. Anyway, Liz has to be back by 5:30 so that I can get to the theater by 6:00. That still leaves you plenty of time to search the apartment, since she's leaving about 12:00."

"And where will you be while all this is going on?"

"Right there. Then I can keep a lookout..."

"If I need a lookout, I already have a partner."

"He doesn't look as if he belongs there. I do. And I can hide you if the repairman comes while you're there."

"I don't want to drag you into any more of this. You've done more than enough. I don't want to endanger you any further."

"James, the danger will never be over until you find out exactly who the traitor is. And let's face it, when are you going to get another such opportunity? We must plug this leak before anyone else dies."

In the end, James had to relent. But before he left Jessica, he promised, "This is it, Jessica. I'll never put you in a position like this again."

"All right. I'll buy that. But let me wipe that lipstick smear off your face before you go off and make the world safe for democracy. No sense letting your pal out in the truck know that we literally kissed and made up."

CHAPTER FOURTEEN

The door swung open under Jessica Minton's black-gloved hand. Her sister's apartment stretched before her. Her brother-in-law's apartment, too. A flash of anxiety made her hesitate. No, she'd come too far to chicken out now. At least her promise to wait for the telephone repairman, so Liz could go out, gave her a legitimate reason for being here. She couldn't feel good about the *real* reason. Closing the door behind her, Jessica was relieved, if still guilty, that she'd told Liz another engagement prevented her from coming over before her sister left. Jess wasn't sure she could pull off this gambit if she had to face Elizabeth before things even got started.

With his connections, James had been able to reschedule the repairman's appointment to give himself time to do his job (and give the repairman sufficient time to do his) before Liz got back. All that efficiency didn't ease Jessica's guilt over Liz and Peter's home being invaded. Jess pulled back her glove to check her watch. When was James getting here, anyway?

Looking up again, Jess now noticed that a half-finished glass of Liz's trademark iced tea and milk sat atop the bar. Next to that was a most fetchingly fresh banana-cream pie — with a slice recently excised. Wasn't that just like Liz, getting even with Peter for going away when she was sick by making his favorite dessert, then polishing it off before he could enjoy even a crumb? Peter had been taking so many trips lately that pretty soon Liz would need a reducing program.

Crossing to the bar, Jess reached for the pie to put it away. It wasn't like Liz to leave something out that might spoil, especially if she planned to devour it herself. Oops, better take off the gloves. No sense adorning black suede with cream or pie crumbs. Lucky for Jessica's waistline, this was one type of pie she wasn't especially fond of. Still, she'd rather worry about gaining a few inches than about whether her sister was married to a Nazi viper or how she could help Liz get over it. Of course she also wasn't forgetting that she would really be in a jam, herself, if Peter were innocent and James Crawford still had no clue to the quisling's identity.

Jessica turned abruptly away, her eyes meeting the poster-board sketches cunningly arrayed on the couch before her. Hint! Hint! from Liz. Her designs of women's clothing. In fact, Jess's tawny velour skirt and matching V-neck pullover with a black jersey were Liz's own creation. She'd told Liz to do more work like this. Not just for her kid sister, but for profit — channel some of that restless energy into creativity. Lately, Liz had been starting to listen to her and make noises about looking for freelance work, just to keep occupied. Peter hadn't been too crazy about the thought of his wife working: silly masculine pride. But Liz might need to earn her own way if Peter turned out to be a fiver. No, don't think of that now!

Sitting down with the sketches, Jess decided that she'd better give the designs more than a cursory look. Knowing Liz, Jess figured she'd be in for a third-degree from her on the drawings.

A soft, swift knock at the door nabbed Jess's attention. She was there in a flash, but her hand hesitated at the doorknob. Her eye went to the peep hole, just as she remembered she hadn't locked the door behind her. The person on the other side of the door pushed it open somewhat cautiously, but not cautiously enough to avoid hitting her nose.

"Ow!"

"Oh, sorry, Jessica! You're all right?"

At least it was James, his leather-gloved hand closing the door and locking it behind him. Gingerly touching her nose, Jess remarked, "This is what I get for sticking it into the wrong places."

"That's a greater danger when you tend to be more on the aquiline side." His finger tapped his own nose. Then he was all seriousness. "We're alone?"

"Liz was out when I arrived. We know Peter took off yesterday. It's just you, me, and 7/8ths of a banana-cream pie."

"Banana cream? Pie?"

"Down, boy. You're worse than my brother-in-law; he could live on the stuff! Besides, Liz has already eaten one slice, and she knows I'd much rather have cherry. She measures her portions down to the millimeter. So, unless you want her to start asking awkward questions about why too much pie is missing..."

"Understood."

"You were a little late, James. Any problems?"

"Not exactly. I had trouble getting in through the service entrance, so I had to come around front and spend some time getting onto the service elevator unobtrusively. Before we start, I want to be sure that there's no chance of your sister coming back too early."

"No. I took care of that. I persuaded her to not just stop at Bergdorf's but to hit Bonwitt Teller, too."

"Ah," James nodded appreciatively. "You're getting good at this."

"Forgive me if I don't take that as a compliment. It's my family we're playing with."

James had been ready to move on to work, but Jessica's words stopped him. "Sorry, Jessica. I'll get you past this as soon as I can."

"It's not just me. It's my sister. If her husband is a Nazi..."

He took Jessica's hands and pointed out, "Look, Jessica, if Peter Hennessey is a Nazi, then it's better your sister finds out and gets away from him. Her not knowing isn't going to clear him. This is the only way. If he is guilty, sooner or later, she's going to tumble to it and become a liability to him — unless you think she'd keep secrets for the Axis."

Jessica shook her head. James squeezed her hand comfortingly and proceeded, "Right then, we have to make the best of our time. Let's get to it. The plans I could find for this apartment weren't clear on where you brother-in-law's safe is."

"Over there," Jessica pointed across the room, to the left. "Behind the painting, the copy of Matisse."

"It's *always* behind the painting," James shook his head, guiding Jessica across the room.

Jessica smiled quietly, and James set to work, saying, "Help me get this painting off the wall. Right, like this. We'll just lean it against this couch. Fine."

"This is the second time you came to crack someone's safe. Do you do a lot of this?"

"Do you mean, am I planning my post-war career? Or did I have an extra-legal sideline before the war?"

"I was just wondering."

"On-the-job training. Now, let me concentrate. I can't be chatting while I work."

He had pulled a roll of tools out of his dark wool jacket while they were talking, apparently in case the safe required something more expert than a good ear for tumblers clicking into place. Jessica stepped back, out the way. That was when they heard the fumbling at the front door.

James shot Jessica a sharp look, but she shook her head, bewildered. He rolled the tools back up, swept the room with his eyes, then jerked his head toward the terrace. Whoever it was was having a bad time with the key. The door rattled again, and James and Jessica had the painting back up. The sounds stopped for a moment, but James wasted no time, sliding the balcony doors open and fairly hurling Jessica through. Joining her, Crawford closed the heavy curtains almost completely, only leaving a crack to spy without being spied. He swiftly, quietly pulled the glass sliders shut, exiling them to the cool fall afternoon.

"I want to see what 'our visitor' will do if he thinks the apartment's empty." James whispered, "If everything's on the level, you can saunter back in as if you'd just stepped out for a breath of fresh air."

Jess had no time to respond. The sound of the front door opening reached them, but the sight of whoever had entered remained frustratingly beyond her.

She tried not to feel too happy to be this close to James. Forcing herself to be practical, instead, Jessica checked behind her to confirm that the fire escape was where she remembered: off the terrace behind them, by the window of the study. Jess touched James's arm and jerked her head in that direction. He glanced sharply back, relaxing when he realized she was only indicating an escape route. Crawford nodded his comprehension before turning back to the crack he'd left between the drapes. He wanted to see who came in.

Jess would have cursed the curtains for hiding a clear view of the person in the apartment, except that they also hid her and Crawford from that intruder. A man approached the safe behind the painting, his back to them, but Jessica knew that back, that suit — although the hat was new.

James's arm tightened around Jess in support as her knees went weak. His glance told her that he felt for her anguish at discovering her faith had been so misplaced. Then he quietly moved away, pulling out his gun. His eyes indicated the fire escape. He wanted her out of there.

Jessica shook her head. James hesitated, but they both knew he couldn't afford to quarrel with her *now*. She was going to see this through to the bitter end. She was going to see him arrest Larry.

Larry dropped a manila envelope onto the couch and removed the painting carefully, quietly. He had a slip of paper. Of course, the combination. Crawford was watching and waiting to catch Larry red-handed — perhaps Larry was framing Peter with whatever was hidden inside that envelope.

While Larry was working the combination, James moved Jessica back from the slider, signaling her to stay put. Miserably, she nodded. Even though Larry was guilty, she didn't want to join in the arrest — or maybe she just couldn't bear to witness his inevitable admission of guilt.

The safe was open. James moved swiftly into the room, interrupting Larry as he put the envelope inside with, "Hold it there, Sanders. Don't make any sudden moves."

In spite of her misery, Jess caught herself thinking, "People actually *said* that!"

"What in the name of...?!"

"Skip it and hand me that envelope, Sanders, but slowly, easily. Keep your hands where I can see them."

"Who in God's name are you? Wait. How do you know my name?"

"Life will be much simpler if I do the questioning. Let's see what we have here."

"All 'we' have are some business papers belonging to a friend of mine. I'm afraid you're not going to make much of a haul for a burglar."

"Business papers? Mmm." A sound of the envelope being ripped open and Larry's angry protest, then James's sarcastic, "Business papers marked 'classified'?"

Jessica stiffened.

"What are you talking about?"

To Jess, Larry sounded stunned. She shivered with anxiety almost as much as from the autumn chill.

"I'd offer to let you have a look, but there's no sense in indulging your act. You don't project 'ingenuous' that well, Sanders. Fortunately for Peter Hennessey, I'm here to prevent you from framing him for your treason."

"Treason?! You're lying about seeing 'classified' on those papers. Why this is a frame up — or worse, you're trying to run some espionage game of your own. You must be the blackguard who's been trying to use Jessica. Or are you crazy? That's it! You aren't a traitor, but a man pushed over the edge by battle fatigue. Get a hold of yourself, Crawford. Take another look. Don't let your mind play tricks on you, man. Can't you see those aren't government secrets? They're just business papers. My friend called me less than half an hour ago and asked me to put that sealed envelope in his vault for safe keeping. That's easy enough to verify."

"Call Peter Hennessey?"

"Yes. Of course. And for God's sake, put that gun down before you hurt..."

"Achoo!" resounded from the terrace.

"What was that?"

"Don't change the subject. I'm taking you out of here, Sanders. There are some very unhappy F.B.I. agents who want to talk to you about..."

"I know that sneeze. Good Lord! You've dragged Jessica into this again. If you've hurt her..."

"Hold it right there, Sanders. In spite of what you've cost us, I don't want to have to use this gun now."

"In front of Jessica? She might get smart, then. See you for the lunatic you are."

"Relax, Sanders, you're not going to rattle me."

"Jessica," Larry called past James, "has he hurt you? Are you all right?"

Should she go in? Was there any point in staying hidden, now that she'd sneezed away her cover?

Jess stepped into the room with, "I'm fine, Larry."

A glance told her that James was not happy to have her in the room, but he didn't say anything. Larry's features were so anguished that she suddenly wondered if he *could* be guilty.

"Thank God he didn't hurt you. He forced you to let him in, didn't he, Jessica?"

Before Jess could answer, James observed, "Odd that the man who sent his partner to kill a woman should suddenly be concerned about her well-being."

"Partner? Kill Jessica? What? Jess, do you have any idea what he's talking about?"

"He's talking about Bromfield, Larry. You know about the knife and the attempt on my life. You wanted to pin it all on James before, but now, here, it all looks so bad for you."

Could she feel any more miserable, saying that? Larry must have read it all in her face, for he tried to persuade her, "Jess, Peter called me at the office and asked me to deliver some papers here on my lunch break. You can't believe this man, take his word over mine. It's insane! I've seen you overly imaginative before, but you can't be as delusional as he is."

"Sanders," James Crawford cut in, "I did some checking on the lodge where Peter Hennessey is staying. He couldn't have rung you up. No telephone."

Jessica couldn't keep the pain out of her features, especially at Larry's sinking expression.

Then his eyes narrowed and he challenged, "No telephones according to *you*." Turning, Larry pressed Jessica, "It's his word against mine until you look at the papers I brought, Jessica. Don't believe Crawford until you have a look at the papers."

"I guess it wouldn't hurt," Jessica began. She still owed that much to Larry, even though the weight of evidence was against him.

James shook his head and said quietly, "Sorry, Jessica. I can't let you do that — and Sanders knows it. The papers are marked 'classified.' You don't have any clearance, and I've bent the rules too much already." Turning to Larry, "Nice try, though, Sanders. Now, let's take a little walk, shall we? There are some chaps from your government who can't wait to have a chat with you."

"Jessica," Larry pleaded, "Don't believe him. You can't trust this man. Think of how he's deceived you before. He'll probably kill me . . ."

Jessica shot James a startled look. He shook his head and tried to calm her, "You go buzz the doorman in the lobby and have him call a policeman. I'll use the officer instead of my partner as backup to take Sanders to the nearest precinct. I'll have my F.B.I. contacts meet me there. That way you know I'm not running some kind of scam. I'm hardly about to kill a man in front of the law, am I?"

"No, no. That makes sense. I didn't mean to hesitate, but Larry just . . ."

"I understand, an instinctive reaction."

"Instinct for betrayal?" Larry accused both of them.

Jessica turned to Larry and explained miserably, "Larry, I wish I could still believe you, but it just doesn't make sense anymore, not with your being caught red-handed here. If you are innocent, if there is another explanation of some kind, the cop will be there to protect you." Turning back to Crawford, she pleaded, "James, you wouldn't railroad Larry, would you? You've got to promise me..."

"Jessica, it wouldn't do me any good to railroad anyone. The traitor would still be at large, taking lives, even yours, likely. I'm not about to let any of that happen. I promise."

"And what *is* your promise worth, Crawford?" Larry sneered with a bitterness Jessica had never seen before.

The expression that came into James Crawford's dark eyes silenced Larry and frightened Jessica a little. But Crawford held back. Instead of speaking his mind, he focused on Jessica, though still with a sharp eye on Larry, and said, "Ring up the doorman. Have him get me that officer, will you? Don't go into details. Just say it's an emergency. We're holding a burglar. I'll straighten it out when the policeman gets here."

A quick glance at Larry, and Jessica nodded to James before crossing the room to the buzzer by the door. Behind her, she heard James telling Larry to take a seat. Then she was on the intercom with the doorman, following James's instructions about arranging for the police to come. So they waited. James had Larry on the couch under the painting, right under the safe that had helped incriminate him. Sitting on the other couch across the room, Jess couldn't bring herself to look at either man. No one was particularly talkative. Yet Jessica really wanted Larry to talk, to find some way to clear himself, even if that would leave the traitor's identity dangerously up in the air.

She couldn't help looking at Larry, then, and the bitter expression he fastened on her drove her gaze away. His harsh words forestalled even that much escape from his anger. "I hope you're proud of yourself, Jessica."

"I think you can leave her alone," Crawford interjected levelly. "A man who betrays two countries, especially for the Nazis, isn't in any position to cast stones. I just wish I knew what made someone like you tick. I wish I could figure out what would make you sign on with a bunch of bastards. Maybe if you'd seen some of what I've seen in France or back home..."

"I'd have slipped over the edge like you?"

James had no chance to reply, cut off by the doorbell and a peremptory voice calling, "Police. Open up."

Catching Jessica's eye, James nodded toward the door without relaxing his guard over his prisoner.

Jess was on her feet instantly. It was a relief to break that tension. An officer, indeed, waited on the other side of the door. As soon as she ushered him in, Larry jumped up, launching protestations and accusations against Crawford that left Jessica almost as flustered as the cop, even though she had witnessed everything. However, James's identifying his government connections and requesting the policemen call in to have his F.B.I. contacts meet them at the precinct smoothed things over, with the policeman, at least. After Jessica gave her statement to the officer, James asked her to remain and wait for Liz. To his mind, too much danger had been circulating around Jessica for Liz not to be alarmed if her sister suddenly wasn't where she was supposed to be, not even if she were left an explanatory note. Jess couldn't have agreed with that reasoning more, but she also suspected James wanted to spare her being dragged any further into the downfall of someone she'd cared for.

James wasn't entirely successful with the latter part of his plan. As soon as he told the officer take out his cuffs, Larry protested to Jessica, "Are you going to let them do that to me, Jessica? Has it come to this? This is espionage. I can't even refuse to talk without a lawyer. I know this business."

A knife in her heart. Wasn't it her fault he was in this mess, if he were innocent? Jess turned to James, a plea in her eyes.

He shook his head, "I'm sorry, Jessica. I have to go by the book. This is too important." He turned to Larry to say, with distinctly less compassion, "Do you think you could leave her alone?"

"Do you think you can stop manipulating her?" Larry shot back.

"All right, Officer," James instructed, as Larry was cuffed. "Get him out of here."

"Wait, James," Jessica caught his arm in the doorway. "What will happen to Larry?"

James wasn't comfortable answering her, but he did. "We'll be questioning him to get the truth. If we find he's innocent, we'll let him go. If we find he's not... there's a military tribunal. He will have decent representation, then. I'm sorry, Jessica. None of this is very pretty. I can't talk any more. I've got to take him in. After we get him in, I'll have someone keep an eye on you, just in case. But I think you're in the clear now. I'll contact you later."

When James squeezed her shoulder, his hand lingered. She could see the green flecks in his eyes, but she could see regret there, too. He might have caught his prey, but that didn't make him feel any better about tearing apart all their lives in the process.

They were gone. Jessica closed the door and started to lock it, then stopped. Against whom? She moved slowly into the living room, surveying it, too restless to sit down. How could she relax when Larry had been led off in handcuffs? How could she have been so wrong about him? It was still impossible to believe completely that he was a traitor. Could she really ever have had feelings for someone like that? Larry just didn't seem the heartless, faithless type. Maybe he had thought the same about her.

Wasn't life just ducky? She'd found out that one fellow who'd seemed to care for her was probably a Nazi spy — and if he weren't, she'd have been responsible for helping to put him through hell. On top of that, the fellow she really had fallen for might never again show up in her life. What more could go wrong?

Jess tromped over to the bar. Maybe she could work off her frustrations by doing something positive, like putting away the banana-cream pie before it went bad. Reaching for the pie, she knocked over the glass of ice tea. *Holy cow!* Liz would kill her if she stained the bar's finish. Okay, Liz kept rags for mopping up spills under the counter of the bar. All she had to do was slip around the other side — Jess was in motion even as she was thinking — and grab one of the rags... Why was that dirty *dish* sitting in the bucket her sister reserved for glassware? Neatness-nut Liz would never allow a plate with a half-finished piece of pie to slime her glasses. The glass in Jessica's hand hit the floor with an unsettlingly loud crash.

A plate of pie amongst Liz's glasses! Oh God, she wasn't alone! Hadn't been since she'd arrived. She and James had unknowingly shared their eavesdropping with someone — someone not unknown to her any longer. There was only one suspect in this case with a predilection for banana cream pie severe enough to risk leaving behind this identifying clue. She had to fly this coop NOW before that traitor figured out what had startled her into dropping the glass!

Sprinting around the far side of the bar, Jessica found herself taking a flyer over an unexpected hassock, tumbling across the floor almost stunned. But not half as stunned as when she raised herself to face the gun with a silencer, held by Peter Hennessey.

"Oh damn," she muttered softly.

"It's not ladylike to swear, Jessica," her brother-in-law smiled, keeping her under the power of his weapon.

Jessica sat up, trying to pull herself together before she spoke. An exit strategy seemed a pretty faint hope with that nasty piece aimed at her, but at least he hadn't killed her right off the bat. Of course blood stains on Liz's carpet had to be a consideration.

"If you were a gentleman, you'd help me up, Peter."

He shook his head, "Nothing doing, Jessica. I'm too smart for that. You ought to be able to figure that out after seeing the way I set up Larry."

"Oh, quite a piece of work, but if you were really bright, you wouldn't have come charging out here with a gun on me," she returned, rising defiantly, but shakily.

"I couldn't let you waltz out the door, Jessica, once you'd figured out I was here all along, not in the woods upstate," Peter countered, quite pleased with himself. "You really ought to learn not to drop things and swear when you're startled. It's a dead giveaway — so to speak."

"Maybe you'd have been smarter if you hadn't been hanging around to be caught, Peter. What are you doing here, anyway?" If she could keep him going until the repairman arrived, she might have a chance — and Peter had an obsession with making sure people knew how much smarter he was than they were.

"I had to sneak back to put my plan in motion, Jess. I figured your colleague would try something like this if he had trouble pinning the rap on Larry. So, I set you all up. It was pretty simple to come back in another car, wait comfortably, and scarf up some pie, until you came to the door. All I had to do then was sneak out the window in the study so I could call Larry from the drugstore across the street and have him deliver an envelope I told him contained personal business papers. I knew Larry would never open a sealed envelope and see that I'd actually given him classified documents. Pretty clever, you have to admit."

"So you tip-toed back up the fire escape and in the study window just to make sure everything went off as you'd planned."

"Simple as pie, so to speak."

"I bet you even fixed the service entrance to slow James down, didn't you?"

"Nice touch, wasn't it? And I made sure to 'accidentally' tell Larry the wrong key to use so you and Crawford would have time to hide and watch him incriminate himself. Thorough, aren't I? Now why don't you stand over there by the bar where I can better keep an eye on you while I decide exactly how to eliminate you. I'd be a fool to kill you here, when I could take you to a place where it's easier to dispose of you afterwards. We both know it's impossible to clean blood stains out of this rug — but get that look out of your eye — if I *have* to kill you now, I will. And I'll cook up a convincing scenario to boot. I'd just rather not make things any more difficult for myself than I have to. Don't worry, though; it shouldn't take long for someone as sharp as me to figure out how to liquidate you without blowing my cover."

Jessica had moved over to the bar as Peter commanded, all the while calculating how to play effectively on her bother-in-law's ego and provoke him into a prolonged argument. Maybe even manipulate him into not killing her. "Don't get so smug, Peter. You've actually outsmarted yourself. Sure, you think you can silence me permanently, but you framed Larry so perfectly that he's with the police now. A pretty solid alibi if anything happens to me, don't you think? James will only have one suspect left. If I were you, I'd lam out of here and set up shop under an alias somewhere else."

Peter smiled devilishly. "Nice try, Jess. I suppose if I did, you'd close your eyes, and count to one hundred to give me a head start? Give me a break. You'd be on the horn to the cops in a flash."

"What horn, Peter? Remember I'm here because the telephone isn't working..."

"And the repairman should be coming along? You were counting on him, huh? Too bad. I checked up and found out that the appointment had been set back. I know exactly how much time I have to take care of you."

"It doesn't matter when he's due, Peter. It's still going to look funny if something happens to me now."

"Don't think so, Jess. One of the Nazi mastermind's minions could have killed you for getting in the way of his mission. Remember, Frederick Bromfield and Sammy Trendler made mistakes that got in my way and look what happened to them."

"*You* sent Bromfield to kill me, and *you* killed him. Why? He was your partner. And *I'm* your sister-in-law for crying out loud! How could you?" Jessica's fist pounded the bar next to her, just missing the pie.

"I had to. You and Crawford were getting too close. At first, I wasn't sure if it was Larry or me that Crawford was after, or exactly how much you knew. I had Sammy Trendler get into your apartment with the key you'd graciously given Liz and me, and she believed was lost. He took pictures of the 'documents' in the package, which I discovered were a hoax — a good one — but a hoax just the same. Too bad you didn't know that the *Abwehr* has had me secretly tutored in engineering for years now. Anyway, all family loyalty was off when I figured that you were in cahoots with Crawford.

"But Trendler was sloppy — and he hit my wife. Bromfield was sloppy, too, on his assignment to eliminate you. He hadn't been very good lately, cracking up after the big arrests of our less fortunate agents. I couldn't afford to let him get caught and finger me the way Seybold and some of the others did their 'colleagues' to save their skins. He became a liability, so I made arrangements to meet him in your dressing room and pay him off right after the show."

"Only the payoff he got wasn't exactly what he'd had in mind."

"Clever girl, Jessica."

"And to think we all fell for your Brussels-sprouts-induced-indigestion story."

Peter's superior smile broadened.

"Peter, maybe you won't be so smug when Liz starts thinking this thing through. Do you really expect her to take it lying down if something happens to her kid sister?"

"Liz will feel much too guilty. You look puzzled. Don't tell me you haven't noticed how well she and Larry get along. How she always turns to him when there's trouble between us? I cultivated that dependency. I knew that one day Liz would grow suspicious of my undercover dealings and that I'd need a defense against her probing. The perfect solution? Guilt. You know your sister fancies herself a one-man woman. If I question her fidelity with a sufficiently wounded mien, she won't dare accuse me. And to have been disloyal with a traitor to boot! That would give me an excuse to leave her and continue my career somewhere else, anew. Pretty clever, huh?"

"And what about your Nazi chums, the ones you report to? Won't they be reluctant to use someone whose cover was nearly blown? Won't they get antsy about how many people suspected you? How many dead bodies you left behind?" If she could just keep Peter talking about how clever he was, she might be able to make him lose track of time.

"I'm a lot smarter than they realize. They know what I want them to know, what I report to them. Remember, I was the head of my two-man cell. For instance, they don't know that *I* killed Bromfield or that you found out about me. I decide if it's in my best interest if they know you're a danger to me. So, are you now going to tell me how Dusty's going to track me down? You're running out of threats, Jessica."

"You forgot James Crawford. He'll know, Peter. He'll know something's fishy because..."

"That fool Crawford can't even begin to challenge me! Do you really think that amateur is sharper than me, has the passion I have? Do you want to know why I am what I am? Do what I do?" In his rising anger, Peter moved closer to Jessica as he spoke. "It's what was done to my parents by your lofty Allied nations. My father, he and my mother came here before I was born. Hell of a lot of good this land of opportunity did him — a strikebreaker smashed his skull when I was ten. My da's folks in Ireland offered to take my sister and me until my mother could save up enough money to put us both through school over here. She worked sixteen hours a day in a factory and scrubbed floors, and it eventually killed her. First, though, she got me back over here, and I worked to get the rest of my education. And let me tell you, my grandparents educated me pretty well on what your country did to my parents."

Unexpectedly, a board creaked around the corner, from the direction of the study. Peter whirled, ready to fire. Thinking fast, Jessica slammed the pie into his face and shoved his gun arm into the air. A shot plowed into the ceiling. Flung away and to the floor, Jess prayed that no one was home in the apartment above. But she didn't have time for much else before Peter, himself, was hurtled to the floor, tackled by the man he'd just scorned.

On top of Peter, James struggled for the gun. The weapon flew away from them both, but James had no opportunity to go after it as Peter disoriented him with a blow to the jaw. Crawford was tough enough to recover quickly, and before Peter could lunge for his weapon the two were a rolling, struggling mass once more.

On her feet now, Jessica scrambled across the room for the gun. Aiming the heavy black weapon at the two scrabbling forms, Jessica commanded with only a slight quaver, "All right you two! Break it up!"

Nothing.

"Hey! Look, you dopes, *I've* got the *gun!*"

At least that worked.

As the two pulled apart and got up, Jess continued, "Okay, put your hands up. Not *you*, James. For Pete's sake!"

"Sorry. Force of habit and all that."

Peter stood, hands in the air, eyeing Jessica narrowly.

"Are you all right, Jessica?" James asked, relieving her of the gun.

"Yes, I think so. A little shaky, maybe."

"Sit down." He moved her to a barstool, still keeping the gun on Peter, then ordering him, "You, Hennessey. Sit. On the floor. Hands on your head. There, that's just fine."

"He looks as if he were going to bite," Jessica remarked bitterly.

"Maybe I still can." Peter's eyes were calculating.

"Maybe we'll put a muzzle on you," Crawford warned. "But don't worry. We'll remove it when I take you to have a chat with a few mates of mine in the service."

Peter just sneered.

James diverted only enough attention to say, "Jessica, I don't trust this little angel. We need to truss him up. Have any rope handy? The drapery cord, perhaps?"

"Mess with Elizabeth's decor at your own peril. But I think there are some jump ropes in the kitchen."

"Jump ropes? How old is your sister?"

"She uses them to exercise, wise guy. Boxers use them, too, you know. You wouldn't cast aspersions on Joe Louis, would you?"

"I wouldn't cast anything on Joe Louis."

"Hey," Peter interrupted. "You've already captured me. Do you have to torture me with your wry repartee? There must be something in the Geneva Convention against this."

Finding the jump ropes didn't take Jessica long. Returning, she handed them to James saying, "Thank God you came back, but how on earth did you know I wasn't alone?"

Taking the ropes, James answered, "Taking Larry away, I had time to give his protests more thought. Peter could have set him up, but I wasn't sure. I couldn't afford to release Larry right off; but I thought if I took Larry away, Peter would get overconfident and slip into my hands — until I remembered the pie. It's the pie that made me realize I should never have left you alone here."

"The pie?"

Quickly, expertly roping Peter's arms to his torso, James explained, "The pie was sitting there, going bad. Your sister would never have let a banana-cream pie spoil, not with all the ration coupons she'd have used to make it. Someone else would have to have left it out. It wasn't you; you don't care for it. But there was someone already under suspicion who, as you said, could live on the stuff."

"Clever culinary deduction, Sherlock!"

"You deserve some kudos, yourself, for your unique defense techniques. For someone who never worked for Mac Sennett, you're rather handy with a pie to the face."

After tying Peter's ankles together and securing them to the leg of a couch, James stood up. "I left the officer outside the building, so I could double back while he radioed for backup and held Larry in case my hunch was wrong. I came up the fire escape. But I couldn't wait when I realized Hennessey was getting ready to take you out of here. You're all in, though. I'm going to get you a stiff drink. Hell, I'm bloody well going to do one up for myself, before the backup gets here."

Jess nodded, letting James move away from her and circle behind the bar. Her thoughts reached beyond herself and a troubled, "Poor Liz!" escaped her.

James nodded sympathetically before agreeing, "It will be a pretty hard knock for her when she finds out about her husband. I can only begin to understand. I guess she'll need your shoulder to cry on."

"We're sisters. We're always there for each other, James."

He hesitated, his expression showing what it cost him to admit, "I had a brother who looked out for me like that before I lost him."

For just a moment, James seemed to welcome what the softening in her features offered him. Then he changed the subject, "I have to talk fast. The police should be here any minute. I can't make you any promises about the future, Jessica. Hennessey's trial will be a closed military tribunal, same as they gave the spies they nabbed off Amagansett. I'll try to keep your identity from getting into the wrong hands, but he may have talked about you to his superiors. You might have to go into custody, be relocated. Why on earth are you smiling?"

"Because Peter told me he was too smart to let his superiors know he was under suspicion; he was handling this solo. The only other enemy agent who knew about me was Frederick Bromfield."

"Who's now dead," James completed. He looked down briefly to finish making the drinks, then pensively walked around the bar to sit next to Jessica, while keeping an eye on Peter. "As I said, the trial will be classified information and witness identity will be hidden as protection against reprisal."

"So I might come out of this all right?" Jessica ventured.

"If you keep your head, yes. The odds are in your favor."

"It seems too good to be true."

"Jessica, just because you want something doesn't automatically put it beyond your reach. Good things happen, too — if you work at them." James seemed to surprise himself. "I haven't put my heart into words like those in a long time. Maybe you're a good influence, Jessica Minton."

"Maybe you'd rather have a fool to make you merry than a wise guy to make you sad."

"I don't see a fool facing me."

"Neither do I."

He started to smile then, but paused before saying seriously, "I have work to do, Jessica. I know I won't be posted here for the duration. Sooner or later, they're going to send me back, and as much as I want to stay with you, I can't say no when I'm needed. I won't be able to tell you where, not even when, I'm going. You won't see me for long stretches of time."

"I'm not going anywhere."

"It may be a long war."

She thoughtfully traced the rim of her glass with her fingertip before deciding aloud, "Time and distance are good, sometimes. They can give you a chance to think and decide if what you want is really what you want."

"Hmm, this is unsettling."

"What?"

"I think I understood what you just said."

Jessica narrowed her eyes.

"Only joking, only joking," he said, a smile playing beneath his mustache. "I wouldn't want to provoke another one of your nasty right hooks."

Jessica smiled this time. Their glasses clinked, sealing their pact — their glasses, then a kiss.

Regarding the two from the floor, the uncomfortably trussed Peter Hennessey observed, "Ugh! Mush!"

Jessica and James did not comment. They were otherwise occupied.

AFTERWORD

I had a lot of fun doing background research for this novel, but I have to come clean and point out that I indulged in some "creative history." The reference to Nazi saboteurs put ashore by submarine at Amagansett Beach, Long Island actually happened in June 1942 not 1943. The event just fit too perfectly into the plot of my story for me to pass it up, and the tale as a whole works better set in 1943. So, please forgive my artistic license. In all fairness, I probably played far less fast and loose with the facts of the incident than 20th-Century Fox did with their 1943 film *They Came to Blow up America*.

That admission on the table, I'd like to give credit to some of the wonderful sources I found for giving *Bait and Switch* its roots in 1943 reality. The periodical *America in WWII* ran some great articles in its regular issues on the Amagansett story and England's Special Operations Executive (S.O.E.). The publishers' special issues, particularly on espionage (*World War II Top Secret*), provided some of the best details on Axis spying in the U.S., the development of the O.S.S., and the S.O.E.'s and the Underground's endeavors in France. Beirne Lay's memoir *Presumed Dead* was also helpful in filling me in on the Resistance's work helping downed flyers evade capture by the Nazis and return to Allied territory. The BBC's *Danger UXB* and *Wish Me Luck* gave me further inspiration. I found helpful general information on the war years, the home front as well as theatres of battle, in *Time Capsule History of the War Years: 1939-45*; *The Good War*; *I Saw It Happen Here*; *Duty, Honor, and Applause: When the Stars Went to War*; *Good Food, Good Girls, Good Fun: The Story of the U.S.O. Hostesses During World War II*; and *When Our Mothers Went to War*. I am especially grateful for wonderful conversations with family and their friends who lived through those tough times at home and under fire. Books that helped me get the feel of the NYC home front included *New York in the Forties* (Dover books picture collection); *Helluva Town: New York City in the 1940s-50s* (Vivian Cherry); *Helluva Town: The Story of New York City during WWII* (Richard Goldstein); *Manhattan '45*, and *Over Here! New York City during World War II* (Lorraine B. Deihl). One of my most interesting founts of information was *The New York Times* in 1943. Not just by checking headlines but by perusing advertisements, radio schedules, stage and film showings, restaurant menus and prices, I found myself submerged in the everyday life of the time. So, a tip of the trilby to the librarians at University Massachusetts, Lowell and Worcester State University for showing me how to have at those microfilm machines. For background on the stage, I was fortunate enough to have the guidance of friends who have worked both backstage and treading the boards: Tasha Matthews, Amber Vayo, and

Colleen Gresh, as well as sources more contemporary to my novel: *Modern Theatre Practice*, *Supernatural on Stage*, *Bright Lights* (Marian Seldes' autobiography), *Life Is a Banquet* (Rosalind Russell's autobiography), and *My Life in Three Acts* (Helen Hayes' biography).

Finally, I have to express my appreciation for some of the 1940s filmmakers whose work spurred me to write my own suspense scenario, to create my own smart-talking gals and guys, nefarious villains, and quirky supporting players trying to make their way down moody, dark streets. Thanks to actors like Joan Bennett, Rosalind Russell, Claude Rains, Claire Trevor, Dick Powell, Paul Henreid, and Humphrey Bogart. Thanks to directors of photography, writers, and directors like Nicholas Musuraca, Stanley Cortez, John Paxton, Daniel Fuch, DeWitt Beaudine, Edward Dmytryk, Vincent Sherman, Leonard Spigelgass, Steve Sekely, Jacques Tourneur, and producer Val Lewton.